DON BERRY

Don Berry (1932-2001) considered himself a native Oregonian, despite
the fact that he was born in Minnesota, with a lineage from Fox Indians.
After attending Reed College, where his housemates included poet
Gary Snyder, who shared his interest in Eastern metaphysics, Berry
began a lifetime of pursuing his many passions: playing down-home
blues and composing synthesizer music, sumi drawing and painting,
sculpting in bronze, exploring theoretical mathematics, and writing for
prize-winning films.

In addition to his three novels about the Oregon Territory (*Trask*,
Moontrap, and *To Build a Ship*), published in the early 1960s, Berry wrote
A Majority of Scoundrels, a history of the Rocky Mountain fur trade. An
early Internet pioneer, he also created a remarkable body of literature
that exists now only in cyberspace.

Moontrap

DON BERRY

introduction by Jeff Baker

Oregon State University Press

Corvallis

A NORTHWEST REPRINTS BOOK

Library of Congress Cataloging-in-Publication Data
Berry, Don.
  Moontrap / by Don Berry ; introduction by Jeff Baker.--
1st OSU Press ed.
     p. cm.
  ISBN 0-87071-039-7 (alk. paper)
  1. Willamette River Valley (Or.)--Fiction. 2. Married people--
Fiction. 3. Shoshoni women--Fiction. 4. Fur trade--Fiction. 5.
Farm life--Fiction. 6. Trappers--Fiction. I. Title.
  PS3552.E7463M66 2004
  813'.54--dc22

                                            2004005744

∞ This paper meets the requirements of ANSI/NISO Z39.48-1992
(Permanence of Paper).

Oregon State University Press
121 The Valley Library
Corvallis, OR 97331-4501
541-737-3166 • fax 541-737-3170
osupress.oregonstate.edu

Introduction

by Jeff Baker

A few years ago, I was standing on the bank of the Clackamas River with Robin Cody, author of *Ricochet River*, a novel set on the same river we were skipping rocks across. We were talking about other novels set in Oregon and how there are only a few really good ones.

H. L. Davis' *Honey in the Horn* is the only novel by an Oregonian to win the Pulitzer Prize, and that was in 1936. Bernard Malamud wrote *A New Life* in Corvallis and based it on a fictionalized Oregon State University, then moved to Vermont before the locals figured out they were being teased.

Cody said he thought the Great Oregon Novel was *Sometimes a Great Notion* by Ken Kesey. No doubt about it, Cody said—*Sometimes a Great Notion* is big, it's raw, it's stylistically inventive, it gets right what it's like to live in this rugged, beautiful land.

True enough, I said. I love that book, and I think it shows Kesey's brilliance way more than *One Flew Over the Cuckoo's Nest*. There's one novel that's better, though, one that has more to do with who we are as Oregonians and how we came so far in such a short time and lost so much along the way. It's *Trask* by Don Berry, and it changed my life when I read it as a teenager.

Cody's next rock whizzed suspiciously close to my ear. He liked *Trask* just fine but thought *Notion* was more ambitious and more successful on more levels. Kesey was aiming higher, he said, and he pulled it off. He wrote about a family, a town, an industry, a way of life. Nobody's come close to getting so much about Oregon into one book and doing it in such an intense, exciting way.

I still like *Trask* better, I said. We agreed to disagree and went back to skipping rocks over the green surface of the river. Three years later, Berry and Kesey were dead. They were Oregon's best fiction writers of the post-World War II generation and, despite obvious differences in temperament and style, had much in common. Both were born elsewhere but considered Oregon their home. Both did their best work before they were thirty in marathon sessions of intense creative concentration they were unable or unwilling to repeat in later years. Both turned away from writing novels in favor of other, more personal artistic pursuits that included living their lives as art, and both spent their last years experimenting with technology that didn't exist when they were ambitious young writers.

There's a statue of Kesey in downtown Eugene. His life is celebrated by his many friends and his novels have never been out of print. His influence on twentieth-century American culture is immense—as a link between the Beat Generation of the 1950s and the counterculture of the 1960s, as a proponent of drug use to expand consciousness, and as a rebel who took every opportunity to cheerfully challenge authority.

Berry's life and accomplishments are less well-known but no less interesting. He was a key figure—along with Gary Snyder, Philip Whalen, and Lew Welch—in the small group of writers who attended Reed College in the late 1940s. A self-taught researcher who never took a history class, he wrote an influential history of the Rocky Mountain fur trade called *A Majority of Scoundrels*. A musician, a painter and sculptor, a filmmaker, a poet, an essayist, and a spiritual seeker, toward the end of his life he put his restless energies into an amazing Web site (www.donberry.com) and became one of the first writers to fully explore the possibilities of the Internet.

His most important artistic achievement is the three novels (*Trask, Moontrap*, and *To Build a Ship*) published between 1960 and 1963 and written in a spasm of sustained creativity unequaled in Oregon literature. All three are set in the Oregon Territory in the decade before statehood and form a loose trilogy that tells the story of our state's origins better than any history book. They are set firmly on Oregon soil and mix historical figures such as Elbridge Trask, Joe Meek, John McLoughlin, and the Tillamook chief Kilchis with fictional characters. Berry believed fiction could tell larger truths as effectively as history and shared the opinion of Ben Thaler, the narrator of *To Build a Ship*, who thought "literal truth is not the important consideration ... history tells us only what we have already made our minds up to believe."

More than forty years after they were first published, Berry's novels speak for themselves and need no detailed explication. (It is interesting but not necessary, for example, to know that unlike Berry's childless Trask, the real Elbridge Trask—after whom the Trask River is named—and his wife Hannah had eight children before leaving the Clatsop Plains for Tillamook Bay.) A brief examination of who Berry was, how he wrote these remarkable books, and what he did with the rest of his life can provide a more complete context in which to appreciate a true Northwest treasure.

Berry was born January 23, 1932, in Redwood Falls, Minnesota. His parents were touring musicians; his father played the banjo and guitar, his mother was a singer. His father left the family when Berry was two and did not see his son again until Berry was eighteen, although they enjoyed a friendly relationship in later years. His mother moved frequently around the Midwest and Berry said he attended six schools in five states one year. Berry was small for his age and extremely intelligent, the kind of kid who had to get adults to check out books for him from the library. In grade school, he was given the nickname "China" for his interest in the far east.

By the time he was fifteen, Berry and his mother were living in Vanport, the city that was destroyed by a flood of the Columbia River in 1948. Berry took the newspaper notice of his death in the flood as an opportunity to leave home and disappear. He attended high school in Portland and was offered scholarships in mathematics by both Harvard and Reed.

In 1949, Berry was attending Reed, working in the bookstore and sleeping on top of a boiler he tended on campus. He was invited to live in a house on Southeast Lambert Street with several other students, including Snyder, already a serious student of Eastern philosophy and on the way to becoming one of the finest American poets of the twentieth century; Whalen, a Portland native who became a prominent Beat poet and later a Buddhist monk; and Welch, another poet whose *Ring of Bone: Collected Poems 1950-71* is one of the best books from the Beat era. The young men formed what they called the Adelaide Crapsey-Oswald Spengler Mutual Admiration Poetasters Society and drank wine, wrote poetry, and goofed off for the better part of two years.

"It was probably the birth canal for the Beat Generation," said Berry, who was more interested in painting than poetry at the time. "It was classic post-war Bohemianism, and also one of the richest experiences of my life. The quality of minds involved was extraordinary, and it was also hugely funny."

As a freshman, Berry was one of the editors of the Reed literary magazine. "I once rejected a poem as being too derivative of Lew Welch," he remembered. "Lew gave me hell later, because he had written it."

Berry, Snyder, and Whalen studied with the legendary calligrapher Lloyd Reynolds, an inspiration to generations of Reedies. Reynolds would tell his students, "You've got a million bad letters in your fist, and the only way to get rid of them is to write them down."

"Lloyd was one of the four great teachers of my life," Berry said. "Not necessarily in any specific detail, but in the sense that he was the first teacher who ignited me, as a candle is ignited from a flame already burning. He showed the most astonishing confidence in my ability. When I was a freshman, Lloyd had me deliver the lectures on Chinese art to his art history classes. Those were the only lectures they received on the subject, and Lloyd seemed content. At the time, it seemed perfectly reasonable to me ... The clichés of a young artist. Lordy, lordy."

Berry left Reed in 1951 to earn a living. He had met his future wife by this time and was beginning to write science fiction, a genre that appealed to him because he could sell stories, learn to write, and let his imagination wander freely. His goal was to write a short story every week and he sold about a dozen between 1956 and 1958. But he wanted to write something different, a commercial novel set in the present day on the Oregon coast, and wanted, he said, "to include some folk stories, or Indian legends, or something to give some local depth and flavor."

Wyn Berry brought home a study by Reed historian Dorothy Johansen of coastal Indian cultures around 1850. Berry's reaction to it, as described in a 1997 email, deserves to be quoted at some length:

> This was not academic history, it was a complilation of
> very personal anecdotes and records of ordinary people—not
> "history-makers."

At one point Dorothy Jo was describing a trip made by Elbridge Trask from the northern coast down to Tillamook Bay (where he later settled) to scout out land. She commented that nobody ever could figure out why he made some particular decision.

Well, I knew why, because it was exactly the decision I would have made under the circumstances. And at that instant, I had a small epiphany about the nature of history. History was actually made by people. People like me, even. This had never occurred to me before, as I had no sense of history myself, and no particular interest in it.

That night I climbed up on the roof of the Red House and sat on the peak to watch the sunset over the fields and the Willamette River. I had demonstrated that I could write commercial magazine fiction. But I increasingly felt that if I wanted this career to last for twenty or thirty years I would have to write something that was deeper, that used more of me than commercial writing, or I would eventually become bored. I have always preferred doing things I don't know how to do.

Watching that sunset, I decided to change direction completely. I decided to write a serious novel of history, and Elbridge Trask's exploratory trip to Tillamook Bay would be the story, and Trask the main character. The next morning I drove down to the Oregon coast, and eventually found the Tillamook County Historical Museum.

The museum was a treasure trove for Berry, who said that the material he found there served as the basis for all three novels. He spent several weeks reading and copying everything in sight, then moved on to the Oregon Historical Society in Portland. He said he wrote *Trask* at the same time he was doing his research, "and by the time I had finished the research, I had also finished the novel."

Maybe so, but there is much that it is in the novel that can't be found in a museum. A bare-bones summary of the plot doesn't begin to do it justice: In 1848, Elbridge Trask, once a trapper and mountain man, has settled on the Clatsop Plains but feels restless. He decides to take a trip to Tillamook Bay and is accompanied by Wakila, a young Clatsop Indian, and Charley Kehwa, a *tamanawis* man or spiritual leader of the tribe, who acts as a guide. The party travels from present-day Gearhart south along the coast across Tillamook Head, Cape Falcon, and Neahkanie Mountain. After a shocking, unexpected tragedy, they reach the bay and are greeted by Kilchis, the chief of the Killamook tribe (Berry notes in *A Majority of Scoundrels* that Tillamook was usually spelled with a "k" sound until 1852). As a result of a power struggle within the tribe and to prove his worthiness, Trask volunteers to go on a vision quest called the Searching, a purification ritual involving fasting and prayer. He survives it, at great cost, and is free.

What is initially most striking about *Trask* is its clear, sure sense of place. Glen Love, professor emeritus of English at the University of Oregon and a great champion of Berry's work, wrote in a short study of his novels that "a regional work of literature may be defined as one in which landscape is character, perhaps the central character, so much so that a change in setting would completely alter and destroy the essential quality of the work."

By that standard, *Trask* is a regional work. With love and precision, Berry describes everything from Short Sands Beach ("the white lines of breakers were tiny as they marched slowly in, and along their humped green backs ran the quicksilver reflections of the sun") to a rainstorm in the Coast Range ("The rain came like whiplashes, driven out of the low clouds with a startling viciousness. It drummed and whacked against the waxy leaves of the salal with such force it seemed certain to tear them from their stems.")

Everyone in *Trask* is unsettled and unsure of where they fit. Trask has traveled the world as a sailor and a mountain man before settling on the Clatsop Plains but now is itching to strike out for somewhere new. Wakila has come of age in a tribe that has been decimated by smallpox and is now succumbing to gambling and alcohol. Charley Kehwa is a spiritual leader who has lived among whites and knows the inevitability of their push for land and power. He sees in Trask a rare white man who respects Indian culture and perhaps can prevent what happened to the Clatsop from happening to the Killamooks.

Trask's restlessness is much more than a mountain man's independence and love of freedom. In an unsure, inarticulate way, he is on a quest to find a deeper meaning to his life long before he goes on the Searching. He explicitly rejects Christianity and Western society but is unsettled by Charley's dreams and premonitions. He looks to nature and looks within himself in a way that reflects a traditional Eastern path toward enlightenment without ever explicitly stating it.

That this takes place in a novel set in the Oregon Territory in 1848, within the context of an adventure story about first contact between white settlers and Indians, is remarkable. It's as if Berry gutted a Louis L'Amour novel and replaced it with Somerset Maugham's *The Razor's Edge*. The Searching scenes are the soul of the novel and the final chapter (added, according to Wyn Berry, when the novel was in galleys) is stunningly powerful, a coda that gives fresh meaning to all that has come before.

"All his senses shared the same bright clarity; the intensity of any simple act of perception was almost unbearable," Berry writes. "The sheer brilliance of color was blinding; the sweet, clear tone of every sound came to him almost as a physical shock, making him catch his breath. The swinging glide of a gull came to have an almost-grasped significance that kept his mind hovering on the edge of joy."

Trask had a troubled publishing history. Berry said his first agent told him "there was no possible way he could submit such a book to publishers, and thought it better if we parted ways. Which we did." A different agent sold the book to Doubleday, where it was turned over to an editor who Berry thought "confused himself with an author." Unwilling to make the requested changes, Berry returned his advance and withdrew the book at Christmas of 1958. Viking Press eventually bought it and published it in 1960, to strong reviews. (The *Saturday Review* called it great. The *Northwest Review* said it was the best first novel by an Oregonian since *Honey in the Horn*.)

Berry already had moved on. *A Majority of Scoundrels: An Informal History of the Rocky Mountain Fur Company* was published in 1961. It is an amazing work, a combination of scholarship and narrative that proves true the cliché about history coming alive and shows why many of those closest to Berry considered him a genius. He did much of his research through microfilms from the Missouri Historical Society and was able to go where some of the finest western historians of the century—men such as Hiram M. Chittenden, Dale Morgan, and Bernard DeVoto—had gone before and break new ground.

Moontrap (1962) and *To Build a Ship* (1963) were mostly written while Berry was traveling, first in France and then around the world. He carried copies of some of the material he had found in the Tillamook museum with him, including a typed copy of pioneer Warren Vaughn's diary that is the backbone of *To Build a Ship*. Wyn Berry, who read and edited all of her husband's manuscripts, said there was something in what the pioneers did and thought that moved Berry.

"He identified with their values," she said. "He thought the kind of quiet, everyday heroism they had was undervalued in the present day, and he felt many of the agriculture people had sold their birthright. The mountain men, the guys who had to adjust to society—he loved them the most."

There are references to Elbridge Trask in both *Moontrap* and *To Build a Ship* and the books make sense when read in succession. There are plenty of discrepancies and departures from the historical record, all of them falling under the large umbrella of artistic license. Berry said 90 percent of *To Build a Ship* comes from Vaughn's diary but the novel is narrated by Thaler, not Vaughn, and has a sensibility that is wholly Berry's.

Like *Trask*, *Moontrap* has a lead character who is a mountain man struggling to find a place in settled society. In this case, the setting is Oregon City in 1850 and the character is Johnson Monday, a trapper who wants to make a home with his Indian wife but has "never really been willing to accept this new world he was living in. He had never committed himself fully, and now he had to pay for it."

Monday pays for his independence early and often, and so do others who live outside the boundaries drawn by the newcomers. Monday's old trapper friend, an unrepentant, uncivilized mountain man named Webster T. Webster, is the comic relief, the moral center, and the scene-stealer of *Moontrap*. Monday wrestles with his dilemmas; Webb curses at his and clings hard to the life he loves. Webb is Berry's most memorable character, one the author said jumped up during the novel's creation and demanded a larger role.

A brilliantly rendered centerpiece of the novel is the trial and hanging of a group of Cayuse Indians for the Whitman massacre six months earlier. The Indians who were hanged almost certainly were not directly involved in the massacre at the Walla Walla mission, a fact that didn't give pause to those who executed them.

After the hanging, Monday and Webb visit John McLoughlin. Berry's sketch of the eagle in his roost at Oregon City, retired from the Hudson's Bay Company and fighting futilely against the Americans who were biting the hand that had so generously fed them, is a poignant snapshot of McLoughlin's final years:

> "I heard there was some trouble about the land," Monday said, embarrassed. The trouble was simply that the Americans, Thurston most prominently, were methodically stripping McLoughlin of all his holdings in the Oregon country, their only legal weapon a campaign of hate against the "damned Jesuitical rascal of a Hudson's Bay man."
>
> "Yes, yes, quite. But it has all been turned over to intermediaries for settlement now, and I am a bit hopeful. I am expecting them momentarily with the papers. But now—" McLoughlin suddenly swept his arms up in a great despairing gesture to heaven. "*Now*, Mr. Monday."

When civilization comes crashing down on Monday, it is Webb who takes frontier revenge for his friend and flees to Saddle Mountain, where he holds off the pursuing mob and builds a moontrap, a more explicitly Eastern practice than anything in *Trask*. Berry said that despite his immersion in Chinese literature and friendship with Snyder and Whalen, he did not study Zen Buddhism until a good ten years after he wrote his novels.

To Build a Ship is different in tone and style than the novels that preceded it. It is narrated in the first person, by someone who is not a skilled mountain man and not a fair-minded friend to the Indians.

History tells us that the kind of me-first moral relativism that consumes Thaler was more typical of the white settlers to the Oregon Territory than the open-minded, live-and-let-live attitude of Trask and Monday. Indians in Oregon were wiped out by disease, killed by settlers or local militia, and moved to reservations, in a very short time after first contact.

"The cumulative death rate for Oregon Indians is estimated by 1850 to have ranged between 50 and 90 percent in some originally heavily populated areas," notes the *Atlas of Oregon*. "... What disease began, warfare completed."

It is to Berry's credit that he wrote honestly and sympathetically about Indians during a time (the late 1950s and early '60s) when attitudes toward them had not noticeably begun to change. Thaler, a rationalist who puts the construction of the ship above anything his conscience might be trying to tell him, is still sensitive enough to recognize that he "has never known a more intelligent man of any color" than Kilchis. When Kilchis asks Thaler why Trask did not come back and tells him Thaler must keep the peace in Tillamook Bay, he knows he is asking the impossible from someone not capable of giving it. The settlers came, and the Indians soon disappeared.

So did Berry. After four books in four years, a National Book Award nomination (for *Moontrap*) and a stack of great reviews, nothing. He wrote a children's book called *The Mountain Men* in 1966, but published no more novels for the rest of his life. Why?

When I made contact with Berry in 1997, via email, that was the first question I asked him. This is his reply:

> At different times I've been interested in different explorations. Some of these explorations involved writing (my primary medium), but many did not. Writing is not my "career." I have no idea what a "career" is. Basically, I have wandered the world physically and mentally, most of the time fascinated and astounded by what I discover, and sometimes putting that astonishment into words, or music, or film, or bronze, or design, or teaching, or philosophy.
>
> The trilogy of Oregon novels and historical works were all done before I was thirty. *Moontrap* and *To Build a Ship*

were written in France while I was travelling around the world with a packsack, a guitar and a typewriter.

I am also hopelessly inept at the business side of art, and don't have the patience to deal with it. I am not a dependable source of a predictable product. The vast majority of my life work—in all forms of art and thought— doesn't fit into market categories. And I don't think a marketing committee ought to determine whether what I write gets read or not.

Berry did not make much money from his novels. Wyn Berry estimated he never made more than about a thousand dollars per year from his writing, excluding movie options, and Berry guessed he averaged about a hundred dollars per year in royalties for twenty years. (There was some movie interest—Jack Nicholson briefly held the rights to *Moontrap* just before he won the Oscar for *Cuckoo's Nest.*) Berry was frustrated that he made money more easily from science fiction than historical novels. At that time, he thought of himself more as a painter than a writer, he wanted to travel and follow his interests wherever they led, so why spend all that time writing novels?

"He never valued his own work very highly until much later in his life," said Wyn Berry, who always was the primary supporter of the family. "He didn't expect great things, but he was annoyed that he wasn't making a living."

However, there was more writing that never got published. Wyn Berry said her husband wrote a sequel to *Trask* that he burned because he felt it didn't work as a story and put another finished novel called *Eye of the Bear* "into the fire." Love writes that Berry destroyed these books "because he realized he had not been changed by the experience of writing [them]." Wyn Berry said he was "a very accurate critic, but fierce in all ways."

Berry did have a regular job for a while, as a writer on the film unit at KGW in Portland. There he met a gifted producer and director named Laszlo Pal and began a collaboration that lasted more than thirty years. Berry worked as a writer on many of Pal's award-winning documentaries and on industrial and institutional films, which he enjoyed because he could immerse himself in a subject and learn all about it. Pal accepted Berry's wandering ways and Berry said that "if I disappear for five or six years, he accepts that, and when I return we can resume work together again as though no time has passed."

Berry wrote some commissioned books, such as *The Eddie Bauer Guide to Flyfishing* and *Understanding Your Finances*, and taught creative writing at the University of Washington and other colleges. He built a bronze foundry on Vashon Island for his sculpture and played in a band called Vashimba that performed the music of the Shona tribe of Zimbabwe. He spent several years living in a boat in Eagle Harbor, off Bainbridge Island.

And he discovered the World Wide Web. His Web site, Berryworks, contains a historical novel set in the goddess culture of Minoan Crete called "Sketches from the Palace at Knossos," eight different short stories, a children's book, some essays (including "On the Submissiveness of Women in Tango" and the beautiful "Snapshots of My Daughter, Turning"), twenty-one chapters about living on Eagle Harbor called "Magic Harbor," a large amount of poetry, art, and philosophy. Some of the writing is excellent and all of it is original and wholly Berry.

He was passionate about the possibilities of the Internet and a strong believer in it as a creative medium. "Long before I set up my studio in cyberspace, I had been exploring in a different literary form—a mosiac of individual pieces, rather than linear narrative," he said. "Each individual piece ... can be read separately, in any order. In Berryworks, you can move from any place to any other place, with a single hyperlink. Everything is available simultaneously."

Everything is available simultaneously, and for nothing.

"I am invariably asked why someone who has been nominated for the National Book Award would simply give their work away," he said. "But I have never been part of that world. It has always been my dream to write exactly what I want to write and give it away to anybody who wants it. Cyberspace makes that possible. And I didn't get paid for probably 90 percent of the other work I've done, so it's not all that different. Economically I'm marginal and always have been, even when the books were new."

Berry was cautious but curious when I contacted him in 1997. He wanted to have Berryworks reviewed as a whole, the way a book is reviewed, and wanted to do everything by email. Six months of electronic exchanges led to phone calls and finally a meeting in a coffee shop on Vashon Island. Berry suffered from chronic pulmonary obstructive disease, the result, he said, of "forty-five years of rolling cigarettes out of pipe tobacco." He needed oxygen for any exertion and carried a portable tank when he left his house. He spent up to ten hours every day on-line but did confess to a weakness for "Xena, the Warrior Princess."

Berry died in Seattle on February 20, 2001. At the end of his life, he knew he would be remembered for *Trask* and *Moontrap* and *To Build a Ship* and *A Majority of Scoundrels* and was pleased and proud that people still read them.

"When I wrote *Trask* I didn't even have any idea anyone would read it," he said. "As to the durability of these works, it is much like watching your children grow up. After twenty years or so you think 'good lord, how did that ever happen?'

"A writer can plan to make a book entertaining, or plan to make a book interesting, and many other things. But a writer cannot plan to make a book last. That is not in our hands."

Moontrap

To Wyn with love
for a certain patience
with the old man on
other mountains, other trails

Chapter One

The old man traveled alone. He came riding from the north, a skeleton rider on a bony horse, plodding methodically along the riverbank. He sat humped in the saddle with the posture of a man who has ridden many miles, and knows there is no speed in haste.

Two locks of hair—long, thick, heavily greased—dangled in front of his ears, set into gentle swaying by the jarring steps of the horse and the endless watchful movement of the man's head. A great limp-brimmed felt hat dwarfed his features. The old man's buckskin hunting shirt folded from the points of his shoulders as from pegs in a wall, and it was a mottled black of grease and dirt and dried blood. His breeches were buckskin to the knees (bony pinnacles, threatening to tear through the leather), but the bottoms of the legs were of blanket cloth. It had shrunk in wetting so that eight inches of grimed and bony leg showed between trouser bottoms and moccasins.

It was not yet dawn. The eastern sky was beginning to be light, a heavy grayness like a pool of dull Galena lead suspended overhead; but it was not yet true dawn. In the cool and neutral light he came to a river crossing his path, and stopped. He dismounted, letting the reins drop to the ground, and his horse began to browse contentedly among the ferns at the river's edge, nosing them gently aside to find the rich grass beneath.

The old man walked to the very bank of the river, cautiously. He scanned both banks with care, watching for movement, listening, alert to any sign that he was not alone. A few hundred yards to his right the fast-moving stream emptied into the larger river along which he had been riding. The large stream, he knew, was called the Willamette. He grunted deep in his throat, and the sound was like the coughing snort of a bear.

"*Wagh!*"

He looked at the meeting of waters, watching the ripples of the fast-running tributary lose themselves in the wider flood. It was vaguely annoying that the Willamette should run north. Sensible river'd run south, he figured. All of them did.

Except the Yellowstone. And the Bighorn. And the Powder and the Rosebud . . . he remembered. He snorted. "Don't make no difference," he said aloud. "Goes against nature anyways."

He was not happy about the river he had to cross. The banks were heavily wooded, timbered almost to the edge, with the thick growth of brush he'd found everywhere in this rain-soaked country matted below the trees. It was good cover. Put a whole damned Piegan encampment in there, and you'd never see it.

He squatted on his haunches and pushed back the brim of the huge felt. Finally he spat down into the river and grunted. He told himself it didn't matter—he was in civilization now, just an hour or so from Oregon City. But suspicion of good cover was a habit of his life, and there was neither way nor reason, now, to change the habits of his life. He shrugged and stood again, absently fingering the ends of one long braid of hair. He'd cross, because there was nothing else to do.

He remounted, swinging easily into the saddle, and let the old horse slide down the bank and into the water. The river itself was little different from any other; so viciously cold it seemed solid, so swift the horse's feet were swept out from under her in the first five seconds.

The water closed around the old man's legs with the painful pressure of drying rawhide. As the horse lost her footing and plunged deep, the vise of cold clamped suddenly around the old man's groin, making him gasp with the shock of it. Together, as one animal, they floundered across the stream and scrambled up the opposite bank, many yards downstream toward the confluence. At the top the horse stopped and shook her head like a dog, stretching her neck to relieve the cramp of cold. The old man kicked her furiously in the ribs.

"*Wagh!* C'mon, y' wuthless hunk o' meat. Hya!"

In her own time, the horse resumed her steady pace, unconcerned. The freezing chill of the water had seeped into the old man's bones, and his testicles ached as though he had been kicked. He put it away from his mind; he had crossed many cold rivers and he was no longer interested in the pain they gave him.

"Damn poor doin's," he muttered vaguely, meaning not the river but things in general. He was mildly disappointed that he had not been attacked; the place was perfect. It was a kind of waste.

He laughed, a short, yelping bark that made the horse's ears twitch. It reminded him of another time, reminded him of a story he'd been meaning to tell himself. "It was some, now," he muttered under his breath. "It was. Was Doc and Gabe and this child as was just down from the Roche Jaune with three inches o' iron in the hump ribs . . ."

The horse's hoofs thumped dully along the trail. With a habit so old he was no longer aware of it, the old man scanned the forest on either side of the trail, watching. To his left the eastern sky soaked up light from the coming dawn, and on the right the broad sweeping flood of the Willamette reflected the silver grayness of the sky in its current, silent in the early morning, glimpsed between the endless ranks of firs.

"Had a hair o' the black bear to him, now. *Well*, he did," the old man muttered. It was a long time ago, but it was very clear in his mind. He traveled along, telling himself a story of men long dead and what they had to say and where they went and what they did there. From time to time he gently eased the horse out to the bank of the Willamette, so he could see more clearly upriver. He could see the great horseshoe of the falls ahead, and the distant, steady murmur of white water came to him. Just below the cascade that stretched across the river was a small island, and there was a faint plume of white smoke rising from it into the still morning air. He watched it.

"Major says, 'Gabe, sorry as hell about the man, but no damned rascal of a 'Rapaho going t' insult my wife, hear?'" His monologue was endless, as life itself was endless. In the telling he became a sort of god, for he restored warmth to flesh long since cold and gave living bodies back to bones picked white and clean in the mountain valleys.

"Gabe says, 'Meek, you know the rules about firin' off a gun in camp.' 'Hell's full o' such rules,' says the Major, cleanin' his gun just as ca'm as ca'm. . . ."

The plume of smoke was from a building built near the edge of the island. A mill, near as the old man could make out, and no threat to him. He tugged gently on the reins and the bony horse moved obediently back inland to the trail. In half an hour he had come into sight of the first of the buildings of Oregon City, perched high on a cliff overlooking the falls of the Willamette.

The old man did not go into the main settlement. He stayed low, on the bench of land bordering the river. From below he could see a few houses of the cliff-perched settlement, one of them large, white, and freshly painted. Though he had never before been within a thousand miles of the place, he recognized the house as being that of John McLoughlin. He recognized most of the buildings he saw, except for the very new ones. In winter camp, sitting half frozen around a lodge fire, a man had a chance to pick up a good bit of information. Oregon City had been described to him once, and as a matter of habit each detail had remained fresh in his mind, waiting for the time it would be needed. He was a mountain man; it was his way.

The old man reined up, surveying the buildings of the upper town, the few frame structures now beginning to be built lower down, on the bench. There was a ferry landing, and he figured it was the ferry McLoughlin had started when he left Hudson's Bay. On the opposite side of the river was another settlement—a few buildings, rather, straggling among the timbered hills. Went by the name of Linn, he recalled.

The sky was now full light, and the old man felt exposed. He had no curiosity about Oregon City at all. He was only regretful he had to pass by now that it was light. It was fully six o'clock, but he could see no signs of activity except the plume of white smoke from the island mill, now directly opposite him.

He thought about it. His fingers moved in the long black lock of hair, plaiting it into a tight braid, then shaking it out again. He felt unsafe among the wooden structures.

"Goes against nature," he muttered, scanning the signs of human settlement. It wasn't like a real village. A real village you could pick up and move and a week later there would be nothing but a few traces of fires and the packed surface where the lodges had been. These wooden shacks were ugly; they didn't belong, they were badly made and offended the land. Permanent. You could never give the world back to itself when you built like that. He leaned over the saddle horn and spat contemptuously.

"Bunch o' wuthless dungheads," he said. *"Wagh!"* But that was the way it was, and there was no help for it. There was no doubt in his mind that the human race was some kind of hideous error on the part of a god intending something more sensible. It made a man mad just to think about it.

He kicked the horse up again, anxious now to get past. The trail changed abruptly into something resembling a street, lined on one side with a few frame buildings. Ugly as the rest of them, with painted signs on the front. He could have read them if he'd been interested, but he wasn't.

Names. Always names. It was a dirty habit they'd got into of naming everything. He supposed the river he'd crossed near dawn had a name of some kind or other. People always put names to the world, the dungheads. Not enough sense to leave things be . . .

Suddenly he stopped, his reverie broken. Just ahead of him a still figure was lying curled tightly against the wall of a building, a shapeless lump rolled in a blanket. The old man eased the horse ahead until he drew even with the silent form. The sleeper clutched the neck of a bottle in one hand, but it was overturned and empty. A stale and foul pool of vomit stained the earth around his head.

The old man sat still, watching. The blanket bundle stirred, vague wakefulness brought by the sound of the old man's horse. A black, disheveled head poked out, and two puffy eyes turned up hopefully. It was an Indian, but one of the coast peoples the old man did not know. The face was flat and broad, with almost oriental folds around the eyes. The man's lips were slack and wet as he stared humbly up at the mounted white man. Blankly the Indian's eyes roved over the towering figure, trying to understand.

"Wiskey?" he said tentatively, and tried to smile. "Wiskey, no?"

The old man said nothing. His face impassive, he leaned forward across the saddle, watching.

The Indian put his head back down and turned to the wall. He let his black head rest still for a long time, but the old man did not go away. Finally he turned back, lifting himself shakily on one elbow, and tried to clear his vision.

The old man watched without expression, peering at him from behind the leathery mask of his face; a mask that showed no feeling. The Indian blinked uncertainly, and for a moment the two were still, watching each other. The Indian levered himself up to a sitting position against the wall, beginning to be afraid. A terrible sharp pain coursed through his skull, but he dared not close his eyes while the other watched so steadily.

"*Klahowya*," the Indian said apprehensively. There was no answer.

Slowly the brown man pushed himself up, supporting his back against the wall, drawing the blanket around him. The blue of his denim jeans was a dirty gray, and the once brightly checked shirt he wore was stained with vomit and the accumulated dirt of months. He began to inch along the wall away from the old man, clutching the blanket with one hand and feeling his way along the building with the flat palm of the other. He felt the corner of the building with his fingertips, and a soft, deerlike whimper sounded in his throat. He turned away from the old man and began to run down the street, the loose end of the blanket trailing behind him in the dew-dark earth. He ran shuffling, not in control of his legs, stumbling and lurching. Reaching a corner he turned, with one panic-born glance back, and disappeared.

For a long moment the old man remained, sitting his horse quietly, leaning over the horn and watching the corner where the Indian had vanished. Then he sat up straight and jerked the horse into movement. When they passed the corner he did not look to see where the Indian had gone.

"So Major cleaned his gun 'n' there wasn't a thing in hell old Gabe c'd do about it. Fined 'm five dollars, *wagh!* But if I recollect me, we never had trouble like that with Meek again."

He had been interested in the Indian, because it was the first tame Indian he had ever seen. It was a new thing for him, and he had all his life been very curious about new things.

2

The sun was now above the eastern hills, and he figured he had still another three hours to go. The land was clearly in his mind; the river trended north and south for another ten miles above the falls. Then, abruptly, it shifted, making an arrowhead point and running east-west. On that point Johnson Monday had his cabin; had his farm.

The old man leaned over and spat on the ground. "Damn dunghead dirt-clodder. *Wagh!* That's *some*, now."

For all he had the country clearly mapped, it was hard to make the picture in his mind of Johnson Monday behind a plow. The Jaybird himself, scraping away at the ground like a mole looking for a home. The old man shrugged, and the heavy locks of black hair swung at his shoulders. No telling what a man would do if he got scared enough; that was the dirty part of the whole human trick.

He grinned faintly. There'd been a time or two when the Jaybird never thought to see his hair again, much less the ass-end of a plowhorse. The old man closed his eyes, seeing how it had been when he and the Jaybird were running together.

"Was up to the Powder," he said reflectively. "Ice just breakin' up, *wagh!*, 'n' colder'n Billy Sublette's heart. 'Here's wet powder 'n' no fire t' dry it,' says I. 'Wagh!' says Jaybird, a-readin' sign. 'This here's Yellow Wolf's band or I'm a nigger. . . .' "

The way it was, the way it had always been, when the world was real. The plodding of the horse turned steps to yards, and slowly the miles disappeared behind him. The sun went up fast above the horizon, then strangely slowed for its imperceptible journey across the center of the day. It burned warm against his cheek, and when he put the flat of his hand against the horse's neck, it was heated from the sun.

"This nigger figures to cache," he told himself. "Man's a damn idjit t' go bangin' about without he looks over the land a bit." He nodded to himself in confirmation. It'd work out, one way or another. He'd see the Jaybird in good time, there was no real hurry. This was new country for him, the Willamette Valley, and he always liked to have just a little time to get used to new country. Get it in his belly.

Well before midday the trail he followed began to rise, as a cliff formed on his bank of the river. Soon he came to the river's turning and looked across at the point of land and the cabin that belonged to Johnson Monday.

The old man was on the outside of the river's curve, and the ground was much higher there. The cliff below him was studded with brush and some small, scrubby trees. On the opposite bank there was taller growth, firs and the like, but the old man could see over the tops easily. The point of land was as he had heard; a sort of arrowhead, almost a peninsula. The center had been roughly cleared, and it was newly plowed. Stumps still dotted the field, half a dozen of them smoldering and floating feathers of white smoke into the still air. The raw patch of earth was scraped out in the midst of the black-green and solid forest that stretched across the gentle hills as far as he could see. Ugly, helpless. An open wound on the earth, the festering sore of some mysterious wasting disease.

"*Wagh!*" the old man grunted, pleased with himself. "That's it, sure god. This child knows all about such." Mankind was a walking plague, a sort of running gangrene getting into every little scratch on the face of the earth and turning it rotten.

He looked across at Monday's field for a long time. Set in the center was the cabin, a forlorn small animal crouched miserably in the sun, hoping for warmth. There was no one about, but the chimney trailed a little smoke. The walls kept the heat out, not like an honest lodge. It would be dark inside, too, the sun never coming in. He thought of his own lodge, with the sun streaming through the skins and the bright designs making everything warm and comfortable.

He shook his head slowly in bewilderment, tugging at the long braid that hung beneath his hat. How the hell could a man who'd known a real home ever live like that, hunkered under a heavy roof? It was nothing to him, but he wondered just the same. One more item in the account book against a man's name.

He shrugged. It was nothing to him. "Wagh!" he muttered. "Dungheads all, 'n' there's no help f'r it."

There was a small island in the river, long and thin, separated from Monday's farm by a narrow, swift-running channel. The island was perhaps a quarter of a mile long, and not more than fifty yards wide. A rocky beach stretched along the river side, and the rest was wooded.

The old man could not see the channel side from where he stood, but he guessed there would be no beach there; the channel current was too swift.

"This nigger'll cache there a bit," he muttered, and turned the old horse back away from the edge of the rocky outcrop. He dismounted and began to backtrack along the trail, looking for a route down to the water. He led the animal back more than half a mile before the edge had gentled enough to get down, and it brought them well below the lower point of the island. The old man toyed with the black braid and looked at the current and the width of the river and the nature of both banks. He shrugged and turned away. If it came to that, they could swim upstream as well as down. It was all equal to him, the horse had to do the work.

He turned back to the animal and surveyed him speculatively. "Y' goddam boneyard. Nothin' but wolf-meat, 'n' the sooner the better. Y'are now."

The horse drew back her lips soundlessly, showing great white teeth in a terrible grimace. Then she reached forward and tried to nibble one of the old man's black braids. The old man slapped her across the nose, and the horse grimaced wildly again, still without sound.

"Wuthless 'n' iggerant," the old man muttered, swinging up into the saddle. "Hya! *Move!*"

Carefully the horse picked her way to the edge and stopped with her forefeet planted in the water, looking across the river. The old man snorted. "That's right," he said angrily. "Drown me. This child knows y'r mind. Y' thinkin' he don't *know? Wagh!*"

He jerked on the reins, pointed the horse's head upriver. The animal stepped carefully into the water, feeling the bottom tentatively with each step. When it was deep enough she began to swim methodically, parallel to the bank, directly upstream. Near the bank the current was not too swift, and they gradually made up the distance they had been forced to backtrack. Twice on the upstream journey the horse swung in to the edge of land again, at flat shelves just wide enough to give her feet purchase. There she stood and rested, her breath coming heavy and fast.

After entering the water the old man had let the reins hang loose in his hands, letting the animal work as it saw fit, trusting perfectly in its judgment. When they returned to the bank to rest, the old man dismounted in the tiny space and squatted silently on his haunches, waiting until the horse was ready to move again.

It took nearly an hour to make up the lost distance, and the old man was content; they were once again nearly opposite the upper end of the island, two hundred feet below the cliff where he had stood before. All that remained was to cross the river. The horse was tired now and rested a long time before starting across; long enough for the old man to tell himself two stories of things that had happened long ago. He sat with his back against a stone, eyes closed, leaning back without tension. The horse was motionless, head down and silent. Both were passive, without will or desire, waiting, because at that time it was necessary to wait.

At last the horse raised her head and snuffled. The old man opened his eyes slightly and looked at her. For a long moment they remained that way. Then the old man stood and mounted and they crossed the river.

3

He explored the island briefly, not so much for defense as to satisfy his curiosity about the way things were. Then he returned to the spot he had selected near the upper end and picketed the horse. The animal immediately pulled up the picket pin and wandered off, grazing.

"Iggerant as a man," the old man muttered, watching the horse meandering away into the woods.

He sat against a tree, wriggling against it to scratch his back. From the voluminous flap of the leather hunting shirt he extracted a redstone pipe bowl, a stem, and a small packet of tobacco. Carefully, pinch by slow pinch, he stuffed the thin shreds into the bowl, not wasting any. He fitted the stem and bowl together, rubbing the stone gently with his thumb and forefinger, turning it around and enjoying the feel and sight of it. Sioux, it was. Only one place on the face of the earth that particular red stone came from. Supposed to be the same stone as the first medicine pipe Wakantanka gave to the People. That was the way he heard it. You couldn't believe anything the lying bastards told you, but that was the way he heard it, and he occasionally let himself believe it for a while.

"This nigger's a long way from home," he said to the pipe.

He smoked in silence until it was finished. Then he stretched himself out full length at the base of the tree and went to sleep. In time the horse wandered back and nuzzled the old man's head. She walked to the place she had been picketed and awkwardly lowered herself to the ground.

They slept for nearly two hours, while the sun passed noon and swung into the west. It was a quiet time, with no sound but the rustlings of small animals in the brush, and no movement but the slow shifting of dappled patches of sunlight through the trees and across the ground.

The old man woke as suddenly as he had fallen asleep. He walked over to the channel side of the island, kicking the horse in the rump as he passed. He waded in up to his waist, wetting the buckskin trousers and moccasins again. During his nap they had begun to dry, stiffening and shrinking painfully. This time they would dry while he was moving, and it would not be bad.

He stood there in the water, looking across at the mainland, no more than fifty feet away.

"This nigger c'd swim that slick," he said contemptuously. For a moment he waited. If he swam he'd just have to walk when he got there, so he decided to take the horse. He had never tried swimming before, but he thought he could probably do it, if it came to that. He knew men that could swim, brown and white both, that weren't half the man he was, so he didn't expect there was any great problem to it.

The horse was standing again, waiting patiently, when the old man returned. "Hya! Y' damn boneyard. Us'll see how the Jaybird's stick's a-floatin'."

The mainland point that faced the island was a sandy beach, the only one the old man had seen along the river. To reach it they had to swim

directly from the upper point of the little island across the mouth of
the channel, going diagonally upstream again. The channel mouth was
shallow, and the horse's hoofs scraped bottom often; sometimes more
walking than swimming. But the same shallowness had its disadvantages,
for the swift-running water was clogged with deadfalls and debris that
had come sweeping down the Willamette in flood season. Some were
visible and easily avoided, but others were submerged, waterlogged
and heavy, with networks of hidden branches making traps below the
surface. Several times the animal lost its balance, nearly throwing them
both into the current.

But the distance was short, and quickly made. They plodded up the
sandy beach a little, and found a well-defined trail leading up through
the screen of trees that separated Monday's field from the river.
Reaching the top of the trail and emerging from the trees, the old man
reined up and looked again at the Jaybird's handiwork. The
black-earthed furrows stretched away from him toward the little cabin,
and the slow twists of smoke from the smoldering stumps were like
candles just extinguished. There was still no sign of activity around the
cabin itself, and he could see no animals.

A bright reflection glinted from something metallic near the wall of
the building, but he was still too far to make it out. Maybe a plow.

He started the horse moving again, skirting the field on the south
side and riding parallel to the river. He was past the point now, and the
river was running east and west. In a few minutes he reached a point
directly between the river and cabin, and stopped again as a flash of
color by the house caught his eye. He was only a few hundred feet from
the building and he sat the horse very still.

It was a woman, just come out of the cabin, and the color he had
seen was her brightly patterned dress. Calico, gingham, some such. He
didn't know about such things. When he was trading everything was
silk, and that was good enough.

He gripped the reins more tightly, as a sudden flash of anger and
contempt surged up in him. "'Pears the Jaybird got hisself a white
woman," he muttered to the horse.

Then he relaxed, and shrugged. It was nothing to him. But Jaybird
had had a Shoshone woman in the mountains, by report one of the

best, though just a girl. The old man had never met her, but it annoyed him obscurely that a man would switch women when he had a good one. But it was nothing to him what Jaybird did.

"Damn iggerant dunghead," he said. Though the Shoshone slut might have been killed or something.

The woman that had come out of the cabin was ungainly. She walked around the corner to the woodpile awkwardly, and the old man was contemptuous of her softness.

"Lazy slut," he snorted. You'd never catch any squaw of his moving like that, less'n she was . . .

He leaned forward in the saddle, and saw that his old eyes had been playing him false. The woman wasn't fat, but heavy with pregnancy.

He kicked the old horse in the ribs and started up toward the cabin. The woman caught the movement and stopped, startled. Then she moved back around the corner with the load of wood, the slow, measured pace taking her out of sight as the old man approached. He heard the door shut.

He let the horse plod up to the door of the cabin and stopped. He leaned forward on the saddle horn, crossing his bony wrists comfortably before him. She knew he was there. He could wait. He closed his eyes and was back in Pierre's Hole the year of '32.

"Powerful drunk," he muttered. "Powerful. Billy Sublette's little brother got off first, him 'n' Gervais, I recollect. 'N' I'm a nigger if he didn't haul along the iceman from Boston 'n' his whole kit, them as hadn't deserted. Name o' Wyeth, him. *Wagh! Well*, now. They hadn't got but a couple miles out . . ."

It was eighteen years and a thousand miles from him, but it was all sharp in his mind. How that no-good Nez Percé come roarin' back to camp with his horse all lathered, hollerin', "Piegan, Piegan!" Hadn't been Piegan anyways, but a village o' Gros Ventres coming up from . . .

The old man opened his eyes slightly and looked at the closed, silent door. He grunted softly, and swung down out of the saddle.

"Nothin' t'rile a man like bad manners," he grumbled.

He walked over to the door and shoved it open harshly. It banged back against the wall, the sound echoing loudly in the tiny room. The inside of the cabin was at first completely dark. There was only the light from one small window in the south wall and the low fire on his right. He stood in the doorframe, letting his eyes accustom themselves to the gloom.

For a moment he thought the woman had gotten out, though he had automatically looked the building over as he approached and seen no other way but the main door. After the reverberating crash of the door against the wall there was no sound.

At last he made her out. She was sitting in the farthest corner, where the darkness was almost total, her back against the wall. She reminded him oddly of a doe gone to cover in a thicket; immobile, silent, waiting. As his eyes adjusted to the light he saw that the woman was not white after all. Brownskin, but dressed up funny in white clothes, like that other tame Indian he'd seen. It was curious.

Across her lap lay a long Hawkens gun, the barrel shining dully. Instinctively his eyes went to the hammer, and he noticed scornfully that it was on half-cock. Her hands lay placid and calm on the rifle, moving no more than the rest of her body.

She was a likely woman, he thought, her pregnant-heavy body a contrast with the sharp, fine features of her face. Dressed up so damn queer there was no way he could tell her tribe or band. But she was mountain Indian sure god, and he figured probably Shoshone. It pleased him, mildly. So the Jaybird had brought his woman down with him; that was better.

He moved forward a step. There was a dull, metallic click, and he stopped. The woman still sat calmly and without motion; but the hammer of the Hawkens was now back on full-cock and ready to fire. She seemed to be a part of the wall, so silent, so passive. He had to admit the Jaybird had some eye for beauty. The woman made him think a little of Mountain Lamb, Meek's first woman, that he got from Milton Sublette. Most beautiful damn animal god ever made, they said. She was Shoshone, too. There was something about them.

It appeared like this one was a bit skittery, though, what with the Hawkens on full-cock and all.

For a long time they looked at each other across ten feet of emptiness, both still. The fire reached a pitch pocket in the wood; sizzled and flared yellow. The highlights in the woman's eyes darted, and a shimmering reflection cascaded across her smooth, dark cheek.

At last the old man raised his right hand slowly, palm forward. He pushed it toward the woman, twisting it slightly back and forth in the mountain sign for "question." The woman did not move, but her eyes followed the movement of his hand.

He continued, his hand darting rapidly before him, and as he signed he repeated the question in words: "Where's your man?" He signed very carefully, thinking she might have forgotten, holding his index finger in the erect-penis sign for "man" when he had finished.

There was no reaction. The woman remained calm and still and did not answer.

The old man closed his eyes. Finally he looked down at the floor. "Ain't here, that one," he muttered. "Can't come round *this* nigger. Ain't here. No horse. Nothin'. *Wagh!*" His throat rumbled with stillborn words while the woman sat impassive and almost invisible, watching.

He fell silent at last, then raised his head to squint around, as if confirming his conclusion. He returned his attention to the woman almost reluctantly, and leaned forward slightly. "Where's—your—man," he repeated carefully, as to a child. It was almost as though he had forgotten asking before.

As he spoke again, he moved forward another step. Almost slowly, the glinting barrel of the Hawkens swung around, and there was suddenly no distance between them at all. The half-inch cavern of the muzzle was very close. The woman spoke at last, and her voice was soft and even, without inflection.

"You go now, old man."

"*Wagh!*" he grunted softly. He looked down at his hands, and frowned, considering some problem that was very far away. He seemed to be listening to voices in his mind; answering questions the woman had not asked.

He turned and walked out the door, without haste. He picked up the reins of his horse and climbed into the saddle. The woman followed him and stood in the doorway, the heavy gun still cradled easily across the crook of her elbow. The old man shook the reins slightly, setting the horse off into a slow walk. He passed her as though he did not see; had forgotten the conversation, his mind elsewhere. About ten yards past, he stopped and swung around in the saddle with his fist on the horse's rump. He stared at her again, frowning, while the two long hanks of hair swung across his chest.

"Tell the hoss Old Webb was to see'm. You do it."

Without waiting for acknowledgment he turned away again. He began muttering to himself in a low monotone as he rode away, taking up the story where he had left off.

The woman watched him go, and gradually the barrel of the long rifle lowered until it pointed toward the ground. She squeezed the trigger and there was a dull snap as the hammer fell on the empty pan.

She closed her eyes and leaned back against the doorframe for a second. Then she moved slowly into the house, replaced the gun on its oaken pegs over the fireplace. From a cupboard at the back she took a newly cured skin and stretched it on the floor and began to trace the pattern of a shirt. It was slow. The child was so large now it was difficult for her to stoop.

Chapter Two

Johnson Monday was low in his mind as he rode along. It was already nearing dusk, and the long column was still a good ten miles from Oregon City. Just across the Willamette, in the shadow of the western hills, straggled the half-dozen shacks that proudly styled themselves Portland, known to everyone but the inhabitants as Little Stumptown. He had been counting on making it home tonight, but it didn't look that way now.

He pulled lightly on the reins, easing off to the side of the line, and looked up and down. At the head rode Colonel Patterson, sitting his horse stiffly, as befitted his rank. The more fatigued he became the stiffer he sat, until by this time of night he had lost all contact with the animal and slapped up and down painfully in the saddle.

Monday sighed and stretched his shoulders. "Goddam wooden sojer." Grouped behind Patterson were some regular army in their dusty blue uniforms. Then came the wagon with the Cayuse prisoners, poking along and creaking until Monday thought his ears would tear off. The Indians, all handcuffed together in the back of the wagon, had contemptuously gone to sleep in spite of the unearthly noise.

The rest of the column was a mixed, straggling mass of the so-called militia—just settlers like Monday, with absurd blue military caps—and Indians. They milled along in the wake of the ramrod colonel like a herd of witless sheep. Everyone was very tired.

Monday sat and watched part of the line go by, silent and sullen, heads down, half paralyzed with fatigue and—for some—grief. No one spoke, and only a few even glanced at him. He recognized the wife of Tamahas, her fat body jelly-shaking with each step of the horse. She stared blankly at the ground just ahead of her horse's hoofs, and her glazed attention never wandered. Monday wondered what she was thinking about, riding so silently to the hanging of her husband.

Some war, Monday thought disgustedly. *It is, now.* Five prisoners and thirty tag-alongs. He wished to christ he'd had sense enough to stay home.

One of the regular army came riding briskly by, maintaining a laudable illusion of energy. Seeing Monday motionless by the side of the road, he stopped and gestured sharply. "Get back in line, mister."

Monday looked at him. "Go to hell, sojer," he said uninterestedly.

The blue uniform, just a boy, surveyed the huge blond figure sitting relaxed before him, hands crossed over the saddle horn. The little blue cap, his only kinship with the giant, perched ridiculously atop a mane of yellow hair. Two hundred pounds of resting mountain cat. The soldier kicked up his horse and rode on.

"Hell," Monday said under his breath. He swung off the road and down toward the riverbank. He tethered his horse to a tree and got a bottle out of the saddlebag, sitting down against a boulder with a sigh. For a long moment he simply stared vacantly across the river, vaguely conscious of the slowly retreating squeal of the wagon in the distance. Then he yanked the cork out of the bottle and tilted it up. Tears came to his eyes and he gasped as he felt the terrible burn coursing down his throat. Even for moonshine it was foul, but it was better than nothing. He wished he had some molasses to put in and he'd pretend it was rum.

He sat disconsolate and depressed, occasionally tilting the bottle, until he heard the soft pad of horse's hoofs coming down the slope. Quickly he corked the bottle, tucked it by the side of the rock and pulled a fir bough up to hide it.

Behind him came a voice, very stern. "Alri', Monday. Give me *bouteille.* It is the colonel who speak."

Monday grimaced. Without looking around he knocked the limb away and pulled the bottle out of its hiding place. "Sit y'self down, Rainy," he said.

The man behind dismounted and tethered his horse beside Monday's. He came around the rock to join the big blond man. René Devaux was a good six inches shorter than Monday's six feet, built light. He was perhaps thirty, but had a dark, adolescent handsomeness that made him seem younger. Like Monday, he wore the little blue military cap that signified his militiahood. He looked disappointed as he slid down to sit beside Monday.

"How you know it was me?" he asked in a puzzled voice.

" 'Cause you gargle instead o' talk," Monday said. "You say y'r r's and stuff funny."

"Is not the case," Devaux said firmly. "I speak perfect, there is fourteen years. Wi'out any accent. Moreover, I have a powerful thirst. I give you a little money?"

Monday handed him the bottle. "On the prairie, Rainy." Absently he swept one open palm over the other in the mountain sign for a free gift.

Devaux choked and coughed. He handed the bottle back, blinking. "Is ver' bad wiskey, that."

Monday shrugged. "Don't drink it."

"Not so bad as that," Devaux said in a hurt tone. "Listen. How you think of the army life, hah?"

Monday snorted.

"Ah, but friend of me, I think you understand wrong. One gives you food, one gives you a blanket, one tells you 'do this, do that.' Ver' simple, the army. Problems do not exist. I am ver' *militaire*, me. *La bouteille?*"

Monday handed the bottle back. He let his hands hang limply over his knees and looked at the ground while the Frenchman drank. When the bottle came back to him he studied the level and swished it a bit, then lifted it.

"*Wagh!*" Whyn't y' join up the regular army, then?" he said.

Devaux shrugged. "Me, I have no problems."

Monday laughed. Devaux, in common with all other former employees of the Hudson's Bay Company, was living on borrowed time and knew it. The recent influx of Americans—and the implacable hatred they brought for anything that suggested the monolithic British company—made Devaux's position hard. Oregon had been officially a territory for only a year, but the pressure was growing every day to "run the damn furriners out." After ten days every new settler from the states talked as though fifteen generations of his people had been born on Oregon soil.

"Moreover," Devaux said, glancing at the big man, "is a problem, I go live with the—what you call, the father of my woman?"

"Father-in-law."

"*C'est ça*. Exactly."

Monday laughed again. "Which one, Rainy? How the hell you choose?"

Devaux shrugged. "Is all equal to me."

"How many wives you got?"

"Is bad luck to count," Devaux said seriously. "Me, I never count. Numerous."

Monday grinned and began to tick them off on his fingers. "Well, let's see. There's that Clackamas, and a Calapuya, and that one down to the Rogue River, what do they call themselves?"

"Kelawatset."

"But she's just a girl, anyway, she don't count."

Devaux was indignant. "She is big enough to make babies. But is bad luck to count, friend of me. No more counting.'"

"What the hell you do it for, Rainy? All those relatives." Monday shook his head. The worst thing about having an Indian wife was the relatives, all of whom instantly became members of your immediate family, down to second and third cousins.

Devaux grinned happily. "No problems, me." He paused, and glanced slyly at Monday. "And you know, René Devaux, he goes—*everywhere!*" He swept his arm in a circle. "And no problems. Friends, everywhere. Family everywhere. Not so bad, moreover."

Monday grinned, never having thought of it in just that way. But it was quite true. Of all the men he knew, old Rainy was safer in the hills than any of them. No matter where he went he had a wife and family and a tribe, and could settle down for a week or a year.

"In any case," Devaux said, and his face grew solemn, "is a promise I make to my *père*, just when I leave Montreal. He say to me, 'René, my son, you go off and you make *beaucoup beaucoup* money, yes. But where you go, you don't leave one single'—*métis*—what you call it?"

"Half-breed."

"'—behind you. You make that promise.'" Devaux shrugged. "Alors, one promises, no? I had fifteen years then, but was already wearing long pants. You understand."

Monday stared at his friend in disbelief. "Rainy, you—for christ's sakes, man, you must have thirty kids or better scattered around here. And if they ain't half-breed, what the hell are they?"

Devaux reached out and touched Monday on the shoulder, his expression troubled. "Is my problem, you understand? Me, I travel— everywhere! The whole world over. And for what I do this? For one only thing!" He lifted his finger, to show the solitariness of his purpose.

"To find one woman—*one only woman*—what is sterile. Because, you know, one has promised." Devaux leaned back discouragedly and shrugged, lifting his hands helplessly. "Is my tragedy. Nowhere is sterile woman. Nowhere."

Monday leaned back against the rock, choking and gasping for breath. At last he said, wiping his tear-filled eyes, "Well, by god, Rainy. Nobody can say you haven't worked at it."

Devaux cocked his head. "One cannot know unless one tries, no? Me, I try them young, I try them old, fat and thin. Nowhere is a sterile woman, she *n'existe pas*. And now I am sad for thinking on my tragedy. *La bouteille?*"

"It's yours, Rainy. Finish it. You're better'n whisky t' cheer me up."

"*Alors, c'est ça.* Pretty soon we go, ah? *Le Colonel*, he is ver' *militaire.*"

"All right." Monday stood up, still grinning. "We'll go back and play sojer for a while."

Devaux slammed the cork into the bottle with the palm of his hand, and stood. "Moreover," he said, "you drink the bottle too much when you are low in your mind, friend of me. Me, I have no problems. I do not let it derange me, not the *militaire* or anything."

They walked back to their horses and mounted. The dusk had come full while they talked, and under the shelter of the trees the growing darkness made the small trail indistinct. Monday could barely make out Devaux's features. The Frenchman was still musing on his philosophy as he picked up the reins and swung into the saddle.

"No problems. Because, you know. When René Devaux has a wife, you know what he is doing with her?"

"I sure god do," Monday said, laughing again.

"No," Devaux said. "You do not." He sat his horse quietly in the darkness, and Monday could see no expression on the smaller man's face. His voice had changed. He spoke quietly, but coldly, all the lilt gone.

"When René Devaux has a wife, he is leaving her in the tribe, with her own people. Is the difference between us, friend of me."

Devaux jerked sharply on the reins, wheeling his horse up the path to intersect the main road. After a moment, Monday gently heeled his own horse, following slowly. "Hya," he said softly.

"Move."

2

Monday and Devaux caught up with the creeping column a mile or so farther on. They let their horses plod along at the slow walk dictated by the screaming wagon ahead. Monday wished to christ somebody had seen to the wagon on the way down, but nobody was interested enough. In the desert country they had come through up the Columbia, all the moving parts had shrunk from the dryness, and nothing fitted properly any more. Every turn of the wheel raised a grating shriek that pierced his ears like the shrill screams of a butchered pig. He wondered if he was the only one in the column bothered by it; nobody else seemed to pay any attention. He gritted his teeth.

It was dark now, but there was a full moon so bright it cast sharply defined shadows, illuminating the column with a pale blue luminescence. The line of riders ahead was a processional of the damned under the ghostly light, and the wagon shrieked incessantly like a soul tortured for eternity. Monday shook his head, trying to rid himself of the eerie thoughts. Devaux turned slightly in the saddle to look at him, then looked away again.

One of the soldiers came riding down the line, checking on the mounted Indians, giving gratuitous instruction, keeping them organized, as if it mattered. As he passed, Devaux said to Monday, loud enough for the soldier to hear, "The *militaire*, he are in control, no? Is a comfort to me."

The soldier passed on. Monday looked at the straggling group of Indians, perhaps thirty of them, who had paid no attention whatever to the organizational instincts of the military.

"They make me nervous," he said to Devaux.

"Womens and childrens?" Devaux said.

"They didn't have to come. Why'n hell couldn't they of stayed home?"

Devaux shrugged. *"C'est normal, ça.* When I am hanged, all my friends and relatives come to see also."

Monday shifted his position in the saddle, stretching his shoulders.

"You also will come to my hanging," Devaux said. "I think maybe is a ver' interesting thing to see, a friend of you who dance in the air, no?" The Frenchman suddenly reached over and grabbed the blue military cap from Monday's head. With a broad swing of his arm he sailed it off into the bushes.

"Rainy, god damn—"

"I think is too tight for you, the chapeau. It makes a pression on the brain, no?"

Monday grinned at him. "Might could be you're right."

Devaux shrugged. "Me, I wear it ver' well."

It was nearly nine o'clock when they reached the outskirts of Oregon City, their entrance heralded long before by the squeaking wagon wheels. The manacled prisoners in the wagon were awake now, and sitting up. Monday saw the lean, bony face of Tamahas turning to look contemptuously at his surroundings. Then, not caring, he lay back down in the wagon bed.

Monday shook his head. It had been Tamahas's hatchet that had destroyed the beauty of Narcissa Whitman, slashing away at that gentle, pale face until nothing remained but an unrecognizable pulp of blood, flesh, and splinters of bone. He was a bad one, Monday thought, the kind of man you could never reach and always made you wonder what God had in mind.

A crowd of sorts had gathered to watch their triumphal entry into the town. They lined the street in thin, scattered bunches. Children scampered around the groups, shouting and playing incomprehensible games. For them it was a holiday, a mysterious hour's reprieve from bedtime, and they profited.

"Murderin' red bastards! Hang 'em!"

Monday heard the shout ahead, and picked out the group from which it came: half a dozen men, standing around nervously. One of them, small and wiry, shook his fist indiscriminately at everyone who passed—Indians, military and militia alike—while he shouted curses. Monday leaned over in the saddle and spat on the ground.

The man continued, raising himself to a peak of obscenity as the wagonload of prisoners passed. Around him the other men were muttering and shuffling their feet in the dusty street. Occasionally the man would glance at them slyly, with a half-grin, looking for their approval. It was absurd. But it could get worse.

Monday looked over at Devaux, tilted his head toward the frenzied shouter ahead. Devaux nodded and they kicked up their horses and rode ahead along the line to the little group, and reined up in front of them. Devaux leaned out of the saddle.

"Eh, my friend," he said, his voice lilting, a wide smile on his face. "Not so loud wi' the noise, eh? You waking up the *bébé.*"

The man scowled at him, his fists clenched. "Dirty murderin' red swine!" he snarled, looking at the line. "Kill 'em, the murderers!"

"Eh, but my friend. Do not derange yourself—"

"Hangin's nothin', they ought t' be drawn and quartered," the man said to Devaux. He raised his voice to a shout again, shaking his fist in the air. *"Hang 'em, hang 'em!"*

Monday eased his horse up between Devaux and the standing man, so the animal's shoulder was almost pressing against the other's chest, making him step back. The man looked angrily up at Monday.

Monday said coldly, "Just what the hell do you *think* we're going t' do with 'em?"

The man looked down at the ground, muttering, then turned to his friends for support. They were mostly interested in something else. A voice said vaguely, "Ah, hell. It's gettin' late. . . ."

Monday and Devaux set their horses into a walk again, moving up the line. When they had gone fifty feet they heard the man's voice raised again behind them.

"An' you goddam mountain men are no better! Bunch o' dirty Indians your own selves! Hang the lot o' you an' be done with it!"

Neither of them turned.

A sergeant riding down the line wheeled his horse and came alongside. "Where's your cap, mister?"

"I lost it," Monday told him.

"Mister, that's United States property. You'll have to pay for that cap."

Monday closed his eyes and his fists tightened on the reins. "See my lawyer."

"Real funny," the sergeant said. "Don't get—"

Devaux took off his cap and placed it on Monday's head. "*Voilà*," he said. "The chapeau, he is found. Ver' simple." He smiled ingratiatingly.

"All right, you smart bastard. Where's yours?"

Devaux reached over again and took the cap from Monday and put it on his own dark head. He spread his hands. "*Le voilà*."

The sergeant was genuinely angry now. "Both of you wise bastards better come with—"

Through clenched teeth Monday said, "Move on, sojer. Just move on is all." His eyes were still closed.

The sergeant looked at the sharp ridges of muscle standing out on Monday's jaw, and the white-knuckled fists clutching the reins. He frowned, puzzled by the violence. "Mister, you're going to pay for that cap, I'll guarantee you," he said, but he turned his horse and rode down the line.

Slowly Monday relaxed, letting out his breath in a long ragged sigh. "I'm goin' home, Rainy," he said finally. "I got a bellyful o' this shit. I can't take any more."

Devaux shrugged. "Is ver' late, you arrive," he said.

"I want to see Mary."

He yanked viciously on the reins, turning the animal back down the street. The horse had been broken Indian-style and had only two gaits, walk and full gallop. Monday kicked him up into a thundering gallop, tearing past the last of the slow-moving line and maintaining the frantic pace until he had passed out of the end of town and was once again on the moonlit road.

Devaux watched him go, then turned back to follow the procession up to the jail, where he was interested in watching the prisoners come down.

"Is all equal to me," he said absently.

3

Late afternoon, the eastern sky slowly dulling down to blackness. The forests of the Willamette Valley lying still and vast, touched with warmth from the lowering western sun.

The old man glided swiftly and silently along the trail, his moccasins skimming the surface of packed, spongy needles. The long buckskin hunting shirt reached halfway to his knees, belted tightly about his thin waist, and the skirt of it slid stiffly around his thighs as he ran. An ancient, heavy flintlock swung easily in his hand, the barrel darting forward and back with his pace.

He whispered softly to himself as his moccasins whispered on the trail, fighting over a battle long since lost. "Antoine Godin, him as was Thierry's boy, *wagh!*—half froze f'r hair, him, and his pa kilt the fall before up to the Salmon . . ."

The old man's eyes flickered quickly right and left, drifting like a soft wind over the brush and the trees and the little valley that fell off to his left. He ran smoothly and without effort, watching everything, understanding everything, never seeming to look at anything. His eyes glided across a light patch on the bark of a giant fir by the trail. *"Wagh! Big 'un, him,"* he whispered as he ran, mentally gauging the weight of the buck whose spikes had rubbed the bark. But the sign was days old. He did not slow, slipping tirelessly through the forest. "Big Bellies they was, but the same as Bug's Boys t'my thinkin'. Out goes Antoine t'meet the headman, *wagh! . . ."*

He stopped; suddenly, silently, as the wind stops. He dropped to squat on his haunches in the middle of the trail, peering at the faint marks where several tiny patches of needles showed their dark moistness against the lighter color of the dry surface. Silent now, he glanced around him. The light was beginning to dim quickly, and he nodded to himself with satisfaction. "This child make 'em come. He will, now," he muttered softly.

He found the cross trail weaving behind a clump of brush. The hill slope above him, to his right, was webbed with an intricate pattern of dark against dark, meandering lines that began and disappeared and started anew a hundred yards away, almost invisible. The old man traced the cross trail among these, following it with his eyes surely and without doubt.

Satisfied that what he sought was not above him, he turned and slipped into the solid wall of brush on the downhill side, disappearing from the main trail with only the whisper of a moving branch. The almost-trail he followed wound randomly down the side of the hill, and he followed it more by feel than by vision. The brush was well above his head on either side, dimming off what little light was left of the day. A few minutes later the trail was cut by another, equally faint, and the old man unhesitatingly switched off to his right, following an instinct that made conscious decision unnecessary.

Before the light had completely gone he found what he expected: a dark room, carved out of the forest itself. Overhead the twining, tangled branches of firs made a lacy canopy, a finely fretted net that was almost solid. The lowest branches were all bare of needles. There was no brush here; beneath the netted roof was a broad, clear floor of matted needles, perhaps twenty feet long and ten wide.

The old man spread his nostrils, taking in the wind, then moved quickly across the tiny clearing to the opposite side. He squatted by the trunk of a giant fir, pulling the plug from his powder horn with his teeth. He did not measure the load, but poured with perfect accuracy, and rammed the ball and patch home with sharp, quick strokes. He turned the flint in its vise to a new edge and snapped it once. Then he primed the pan and laid the gun across his lap on full-cock.

Now he fell into a still somnolence, motionless, silent, breathing soundlessly through his open mouth. He closed his eyes and waited. His mind rested, placid and calm as a still lake in summer. The old battles and old dreams did not intrude. There was only the sense of waiting calm, the functions of life suspended in the sweet and perfect gentleness of waiting. Around him the clear space was still and darkening.

He could not have said how long he waited. He was still, hovering somewhere between two worlds where there was no time, but only the eternal contentment of suspension. A fir bough creaked in the dark whisper of wind, but he did not open his eyes. An animal snuffed suddenly nearby, but he knew it was not his, and did not break the tenuous web of passive calm in which he existed.At last she came, silently down the trail as he had come, pausing sometimes along the way to browse in the brush, nibbling off the soft new growth, but always moving steadily toward the clearing.

The old man perceived her coming with tenderness, and tenderly raised the long rifle, resting the muzzle across the Y of the wiping stick. In his mind there ran a soft and sibilant chant, a charm to insure good hunting and the forgiveness of that which was killed so he might live.

She stood at the edge of the clearing, her light buff body faintly luminous against the black-green of night-darkened foliage. She paused, hesitant, snuffling at the air, and the old man let her breathe for the two of them. She looked across the clearing at him and he remained still. At last she turned her fathomless dark eyes from him and took a short, hesitant step into the clearing. The web of branches overhead shook in the sudden thunder that filled the forest opening. The broad puffball of white smoke rolled up, picking a devious, tendriled way through the branches above.

She shuddered with the impact and turned at last to see the old man who sat calm behind the forked stick. Her falling shook the clearing faintly, like the distant vibration of thunder.

The old man stood, stretching his stiff joints, cramped from the waiting without time. He drew the heavy butcher knife from its sheath at the back of his belt. Arterial blood pulsed sluggishly over his hand as he slit the hide over the breastbone and peeled it back. Quickly he made the deep incision through sheath and muscle, plunging his arm deep into the cavity of the chest, groping with his bony fingers for the warm heart.

He stood back from the fallen doe, breathing heavily with the effort of it. He slit the heart, opening the chambers, and drank the rich blood with a strong sense of gratitude. He made his meal of the raw dark meat, and it was enough. When he was finished he drew the blade of the butcher knife across the front of his shirt to clean it. With a grunting sigh of fatigue and content he settled himself down, lying close against the dead doe and drawing into his own body the heat that so quickly drained from hers.

He fell immediately into sleep, though all the time he had intended to tell himself the part where Godin shot the Gros Ventre chief and came galloping back to camp waving his red blanket and swearing.

Chapter Three

It was past midnight when Monday turned off on the trail that led down to his point of land. Unable to take the ferry across at Oregon City—they had stopped extending him credit six months ago—he had to ride down the east bank of the river, a mile past his cabin, wake up Peter Swensen and talk him into ferrying him across.

Peter grumbled, but he didn't really mind, Monday thought. Nothing ever seemed particularly serious to Peter Swensen; no inconvenience could weigh heavily on a man who anticipated the end of the world daily.

Monday sighed, shifting his position in the saddle. It was all so simple, if you could only see it right.

Back in the States, Peter had belonged to a sect which, through careful analysis of the Scriptures, had determined that the world was to end in '41. Peter didn't know exactly how they did it, but he believed it. He had paid eight dollars for a white robe and gone to stand on the nearest hill at the designated time, and nothing had happened except that two of the faithful had sneaked off into the brush after a time, and the girl later became pregnant. It didn't seem a very auspicious sign to Peter Swensen. The truth was, he rather fancied the girl himself, but hadn't felt entirely comfortable about meeting Judgment Day with his pants down. Having lost the opportunity by reason of faith, Peter's attitude toward both women and religion became ambiguous.

After a couple of years he emigrated to Oregon, depressed but still hopeful. It stood to reason that the world was bound to end sometime; it had been promised him, and he expected it. He had lost faith in the promisers, but the promise itself remained clear in his mind.

Monday shook his head. It was strange how little it took to make a man happy. Something solid to build his life around, even if it was the end of the world. He could see how it might be a great comfort.

Soon he came out into the clear, and his field lay black in the moonlight ahead of him. The cabin roof was silvery gray; the moon seemed to spread a thin, metallic sheen over the land, like a daguerreotype he had once seen.

The only movement was the slow drifting of ghostly white wisps of smoke from the smoldering stumps, and Monday smiled to himself. Mary had doubtless been out every day, making sure of the burning. It was a slow process, an eternal process, burning out the stumps. Letting the relentless fire creep down through the root system, clearing his land for him. And what did he have in the end? A bare space, an absence of trees. And still, each year, more clearing, more stumps, more burning.

Moonlight was flooding through the little window in the south wall when Monday closed the cabin door gently behind him. He stood for a moment at the door. The pale light slanted off to the left wall, lighting in silver and blue shadows the bed and the still form of the woman there. Her head was turned to the side, facing him. The moonlight washed gently across the firm contours of her face and was lost in the deep blackness of her hair.

Monday let his eyes trace the rounded swell of her belly beneath the blanket, faintly outlined now in the luminous glow of the moon. He suddenly realized her eyes were open, watching him. Silently he went to kneel beside the bed, putting his hand softly on the rounded hill of pregnancy. "Mary," he said quietly, "I'm not going away any more."

The woman looked silently up at him, her deep eyes highlighted by the reflection of the moon. For a long time they remained that way, still, looking at each other and finding again the lost features. Finally she stirred.

"You are gone a long time," she said.

Monday bent and kissed her softly, tasting again the warmth and freshness of her lips. "I'm back now," he said.

"You have not eaten." She struggled up to a sitting position, the blanket falling away from her breasts, now growing full and heavy.

"It doesn't matter, Mary. Please."

"I fix something," she said. Awkwardly she put her legs over the edge of the bed and reached for the shapeless nightdress she never wore. Monday reached to help her. "No," she said. "The fire."

The blond man stood and went to the fireplace, knelt down to find a glowing coal. He built a tiny cone of kindling and with the wooden tongs carefully put the black-red coal beneath. In a moment the yellow flame had spurted, and he began to lay the larger wood.

Mary had gone to the cooler deep beneath the floor at the back, and brought back a deer steak. "You sit down," she said, bringing the meat to the fire.

Monday went to the table against the opposite wall and pulled it out into the center of the room to be closer. He sat on a bench, facing the fire, with elbows back against the table. As his wife worked to make the meat ready, he watched her move, following every twist of the hand, the arch of her back, the swinging black hair.

The woman impaled the steak on two sharp sticks leaning toward the fire, and in a moment there was a sizzling as the first drops of fat melted and fell.

"Mary, come here," Monday said.

The woman came to the table and sat beside him. He put his arm around her shoulder and she leaned her head against him, watching the fire. They sat with the warmth of each other and the fire, without speaking. After a while Mary gently moved his arm, and returned to the fire to turn the steak.

"Who was it?" she asked, not turning.

"Tamahas and the rest of them. Everybody at the mission was mixed up in it. About two hundred Cayuse and a few Nez Percé."

"Who did you bring back?"

"Tamahas and four other headmen. Old man Kiami says he didn't do anything, but he isn't afraid to die."

"Five men," Mary said.

"Better'n nothin', ain't it?" He shrugged. "Anyways, the massacre at Waiilatpu was better'n two years ago. This puts an end to it."

"Nothing new, then? About why they did it?"

Monday shook his head. After a moment he said, "How—how have things been here, Mary? You get along all right?"

"Yes. It was all right."

"You didn't get too lonesome? Or anything?"

Mary turned from the fire and smiled slightly. "Peter Swensen, that one came every day." She gestured toward the wall. "He plow your field, you will see it in the morning."

"I'll be damned," Monday said. "What'd he do that for?"

"He said his horses were forgetting how to do it. Keep it in their minds."

Monday laughed. "He's got land of his own he could plow, up on that mountain of his." Swensen had staked out his 640-acre land claim on the rough hill north of Monday's farm, and it was generally known as Peter's Mountain. But he refused to live there until he could build the right kind of place. What with the end of the world coming and all, it hardly seemed worth the trouble, so he simply squatted on the ownerless land on the river, and waited.

"He says is all a waste of time," Mary explained. "But he don't want his horses to forget. So he plow your land, because it is closer."

"I just saw him and he didn't say he came by so often," Monday said absently.

"I know all about the end of the world now," Mary said. "You ask me anything, I tell you." She was silent for a moment. Then she said, "Is it true, what he says about the end of the world?"

"No," Monday said. "I don't think so, anyway."

Mary nodded. She went to the cupboard and got down a wooden platter, deftly forked the steak on to it. She put the fork by the platter and sat down beside her husband. Monday reached the butcher knife out of its sheath, wiped it off on his shirt front.

"Much business down here now," Mary said. "Joe Meek coming down maybe two, three times a week. See if anybody making whisky or hiding niggers, he say."

"Fat lot Meek cares, even if he is marshal," Monday said. Suddenly he stopped, a forkful of meat halfway to his mouth. He put the fork on the platter and turned to Mary. "Who else was here? Just passing by, I mean."

"Virginia came down to talk, you know Virginia."

"Sure, I know Virginia," Monday said. Meek's Nez Percé wife, who never left home any more than Mary did, and for the same reason. "Who else?"

Mary looked at him, smiling. "Maybe I don't need to tell you more."

"No, maybe not," Monday said. He could probably count them off himself: Meek and Doc Newell and Ebberts and their wives. Smith and Trask, maybe, all the way from the coast. Russel from down in the valley. Just passing by on sudden, unexpected errands that took them on the long and inconvenient detour past Monday's place. Stopping at Swensen's for a little chat, cursing one another and telling lies. Men that hadn't seen each other, some of them, since they left the mountains, suddenly meeting by accident where the river turned and a woman waited alone for her husband. Monday picked up his fork, turned it between his fingers, looking down at the piece of steak.

"Tell you something, Mary," he said. "You meet a—funny kind of people in the mountains."

Mary smiled very faintly. "The Shoshone are mountain people," she said softly. She put her head against her husband's shoulder, feeling the cords of muscle roll as he drew the knife through the steak again and lifted it to his mouth.

2

Early morning, the forests and hills of the valley emerging slowly from the bottomless dark to stand against the graying eastern sky, flat, without depth. The old man woke clear-eyed and instantly, moving cleanly from sleep to waking, without transition.

The body of the doe was cold now, making skinning difficult. The fleshy surface of the hide was cold-congealed, clinging stubbornly to the muscles below. The old man worked patiently, holding the hide taut away from the body and drawing the edge of the knife gently along the joining line to separate the membrane. He took only enough of the hide to make a carrying bag for the meat. He butchered out the rear quarters, regretfully taking only the best cuts and piling them on the square of skin that lay beside the stiffening body of the animal.

Two corners of the hide square ended in the long projections that had been hind legs, and these he tied across the top of the meat pile. Holding the other corners together over the top, he slipped a cherry-wood awl from the pouch at his belt and perforated the skin. Deftly he incised out the tendon at the rear of the leg, passed it through the perforation, and tied the bundle up securely.

He staggered at first, hoisting it to his shoulder, but quickly caught his balance and shrugged the bulk of the pack into a comfortable position. As he left the glade he glanced back at the dismembered doe, regretful and disturbed that he was able to take so little of her. He knew he was betraying her and his promises to her. But there was no help for it.

"*Wagh!*" he grunted. "Bad doin's when it comes to that."

He put the bag down on the ground and went back to the carcass of the animal. "Nothin' for it," he muttered. He grabbed the forelegs and dragged the doe over under the tree near which he had shot her. The next half-hour he spent laboriously hoisting the carcass up into the branches, where it dangled suspended by the tied front legs. He was panting when he was finished, but he felt a little better about it. She wouldn't get flyblown anyway. He tried to put the guilt away from his mind as he hoisted the bag again and began to climb back along the twisted skein of trails to the man-trail above him on the slope.

The light of morning was full when he reached the trail and turned back the way he had come the evening before, back to his new camp. He quickened his pace with the easier going, moving along the needle-pack with the quick glide of moccasins that was more like floating than walking. The weight of the meat was heavy for him, and once he had to stop to rest, conscious of the stiffness in his joints. For a few moments he squatted motionless in the middle of the trail, his bony wrists thrust out of the too short buckskin sleeves and dangling limp across his knees. He stared straight ahead, breathing evenly, resting. Then he shouldered his meat again and moved on, taking up his story where it had been ended the night before by the need for silence.

"Th' Gros Ventre headman rides out, wavin' some kind of flag, might could've been Union Jack or other. Didn't shine with Godin though, *wagh!* 'n' him half-froze for a little Blackfoot hair on account his pa.

That nigger rides out to meet'm with a Flathead riding flank 'n' Betsy on full-cock . . ."

The trail followed the contours of the hill, gradually dropping lower on the slope. He was heading south now, down off the mountain toward the river. Before the trail joined that road that led toward Monday's place, the old man left it, cutting off to the right toward the valley of a tiny stream. He entered a thick stand of spruce, the light within it gloomy and cold. It was a trifle less brushy, and a little easier going.

The spruce extended nearly to the bottom of the tiny ravine, and as the old man listened he could hear the faint trickling sounds of the stream. Near the edge of the spruce island, where the forest suddenly turned back to firs, he stopped. Grunting, he heaved the bag of meat off his shoulder and rested it on the ground. For a long moment he stood silent, mouth open, listening. He was within twenty yards of his camp, though he could not see it through the trees. He picked out a faint rustle that he took to be the sounds of his horse browsing, dragging its rawhide rope in a broad circle around the picket. His mind separated and evaluated the sounds of tiny animals in the brush, the swaying and creaking of limbs together, the trickling conversation of the stream. The pattern was full and rich and safe; the sounds of the world went on as they should, except in a small circle of which he was the center. He waited, still, until the birds near him began to chirp again without the raucous excitement of their alarm call; until the brush near him rustled again with the sound of small creatures returning to life after their moment of paralyzed fear of the giant intruder in the world.

He was satisfied. But still he lashed the meat bag to the highest branch he could reach and set out again, making a wide circle around his camp. He moved with difficulty through the tangled brush, unable to follow even the animal trails. He watched carefully as he circled, his eyes flitting over the undergrowth, caressing the tree trunks. He lay on his belly near the edge of the stream itself, peering upstream and down before he crossed quickly and disappeared into the brush on the other side. Nowhere along his course was there any sign that a creature of man size—or man clumsiness—had crossed that circle.

The entire circuit took more than half an hour, but when he reached the hanging bag of meat again he was content. He had known to start with that he was perfectly safe, here in the middle of civilization. But he also knew the names of men found dead in places where they were perfectly safe. He did not regard the half-hour scrutiny as wasted; it was how he had learned to live.

His camp was a small grassy patch, a tiny glade on the outside of a bend of the stream, where he could see up and down with comparative ease but would himself be hidden by the clump of brush at either end of the clearing. The stream itself was tiny, not more than six feet across and ankle deep.

He approached camp from upwind, giving the bony old horse his smell so she would not whicker in alarm. She stiffened as she heard his approach through the brush, snuffed at the air and dropped her head back to the grazing, taking no notice of the old man when he finally appeared in the tiny clearing with the skin bag over his shoulder.

It had now been over four hours since he had wakened, and he was hungry. Regretfully he set the skin of meat to one side until he could tend to the matter of food.

He stripped off the greasy buckskins and stood naked by the edge of the water. The old man's body was thin and hard, and very white. Sun marks began abruptly at the middle of his forearms, extending down his hands as though he had plunged his arms into a vat of dye only so far. His face and neck, too, were dark, and a deep V of brown pointed down his bony chest; the rest was white.

He walked into the middle of the stream and sat down in the swirling shallow water. Even when he sat, it barely covered his hips, piling up at his back in a tiny cold wave that bumped and rolled around his spine. He scrubbed hard in the icy water, purifying himself and wondering how he was going to go about it. The problem was one he had come across only lately—too often, lately—and he was not settled in his mind how to deal with it; no ritual he knew was adequate. In normal life it didn't happen. He had to devise something of his own, and was uneasy about it because he was not gifted in that way.

The deer spirit was angry at him, he knew. He had sung the song before starting to hunt, and then again in his mind when he first saw her. The doe had listened, had understood his need and accepted his promise that the flesh would die, only to live again. Understanding and accepting, she had permitted herself to be killed; the bargain was immortality. But now the old man, through his loneness, was unable to bring her back to life again, and the guilt of it was strong.

He could, perhaps, plead his weakness; he was old, and could carry only part of the meat. The organs he had taken, but much of the muscle and all of the intestines had been left behind. They were wasted; they would never live again in the body of a man. No arrow points would be made from her bones, no pestles, no medicine sticks, no needles. Her tendons would never be used to make clothing, to bind up new moccasins, to seam the edges of a lodge. Her brains would never be used to tan skins. Her hide would never make shirts to keep a man warm when the snows came.

So much wasted, so much dead that would never return to life. A betrayal of the compact that had existed between man and animals since the Beginning. But it was hard for a man alone to make good. Without a tribe, without even a family, he couldn't use everything. There was in the old man's mind a faint suspicion that perhaps he ought not to sing the promising-song before a hunt. But then he would die, violating the laws of the world. What animal would permit itself to be killed, unless promised new life?

The old man sighed, sitting in the cold stream, and began to scrub himself again. He would simply have to go through with the inadequate ritual he had devised, and hope the deer spirit could understand how strong his need had been. Perhaps it was enough; he didn't know. A man had to walk softly in the world if he would walk there long.

Shivering, he stood out of the stream and returned to the bank. With handfuls of fern he rubbed his body partly dry, but the chill remained. He squatted on his heels beside the water, smoothing a space with his hand at the edge. With a stick he drew the crude outline of a deer. He had no color, no medicine sticks, nothing with which to contact the spirit in the drawing, nothing to make it vital. He went over to his pile of clothing and got the butcher knife. Holding his arm over the scratched image in the dirt, he slit a line across the top of his wrist. Bright blood beaded the edges of the incision, pooled, and began to drop slowly off his arm. He tried to make some sort of pattern, but the blood soaked so quickly into the earth and diffused that he had to be content with merely staining the ground.

It did not seem enough to him. As he had only himself to make it holy, he urinated on the image in addition to the blood. Still dissatisfied, but knowing it would never be exactly right, he began to address the deer spirit.

The old man did not have the medicine in him to make a song, or he would have done that. It would have been more acceptable, but the words did not come to him properly. The spirits detested bad singing, and the old man was unwilling to take the chance of offending them further with a bad song.

In the end, he simply explained how it was with him. About the pain in his belly if he went without food too long. About his age and infirmity, which he exaggerated. He told the deer the names of men who had starved to death, and where it happened, and the terrible agonies they had endured. He described in careful detail all the torments of hunger, hoping to make the one thing stand for all human need.

It took a long time, and at last he ran out of words. He remained squatting there, trying to think if there was anything else he should have said. At last he shrugged and stood up. He had done what he could. It was out of his hands now. He brought his fists together in front of his body, then separated them, in the sign for "It is finished."

He dressed, rubbed out the deer image with the toe of his moccasin, and began to untie the bag of meat.

3

Monday woke when the false dawn was beginning to lighten the southern window. He was motionless, looking at the rough plank ceiling above and feeling the hot length of his wife's body along his own. For a long time he did not move, letting his mind wander absently from sleep into waking, savoring the peace and comfort of it. It seemed a long time since he had wakened without a knot of tension in his belly, and even longer that he had not felt the electric touch of naked skin brushing his thighs and shoulder. He turned his head to look at Mary. She lay on her back beside him, her face turned up, peaceful and helpless with sleep. The blanket had been drawn back in the warmth of the early summer night, and he reached over to stroke her full breast, his hand softly pressing the warm flesh. He bent to kiss her soft and yielding mouth, still partly open in sleep, and her eyes opened. She moved beside him, brushing her hips and thighs against his body gently. He wanted to make love to her, but felt he dared not because of the child. She reached up and drew his head down, pillowing it against the softness of her breast while his hands caressed the smoothness of her arms and thighs, and moved tenderly over the swell of her belly. For a long moment they lay close together, conscious of nothing but the closeness of each other. Then, suddenly, beneath his hand he felt a sudden jerk, as the unborn child kicked. It startled him, and he lifted his head in surprise. Mary laughed and put her hand against his cheek.

"He does that all the time, you know."

"My god," Monday said. "Don't it wake you up?"

Mary lifted her shoulder slightly. "Sometimes," she said. She drew herself up to a sitting position, and Monday laid his head back on the pallet.

"It is how he knows where he is," Mary explained. She moved slowly off the bed and reached down the long nightdress from its peg.

"You think he knows where he is?" Monday asked curiously.

"Yes, I think," Mary said. "He kicks, he turns, he move around all the time now. Now he know exactly how big is the place he is in. He know how far away is the outside. This is why he kicks, to try himself against his world."

"Like all the rest of us."

"And you know," Mary continued seriously, "when he comes out, he will think is *him* who does it." She leaned over to kiss her husband, buttoning the last buttons of the nightdress. "All men born like that. Is why men are the way they are. First thing they do in life, they make a woman to open her legs for them."

Monday laughed. "But you know, baby girls do the same thing."

"That is true. But only the men so stupid they think is *them* who do it. Because is the woman. Always."

Monday reached for her again, but Mary twisted away with something of her old, doelike grace. She moved over to the fireplace and swung the coffee pot in on its long hook, blowing at the still fresh coals from the night. Monday lay back, looking again at the ceiling.

"Now," Mary said, "the little man in me is angry. All the time now he figures how to kick himself loose."

"It ain't such a hell of a bad way to start living," Monday said comfortably.

"No, but all the time I wait, because for *me* is the work, you know. And I smile to myself, because when it is ready, it is ready. He change his mind, I change mine—it makes no difference. He will be free. It is how the world is, only men like to think they *make* it that way." Mary shrugged. "It is a weakness in the head, that women understand better."

"You're pretty high and mighty," Monday said. "You keep on talkin' like that, I'm like t'give you a good lodge-poling."

"When it is ready it is ready," she said indifferently. "He comes. And he is so angry because he has no choice. So he holler. And then all his life he pretend he is strong and free, because he is ashamed of how weak he was at the beginning. Is the way men are."

She went about the business of preparing breakfast, and there was silence in the cabin. At last she said, "How many men you lose?"

"Gettin' Tamahas? None. There was no fighting. Hell, if they'd decided to take out, we'd never of caught 'em."

"They give themselves up, then?"

"Yes."

"Why would they do that?" Mary said, puzzled.

Monday laughed shortly. "Hell, Mary. You know there's only one thing on god's green earth could make them do that. Hudson's Bay sent Ogden up to talk 'em down."

Mary grimaced slightly. "He is a very hard man, that Ogden. The Shoshone know Ogden."

"Wagh! They *do*, now," Monday said. "Before you were born the Shoshone knew Ogden. Anyhow, he talked Tamahas and the others into giving up."

Mary frowned and turned away from the fire. "You tell me something."

Monday grunted.

"When Americans come here first, they go to Hudson's Bay at Vancouver. Because they all of them starving to death when they come."

"Mm."

"And they get food, and they get clothes and seed and cattle and tools and plows and all. And they never pay any money for all that."

"That's about right."

"Ten, twelve years now that happens. And if there is trouble, is always the Hudson's Bay men who settle it. Like the trouble at Waiilatpu. Was them who buy back the prisoners at the start, because the Americans got no money. Was them who chase down Tamahas, really, and say, 'You better come in here.'"

"Sure, but hell, Mary, you know they're the only people in this country that can *do* anything."

"Yes, but this thing I cannot understand. Why do the Americans then all hate Hudson's Bay? This is what I cannot understand."

Monday squirmed uncomfortably on the bed. Finally he said, "Well, you know, the Mission Party—I mean, this country is American by rights, anyhow—"

"You talk crossways, like the Absaroka," Mary said calmly.

Monday thought about it some more, and finally shrugged. It's just the way people are, I expect. The one thing they never forgive you for is if you do 'em a favor. Without McLoughlin and HBC there wouldn't be any settlement here at all. Just a pile o' bones. So now the settlers hate his guts. Just the way people are."

"White people, maybe," Mary said, turning back to the fire.

Monday said nothing for a long time. Finally he raised himself to a sitting position on the edge of the bed and reached for his pants. "It's what they call politics, Mary," he said, frowning. "It's sort of hard to understand."

Mary smiled faintly at the fire. "Yes," she said. "Is hard to understand."

Behind her Monday dragged his pants on. It wasn't something he thought much about. You just lived with the way things were and tried to get along, that was all. And since the people he had to get along with were the Americans, Mission Party and all, there were some things it just didn't pay to get upset about, else you were in trouble all the time. "Hell," he muttered. "Hudson's Bay c'n take care of its ownself. I got problems o' my own I ain't solved yet."

The main trail south into the Willamette Valley from Oregon City was on the opposite side of the river from the settlement itself. It did not border the river, but ran inland perhaps a mile. From the ferry landing across from Oregon City it wound south over the heavily wooded prominence of Peter's Mountain, finally coming to the river again across from Swensen's shack.

In this spring of 1850 there were three major settlements along the river; for, whatever other trails existed, the river was the road, the bloodstream of the colony. Oregon City was at the falls, and some forty miles upstream the Methodist Mission settlement lay in the fertile heart of the Willamette Valley. Between these, perhaps fifteen miles upstream from the falls, was the Champoeg settlement of retired Hudson's Bay Company men; most of them French-Canadian freemen like René Devaux, who had chosen to forgo their free transport back to Montreal and remain in the Oregon Country.

From the main road, a dead-end trail cut in toward Monday's farm, running down the center of the arrowhead point and ending at Monday's cabin. It was down this trail a visitor came riding in the late afternoon, a beautiful bay mare pacing slowly from the north.

The man that sat her was small and trim, the cuffs of his pinstripe trousers tucked neatly into riding boots. Across the stomach of his tightly buttoned waistcoat was a conservative golden chain, from which swung a small nugget. He rode easily and confidently, his hands lightly grasping the reins.

Monday sat at the door of the cabin, the long, slim head of a double-bitted ax cradled on his knees while he stroked the cutting edge with a file. Hearing the horse, he looked up.

To Monday, the small man perched atop the great horse appeared slightly absurd; he was accustomed to the sight of large men straddling the tiny Indian horses, their legs dangling until they almost seemed to reach the ground.

He put the file aside and said without turning, "Mary, come here."

Mary came silently to stand in the doorway behind him and look over the top of his head at the approaching rider.

"It's Thurston," Monday said.

Mary went back into the house for a moment, and returned with a bucket.

"I go find some blackberries," she said. She left the porch and moved slowly down toward the thickly clustered vines near the river. Monday stood up, leaning the ax against the doorframe, and watched him come.

Chapter Four

The small man reined in his horse, looking down at Monday with a sudden ingratiating smile, as though he had just remembered. He was cleanshaven, his hard, thin face as smooth as though it had been scraped with glass.

"Afternoon, Mr. Thurston," Monday said.

"Afternoon, Monday. Fine day."

"It is, now. Got a pot of coffee on."

"Well, now," Thurston said, dismounting. "That's very hospitable." He looped the reins loosely around the tiny rail and came up to the porch, extending his hand. It was small and delicate, but he gripped with deliberate strength, as though there were a contest in progress.

"C'mon in the house," Monday said. He felt embarrassed, as always when Thurston gripped his hand so hard and stared up, reproving him for his undisciplined size.

Monday fumbled at the fireplace, pouring the coffee, while Thurston sat relaxed at the table, watching him carefully, his face drawn and expressionless. Monday put the cups on the table, and a few drops spilled over the rim. Thurston drew slightly away, and Monday muttered something about his own clumsiness and went to get a rag from the back to wipe up the small puddle on the table. When Thurston was around his fingers were always numb and awkward, as if half frozen; spilling things and knocking things over like a schoolboy. When he had wiped up the coffee he was rewarded with another of the sudden, flashing smiles from the small man, showing his perfectly even white teeth.

"Well, Monday. Fine day," Thurston repeated.

Monday nodded and sat down across the table. Thurston leaned forward, cupping his hands around the mug.

"You wouldn't have any sugar about, would you?" Thurston asked. "I can't abide coffee without sugar."

Monday shook his head, looking at the table. They hadn't had any sugar for six months. "Sorry, Mr. Thurston," he said. "They—up to Oregon City, you know. I been late every time a ship come in—"

"Well, no matter," Thurston said in a friendly way. "It makes no difference, does it?" He carefully took his hands from around the cup and sat back, leaving the steaming coffee in the center of the table as a silent reproach. Monday looked at it helplessly.

"Well, now, Monday," Thurston said. "I didn't see you in Oregon City last night. When the regiment came in."

"Regiment?"

"With the Cayuse prisoners," Thurston said, faintly annoyed.

"Oh. No. Well, we got 'em in. I thought I better come home then."

"Most of the men stayed with the job until the Indians were safely in the hands of the marshal."

Monday cleared his throat. "Well, Mr. Thurston, I didn't think I was—needed any more. You know, it was all over, we had 'em in and all."

Thurston leaned forward again, never taking his eyes from Monday's face. "Monday," he said seriously, "that's your problem. That's your big trouble."

"Trouble?"

Thurston sat back again, regarding the blond giant across the scarred planks of the table. With one finger he flipped the gold nugget on his watch chain.

"Your modesty," he said finally. "Your modesty." The smile flashed, and was gone. "Thought you weren't needed! Indeed! Monday, don't you realize that a man of your caliber is *always* needed? Why, you could be the very backbone of our society here. Now you know that, don't you?"

"Well, I never thought very much—you know, Mr. Thurston, I try to get along, but as far as backbone and all that—"

"Modesty again, Monday," Thurston said, amused. "Admirable, but, you understand, misplaced. You must recognize your own worth, you must take your proper place."

Monday coughed.

"Well, no matter, eh? I came to congratulate you on your part in the campaign, Monday. It was well conceived and well carried out; a complete success, I dare say, and something the community may well regard with pride."

"There wasn't a hell of a lot to—"

Thurston held up his hand in protest. "Modesty, my friend? I know what these things are like, believe me. Hunger, thirst, constant danger. And doubly difficult, I dare say, what with the damned conniving and plotting of the Jesuitical underlings of Hudson's Bay. Twice the danger, with them inciting the Indians against us at every opportunity."

The only thing Monday had been particularly aware of on the expedition was being bored and saddle-sore. But, as always with Thurston, he thought he was beginning to lose the thread of the conversation. He frowned. "You know, though, without Ogden and HBC them Indians wouldn't ever of come down. We'd maybe have a honest-to-christ war on our hands."

Thurston threw his head back and laughed heartily. "Monday, surely you aren't allowing yourself to be taken in by *that* story? Naturally, the Jesuitical plotters attempt to turn everything to their own advantage."

"But it was HBC that bought back the survivors in the first place—"

"A gesture, my friend, I assure you. What did it cost them? A few blankets, to throw us off our guard. And as far as persuading the Indians to give themselves up . . ." Thurston pursed his lips disdainfully that anyone could be taken in by such a tale.

"But even the Indians say—" Monday said, frowning, still trying to get things straight in his mind.

Thurston smiled ruefully. "Yes," he admitted. "I dare say they've been sufficiently well rehearsed. The voice of the Pope, you know . . ."

Monday looked down at the table. He had never understood exactly how the Pope kept getting involved with Hudson's Bay, except that McLoughlin was Catholic, as were most of the Canadians. But sometimes it seemed as though the Pope were in personal charge of HBC's Columbia Department. The Mission Party always gave that impression, and now Thurston . . .

"Well, I don't know about all that kind of thing," he said finally. "I just try to get along, Mr. Thurston."

"Believe me," Thurston said kindly, "it is not necessary for you to worry about it. After all"—he laughed—"is it the function of the backbone to worry? Hardly! There are those of us competent to stay one step ahead of the Jesuits, I dare say."

"Well," Monday said vaguely, "I expect it'll be all right, anyway. . . ."

"Of course. But Monday, good lord, man—I'm forgetting my purpose! I came to congratulate you, not exchange political ideas, fascinating as that may be."

"Well, thanks very much, Mr. Thurston, but I—"

"Frankly, Monday," Thurston said reflectively, "there was a time—you don't mind my being frank?—there was a time I was deeply concerned."

"About me?"

"Perhaps, more accurately, about your loyalties; about your willingness to take the responsibility of a citizen here."

"I've always tried to be as—"

"In order to establish a society here—a real society—a man must place his loyalty to the community before self-interest. The community first, the individual second. You agree? Cooperation is the key, Monday. Menaced on all sides, the Indians, the underlings of Hudson's Bay—cooperation is the key to survival; we must work together.

"I dare say the situation is not too different from that you encountered in the mountains, Monday. In order to survive the perils of your trade, you hardy mountain men banded together, working as a unit for the common good. The group is always stronger than the individual alone."

In spite of his uneasiness and confusion, Monday grinned. "Well, it didn't work exactly that way, Mr. Thurston."

Thurston waved his hand negligently; the details were not important. "Nevertheless, I think my point is well taken. The self-interest of the individual must be subordinated to the common good. Else—there is chaos."

Monday nodded. He suddenly realized his coffee was getting cold, and gulped some down.

"And in any event," Thurston said, "my concern has vanished. I can't tell you how heartening it is to see you accept your responsibilities, such as the late Cayuse War. You are leading the way, and from your example I fully expect great changes in this community. The relations of the mountain men with—shall we say?—the more respectable elements have not been of the best. There is, perhaps, a difficulty in adjustment, a reluctance. In fact, it might best be described as a failure of discipline."

Monday smiled again. "Discipline wasn't hardly ever a strong point in the mountains. We did pretty much as we pleased."

Thurston shook his head ruefully. "Yes," he said sadly, "like willful children. Or the savage Indian himself. You see the connection there."

"I expect," Monday said hesitantly.

"And, like all children, we mature; we become sufficiently adult to realize that our place, ultimately, is as part of the community. Oh, Monday," he said, with a confidential smile, "I've had my—moments of irresponsibility, too. You needn't think I've been without one or two—peccadillos, shall we say? I dare say I've been as bold as any, in my time. But that is over now. One sees one's responsibility and acts accordingly." He shrugged. "It is a question of growth."

"I expect it's something like that."

"A few minor failures—what can one expect? Absolutely unimportant. For example, that Indian servant you keep around, the woman. But, in time, with your growing sense of community—"

"That's my wife," Monday said, feeling the sudden coldness in his chest.

Thurston smiled tolerantly. "Between men, Monday—is that really necessary? There are certain natural needs to be satisfied—one understands. But, the dignity of a title? Really. Let's view these things honestly. After all, we have our—biology, haven't we? We can wink at a thing or two, even if the Methodists cannot." He laughed.

Monday stood, placing his hands flat on the table. "Thanks for coming by, Mr. Thurston."

The smile faded from Thurston's face. "Sit down, Monday," he said quietly. "There's one more thing."

"I got work to do."

"I said, sit down." Thurston did not raise his voice.

For a long moment they were static, the huge form of Monday braced against the table, leaning tensely forward; Thurston, relaxed, legs crossed, fondling the gold nugget that hung from his watch chain, looking calmly up.

Then, reluctantly, and without volition of his own, Monday sat down. He clasped his hands in front of him.

"No need to take offense, Monday," Thurston said calmly. "I would simply indicate that the presence of that woman is a handicap to you. Perhaps an insurmountable one, in time. It is surely clear enough that while the Indian remains, it will be impossible—"

"You said there was one other thing."

Thurston shrugged negligently. "Very well," he said. "But in time I am certain you will see the nature of the choice that exists for you. The other thing, Monday, is that you may be called upon to give a bit more of your time in the interests of the community."

"What now?" Monday said.

"There are reports of a wild man in the hills about here. In time it will probably be necessary to form a vigilance committee to root him out."

"What's he done?"

"Done? Nothing, as yet. But the danger he represents is clear enough."

"Where the hell's the danger if he ain't done anything?"

"Monday, please. You are being deliberately naïve. For one thing the Indians are convinced he is *the* Wild Man, from the absurd mythological time of the First People. You understand, it causes unrest."

"Who's seen him?"

"He threatened one unfortunate in Oregon City itself. The Indian reports he had blood running from his eyes, was waving a rifle, and disappeared in a cloud of smoke."

Monday looked up in surprise. "You believe that?"

"Of course not. The Indian is telling the story for fifty cents. But that the man exists, there is no doubt."

"Just some old solitary roamin' around," Monday said.

"Doubtless. But that is precisely the question. It is unnatural for a man to be what you call a solitary."

"Maybe it is, maybe it ain't," Monday muttered, looking down at the table again. "Man wants to run 'lone, leave 'm be. That's his business."

Thurston stood at the table. "Fortunately, Monday, it is not a question you are called upon to decide. A man like that is not—whole. He is not in possession of his faculties. When you speak in that way I am reminded of your mountain background, and I find it discouraging. A man who 'runs 'lone' as you phrase it, is a threat to those who would work together. He must be dealt with. I should think that would be clear to you; in a sense it has been the subject of our conversation."

"Mr. Thurston, I ain't going to—"

"Monday," Thurston said impatiently, "I have no intention of arguing the point any further. You may be called upon to assist in this matter, and I have every expectation that you will do so. It should not be necessary to point out that your relation to the community is involved in this request, too."

Monday looked up finally. His hands remained tightly laced on the table in front of him. "That sounds awful much like a threat."

Thurston shrugged. "Not in the least. I find threats quite unnecessary. All that is required is a clear understanding of the situation that exists. I had thought your eyesight was improving, but I discover there are still areas of blindness. I sincerely hope, for your sake, that the difficulty is temporary. Good-by, Monday."

He turned and walked quickly out the door. Monday heard the rustle as he took up the reins and turned the horse back up the trail. He listened until the sounds of the horse's hoofs on the packed trail were no longer audible.

He cradled his head in his hands and stared down at the scarred table planks, tracing with his eyes the nicks and scrapes of knives carelessly dropped, the darker stains of spilled coffee and the blood of rare meat. Suddenly he raised his head at a sound near the back of the house. In a moment Mary came through the door, carrying the bucket.

"How long you been back?" he asked.

"I have just come." She went to the cupboard at the back and got a leaf of paper to dump the berries on.

"You didn't get much," Monday said, looking at the small pile.

"Many were not ripe," Mary said. "There is enough for a pie, if we could get some flour."

Monday put his head back in his hands. There was no way to tell whether she had heard Thurston's comments or not. It was one of the many things he would never know.

"Mr. Thurston did not drink his coffee," Mary said, taking the full cup from the table.

"He likes sugar in it," Monday said.

2

He woke feeling dull and depressed in the morning. A random thought came to him as he struggled up out of the darkness of sleep, blurred by half-consciousness. They just won't leave me alone, he thought blearily.

Yesterday he had wakened clean and fresh, with only the consciousness of Mary's body and his own, side by side. This morning he was back in a world of complexity he had not made. Seemed as though just as soon as a man got to feeling loose, somebody had to remind him of the way things really were.

Mary was already up, moving about the fireplace. Monday turned his head to watch her. With a long scoop she was dipping up the feathery gray ashes and dumping them into the ash hopper that stood at the side of the fireplace.

Monday hoisted himself up to his elbows, blinking with sleepiness, and rubbed the back of his neck. It was always hard for him to wake when there were things he didn't want to do.

Mary turned briefly to see him rise, then returned to the slow, gentle pouring of the ashes. Monday watched the pale cloud of gray that floated up as the stream ran into the hopper.

"Makin' lye?"

"In a week, maybe," Mary said. "We have not much soap left. And I could use it to sweeten the sourdough, if we got some flour."

She could make a pie, if they got some flour. She could make sourdough, if they got some flour.

"I'm going to put the field in wheat," he said. "We'll have plenty of flour in the winter."

But even as he spoke he knew it wasn't certain. There were only two mills in the country, one at the Methodist Mission upstream and the other on the island at Oregon City. There was no credit at either place, and the percentages were always too high. Worse was the simple fact of being there. At the mission mill they saved his soul for God, while they cut his purse strings, and at Oregon City the mill was run by friends of Thurston, which was almost as bad. He had come to dread both places and always found some excuse to avoid them.

He swung his feet over the edge of the bed and reached for his boots. Before he could put the field in wheat he had to have the wheat. Thank god for Swensen, he wouldn't have to plow. The endless, wearisome, monotonous trudging back and forth behind the animals, and them borrowed . . . A man wasn't made for work like that, the same movement over and over again, endlessly using exactly the same muscles. It made him ache at night.

He would get the seed wheat from McLoughlin in Oregon City. If McLoughlin didn't have it, he'd see that it came out of the Hudson's Bay storehouse in Vancouver. There'd been a hell of a bunch of people through here in the last ten years, and McLoughlin had seen that none of them starved. Lost his job for it, too. And the directors in London had charged his personal account sixty thousand dollars for the things he'd given to the Americans to keep them alive those first bad winters.

What the hell was wrong? Seven years here, and he still had to go on his knees begging for seed wheat. Short of seed, short of soap, short of flour, short of clothes, even short of powder and ball. In the mountains it had never seemed so complicated, just to stay alive. He couldn't recall ever giving it much thought. And now, already, the eternal damp was beginning to rot the foundations of the cabin and the beams of the roof, and they would have to be replaced before winter came again.

He sighed, dragging on his trousers. "Mary, sometimes I think I just wasn't cut out for farming."

Mary shrugged. "There is much to do," she said.

"Seems like I take two steps forward and fall back three. I'm gettin' farther behind all the time."

"Is bad luck, maybe."

"A man can take just so long a run of the bad," Monday said. "Then he's got to have some good, or he goes under."

Mary finished scooping the floating ashes and wiped her forehead with her wrist. Her husband's back was turned, as he took the linsey-woolsey shirt from the peg on the wall above the bed. Mary looked at him for a moment and turned back to the coffee pot. "You will be here today?"

"No," Monday said morosely. "I got to go into Oregon City. See about the wheat."

After a moment Mary said, "Is maybe better you stay here a day."

"Why?"

"You are gone a long time. The meat is gone, now."

Monday closed his eyes. "Meat, too. Christ, we don't have anything."

"Everything else we can do without. Meat, we cannot do without meat."

"All right," Monday said. He started taking off the cloth shirt, his farmer's shirt, and suddenly the depression began to lift. He reached up for the buckskin hunting shirt, and in spite of himself began to smile.

"By god, that's not a bad idea, Mary." In his mind he could already see the branch moving, the faint shadow of a buff body over the sights of the gun, could feel the waiting tension. "The wheat can wait a day, can't it?"

"Yes, I think so," Mary said.

His movements became quicker, more sure. He yanked off the stupidly heavy boots and reached under the bed for the feather-light moccasins. Just getting the boots off, he felt ten pounds lighter. The moccasins were his own feet, shaped by the wearing until no other man could feel comfortable in them. He stood up, shrugging his shoulders, loosening his body for the hunt.

"You don't want breakfast first?" Mary said.

"No," Monday said seriously. "I best get out early." He was suddenly impatient to be gone and could not wait.

Mary nodded.

Monday took down the gun from its pegs over the fireplace and checked the flint. He poured a little powder into the horn, and took several balls.

"You take enough?" Mary said, watching.

"I only need to shoot once."

"What if you miss?"

Monday scowled at her. "She's got hindsights and a foresight," he said sharply.

"Just a question that I ask," Mary said innocently, raising her hands.

"I c'n still shoot a gun," Monday muttered, not seeing her faint smile. He snapped the hammer sharply several times and nodded to himself.

Lightly he moved to the door, stepping out into a flood of early-morning warmth. The sun had just passed the screen of trees to the east, and was rising quickly, losing the redness of dawn. He stood at the door for a moment, looking at the world, letting his eyes sharpen themselves against the wall of foliage that surrounded his little clearing, feeling the sharp cleanness of the air.

"Good, I'll get goin', then."

Quickly he saddled the horse, muttering softly to him, rubbing his muzzle. Mary stood in the doorway watching her husband's impatience without expression. He mounted and Mary walked over to the horse. Monday bent down from the saddle and kissed her perfunctorily on the forehead. "Got to get movin'," he said brusquely.

Mary stepped back and he swung the horse around, setting off up the main trail for Peter's Mountain and the thick cover of brush where the soft and subtle bodies of the deer were waiting for him.

She watched him go, then turned and went back into the dark house. With difficulty she stooped at the cooler beneath the floor and began to rearrange the paper-wrapped packages. She put all the fresh packages of meat that Swensen had left near the back, where Monday would not notice them. Then she got out the half-completed shirt and took it to the front porch, where she could work in the warmth of the sun.

3

Once on the trail he lost the tensions across the back of his shoulders, the feeling of tightness that had slipped into him with the thoughts of seed wheat and no flour and begging and the mission and all the rest of it. He began to feel relaxed and easy again. The horse's hoofs fell softly, like the pad of a cat, and overhead the branches of fir moved slowly, a creaking, shifting roof over the endless tunnel that was the trail.

Here in the woods the concerns of civilized life receded into nothingness again. No worry about Thurston or the farm or that vicious thought of raising money that always twisted his guts. And most of all, no question of whether he was doing the right thing, the thing he was supposed to do. Right and wrong were merely words again, noises of no distinct meaning. There was only the powerful consciousness of the world around him, as it existed, without trying to make up words to fit it. Monday realized it had been a long time since he had been able to feel the good world-feeling, the balanced emotionless awareness of himself and the world, and what was passing between them. He nodded to himself, watching the brush to either side close in, taking a growing joy in the simple act of perception.

When he had ridden in this way for half an hour, the trail narrowed so that it was not easy for the horse to pass without brushing against the undergrowth at either side. The sense of being penned was making the animal nervous, and Monday reined up. He dismounted and rubbed the horse's muzzle gently. "Easy, easy. Can't worry about it," he whispered. Gradually the skittery animal calmed, drawing a sort of peace from his master. Monday felt perfectly neutral and suspended now, almost without volition.

There was good grass growing beneath the ferns. He unsaddled and picketed the animal there, murmuring reassurances. The rest of the way he would make on foot. He had been skirting the edge of a hill, and near the bottom at his left would be a stream, in the summer probably almost dry, but for now it would give cool clean water that the deer would prefer to that of the main river. Good cover, easy water, and good forage. Paradise.

When the horse had begun to browse without tension, Monday slipped into the brush on the downhill side, working toward the base of the valley. When he had gone a few hundred yards, he stopped abruptly, lifting his face to the breeze. He caught a faint, acrid smell of burning.

Involuntarily he wheeled, starting back to his animal with the instinctive panic fear of fire in the forest. Then, angry at his own fear, he calmed himself and looked around. The smoke was so faint that he missed it entirely at first. Then he saw it, a misty thread some distance up the tiny ravine, swinging toward him in the breeze. It was almost invisible, appearing and disappearing like a spider web twisting in the beam of sunlight. Had he not been directly downwind he never would have caught it at all.

He frowned, puzzled. A smoldering log would surely give off more smoke than that; and an open fire would cover more ground. It looked like nothing so much as a small campfire, but who would be making camp in the hills in the middle of the day? The tame Indians around Oregon City never hunted, and the others didn't like to come so close in.

Suddenly he remembered Thurston's talk about the solitary roaming around out here. Wild Man himself. By god, that's him, he thought, grinning to himself. I'll just have a look at that 'un.

If it was Wild Man, Monday thought, then he'd be like to have Younger Wild Woman some place about. She'd keep y'r lodge warm, wagh! And while you were still on top of her she'd start eating you up and spitting out the pieces. It was a serious fault in the Younger Wild Woman.

He was content as he began working his way down to the stream, his mind roving over the old, familiar stories. It felt almost as if he were in the mountains again, tracking, moving along the almost imperceptible animal trails to see who else was about.

Reaching the base of the valley, he stepped into the little stream, feeling the chill water grip his ankles. He began to plod upstream, the gurgle and sputter of the water covering the sound of his approach.

As he rounded a bend he caught sight of the fire, and of a bony old horse picketed on the point of the next curve. He moved slowly to the side of the stream and studied what he could see before going on. The camp seemed to be deserted. He thought he could see nearly the whole extent of the clear area, and no one was in sight.

He moved back into the stream carefully, glad he was downwind from the strange horse. As it was, the animal did not catch his scent until the last minute, then whickered nervously and crab-sidled away from him as far as the picket rope would permit.

"Just take it easy, easy now," he said. The clearing was deserted. A bloody skin, tied up into a bag, lay not far from the fire. He suddenly realized the fire was far too fresh, and a piece of meat lay beside it as though dropped. He jerked his head up, knowing it was too late.

A muffled, animal snort in the brush made him swing around, just in time to see the flash of an igniting powder pan. A ball whirred past him, ripping into the brush behind, to the sound of thunder.

Monday fell flat, lifting his own gun as the old man came stooping out of the underbrush, his hat flopping limply around his ears, two long plaits of hair swinging. He carried his long rifle, still smoking, loosely in one hand. He muttered angrily as he crossed the clearing toward the prone Monday.

"Took y' f'r a Injun, I did. *Wagh!* Come near t' throwing down on y', god damn y'r eyes."

"Webb! Jesus god, Webb!" Monday stared up from the ground in astonishment, his rifle barrel falling to the ground. The old man walked past him to the fire, grabbing the hunk of dropped meat and drawing his butcher knife, still grumbling.

"Y'almost kilt me, Webb," Monday said, sitting up and staring at the old man.

Webb snorted and cut himself a piece of meat. "Learn y' somethin', y' damned pork-eater. Come a plunderin' into a man's camp thataway. Y'allus was a turrible dunghead. How be y'anyway, hoss?"

Chapter Five

D amn me, Webb! I plain can't get over it, seein' you here. What do y' feel like, y'old coon?"

"*Wagh!* Half froze f'r 'baccy, this child is. Got any about y'?"

"*Well*, I have."

Monday fumbled out his tobacco pouch and handed it to the old man. From the recesses of his voluminous hunting shirt Webb produced the red sandstone pipe bowl and the long wooden stem, fitting them carefully together. He lit up and closed his eyes luxuriously, letting puffs of white smoke curl out of his nostrils.

Monday watched him curiously, full of an obscure restlessness. He felt just as he had when he sat around a mountain fire for the first time, at the age of nineteen, and watched this same man smoke and talk and drink and curse and lie. Webb had looked then exactly as he did now, except for the long plaits of black hair that now dangled beneath the limp felt hat. To the young *mangeur-de-lard* on his first trip, Webb had been the personification of mountain wisdom; infinitely old, infinitely experienced, infinitely wise.

Thirteen goddam years, Monday thought, the spring of '37. He suddenly realized he had been down here in civilization longer than he had spent in the mountains, a full year longer. It was a depressing thought. Nothing had happened here worth mentioning, except anger and humiliation and failure. But the mountain years had been full, as a man's life should be full.

Even the winters, holed up with the Crows on Wind River with the snow packed around the lodges—there'd always been something going on, and Webb was always in the middle of it. The old hoss could read and write, for one thing. Had, in fact, taught Monday himself to read, sitting around the Absaroka fires through the long, cold nights, whiling away their time until the spring thaw allowed them out for the hunt. The Rocky Mountain College they called it, and more than one grizzled mountain man had cut his literary teeth there, puzzling over the strange printed sign with the same intensity he gave Indian sign or beaver sign.

Monday grinned to himself, thinking about it. Shakespeare, the Bible, and above all, *The Scottish Chiefs*. The Shakespeare and the Bible were carried about with the camp goods, but Webb had his own private copy of the long novel, four tiny leather-bound volumes no bigger than the palm of your hand. He could remember the old man's utter rage when Monday, the green student, couldn't follow the sense of Miss Porter's long, periodic sentences. (Y' *goddamned dunghead, wagh! Fit f'r nothin' but wolf-meat, that is a fact! Well, this nigger's had a craw full o' y'.* . . . —snatching the book out of Monday's hand and stalking off.)

For some reason he'd taken Monday under his wing those first years, easing him through the intricacies of mountain life with a sure, if occasionally rough, hand. Not once, Monday thought, but a dozen times, he owed his life to the old man. Though at times he wasn't sure his life was worth the price; there was always the cussing out later. (*If'n this child had as much money as you got stupids, why, he'd be a-puffin' on a big cigar an' struttin' in Saint Looy alongside Chouteau.* . . .)

He looked just the same, smoking his pipe with all his attention and ignoring a friend he hadn't seen in seven years. Webster W. Webster, M.T. That was how he signed himself, the M.T. standing for the only education he admitted to straight out: Master Trapper. And it was no more than truth.

"Well, coon," Monday said. "How's it come for your stick t' be floatin' out this direction?"

"*Damn* y'r eyes," Webb snapped. "Ain't you learned yet t' leave a man in peace when he's a-smokin'? *Wagh!*" But at the same time he spoke he made a V with two fingers and moved it upward from his forehead in a spiral, sign-talk for "medicine."

Monday nodded. If Webb's being here had something to do with his medicine, Monday would just have to wait until the old man said what he had to say; or perhaps he would never know. It wasn't something you asked about.

"Roll out y'r doin's, Jaybird," Webb said contemptuously. "Seems like y' got y'r mouth all set f'r talkin'."

Monday looked down at the ground for a moment. "Not much to tell, hoss," he said at last. "Left the mountains same year as Bridger built his fort down to the Green, 'forty-three it was—"

"*Wagh!*" Webb deliberately leaned over and spat into the fire. "That's what killed the trade, Bridger 'n' his goddamn fort."

"—come down here to the valley to settle. That's it." And little enough, Monday thought. Try to put the mountain years into one sentence.

Webb nodded, his eyes roving absently over the opposite slope. "Well," he said at last, "leastways y'ain't gone to percussion guns like ever'body else."

"Nor you neither," Monday said, grinning.

"*Wagh!* Hell's full o' percussion guns all rifled inside. This child never saw a nigger could charge a percussion gun on horseback runnin' buffler. Nor make a fire with a percussion cap 'stead of a flint. Y' ever try t' ram a ball down a barrel with all them little grooves inside?"

"They say she shoots straighter like that," Monday said reasonably.

Webb snorted. "This child make 'em come without no goddamn little grooves in his gun. Goes against nature t' have them little grooves in there."

Monday shrugged. There was no use saying anything; Webb could easily prove that if God meant guns to be rifled He'd of made wiping sticks with ridges to fit. "Where the hell's ever'body got to, coon? Where's Bill Williams?"

"See that child in hell, *wagh!* He's cached up snug down to Taos."

"Taos! Never thought I'd see old Bill in a town!"

"Got to. Took hisself a Ute wife or three, 'n' living with a pack o' the dirty red bastards up to Bayou Salade. *Well*, now! Come a couple o' summers ago, 'forty-seven I think it was, he takes the whole year's catch o' the band down to Taos to sell."

"Nothin' wrong with that," Monday said.

"Shut y'r damn mouth," Webb said. "The nigger sells the furs, goes on a spree. He did now. Two, mebbe so three weeks. Had a turrible dry, I expect. Wakes up still dry, 'n' all his people's money gone. Hires out f'r a guide to the Army, 'n' takes a party o' them pretty Blue Boys right plumb back t' his own lodge. Well, *wa'nt* there whoopin'! Seven

Utes from his band went under that spree. They ain't forgettin' he led them sojers, nor the furs neither. Old Bill don't want to get nowheres near the mountains if'n he feels like keepin' his ha'r."

Monday looked at the ground. He picked up a twig and drew a circle in the dirt. "Hard times when it comes t' that," he said quietly.

"Must've been a real turrible dry he had," Webb agreed. "But them Utes'll raise him one day, *wagh!* they will. They'll make him come, then. He may of lost his topknot already, f'r all this nigger knows." The old man spat contemptuously in the fire. "I ain't been followin' Bill's doin's lately."

"What's beaver in Taos?"

"Dollar."

"Saint Louis?"

"Same."

Monday cleared his throat. "Ain't gettin' any better."

Webb turned on him angrily. "Beaver's bound t' rise," he snapped. "Goes against nature t' sell beaver a dollar a plew. She'll rise."

Monday looked at the old man in surprise, then turned away. He wondered if Webb could really believe it. The refrain had been going around since '37, and it hadn't risen yet.

"Hard t' live," he said. "Dollar a plew."

"Wagh!"

After a moment Monday said absently, "Trask and Tibbets and Solomon Smith're settled down to the coast. Meek and Doc Newell and me and a few others here in the valley."

Webb spat into the fire again. "Farmers."

"Approximately."

Webb turned to squint suspiciously at him, one eye closed. "That dirt-cloddin' shine with y', boy?"

Monday looked at the twig in his hand. He put it down on the ground where he had found it. "Not so much," he said.

Webb nodded. "Goes against nature, rip up the ground with a plow. It does, now."

"No help for it," Monday said.

"Wagh!" Webb spat again. "Man was made t' run buffler, not poke around makin' holes in the ground."

"Webb," Monday said hesitantly, "listen, coon. That's all over. The hunters are dyin' out and the farmers takin' over. That's how it is."

"Y' goddamn dunghead!"

Monday shrugged, frowning. "How it is," he repeated. "Sometimes you got to swim with the current, hoss. She's too strong."

"This nigger'll swim how he pleases," Webb said angrily. "Current, *wagh!* Y're a farmer right enough. Current!"

"Ain't no need to get y'r back up, hoss. I'm just sayin' is all."

"Never thought t' hear the old Jaybird a-talkin' like that. You sure god turned out bad, boy, y' hear?"

Monday shrugged. "Times change, coon. A man goes along or goes under."

Webb thought about it for a long time. "This nigger's out o' baccy," he said sharply.

Monday handed him the pouch again and watched while the old man filled up. Webb tamped the tobacco carefully into the bowl, watching it suspiciously all the time. "How d'the honest-to-jesus farmers take on t' old mountain men," Webb said uninterestedly.

"Well—different, I expect. Meek gets along good enough," Monday said.

"Heerd he was marshal or summat," Webb said.

"So."

Webb snorted. "Some marshal, that 'un."

"He ain't too bad," Monday said. "Anyways, what the hell they going t' do with a man like Meek? It's make him marshal 'r have half a dozen marshals t' handle him."

"Leastways he ain't diggin' up the ground."

"He tried it for a couple years, but it didn't work out too good."

"Good enough f'r you, though," Webb said, looking at him through a plume of smoke.

"Good as a man c'n expect," Monday said. "It ain't easy. There's more t' this kind of doin's than you'd think. A man's got—responsibilities." He wished for a moment he could tell Webb how hard it was, find some way to make the old man understand. But there was nothing he could say but what Webb would just call him dunghead again. He raised his hands and let them fall. "It ain't so easy," he repeated.

Webb puffed contentedly on the new tobacco, staring out at the hillside as though unaware Monday was there.

"Anyways," Monday said, anxious to get to some other subject, "what're you doin' nowadays, hoss?"

The old man made a fluttering, winglike motion with his hand. "Livin' with the Crows," he said.

"What band?"

"Kicked-in-their-Bellies. We winter up to Wind River."

"When you figure t' get back?"

"Don't figure t' get back," the old man said calmly. "This child's a-fixin' t' die."

2

Mary was scouring the plank table when she heard the sound of a horse coming down the trail from the north, and knew it was not her husband's. She put aside the pumice stone and went to the corner where the old rifle now stood. Dusk had fallen, and she knew the light of the candles would be visible from outside.

She took the gun and went to sit in the chair at the back corner of the cabin, away from the door. The flickering light of the candles cast long darting shadows in the room. She put the rifle across her lap and sat still, making herself small. She watched the door, motionless, listening to the sound of the rider dismounting, the sound of the reins being thrown over the rail, the firm footsteps on the porch.

She did not move when the knocking came, but sat still as a doe with her hands folded on the stock of the gun. It came again, and the candles fluttered and the dark shadows danced.

Then there was a voice, a woman's voice, but firm and strong. "It's me, child. Doctor Beth."

Mary stood and went to the door. She opened it and stepped back to let the woman pass in. Dr. Beth was a big woman, built square and stocky, but she moved lightly, like a girl.

"I was just passing by, child, and I thought I'd drop in if I'm not bein' a trouble to you."

"No," Mary said. "You come in, please."

Dr. Beth glanced at the rifle Mary still held, but said nothing. She came into the room and sat down at the table, facing the fire, while Mary returned to the corner and stood the rifle up. Beth watched her carefully, the slow, measured movement, the size of the swelling belly. She was awful young, Beth thought, not more than twenty or twenty-one. Monday must have taken her to wife at fourteen or so. A third of her life spent this way. No wonder she was so hard to reach. Beth shook her head and turned back to the fire.

"There is—no tea," Mary said apologetically. "And the coffee is for the man."

"Makes no difference, child," Beth said. "I can't stay long. I just wanted to get off that animal for a minute."

The white woman watched the fire for a moment in silence. "Well, Mary," she said at last. "How's it coming along?"

"He is coming pretty soon, I think," Mary said.

Beth nodded. "A few weeks, I'd guess. You're sure you can't remember the last time you mens—the last time you had the moon sickness?"

Mary shook her head silently.

It wouldn't be so bad, Beth thought, if the girl had stayed with her people long enough to learn from the other women what to expect from birthing. As it was, she had no way of knowing except what she could remember seeing as a child. She simply waited, alone, and with no one to ask.

"He's moving around a lot now," Beth said.

"Yes."

"You know, child, sometimes there are—troubles, when the baby comes."

Mary said nothing.

"Sometimes they come wrong end to, and it can be hard."

"Yes. Woman die sometimes."

"If there is someone else around, sometimes they can help," Beth said. "Sometimes there are ways to turn the baby around, if that happens."

"Yes," Mary said.

"You understand, when you feel the baby coming, you should send your man for me."

"Yes."

Beth sighed and leaned back against the table. There was absolutely no way to tell if she was reaching the Indian girl or not. She simply sat with her hands quietly folded and said "Yes."

Beth knew the baby was coming breech. The one time Mary had let herself be touched, Beth had felt the head up high, too high. Sometimes they switched ends in the last couple of weeks, sometimes not.

"Listen, child," Beth said. "I have to touch the baby again. Do you understand? I want to see how the baby is."

"No," Mary said quietly.

"Mary, listen—"

The Indian girl lowered her eyes and looked at the floor. "I think it is better if you do not come here any more," she said.

"I'm just trying to help," Beth said. "I don't want to hurt the baby."

"No," Mary said. "But I think is better. Because—I am Siwash. I am Shoshone."

"So?"

"I think maybe—the white women not like you to touch me, and then touch them."

Beth stared at her, the calmly folded hands, the gentle patience of her body. The Indian girl had spoken quietly, with neither anger nor pity for herself; stating a fact of minor importance.

"Mary, you don't understand—" Beth started.

Mary looked up, her face lit warmly by the flickering of the fire and the lighter glow of the candles. "I understand," she said.

Beth felt suddenly tired and unable to find anything to say. All the high moral talk that came to her mind—none of it would make any difference. It was just talk. The girl sitting quietly beside her knew the way things were, and the theory could never compete with the reality.

Mary stood up. "The man is coming now," she said. She had been listening to the sound of the two horses approaching while they talked. They were just outside now, and the girl reached down to swing the coffee pot near the fire.

As the soft sound of moccasin-shod feet sounded on the porch, she started toward the door. As she was reaching for the handle, it swung open. At the threshold was the terrible figure from some nightmare of long ago.

The old man peered at her as though over the sights of a rifle, his bright, indifferent eyes holding her pinned immobile; then she was dismissed. He pushed past her into the room, bent and shuffling, muttering something she caught only as ". . . no gun, anyways."

He moved over to the fireplace, glancing sharply at Doctor Beth but not greeting her. He squatted on his haunches before the fire, grumbling and looking around the cabin, the long rifle planted upright between his knees and clasped in both hands.

Monday came in then, and the solid familiarity of his shaggy blond head and wide grin broke the web of fright that held her. "Damnedest thing, Mary," he said. "Just ran into old Webb out in the hills. He come all the way from the mountains to see us."

"Yes," Mary said. She closed the door softly behind her husband.

"Doctor Beth!" Monday said, surprised. "Saw the horse, but I didn't recognize her. That's a good-lookin' animal."

"New," Beth said shortly. She was watching the old man's back as he squatted before the fire. Suddenly she said in a hard voice, "Old man, don't you know enough to take off your hat in a house with women?"

Webb's head turned slowly to survey her, and he made a grunting *"Wagh!"* very softly. After a moment the leathery skin around his eyes crinkled with what might have been amusement. He leaned his rifle carefully against the fireplace and slowly lifted the limp hat with both hands.

Dr. Beth leaned forward, full of sudden interest.

The top of Webb's head had been scooped out. An area the size of a man's palm was sunken in nearly an inch deep below the sides, a gaping cavity in the crown that seemed impossibly deep. The crater was rimmed with heavy ridges of scarred tissue, and the inside was a dull, bluish gray; the very bone of his skull.

"Well, damn me," Beth breathed, leaning forward to inspect the exposed skull more carefully. A leather headband circled his head just below the cavity, and from it were hung suspended the two long locks of black hair that dangled from beneath his hat brim.

Monday suddenly laughed, and the sound was abrupt and shocking in the silence. *"Wagh!* you ol' coon! They got to y' at last!"

Webb had obligingly tipped his head forward for Beth's interested inspection. *"Well,* they did," he grumbled. "Lifted this child's ha'r slick as a hound's tooth." He looked up at Monday triumphantly and bounced one of the headband plaits in his hand. "This here's the Piegan nigger as lifted her, though. "An' this'n here's a friend o' his." He flipped the other scalp lock over his shoulder.

Monday leaned over to peer into the crater. "She's a damn strange color, now," he said speculatively.

"That's *bone,* boy," Webb said proudly. "She'll weather down some."

"How'd you dress that?" Doctor Beth demanded sharply. She was fascinated and delighted, never having seen a scalped man alive before.

"Wagh! Hell's full o' dressin's," Webb muttered. "Slapped a fresh-kilt beaver pelt on top and pegged her down with a string. Had that by-god beaver tail a-slappin' at the back o' my neck f'r a week or better." He chuckled at the remembrance, a thin, breathless, rasping sound.

Monday frowned, started to speak, and hesitated. "Hoss," he said seriously, "I don't mean t' call you a liar, or nothin' . . ."

Webb looked up with annoyance. "Best not," he said. "Can't y' see the damn bone your ownself?"

"No, it ain't that. But—how c'n you be sure that Piegan topknot you're wearin' is the same as lifted yours?"

"Why, y' damn dunghead! I took it off'n him right there, *wagh!* I did, now. Was runnin' my line up to Marias River with a Pikuni Blackfoot name of Baptiste. He wa'n't full-blood Piegan, but a breed. Half white an' half Injun, an' that's damn bad blood both sides. *Wagh!* Heerd somep'n in the brush, an' first thing I knowed I was eatin' mud."

"Wagh!" Monday said. "That's *some,* now."

"Baptiste, he had both moccasins planted in the middle of my back, just a-rippin' an' a-tearin' away at the old topknot. Must of dazed me f'r a minute, for I can't recollect him takin' the knife to 'er. *Well,* now."

"There's doin's," Monday exclaimed, lapsing into the almost ritual encouragement of the story-teller.

"That made me *so* mad, but I didn't say nothin'. Truth is, I was a leetle mite confused, though you can't hurt a mountain man by hittin' him on the head. Baptiste, he had one turrible time liftin' that ha'r, he did now. Pretty soon he gets her off, though, an' leans down to wipe 'er off a bit on the grass.

"*Wagh!* Up jumps this nigger, like to eat a painter. Couldn't see nothin' whatsomever, account of all the blood. Fetched that child up by feel, I did, *wagh!* Smote 'im hip and thigh, like the Scripture recommends, till I guessed he wa'n't *about* t' run off."

"You *did*, now!"

"Outs with my knife, same as I got in my belt now, 'n' slips it inter his hump-ribs slick. Then I takes my turn a-dancin' on *his* back 'n' liftin' ha'r a while."

"*Hoo*raw, coon!"

"An' *wa'n't* there whoopin' when I gets back t'camp! This child was livin' with Heavy Runner's band at the time. One thing you got to give the Piegans, boy, they give a right smart *coup* dance. And they never 'low but four scalps off'n any one head, not to count *coup* on, anyways. Them dunghead Rees take half a dozen or better, just little-bitty pieces 'n' get half the tribe puffed up on one man's hair.

"Well, now. It wa'n't long thereafterwards that Heavy Runner's band come down with the smallpox, wagh!" Webb swept his right hand under the left, signing "gone under." "Ever' one o' the niggers. It were a fearsome stink in camp, now, and the hollerin' were somep'n to hear. This child didn't set toe *near* them lodges, he didn't. Turned around smart and high-tailed it down to Absaroka country, 'n' been livin' with the Crows ever since."

"That's *some*, now," Monday said admiringly. "Didn't ever figure you had enough hair t'be worth takin', myself."

"No," Webb said, fondling the long black strands that hung from his headband. "This nigger got the best o' the bargain, that *is* a fact. The Absaroka call me Has Three Scalps, my own 'n' two others. Lost m'own some'ers along, but it wa'n't no 'count anyways. Gettin' ratty, it was, like a summer pelt."

"How long it take that to heal?" Dr. Beth asked. "You put any kind of medicine to it? How long you keep it covered?"

Webb was flattered and pleased by the attention. He became almost embarrassed as he tried to remember. "Fact is," he said uncomfortably, "this child never did pay too much mind afterwards. If I'd of knowed somebody was to be so hell-fired interested, why, I'd of wrote 'er down or somep'n."

"You aren't much help," Beth said accusingly. "That ever happen again, you pay better attention."

"Yes'm," Webb muttered unhappily. "I surely will." He suddenly pulled the hat on again. "But I don't guess it's like to happen twice," he apologized.

Beth smiled at Webb's discomfiture. She stood from the table. "I best be movin' on, now," she said. "Mary, you think on what I said."

"About what?" Monday asked curiously.

"Woman talk, Mr. Monday, and none of your concern." She went to the door and opened it. She turned back briefly and said, "An' don't you go pokin' into things that don't concern you." She closed the door before Monday had time to answer.

"Some punkins, that 'un," Webb said admiringly. "Right peart for a woman, an' a white 'un at that. Had me a Nez Percé wife oncet summat like that 'un. Lodge-poled the bitch from Powder River t' Bayou Salade an' back again, for she *wouldn't* quit. Finally swapped her off f'r a Hawkens gun 'n' three pounds o' powder."

"What's she got her back up at *me* for?" Monday said. "I didn't do nothin'."

"Nothin'," Webb muttered. After a moment he added mysteriously, "Y' don't have to."

3

Webb and Monday unloaded the meat they had brought down, and Mary put it all out on the counter for wrapping. There was a stack of *Oregon Spectators* in the cupboard, carefully collected from the newspaper office when the paper was being run by Doc Newell. They were reject sheets, crooked on the press or double impressions, but most of them were still legible.

Webb watched with interest as Mary took the stack down and began to roll up the chunks of meat. He grabbed a sheet from the top, muttering, and took it to the fire.

"Goddam, coon, y' look like a English gentleman," Monday said. "Y' do, now. Sittin' there with y'r paper in front o' the fire, an' all."

"Jaybird," Webb said patiently, "y're just a heap o' shit with teeth, 'n' for oncet I wish y'd cut out clackin' the teeth 'n' lie there still."

"Hell, Webb," Monday said dubiously, "you can't read now, can y'?" Webb's proudest achievement was his reading, and it was an almost sure way to make him come.

This time, though, there was no violence—though Monday had seen knives drawn over the same question in the past. Webb calmly turned the page. "This nigger c'n read slick," he said equably. "He c'n read never mind what. If'n they c'n write it, he c'n read it, 'n' that's truth."

Monday grinned at his back. Mary had turned slightly around, and Monday winked at her. She smiled and turned back to the wrapping of the meat. Webb crouched on his haunches in front of the fire, the two long Piegan scalps dangling down between his knees as he read. For a long moment there was only the sound of the crackling fire and the rustling of the papers as Mary wrapped the meat.

Then Webb said angrily, "What 'n hell's 'ova' mean?" He looked accusingly at Monday as though the big man had perpetrated the word himself.

Monday looked at him, surprised. "Means 'above,' coon. Y' put y'r gun ova the mantel."

"That's *over*, y' damn dunghead," Webb snapped. "Ova, o-v-a."

Monday rubbed his forehead. "I don't believe that's a real word," he said finally. "It don't sound right."

"It's *got* to be a word. Right here in the paper, ain't it?"

Monday went over to the fire and looked at the column where Webb was pointing. It was a long poem, fifteen or twenty stanzas, with the title ADVENTURES OF A COLUMBIA SALMON. The paper was several years old and yellowed, but the type was still legible enough. Webb was on the second stanza:

> 'Tis a poor salmon, which a short time past
> With thousands of her finny sisters came,
> By instinct taught, to seek and find at last,
> The place that gave her birth, there to remain

'Till nature's offices had been discharged,
And fry from out the ova had emerged.

"They got a literary association over to Oregon City," Monday explained. "Call it the 'Falls Association,' an' they're always doin' somethin' like that in the paper."

"Don't give a *damn* where it come from," Webb said querulously. "Just what's it *mean*, ova?"

"That's what I'm sayin'," Monday said. "It's literary. When they put stuff in you can't understand, that's literary."

"If'n it's a word, this nigger c'n understand it right off." Webb snorted.

"Well, you read better'n me," Monday admitted. "What's this'n here mean?" He pointed to the third line of the stanza, the word "instinct."

"*Wagh!*" Webb snorted. "That's 'instinct.'"

"Hell, I c'n sound it out if I want to," Monday said. "*That's* nothin'. Anybody c'n sound a word out if he wants to. But what's it mean?"

"Iggerant child, y'are now. Instinct, that's when you do something you don't know *what* y're doin'."

"That's just stupid, to my way o' thinkin'," Monday said.

Webb stood, clutching the paper tightly in his fist and glaring at Monday. "Nobody *ast* y' for y'r dunghead *opinion*," he said furiously. "Just do you know what 'ova' means."

"Don't get y'r back up, hoss," Monday said placatingly. "Mary, 'ova' ain't a Shoshone word, is it?"

Mary thought for a moment. "No," she said, shaking her head. "What does it look like?" She came over to the paper. Webb had partly crumpled it in his anger and they had to smooth it out on the table.

"C'n she read?" Webb demanded of Monday while Mary looked at the column.

"Hell, yes," Monday said with pride. "I bet she c'n read better'n you."

"Never heard of a squaw could read," Webb muttered. "Goes against nature."

Mary said, "I think maybe 'ova' means 'frying pan.' See, is where they take the fry out of."

"That's it, Mary got it!" Monday said. "See, right there. 'Fry from out the ova.' That's it."

Webb puzzled at it for a moment. "Fry means baby fish, don't you even know that?"

"Hell, yes. Ain't you ever had baby fish fried? An' see there, it says about 'nature's offices.' That means when you're hungry, don't it?"

Webb muttered something unintelligible, tracing the lines with his finger again, trying out the meaning. Then he stood straight and looked Monday square in the eye. "Then the son of a bitch don' make any sense."

Monday shrugged. "That's account it's literary," he said affably. "Like I said. Listen, hoss, you don't want t' worry too much about this literary stuff or you go crazy."

"The bastards," Webb growled, staring down at the paper. "The dirty, lousy, rotten—*men!*" Deliberately he crumpled the sheet into a tiny ball in his fist, his teeth clenched in anger. Slowly he bent to put the wadded ball on the floor, his movement tense, almost shaking with rage. Methodically he began to stamp on the paper, mashing it flat with his moccasins and cursing in a steady stream.

"*That* ain't what God made words for!" he snarled.

Monday started to laugh, and the sound only made Webb more furious. He looked up at Monday, and for a moment Monday thought he was going to be attacked. He held his hands helplessly in front of him, weak with laughter, while the old man raged incomprehensibly. Finally Webb stalked to the door, snatching his rifle from beside the fire. He slammed the door back, and with one last implacable curse stormed out into the night, to make his camp under the open sky.

Monday sat helpless at the table, unable to speak. Mary went back to the counter, but she too was smiling. It had been a long time since the cabin had been full of cursing and laughter.

After a few moments the door exploded inward, slamming loudly back against the wall. Webb came in again, staring challengingly at Monday. He went over and picked up the mutilated newspaper and shoved it defiantly in the flap of his hunting shirt. He stood for a second, arms belligerently akimbo, waiting for Monday to say something. Seeing that the big man lacked the courage, Webb spat in the fire and went out again. Monday put his head down in his hands and began to shake again.

From the counter Mary said, "I think maybe he eat it, now." Her hands deftly rolled the packages and put them to one side.

"No." Monday gasped, wiping his eyes. "If I know the coon, he just can't stand to quit without finding out how it came out. How he is."

Mary smiled. "He is not like the others, that one."

"He's still the same as ever, god damn him. Just like he used to be."

"He is Absaroka?" Mary asked.

"No, he's white—he's livin' with the Crows, is all."

Mary shrugged. "Was that I meant. It makes no difference to the Absaroka. He lives there, he is Absaroka. Same as when you were Shoshone."

"I expect," Monday said, never having thought about it.

"He is very much mountain," Mary said. "He is free, not like white men."

"White men are free too, Mary," Monday said, frowning. "It's just a different kind of life, is all."

"May be that way," Mary said quietly. "You know, that one, he is the Wild Man Thurston talk about."

Monday laughed. "*Wagh!* He is, now. Won't Thurston be surprised when he finds out it's just an old friend."

Mary finished the last of the meat and stooped down to open the trapdoor to the cooler. "No, I think he not be surprised. But he will be angry."

"Angry? Why the hell angry? Webb ain't going to hurt anybody."

Mary stacked the packages carefully and methodically, moving slowly because of her bulk. "I think maybe he hurt you."

"Webb?" Monday laughed. "Hell, he's just playin'. It's like old times, Mary."

"No, is because the old man is—Absaroka. It hurt you to have a friend like that here. Thurston, he does not like mountain people around here. You know."

"Hell," Monday said, "nothin' I c'n do about what Thurston likes or not."

"But it hurts you just the same."

"Mary—listen, Mary. You worry too much about things you don't understand. If Thurston don't like my friends—it don't make any difference. I'm doin' the best I can here."

"No," Mary said quietly, turning to look at him. "You smell mountain. Now, the old man here, you start to talk mountain again. And you will never be one of them here, you smell mountain. You have mountain ways, mountain friends"—she hesitated briefly— "mountain wife."

"Enough, woman." Monday stood, resting his fists on the table. He had spoken in Shoshone, and Mary became silent. She closed the trapdoor over the cooler and stood, brushing the dust from her gingham skirt. She went to the fireplace and hefted the pot, shaking it to hear the liquid.

"There is coffee," she said.

Monday looked down at the table, leaning on his knuckles. "I'm going to take a walk down to the river."

"I heat it again when you come back," Mary said.

Chapter Six

I

The moon was risen. It cast sharp shadows in front of him as Monday walked down to the river bank and sat himself. Below the bluff the Willamette rolled silvery and silent. Across the river the trees were cut-out silhouettes against the lightness of the sky, motionless and seeming very far away in the black and silver dimness of the night.

She was there all the time, he thought. Listening to Thurston talk about "that Indian servant" and "biological needs." Though, at the root of it, Monday supposed it didn't matter. It wasn't new. Times enough in the past seven years, scraps of conversation, sidelong glances, wrinkled noses as she passed in the streets of Oregon City before Monday had gotten enough sense to keep her home. It was nothing new to Mary, or to him.

Meek and Newell both had Indian women, Nez Percé sisters. How the hell did *they* stand it? Virginia Meek just stayed home; there was no way to tell what she felt, if she felt anything. But then, Joe had a "position"; being marshal probably made quite a bit of difference.

Monday shook his head. There was no answer. Except the one some had found, getting rid of their women and getting white girls. But it was no way out for men like Meek and Newell and himself, who had their women not as a convenience, but because they wanted them and loved them. Until he'd bought Mary he'd never had any notion of having a woman permanent, and in fact it wasn't in his mind then. Like the two that had come before her, somebody to keep a lodge for him and mend his moccasins and warm his body in the cold winter nights. But, over the years . . .

Well, the hell with it. It was just the way it was. It was hard and you had to put up with it and try to get along as best you could.

He stood up, stretching his shoulders, trying to ease some of the tension out of them. What frustrated him most was the way things kept becoming problems; things that didn't have any *right* to be problems. What the hell difference did it make to Thurston and the rest of them if he *did* have an Indian woman? That was what he couldn't understand. Their lives were not changed by it, not even affected. In the end he supposed it was the same as Thurston wanting to hunt down an unknown solitary, just because he was solitary. And the new talk about sending an expedition into the up-country tribes that never hurt anybody and wanted nothing from the whites except to be left alone. It was just that they were there.

There was something they couldn't stand about having Indians around. Something that got inside their minds and ate away at them like maggots in rotten meat, and they couldn't rest until they'd wiped out the "threat." A dozen times or better Monday had tried to figure out what the "threat" was, that they were always talking about. Only thing he could ever puzzle out was that the Indians lived a different kind of life, and the settlers couldn't tolerate it. They had to try to change them to farmer-thinking; make Christians out of them, and when that didn't work—hell, there was always the military. It didn't seem enough to produce the kind of reasonless, blind hate but—it seemed to be the way it was. They just couldn't stand to know that somebody was around that didn't live the way they did.

Monday started walking back up to the cabin. Every time he got to thinking about it, it made him low. It was so damned unfair. And to have Mary thinking he'd be better off without her—it was just too goddamn much. An Indian woman who could not be a wife to her man was—in her own mind, at least—nothing. In the moment she had no use, she ceased to exist. And it was what Mary was feeling.

"God *damn* them," he muttered.

Well past the cabin to the north he saw the small flame of Webb's campfire, just at the edge of the trees that walled in the field. There was no use muddling over it all again. He'd reached the old wall, where his thinking butted up hard and stopped. Each time he thought he might somehow plow on through, but he never did. He'd go listen to the old man lie a while, and maybe it would cheer him up.

Webb's blankets were empty when Monday got there. He threw another chunk of wood on the fire, standing close as the yellow flames licked up, so his face was lit.

"Come on out o' there, y' damned ol' squaw," he said loudly.

A few yards from him the brush at the edge of the trees rustled. Monday would have sworn the little patch wouldn't hide a rabbit, but the old man's angular shape slowly unfolded from the ground, as though appearing from a pit. He shuffled over to the fire, lowering the hammer of his gun and sniffing contemptuously.

"Y' damn leadfoot dunghead," he muttered. "This nigger like t' filled y'r guts with Galena, *wagh!*"

"Look here, hoss," Monday told him. "You got no call to be so skittery around here. We got all tame Injuns."

Webb snorted, squatting by the fire. "Y'allus was a iggerant nigger, an' pokin' holes in the ground ain't made you any smarter. One time right quick I'm fixin' to put a ball atween y'r eyes. Learn y' not to come knockin' around a man's camp 'thout so much as a good holler."

"Won't learn me much if'n I'm dead," Monday observed.

"*Wagh!* That's truth! Y'allus did learn real hard. But leastways I wouldn't be bothered with y' no more."

Monday leaned back on his elbows, beginning to feel more easy, his mind sloughing off the turbulence and tension. "How'd she come out?" he said, meaning the poem.

"Hell of a damn thing," Webb muttered. "Dunghead fish gets caught by a fisherman an' gets loose. Otter grabs 'er, she gets loose. Eagle gets holt of 'er, an' another eagle whomps him, an' she falls back to the river. All *kinds* o' goddamn things happen! Then she gets to the falls that she's got t' jump over. *Wagh!* Well, now. She doubles up an' gives a try—then you know what the damn fish done?"

"No, hoss. I didn't read it."

"*Dies!* She goes under slick. After all them *awful* things, that dunghead fish tries t' make a leetle jump, 'n' *dies!*" He held his hands up in bewilderment. "It wa'n't no kind o' poem t' end like that, now was it?"

"Don't seem like it," Monday admitted.

"*Hell*, no. No kind o' poem at all. Fish ought t' have more guts than that, is what I say. This nigger could've jumped them falls slick, 'n' got that damned fry out o' the ova or *what*ever. Even the fish around this country got no more guts than the people."

"Well, that's literary, like I tol' you," Monday said reasonably.

"All bullshit, anyways," Webb muttered. "Puttin' in things a man can't understand."

Monday shrugged. After a moment he said, "Where's y'r stick floatin', coon?"

Webb stared into the fire, then glanced up at Monday. He turned back to the fire and blinked. "Was down to the Bighorn," he started absently. "Met up with a old Crow shaman down there. Says to me, 'Old man, you going to die pretty soon. You best go see y'r family first.' Approximately what he tol' me, except it took three days f'r the dancin' and all."

"Hell, hoss. You oughtn't to take that kind of medicine too serious. You going to outlive us all, just out o' pure mean."

Webb spat in the fire. "It ain't I *b'lieve* the dunghead. They's all a pack of lyin' sonsabitches, them shamans."

"They are, now."

"Still, I expect the lyin' nigger's right, f'r oncet. This child went around t' all his Crow people, 'n' it still didn't feel right. Figgered I had to come round an' see what's left of the old mountain men, bein' as how they was sort o' family oncet. The bastards."

Monday rubbed his forehead, leaning up on one elbow. "What about y'r own children?"

Webb snorted. "Pack o' wuthless no-'count breeds, they are. Man oughtn't to be allowed t' see his children after they c'n walk, else he's like t' kill them or hisself out o' pure mean disappointment. But they's good boys, all of 'em. Give them an' their mother what I had, lodge, some horses 'n' foofaraw like that, 'n' come off."

"You takin' that shaman too serious, t' my way o' thinkin'."

Webb looked at him again, then back to the fire. "This nigger's old, Jaybird. Little bit older'n God, I expect. I been here since the Beginning, I have, now."

"How old are y', hoss?" Monday asked curiously.

"Hundred and twelve," Webb said promptly. "I come out when the trade first started. I was seventeen an' with Ashley's first party up to the Roche Jaune."

"That was 'twenty-two," Monday said. He figured in his head. 'That makes you forty-five years old."

Webb nodded. "Thought it was somep'n like that. Forty-five or a hundred 'n' twelve. Round in there. I been here since the Beginning."

Monday suddenly realized that Webb was, in his own mind, being perfectly accurate. He meant the beginning of the mountain trade; the only universe whose creation meant a damn anyway.

"Forty-five ain't old, hoss. You got good years ahead."

Webb looked up at him, and Monday was shocked by the raw grief in the old man's face. A second later he thought it was a trick of the flickering firelight, for Webb's face had not changed visibly, yet there was no sign of emotion. "Good years behind," Webb said flatly. "This nigger's fixin' to die."

"Bill Williams is older'n you."

"He's fixin' to die, too, if'n he ain't dead."

"Well, damn it, Webb! *Ever'body's* got t'die sometime!"

"*Wagh!* That's the idee, y'iggerant dunghead! Ever'body's got to die *some*time. An' my time's now."

Monday grimaced in disgust. "Webb, you ain't talkin' *sense.*"

Webb poked viciously at the fire. "Ain't nothin' wrong with my talkin'," he muttered. "You just ain't understandin', is all."

"What the hell is there t'understand?"

"I reckon a man c'n die if he says so."

"Hell yes! You c'd fill y'r ears with powder and light it off, if y' wanted to. Nobody stoppin' you."

"Ain't going t' die like that," Webb said calmly. "This child's fixin' to die like a man."

"Dead's dead," Monday said sharply, angry at the old man for talking this way.

Webb looked up at him quizzically, still toying with the smoking stick. "You been away from people too long," he said finally. "Made you weak in the head." He poked at the fire again.

Monday was dumfounded. Crazy old Webb, solitary as an owl, claiming *he* had been away from people too long.

"All right," he said finally. "Roll it out, then. What's a good way t' die?"

"Way the old war-chiefs used to do 'er," Webb said speculatively, without hesitation. "Man gets old, gets ready to die. He paints hisself up for war, an' tells the people what he's after. He's a good old man, an' ever'body loves 'im. Takes his gun an' runs off to the woods.

"Then the young men paint up, too, them as wants to go after 'im. Paint up like Blackfoot, maybe, or some other. His sons get first crack at goin'. They hunt 'im down, makin' like Blackfoot, an' the old man goes under fightin', the way he's a mind to. Who kills 'im gets scalp an' all. Naturally, the sons go after 'im good, not wantin' anybody else t' have his scalp an' horses an' such."

"Why make a game out of it? Why not just shoot the old man and have done with it? No cause t' go play-actin'."

"Ain't no game," Webb snapped angrily. Then he leaned back and said, more quietly. "No game. I mind me of old Walking Bird, him as took four o' the young men afore they got 'im. Three days, an' they had to call out the Dog Society f'r help." Webb chuckled raspingly. "Oh, he come round 'em smart, he did, now. Kilt four. No game to it, she's war right enough. Them as hunt got to watch out. Man feels inclined t' lift a leetle hair, he c'n show what he's worth, an' pick up a few horses besides. If'n he's good. If'n he *ain't* good—" Webb swept his right hand under the left.

Monday shook his head. It all seemed a long way from him now. Things had changed so much. Seed wheat and missionaries . . .

He suddenly noticed that the old man was watching his face intently. "Now, look, hoss," he said slowly. "If you're thinkin'—"

"Ain't thinkin' nothin'," Webb said sharply. "Weakens the brain. You ast me an' I tol' you."

"Webb, listen, coon, I couldn't—" Monday scrambled to his feet.

"I ain't ast if you could or couldn't *any* damn thing!" Webb's voice was harsh and cold, almost a shout. "Shut y'r pan an' get the hell out o' my camp!"

"Webb—"

"*Git!* y' damn dunghead!" The old man snatched up his rifle, throwing the hammer back to full cock. The two black scalp locks swayed violently.

Slowly, Monday turned away from the fire. He started to move into the empty field, then looked back and said quietly, "Y' didn't prime y'r pan, hoss."

Webb looked down at the open pan of his gun and began to curse slowly and steadily. Monday walked away toward the cabin, listening to Webb's low voice behind him until it was no more than the wind that slipped and rustled through the trees.

2

Monday woke late again in the morning, feeling unrested. As Mary heard him stir she poured a mug of coffee from the pot and put it on the table. From the smell of it Monday could tell it was not real coffee, but parched-barley coffee. Glumly he swung himself to the edge of the bed and sat with his hands resting on the edge, staring down at the plank floor. At the edges of the boards there were still dark stains where the winter's wetness had seeped up. By the end of summer they would be nearly dry, and then the insidious damp would begin again. He shook his head and stood up, grabbing his shirt from the wall, trying to gather himself together sufficiently to do what he knew had to be done, sooner or later.

He moved stiffly to the table and sat down before the coffee, cupping it in his hands.

"You are going to Oregon City today?" Mary said.

Monday grunted and took a swallow of the scalding coffee. "Expect I got to."

Mary began to broil the deer steak. In a moment she turned to Monday and smiled gently. "The old man, he holler at you last night."

"Mm." This time there was no pleasure to be evoked in the remembrance of their conversation. Mary turned back to the fire.

"Every year," Monday said absently. "Every year I say to myself, This year McLoughlin's goin' to get tired o' puttin' me down in his little book. This year he's goin' to say no."

"Someday, maybe," Mary said. "But you worry about it then."

"Seems like I used to live without having to beg ever'thing I needed."

"Is easier to live by the gun."

Monday frowned. "Yes, but why? What I mean, why is ever'thing so damn mixed up, why is ever'thing so hard down here?"

Mary looked up from the fire and met her husband's eyes. He looked at her, half-silhouetted against the fire. Her eyes are like a scared doe's, he thought absently. Big and bright.

"I don't know," she said finally. She looked at the floor for a moment, started to say something, and stopped herself. "I don't know," she repeated, turning back to the fire.

"There's so many twists to ever'thing," he mused. "Man's got t' walk so soft all the time, worry about what he says, worry about what he does, there's always a thousand things to worry about, an' I plain can't keep track of 'em all."

"They are not important, maybe, what you worry about."

"That's just the hell of it, Mary. They *ain't* important, an' I know it. But down here you got to worry about it anyways. What people are going to say, what they're going to think. Y' know, by christ, I got so bad there for a while that if somebody said good morning I'd think, but what's he *mean?*"

Mary nodded silently.

"It's like a rip-tide down to the ocean. There's a hundred little currents underneath you can't see, ever'body mad at ever'body else, or jealous, or somethin'. It's too complicated for me. I'm a simple man, I just try to get along, an' do what I'm supposed t' do."

"It will get better," Mary said. "Is hard to learn the new ways."

Monday sighed. "I expect," he said. "Webb says I allus did learn hard." He drained the last of the coffee and went to the door. As he opened it the sun streamed in yellow and warm across the floor, and suddenly there was light and warmth reflected all through the cabin.

"What do we live with the goddamn *door* shut for?" he demanded angrily of no one in particular. Outside the clarity and sharpness of the early summer morning were clean and fresh.

"Like a bunch of goddamn animals hiding in a cave," he muttered.

"Is a very beautiful morning," Mary said, coming to stand at the door and feel the warmth of the sun on her face.

"Nothin' to *hide* from," Monday said. Even as he spoke a part of him stood off and realized he was working himself up into anger because of what he had to do in Oregon City. Even realizing, he was unable to control his rising temper. "In a Shoshone lodge we'd of had the sun two hours ago. Act like we was *scared* of it, or something." Angrily he grabbed the epishemore and saddle from the rail and went off the porch to saddle the waiting horse.

Mary stood with her eyes closed in the doorway, letting the light breeze rustle in her hair and the sun bring warmth to her skin. She thought of mountain mornings, when the sun brought joy, and the red rising of it streamed into the camp circle and the lodges glowed inside from its brilliance and the women chattered as they went about their work, happy and free. She remembered it very clearly, though it was a long time, now.

"Is just the way they make houses here," she said absently.

"Bunch o' slaves, we are," Monday said, throwing the saddle on.

"You forgetting your breakfast," she said.

"I'll get it when I come back. I ain't hungry right now."

Mary went back into the cabin, leaving the door open. Monday tightened up the cinch and stood back, looking around. As his glance crossed Webb's "camp" a couple of hundred yards away he thought briefly he'd take the coon into Oregon City and show him what civilized life was like. Suddenly he stopped, his eyes returning to Webb's tiny fire.

Oh, no, he thought. It can't be.

He mounted the horse, keeping his eyes on the camp, his depression and anger suddenly flooding away. It was so. Webb's rifle leaned against his saddle on the ground, muzzle to the sky. For a moment he couldn't see the old man; and finally spotted him, a good twenty feet from the fire and from his gun. The old man was turned away from Monday, squatted down in the bushes tending to his morning duties.

Monday eased the horse into motion, slowly. Please, God, he thought anxiously, don't let him turn around. He kicked the horse into a gallop. The newly turned soil at the field's edge muffled the hoofbeats, and Monday had covered half the short distance in brief seconds.

A sudden scream ripped from his throat, the yipping war-cry of the Blackfeet.

The old man came out of his squatting position like a startled quail, seeming to dart straight up and change direction in midair. He started to run, but his buckskin breeches were down around his ankles and tripped him up. The dash ended in a long, flat dive toward the gun, his angular body stretching across the space like a bony cloud, hands outstretched and clawed.

Yelling wildly, Monday leaned down off the side of the saddle and thundered through the camp. Just as Webb plowed into the ground a few feet away, Monday's hand closed around the upright barrel of the gun and snatched it away. His yipping cry turned into a howl of pure triumph, and he hauled back on the reins sharply, the horse rearing high and pawing at the air.

He brought him down and turned back. He stood straight in the stirrups, shaking the long rifle and yelling at the old man. Webb was just unfolding himself from the ground. He stood straight and began to yell back, shaking his fist helplessly, stark naked except for his hat, which had somehow remained fast, and the sad, limp pile of breeches around his feet.

Still raging, he grabbed up his pants with one hand and snatched a burning fagot from the fire with the other. Waving the torch he began to charge Monday, cursing as he came. He ran awkwardly, clutching his breeches with one hand, but with amazing speed. When he got near enough he heaved the flaming stick. It passed just over Monday's head, frightening the horse. Monday howled again and kicked his heels in. The horse jerked wildly and broke into a gallop, straight down on the old man, who was now only a few yards off, still coming fast.

Webb dove again, as the horse thundered by like an avalanche, passing over the spot where he had been standing. Monday reined up and doubled forward in the saddle, helpless with laughter.

"Gimme my *gun!*" Webb was screaming, over and over like a mad, hysterical bird. "Gimme my *gun!*"

"Hey!" Monday hollered back. "Y' damn iggerant dunghead!"

"I'll have y'r ass f'r breakfast!" Webb shrieked at him.

Monday walked the horse slowly back, his belly hurting from laughing. Webb darted for him, still holding his breeches up with one hand. Monday lifted the rifle high over his head and out of reach.

"*Never* get y'r gun back that way," he cautioned. "Never, never. Be nice, now."

The old man stopped short, helpless and almost inarticulate with rage. At last, snarling curses, he marched back to his grounded saddle and tied up his breeches with a thong. Angrily he grabbed his floppy hunting shirt and threw it on, belting it as though he were cinching a stubborn horse.

Monday eased his horse over. The animal side-danced, uncertain about the strange thin monster they approached. Monday still held the gun high. "Y'ain't going t' shoot me if'n I give this back, are y'?"

"Ain't promisin' nothin'," Webb snapped. "Give 'er back 'n' see."

"Got to promise or you don't get 'er," Monday told him calmly.

"All right," Webb said angrily.

"All right, what?" Monday asked.

"God *damn* y'r eyes! Don't y' trust me?" It put the old man half in a rage again, not to be trusted.

"Not an inch; you pulled that stuff before. Y' got t' say it straight out."

"Y' damn iggerant—"

"Be nice, now," Monday warned him.

"All right. I ain't going to shoot y'," Webb said quickly. "Now *give* it me!"

"Now that's real kind," Monday said. He lowered the gun.

"Leastways not right this minute," Webb muttered, snatching the rifle. Having it in his hands, he seemed to reconsider, and Monday had to remind him a promise was a promise. Silently the old man finished his dressing while Monday leaned forward on the saddle horn and watched.

"You got into some bad habits, hoss. Leavin' y'r gun out like that."

"Ain't going t' talk to no nigger that done something like that," Webb said. "Takin' a man's gun—it ain't right. It ain't now."

"Thought you was gone beaver f'r a minute there, didn't you?"

"Wagh!" Webb grinned faintly, turning away so Monday couldn't see. "They's more'n one nigger gone under with his pants down, 'n' *that's* truth."

"Hell of a way to meet y'r Maker," Monday observed. "No dignity."

"He made y'r ass too, y'iggerant dunghead. Y' ain't going t' surprise *Him* none."

Monday leaned farther forward in the saddle. "Say, coon," he said seriously, "tell me somethin'."

Webb muttered something that might have been assent, pulling on a moccasin.

"Y' *allus* use poison oak t' wipe y'r ass with, or is it somethin' new you're tryin' out?"

Webb stopped short, the moccasin half on. He looked up at Monday with an expression of utter horror growing on his face. He gasped, and it was too much for Monday. He couldn't keep his face straight, and started laughing again.

Muttering viciously, Webb turned his attention back to the moccasin and jerked it on. "Y're *some*, y'are now. Y' smart bastard."

Monday sat up straight in the saddle and took a deep breath of the morning air. The sun was rising rapidly now and it was hot on the back of his shoulders. The sky was pale blue and cloudless, and the deep black-green of the firs stood out sharply. It was too beautiful a day to waste.

"Tell y' what, hoss," he said. "I got some stuff t' do in Oregon City, but it c'n wait. What do y' say we go take a swim down to the river? Them kind o' doin's shine with y'?"

Webb stood, flexing his shoulders under the buckskin shirt and looking around at the countryside lying peaceful and green in the warmth of the morning.

"Wouldn't hurt none, I expect. Ain't such a bad day, f'r the kind o' day it is."

Monday grinned down at him.

Webb mounted up and the two turned back toward the cabin and the trail that led down to the sandy beach at the point of the river's turning.

"By *god*," Monday said, thinking about it. "You looked like a bird, sure enough."

Webb muttered under his breath.

Monday leaned over and clapped the old man on the shoulder. "Just like old times, hoss. Don't get y'r back up."

Webb's mouth twitched. "Was, now," he admitted grudgingly.

Just the way it used to be, Monday thought. Been a hell of a while since he'd had any real horseplay. Seemed like it was getting grim around. He never seemed to have any plain *fun* any more, that was the trouble.

"Just like old times," he repeated softly.

Chapter Seven

Mary was bringing a chair out into the sun, and she looked up in surprise when they passed the cabin. Monday hollered at her that they were going for a swim first, and she smiled. The two horses eased down the small rise by the house and made their way to the bluff where Monday had sat the night before. There they turned left to follow the bank down to the sandy beach. Monday was beginning to feel good.

"Say, hoss," he said to Webb. "When'd that animal o' yours die, anyways?"

"She ain't dead, this 'un," Webb said contemptuously.

"Sure can't tell it t' look at 'er." Monday shook his head in wonderment. "Looks like wolf-meat sure enough."

He glanced sideways at the old man and saw the muscles in the lean jaw work as Webb clenched his teeth in anger. They rode on a few yards in silence. Then Webb jerked harshly on the reins, twisting his animal's head back with the suddenness of it. Monday reined up too. Webb looked at him silently for a moment, leaning forward on the horn. Finally he spat on the ground between the two animals.

"Dollar says you got shit f'r brains."

"Done and done," Monday said. He eased his horse back even with Webb's, relaxing his grip on the reins to give himself plenty of surplus. He shrugged his shoulders, loosening his muscles under the hunting shirt.

A red-tailed hawk swirled past overhead and gracefully glided to a perch in a tree fifty yards ahead of them, toward the beach. Webb pointed at the bird. "When she flies," he said.

They sat quietly watching the hawk. Monday held the long ends of the reins out to the side, ready to whip. Webb sat comfortably relaxed, only raising his hands a little from the saddle horn. The hawk surveyed the field, watching for the scurry of some small animal. Its head turned slowly, scanning with care. It raised one wing, and Monday's breath stopped. The hawk tucked its head under the wing, searching out an annoying mite. Monday relaxed.

He was beginning to think the damn bird was going to build a nest in the tree. Suddenly and simultaneously the hawk's talons released the branch and Webb shouted *"Hya!"* kicking his heels into the horse's flanks.

Monday's animal jerked, then bolted as he slapped the reins to him. Webb had taken the start in a furious explosion of hoofs. Monday's horse took two jerky steps, then fell into pace and thundered after. The hawk's slow glide faltered, and it veered off startled as the two great animals charged past beneath.

Webb began to howl. *"Hoo-o-o-ohya! Hya! Hya! Hya!"*

Monday heard himself begin to shout, too, as he drew abreast of the other animal. The horses were stretched forward now and the drumming of their hoofs was like a cascade of thunder rolling down from the hills. On Monday's right the trees bordering the river whipped past in a blur of motion, the wall of trees toward which they charged came up at them like an ocean roller.

Beneath Monday's knees the muscles of the animal throbbed with a rhythm of pure power and he howled his delight in it as he pulled ahead.

Then, suddenly, it was over and the trees were upon him and he reined up, the horse rearing and pawing at the air to avoid charging headlong into the near-solid wall of foliage. Webb was just behind, and in the twisting suddenness of the finish the two animals collided in air, fighting for balance. At last they came with all four hoofs on the ground again, dancing away from each other suspiciously while the men hauled on the reins to bring order back. When they were finally at rest, their heads hanging from the effort of the sprint, Monday swung down out of the saddle.

He whacked Webb on the back. "Hooraw, coon! Y' owe me a dollar!"

Webb rubbed the muzzle of his horse. "Y' done good," he said. "Y' done all right."

"Gimme my dollar!" Monday demanded triumphantly.

Webb turned to him slowly, lifting his hands in disappointment. "Now where the hell would I get a dollar?" he asked reasonably. "You know I ain't got a dollar."

"Y' bet me a dollar, y' owe me a dollar," Monday said gleefully.

"Ain't built for the short haul," Webb said speculatively, looking at his horse. "Little sprint like that don't mean nothin'. This child'll race y' from here t' Wind River, 'n' *then* we'll see."

Monday laughed. "Let's get that swim, coon." They started down the trail to the beach. Monday knew he was a dollar richer. Maybe not this year, maybe not in the next ten. But someday he'd have a dollar because of that little sprint. Someday, maybe, an old Absaroka woman would come riding up to his door, a thousand miles from home, and hand him a dollar and he'd know what it was for.

The river spread before them, glossy in the morning sun. The surface was almost smooth, with long swelling ripples moving slowly in the direction of the current. To their left was the tiny island where Webb had made his first camp, and directly across the wide flow was the tall cliff where he had stood to look on Monday's field for the first time.

The sun flooded over the sandy beach, and already it was warm to the touch. Monday hastily kicked off his moccasins and scrambled out of his breeches and shirt. He loped down the short sloping beach and into the water; a long flat dive split the surface cleanly. He came up gasping and hollering. "Hooraw, boys, she's colder'n a dead man's balls! C'mon in, hoss!"

Webb sniffed suspiciously. "This nigger's goin' to have a pipe first," he said. Remorselessly he went over to the pile of Monday's clothes and rummaged around for his tobacco pouch.

"Get the hell out o' there!" Monday shouted, treading water. "Smoke y'r own damn tobacco!"

"May need m'own later, y'iggerant dunghead," Webb explained calmly. He tamped the pipe full of Monday's tobacco and went back to sit on his haunches, high up on the beach. Monday dived under and came up spouting water like a whale. He swam on his back for a while and turned a backward somersault in the water, his feet scrabbling in the air as he turned over.

"Y're damn fancy." Webb snorted when the other man surfaced. Monday grinned at him and went on playing in the water.

Webb continued to smoke, regarding the river through half-closed eyes. After a little while Monday came out, shaking his shaggy head like a dog. He stretched himself out on the sand, feeling the warmth and the digging of the sharp particles into the skin of his back and buttocks.

"God *damn!*" he said. "That feels good, hoss."

Webb grunted.

"You best get in afore I use up all the water," Monday said.

"This child'll go in when he's damn good an' ready," Webb told him.

"You a pretty good swimmer, hoss? Never recollect seein' you swim."

"*Wagh!*" Webb snorted. "This child's the best swimmer *you* ever seen. When he's a mind to."

"Tell you what, then. I'll give y' a chancet t' get y'r dollar back. Race y' acrost the river an' back. That shine with y'?"

Webb looked at the riverbank on the other side and estimated it at a hundred and fifty yards. As he watched, the trees on the other side receded and the river widened to what he guessed must be damned close to a mile and a half.

"Hell," he said. "Y're a fine one, y'are now. You used to the water already, ain't no wonder y're ready to race me."

"But I'm already plumb tired," Monday said. "Listen, I'll give y' a leetle head start, on account you're so old an' feeble."

"Old an' feeble, my *ass!*" Webb snapped. He looked down at the bowl of the pipe and turned it around in his hands. After a moment he said, "Anyways, I got t' have a leetle run at it."

"Take all y'want, hoss," Monday said amiably enough. "Y' c'n take the whole beach, for all I care."

Webb sniffed again angrily and put the pipe down on the ground. He stood up casually and walked back up the slope to the edge of the trees. Monday stood and watched him, ready to follow.

"You don't get no run,'" Webb said threateningly.

Monday shrugged.

Webb rubbed the side of his nose with one finger and looked at the river. Absently he licked his lips, and stuck one hand inside the hunting shirt to scratch himself.

Then he clenched his fists and his body inclined forward tensely.

"Hey, listen, hoss," Monday said, puzzled. "Ain't you going to take your clothes off?"

Webb stood straight, grunting something Monday could not make out. Slowly he took off his clothes and made a neatly folded pile of them. As he worked, he occasionally glanced out of the corners of his eyes at the river, as though to make certain it was not creeping up on him.

Once naked he danced around a little to loosen his muscles. Then he took a half-sideways stance toward the river, his fists clenched, his arms held slightly out at the sides. He squinted his eyes narrowly and blinked rapidly a few times. Then, with a great bellow of rage, he was off.

He bounded down the beach completely out of control, his bony arms flapping like the plucked wings of a monstrous chicken.

Monday watched with the fascination of pure awe, as the flashing brown-and-white skeleton careened past and plunged for the water like the blind charging of a wounded buffalo.

Webb hit the water at terrifying speed, churning the shallows into wild commotion. His legs plunged up and down powerfully, driving him deeper until the beach suddenly shelved off and he plunged into the hole.

His bead bobbed up after a second, roaring and sputtering, and he began to pound the water viciously with both arms. He was still perfectly vertical and he slashed wildly at the water while great circles of splashing confusion began to foam around him. Spasmodically he sank straight down, disappearing briefly from Monday's sight, while the bony arms continued their systematic punishment of the surface. He would come up again choking and hollering, but whatever else happened, the arms thrashed independently, working a terrible havoc on the peaceful river.

"Oh, sweet jesus," Monday whispered. He was held motionless in shock for a long moment. Then he raced to the edge and dived in. The momentum of his dive carried him to Webb, and he surfaced just behind the old man. He grabbed his chin and began to stroke the few feet back into the shallows. It was hard going, because Webb's arms continued to flail around him, sometimes clouting Monday at the side of his head. Shortly Monday's feet felt solid ground. He stood up and, with one last powerful heave, threw the light body of the old man into shallow water. Webb sank, horizontal at last in the shallows, and sat up, sputtering and raging. Monday grabbed him under the armpits and hoisted him to his feet, turning him to face the beach.

Webb shook him off angrily and stalked up the beach to his pile of clothes. Wheeling around suddenly, he crouched forward, his mouth set in a vicious snarl. He tensed himself, dripping puddles of water all around, and suddenly began to gallop toward the water again like a giant bony duck. Monday threw himself at the old man's legs and Webb went tumbling across the sand. Monday scrambled up and dived for the old man, pinned his thin shoulders to the ground.

"Jesus god, Webb, whoa back!"

"What the hell'd you go an' do *that* for!" Webb hollered into Monday's face. "I was just gettin' the *feel* of it!"

2

When Webb had calmed enough that Monday felt it was safe to release him, he let the old man up.

"Y' damn near *drownded* me!" Webb said, feeling his jaw and throat where Monday's heavy hand had gripped him.

"Jesus, Webb," Monday said. "Why didn't y' just *tell* me y' couldn't swim?"

"This nigger c'n swim slick," Webb snapped. "He just swims a leetle different style than some."

Monday leaned back on his elbows. "But damn, hoss. Y'r style, seems like it's better for up-and-down than back-and-forth."

"Ever occur t' that thick skull o' y'rs that maybe that's what I *like?*" Webb said sarcastically.

"All right, coon, all right. Whoa back, now."

Webb sniffed, wiping his nose with the back of his hand.

"Tell you what, though," Monday said, leaning forward. "Bein' as how you got y'r own style down real smart, maybe you'd like t' learn the other one?"

"Wouldn't hurt nothin', I expect," Webb admitted grudgingly, after a moment's thought.

"S'pose we swap, then," Monday said. "You teach me your style, an' I'll teach y' mine."

"Well, hell, boy," Webb said modestly. "There ain't a hell of a lot to 'er. "

"Now *my* style," Monday said, "a man's got t' be more or less flat in the water. Y' get y'r head down an' y'r feet up."

"Y'iggerant dunghead," Webb said. "Don't y'even know *that?* Y' get y'r head down, y' get drownded. Goes against nature f'r a man t' get his head down in the water."

"Listen, coon. I'll show you, all right? Is that fair?"

Webb shrugged, perfectly indifferent to it.

Monday stood and walked along the river for a bit. Down the beach from them, nearly opposite the mouth of the channel that cut the island off from the mainland, drift logs had piled during the winter floods. Monday picked around them until he found one he thought would serve as a decent float.

"Hya! coon. Give me a hand here."

Webb came over and the two of them rolled the log to the water.

"Now listen, hoss. You grab onto one end, an' keep y'r head up."

Webb silently did as he was told, and Monday hauled the log out into deeper water. As Webb's feet left the solid footing of the beach, his face tightened into an impassive mask of indifference.

"Just stick y'r face in the water oncet," Monday said.

Webb did, and snatched it out again, sputtering.

"Y' got t' quit breathin' first," Monday said patiently.

Webb looked at him suspiciously and tried it again. He stayed under so long this time that Monday had to tap him on the shoulder to make him bring his face up.

"That's the style!" Monday said. *"There's* doin's."

"Hell, there ain't nothin' to that," Webb said. "All y' got to do is quit breathin' when y'r under, is all."

"That's just the *start*, hoss," Monday told him.

They were drifting gently in the current and were now opposite the point of the island. Monday had been clinging to the side of the log. Now he let go and came around the end Webb was holding.

"All right, hoss, now you watch me. Move over."

Monday took the log in his hands and began a steady, powerful kick with his legs. Gradually the log began to move upstream.

"Now—you come in," he said, panting.

Webb began to kick, and his legs rose to the surface behind him. He glanced apprehensively at the white limbs trailing him.

"Let 'em come up," Monday said. "They're supposed to."

"Ever' time they come up m' head wants t' go down," Webb complained bitterly.

"That don't matter—"

"Don't matter t' *you*, maybe. Matters like hell t' *me*."

"Now listen hoss, y' trust me, don't y'?"

"Hell no."

Monday sighed. "C'mon hoss. Kick."

Gradually the awkwardness worked out of Webb's kicking, his natural physical instincts overcoming the tension. He began to kick powerfully, his jaw set, as though he intended to shove the log all the way to the source of the river.

"Now take it easy, coon," Monday said. "Y' don't want t'—"

Suddenly the top of the log just ahead of them exploded into shards of flying splinter. Instinctively both men ducked, and Webb came up spluttering.

Monday dived under and came up on the side of the log toward the beach, his head down behind the float. "Get around here," he snapped.

The echo of the shot was still reverberating from the cliff. Monday hoisted himself suddenly and scanned the opposite bank. He could just make out the white powder smoke. He ducked his head just as another ball crashed into the top of the log and whined off behind them.

Webb had gradually worked his way to the side of the log, beside Monday.

"Get y'r hands off the top," Monday said.

"What the hell'm I going to hang on to?" Webb snarled at him.

"Hang on to the bottom or something."

Another crash of an exploding charge came from the cliff and the water just in front of the log sprayed high. Webb began to curse.

"The sonsabitches," he muttered. "The dirty dunghead sonsabitches."

"They's at least two of 'em," Monday said. "One man couldn't reload that fast."

"They're firin' as fast as they c'n load, if'n there's two," Webb said. He had automatically been counting the seconds between shots.

"We got t' get out of here," Monday said. He looked back over his shoulder at the beach, about thirty feet away.

A flash of white smoke on the cliff, and the solid thunk as a ball buried itself deep in the log. Both swimming men felt the impact clearly as the shock was carried from the log to their hands.

"Dungheads," Webb muttered. "Whyn't they shoot *under?* Get us slick."

"Ball won't carry in water. Get this thing movin' back t' shore."

"You'n y'r goddamn swimmin' lessons," Webb growled. But he began to kick, and very slowly the log began to move broadside toward the beach.

The next shot whizzed just over the top of the log and sprayed water behind them.

"Where's y'r gun?" Monday said.

"Up by the goddamn clothes, same as y'rs." What with walking down the beach to find the log, and being carried farther down by the current, they were a good fifty yards from their weapons.

Two shots came simultaneously, one shattering against each end of the log, spraying splinters.

"Had my druthers," Webb said, "I'd ruther be up on that cliff a-shootin'."

"You 'n' me, hoss."

At last their feet touched bottom, and they dragged the log back until they were crouched behind it in waist-deep water, not daring to poke their heads over the top. After the two shots at each end of the log, there had been no more firing.

"Bastards is waitin' for us t' run," Monday said.

Webb shrugged. "They goin' to wait one hell of a while for me," he said.

"We can't sit here all day," Monday said. "My ass is gettin' cold."

"Be a vast lot colder with a half-ounce o' Galena in it."

Monday looked over his shoulder at the beach again, where the drift logs were piled. "We best cache ourselves ahind them logs," he said. "Maybe we c'n work up the bank and back o' the trees to get our guns."

"Y' figger the boys is just going to let us sashay across? Them logs is a good twenty feet yet."

"What the hell choice we *got?*" Monday said.

"We got t' get one o' the bastards t' discharge," Webb said. "Then break for it. With only one ball left, the other'n c'n only get one of us."

"Still one too many, t'my thinkin'."

"Y' got a better idee?"

Monday shook his head.

"Get set," Webb said. He poked his head over the top of the log and a crash of gunfire sounded across the river. The ball whined off across the beach, and both men were up and running in a wild zigzag for the shelter of the logs. The second blast came, and a huge gout of sand spurted up between them.

Then they dived, tumbling behind the biggest log, scrambling close into the lee of it. Monday grinned, huddling close to the wet wood. "Made 'er, coon."

Webb snorted. "If it'd been *this* nigger a-shootin', one of us'd be lyin' out on that beach."

Monday scanned the bank behind them, looking for a fast way up into the trees.

"You 'n' y'r swimmin' lessons," Webb muttered. "You 'n' y'r tame Injuns."

"God damn, Webb, it's a fact. Hell, I ain't been shot at in *years*, 'cept when I come into y'r camp. I can't under—"

Suddenly he stopped short. "God damn," he whispered. He leaned forward and grabbed two sticks of driftwood the size of his wrist and several feet long.

"Gonna beat 'em to death?" Webb asked curiously.

"Just going t' try somethin'," Monday said. "Get down."

With one sudden motion he plunged both sticks vertically into the ground behind the log, so they projected over the top. Quickly he dropped his head again.

There was a long pause. Then, suddenly, there came the enormous roar of the guns across the river. Both sticks splintered and the pieces showered off behind them. Webb's eyes opened wide in astonishment. *"Wagh!"* he said. "That's some—"

But Monday was suddenly standing upright, in full view, shaking his fist at the cliff on the other side.

Webb heard a deep voice across the river roar with laughter and shout, "Hey, Rainy! Look who's here!"

"Enfant de garce!" came the echoed reply.

"You bastards!" Monday hollered. "You sonsabitches!"

Cautiously Webb poked his head over the top of the log and saw two men standing on the opposite cliff, their rifles butt-grounded, doubled over with laughter.

"Who the hell's—" Suddenly Webb recognized the stocky figure of Joe Meek. The other man he did not know.

"Hey, friend of me!" the slighter man shouted. "You wish maybe come hunting with Joe and me?"

"Hooraw, boys!" hollered Meek. "Us'n caught the trail o' some bare-assed ducks! Ain't seen a couple come flyin' past y'r log, have y'? One of 'em real bony, couldn't miss 'im." Then he doubled over again, holding his rifle for support.

"God damn y'r eyes, Meek," Webb howled at him. "I'll bare-ass duck you when I get m' hands on y'!"

"Well, get ready, then," Meek said. "Us'n comin' to pay a leetle social visit."

Monday set off up the beach to their pile of clothes, and Webb followed. Meek and René Devaux brought their horses out of hiding and mounted, starting along the cliff trail to swing down to Swensen's unofficial ferry. Occasional bursts of laughter came echoing over the river to Monday and Webb.

Just as they reached the turning point of the trail and were about to enter the trees, Meek shouted, "Hooraw, Webb! Di'n't even say g'morning. What d'y'feel like, y'old boneyard?"

"Half froze f'r marshal hair," Webb shouted. Meek laughed and led his horse out of sight, followed by Devaux.

"Bastards," Monday growled as he pulled on his pants.

"That Meek always did have a hell of a sense o' humor," Webb said. "Wagh! he did now. I recollect one time up to the Roche Jaime . . ."

3

Devaux and Meek reached the cabin about two hours later, charging down the trail and whooping. Mary, forewarned, had put a huge pot on the fire to boil, throwing in chunks of meat indiscriminately like a camp pot.

"C'mon in 'n' have meat," Monday said, standing at the door. Meek and Devaux tumbled off their horses and poured through the door. When all four men were in the cabin it seemed full to bursting, with everybody talking at once and laughing and gesticulating.

Mary moved silently among them, almost invisible, seeing that there was plenty of meat in the pot and that everything was comfortable. She had pulled the table out of the center of the floor and placed it against the opposite wall, leaving a clear space on the floor before the fire.

Meek leaned over the steaming kettle. "Wagh! Half froze f'r meat, this child."

"Hey!" Devaux said excitedly, pointing at Webb. "Is you!"

Webb looked up calmly. "So."

"I don' hardly recognize you with you clothes on!"

"By god, Rainy—" Meek said.

"Hey, friend of me," Devaux said to Monday, "you know, I never have the honor of the bony one."

"Hell," Monday said. "I figured ever'body— Rainy, this here's Webb. Webb, Rainy Devaux, he's a old Hudson's Bay freeman."

"What we used t' call Nor'west company in the mountains," Meek said.

Devaux leaned forward from the waist in a stiff bow, extending his hand. *"Enchanté."*

Webb took his hand suspiciously, squinting at him out of one eye. "By god, y're a queer one, y'are now. What's this here 'onshontay'?"

"Means 'I'm glad to meet y',' " Monday said.

"Then why'n hell don't he just say so?" Webb demanded. "Who you run with?" he asked Devaux.

"Me, I was with Ogden sometimes. Sometimes out of Fort Vancouver."

"*Wagh! Was* you, now!" Webb said. "You wa'n't with Ogden up to the Snake, winter of 'twenty-four, 'twenty-five, now?"

"*Enfant de garce!* I remember him well, that winter!"

"*Damn* y'r eyes, now," Webb said with delight. "Listen here, coon, this nigger was with that American brigade come aplunderin' into your camp."

"No! *Incroyable!*" Devaux said, his eyes wide in astonishment.

"By god, *there* was doin's, sure god," Webb said, chuckling. "I recollect was ol' Johnson Gardner was booshway that trip . . ."

Webb and Devaux squatted on the floor, turning to face each other, and started a long gesticulatory conversation, completely forgetting the others.

Monday was calculating rapidly in his head. He turned to Meek. "Well, what're y' feelin' like, coon? Y'know, that Rainy, he's a turrible liar. He couldn't of been more'n four, five years old that winter."

Meek shrugged. "Man wants t' talk, he wants t' talk. Rainy ain't going t' stop 'im just 'cause he was born a few years too late. Rainy ain't so much a liar as he is polite. That's cause he's French, y' know."

"*Well*, he is." Monday laughed. "Listen, hoss. How's y'r stick come to float out here?"

"Well," Meek said, rubbing his chin thoughtfully. "I'll tell y', now." He glanced slyly up at Monday, and his dark eyes crinkled slightly at the corners.

"*There's* trouble," Monday said apprehensively. "Ever' time you get a look like that a man like to run cache hisself."

"Figured as how y' might like t' see the trial o' them Cayuse," Meek said. "We'll try 'em t'morrow, an' if'n there's still light, we'll hang 'em afore dinner. Otherwise we'll hang 'em the day after."

"They got the courthouse finished yet?"

"*Wagh!* They's still workin' on 'er," Meek said. "Didn't figure t' have no business so soon, I expect."

"Wouldn't mind seein' that," Monday said. "I got to go into Oregon City anyways, sooner or later." He grimaced at the thought of it, then put it out of his mind.

Meek dug into the pocket of his jeans and pulled out his marshal's badge. Ostentatiously he pinned it to the front of his shirt. Monday watched him suspiciously.

"Well, Marshal," he said tentatively. "What c'n I do f'r y'?"

Meek leaned forward intently. "Gimme two dollars and a half."

"Ah, Meek," Monday said. "You know I ain't got a half-dime t' my name. Now what kind o' thing is that? What for?"

Meek pulled a rumpled piece of paper out of his pocket and spread it out on the floor, studying it intently.

"Says here you owe the United States Government two dollars and fifty cents."

"God damn, hoss. I said from the beginning I wasn't going to pay no taxes, an' it still goes. They got no right t' take a man's money away from 'im."

"This ain't taxes, this is f'r that cap y' lost."

"Two dollars and a half! For that goddamn little blue *cap?* Marshal, damn, that ain't reasonable!"

" 'Reasonable' ain't my business," Meek said, shrugging. "Two dollars and a half is what she says, 'n' I come to make 'er straight."

"Listen, Meek, can't y' pretend I wasn't home 'r something? That's a vast lot o' money."

"Wagh!" the other said cheerfully. "Done and done. Meek's forgot about the whole thing."

Monday relaxed.

"The marshal ain't forgot nothin'," Meek said. "Gimme two dollars and a half."

Monday turned to where Devaux and Webb were sitting. They had gotten into a terrible argument of some kind and Webb had his hand behind his belt on the hilt of his butcher knife. Devaux was in the process of talking the old man out of whatever it was he had in mind.

"Rainy," Monday said, *"you* lost that cap. You're the one ought to pay for it."

"What cap is that, friend of me?" Devaux looked up from the conversation.

"That military cap, you know."

Devaux shrugged. "I know nothing about a cap. Me, I turn *my* cap in to that sergeant. You lose your cap? You should have better luck." He turned back to Webb, whose knife was still half drawn. "No, friend of me. I say nothing about Absaroka in *general.* I say only that in every hundred Absaroka, you find ninety-nine sons of bitches."

"What the hell c'n I do about it?" Monday said to Meek.

"Y'either got t' give me the money or give me a note f'r it," Meek said.

"If'n I give y' a note, I don't have to give y' any money?"

"Not right now, anyways."

"Well, hell," Monday said. "That's fair enough. I got some paper around. Mary—"

Mary had already gone to the cupboard and was getting out the ink and pen, and a scrap of paper. It had once been a letter, and had been bleached out for re-use. Traces of the previous message still trailed faintly brown across the surface.

"It's got somethin' on it, that don't matter, does it?" Monday said.

"No, that don't matter," Meek said. "Why should that matter?"

"I don't know," Monday said. "All this legal kind of stuff."

Webb stood suddenly and snatched the paper out of Monday's hand. "Here, y' damn dunghead, lemme do that. This nigger c'n write out a note slick. He done it a hundred times or better."

Webb crouched over the paper on the floor, slowly tracing the letters. "This ain't no kind o' pen," he muttered. He went over each letter twice, thickening the downstrokes carefully.

"*Enfant de garce!*" Devaux whispered. "That is really writing!"

Webb wrote a beautiful, looped hand that cascaded gracefully across the page, looking like the twisting of grasses in the wind. Every once in a while he held the paper up to gauge his work. "That goddamn 'h' ain't right," he grumbled. He sniffed, and put the paper back on the floor.

It took a long time, and when he was finished Webb wrote tinily in the corner: *Webster W Webster, M.T., scribebat.*

The others were all watching over his shoulder curiously. "Damn, that's pretty," Monday said. "What's this here *scribebat* mean?"

"Means I wrote it out," Webb said. "Don't y' even know *that?*"

"Where'd y' learn how to do that, hoss?"

Webb shrugged negligently. "Learnt it off'n one o' Mackenzie's clerks one winter up to Fort Union. That there *scribebat*'s Egyptian, or summat."

"No, I think she is Latine," Devaux said.

"Some furrin thing or other," Webb said.

"Well she's real pretty," Monday said, holding the note up to the light. It read:

> *I, the undersigned, do hereby bind myself and promise to pay the sum of two dolars fifty cents (2.50$) in good merchantable beaver furr or the equivalent. Because I lost a hat.*

"I figgered I better put that in about the hat," Webb said. "I don't usually."

"I ain't sure it ought to say about the beaver, though," Monday said dubiously.

"Y'iggerant dunghead! That's the way a note *reads!*"

Monday shrugged and looked it over again. He shook his head in admiration and handed the paper to Meek. "That's *some*, now."

"You got t' sign it, now," Meek said.

"Sometimes I go back an' fill in all them little holes, like in the o's," Webb said. "But I like t' do that in red or somethin'. If you got any red around, I'll do 'er."

"Sorry, hoss," Monday said apologetically. "Don't think we have."

Webb looked a little disappointed but he didn't say anything.

Monday signed the document and Meek put it in his pocket, carefully buttoning down the flap. Just as methodically he unpinned the badge from his shirt and stuffed it back into his pants.

"Hooraw, boys," he said, "this nigger's half froze f'r meat. Give us a bit, there."

⊂━⊶

"Meek," Monday said, "y'ever hang a man before?"

"No sir," Meek said definitely. "Never did."

"Wagh!" Webb growled. "Hangin' ain't no way t'die."

"Friend of me," Devaux said, "is because you think like Indian. All Indians afraid of hanging. Me, I am a white man, I think hanging as good as anything else."

Webb shook his head. "Goes against nature t' hang a man," he said. "All that chokin' and all."

Monday said thoughtfully, "Me, I don't think I'd like t' be the man as pulls that trap. Y' don't figure it'll bother you none, seein' 'em dancin' around there?"

Meek leaned back, looked at the fire. "Jaybird," he said absently, "y' recollect that Nez Percé woman I used t'have, before Virginia?"

Monday shrugged. If Meek didn't want to talk about the hanging, that was his business. "I recollect her," he admitted. "Tell y' the plain truth, though, I never did think too much of 'er."

Meek nodded. "Got 'er just after Mountain Lamb went under from a Bannock arrow."

Webb began to chuckle, a dry, rasping sound. "Run away from y' slick, that Nez Percé."

"Wagh!" Meek said, grinning. "She did now. Rendezvous of 'thirty-seven, it was. Powerful drunk them times. I woke up mebbe two, three days after, m' woman was lit out. Went with Ermatinger from HBC 'n' some missionaries. Took me a kettle o' alcohol an' took out after 'em."

"Did you, now!"

"Wagh! Hard doin's it was, too, desert an' all that kind o' stuff. Anyways, that bitch wouldn't lead nor foller, so I give 'er up. Next winter I spent up to the Forks o' the Salmon, with old man Kowesote's village. I says to him, 'Look here, Kowesote. That there woman I had run off from me. Now, how about you give me another one.'"

"Enfant de garce! What he say, that one?"

"He says, 'No,' flat out. Wagh! he did. He says to me, 'Meek, you already got one Nez Percé woman, 'n' the Bible says you can't have another one.'"

"Wagh!" Webb snorted. "Here's wet powder 'n' no fire t' dry it!"

"*Was* now," Meek said. "Well, I says to him if a man's wife runs off, that was like a divorce, an' he's got a right to get another one. Still the nigger says no. Then I shows him in the Bible that lots of men got plenty o' women all around. Took me 'bout two weeks, explainin' about Solomon and David and all them kind o' doin's."

"*Wagh!* You did now!"

"Well, finally the old man comes around t' my way o' thinkin'. An' the Bible's. But that got his back up, right enough. An' he says to me, 'Meek, if all that stuff's in the Bible, how come the jesus-men say I got to give away all my wives except one?' Oh, the nigger was mad, then. 'Well,' I says, 'you better ask them about that.' *Wagh!* I don't reckon that Spalding, him as was missionaryin', thanked me none."

"Hooraw, coon!" Webb stamped the butt of his rifle on the floor. "How'd she come out?"

"Got me the best o' the bargain," Meek said. "Old Kowesote give me Virginia, an' that's the best woman a man ever had."

"*Them's* doin's, right enough." Monday laughed. "Say, don't I recollect you had a baby from that Nez Percé woman?"

"*Wagh!* I did now," Meek said. "Prettiest little baby girl you *ever* seen. Named 'er Helen Mar Meek, after that woman in *The Scottish Chiefs.*"

"Reg'lar fireball, that 'un! That Nez Percé woman took off babe an' all. Hooraw."

"Not exactly," Meek said. "Had the babe myself, little Helen Mar. Give her to Narcissa Whitman t' take care of, when they was coming through the mountains."

Monday had suddenly frozen still, and the cabin was silent.

"That's sort of what I was gettin' around to say," Meek said. "Had m' little girl up to the Whitman mission, learnin' t' read an' write an' cipher an' all."

He looked steadily into the fire, watching the flames flicker and jump. Finally he said thoughtfully, "So I figure it ain't going t' bother me none to pull that trap tomorrow. I expect when Tamahas goes down, I'll just step up and put the heel o' my moccasin on that knot, an' tighten 'er up a bit."

Chapter Eight

Before the visitors rode off up the trail, Meek had said casually, "Say, Mary. Y' know, Virginia's gettin' one o' her spells again." "Something I can do?" Mary said, turning from the fire.

"Might could be," Meek said thoughtfully. "Me out an' aroun' so much, Virginia gets mighty lonesome. Homesick, like, for somebody to talk to."

Mary glanced at Monday.

"Hell," Monday said. "Have 'er stop down any time. She's allus welcome here, y' know that."

"Well, that ain't exactly what Virginia had in mind," Meek said. "She says she'd like t' have somebody come stay with her awhile."

Monday frowned. "Well, damn, coon. I don' know—"

"Be a powerful favor t' me," Meek said. "Anyways, you think about 'er."

"It's just with the babe comin' and all," Monday explained.

"Well, if it comes t' that," Meek said patiently, "y' know there ain't anybody better'n a Nez Percé when it comes t' havin' babies. Ain't that right, Rainy?"

"Is so," Devaux said sadly. "They having them all the time. My Nez Percé wife, sometimes she have babies when I not even been around for a year. They are ver' skillful."

"I wouldn't be surprised any if Virginia might be quite a help with somethin' like that. Anyways, I thought I'd say."

Then they had gone, riding up the trail toward the pay ferry, where Meek intended to bluster his official way across without paying. Devaux thought it would be interesting to watch, though he was fairly confident he himself was going to have a long swim, even if Meek had made him a temporary deputy. Webb rode along, thinking to look over the country a bit.

"Y' know," Monday said to his wife, "writin's a very useful thing. Just write out that little note and it saves me two dollars and a half."

"Still," Mary said, "you have to pay it sometime."

"Surely do," Monday agreed. "But I c'n worry about it then, can't I?"

"Yes," Mary said.

"God damn government anyways," Monday muttered. "You'd think bein' as big as they are they wouldn't worry about somethin' like a little blue hat. Send the marshal after me! I don't b'lieve I'll *ever* pay that."

"Is better you pay it," Mary said surprisingly.

"If'n I start givin' in now, where's it goin' t' *end?*" Monday complained. "What's it goin' t' be like when Oregon's a honest-to-god *state*, if'n it's this bad just bein' a territory?"

Mary shrugged. "You say you want to get along here, is not the way to get along."

Monday sighed. "I know it. I'm just gettin' it out o' my craw is all. I'll pay it sometime when I get some money. But I don't like it."

"You don't have to like it," Mary said. "Just do it."

Monday sniffed. "You sound like Thurston."

"It is like the buffalo hunt," Mary said absently. "The hunting chiefs make a council, and they say, 'No man to run ahead of camp.' They say, 'No man to fire a gun until all the men are around.' They say, 'All the women, you stay away.' They say, 'No arguing about horses when you get near the buffalo.' Many rules to the buffalo hunt."

"Hell, yes, but they all make sense."

"You go by what the hunting chiefs say, and stay with the village, or you go against them and leave the village. Is just the same here."

"You think I ought to jump when Thurston says 'Frog.'"

Mary turned to him, then looked down at her hands folded quietly in her lap. "I think nothing," she said finally. "I say, you wish to be Shoshone, you must do what the Shoshone headmen say. You wish to be white, you must do what the white headmen say."

"Seems like there's a hell of a lot more rules here, though, an' half of 'em you can't even see. Christ, a man can't *move* without worryin' what somebody's going t' think."

Mary shrugged. "With the mountain people is maybe more simple. In the mountains some things are forbidden, everything else you can do. Here, some things you can do, everything else is forbidden. Is two different ways to think about laws."

Monday rubbed his forehead. "Hell, I don't know. It makes me nervous just thinkin' about it."

It was late afternoon, and the sun was already in the west. Monday realized that Webb and the others had been there talking almost the whole day, and once again he had avoided Oregon City. Mentally he shrugged. Tomorrow he would do it, for sure.

"Mary," he said finally, "would you like to go stay with Virginia for a little while?"

"My place is here," Mary said. "You will not eat if I don't remind you."

"I'll eat," Monday said, annoyed. "Anyways, that wasn't what I ast you. Does it feel like the baby's comin' soon?"

"Yes," Mary said hesitantly. "More all the time."

"You ain't scared, are you?"

"No. But he is coming faster now. Like when stones roll downhill, they move slow at first, but very fast near the end."

"When do you think?"

"Doctor Beth, she says maybe two weeks, maybe three. Me I think not one week, maybe."

Monday stood up suddenly. "Not a week!" He abruptly realized the vastness of his ignorance; he had no faint notion of what was to be done, and a kind of panic grew in him.

"Very fast, now," Mary said quietly.

"Well—would you like to go and be with Virginia? Would that be good?"

Mary looked at him for a long time without answering. At last she said quietly, "Yes, I think."

2

Early in the morning Monday rode over to Swensen's and borrowed a horse for Mary. By the time he had returned she was ready to leave, sitting quietly in front of the house in the sun.

"Where's y'r stuff, Mary?"

"It is all here." She had a flour sack filled with her belongings, and Monday realized she'd had the sack tucked away somewhere for better than six months, waiting for a use to appear.

"By god, y' travel light, I'll say that."

"I need nothing," Mary said.

He helped her mount and they set off. He wouldn't dare try to bluff his way across the pay ferry, as Meek did, so they had to go by way of Swensen's. It meant an extra two hours, but there was no choice. On the way across Swensen grumblingly tried to engage Monday in a conversation concerning the end of the world, but for once the big man was having none of it.

He pointed proudly at the swell of Mary's belly and said, "Peter, old hoss, it's just the beginning of the world for some."

"Is all a terrible waste of time," Peter muttered, but he looked at Mary and they smiled at each other.

It was well past noon when the two horses plodded into Oregon City. The streets were almost deserted, and for a moment Monday was puzzled.

"By god," he said suddenly. "It's the trial, ever'body's at the trial."

Mary nodded. "You want to go, I can go to Virginia's alone, now."

"No, it don't matter," Monday said. "I ain't that interested."

Meek's cabin was about fifteen minutes out of the center of town, a small frame building with two rooms, painted white. Virginia came to the door to meet them. Behind her were three small shadows, dark-eyed and curious. Slowly Mary dismounted and walked to the door, carrying her flour sack. The two women greeted each other quietly, without emotion.

"My husband's lodge is open to you," Virginia said. She was taller and heavier than Mary. Not, Monday thought, a likely woman at all. But she had been a good wife to Meek.

"Your husband honors me," Mary answered. She shook hands with Virginia. Then, in turn, each of the three children came forward, silent and wide-eyed, to shake hands.

"How are y', Virginia," Monday said, taking her hand. The children all stepped forward again, and he went down the line, taking each small brown hand in his own gently. He grinned as he stood straight again, reminded strongly of the mountains. He'd sometimes spent half a morning shaking hands, coming into a strange village. Men, women, and children lined up for the handshaking, and with a village of seven or eight hundred it could take quite a while and be a hell of a strain on a man's wrist.

"Joe is at the courthouse," Virginia said. "Many problems today."

"I expect," Monday said. "Thought maybe I'd drop down myself when we get Mary settled 'n' all."

Virginia shrugged and smiled at him. "Settled now," she said.

Monday looked at Mary and she smiled, nodding. For some odd reason Monday felt embarrassed. "Well—" he said hesitantly.

"You go to the trial now," Mary said. "I am settled."

"Well, if you're all—I suppose I might as well. I'll come back after an' see how things are going."

He turned and went back to the horses. "I'll leave Peter's horse here, all right? In case—in case you might need him or something."

"All right," Virginia said.

"Well, take care of yourself, Mary."

Mary nodded and put her sack inside the door. Virginia came over to him and said, "You not worry about anything. We take care of each other."

Monday nodded. "Thanks, Virginia."

The Nez Percé woman went back to the porch and she and Mary started inside. The emotionless reserve of the formal meeting was gone now, and Virginia chattered like a kingfisher as they went in the house, her arm around Mary's shoulders.

Monday grinned as he pulled his horse around and started down toward the center of town and the courthouse. "Damn squaws," he muttered, smiling to himself.

There was a mutter of raised voices inside the courthouse as he tied the animal up in front. He pushed open the door, inadvertently shoving several people out of the way. One of the lawyers was orating wildly, but Monday couldn't tell whether it was the defense or prosecution.

He was hollering about God and justice and several abstract principles that could have applied to either side.

The room was small, and jammed with spectators, and the stink of humanity was heavy and sour. All the bench seats were taken, and the stairs leading up to the second story were crowded with watching Indians.

Meek was up in front of the rail, presumably to keep order. Monday spotted Webb against the wall to his right, and started to push his way through the standing crowd.

"Hooraw, coon," he whispered. "How's she goin'?"

"Not bad doin's," Webb admitted grudgingly. "Pretty vast lot o' talkin' goin' on."

Monday let his eyes rove over the center of attraction. Judge Pratt was listening attentively, leaning forward on his elbows. The jury box was more or less indifferent. Puzzled, Monday saw that many of the jurymen had on work clothes, with a variety of tools poking out of one pocket or another. One of them had a tool-box on his knees and was rummaging through it, looking for something.

"What the hell's that?" Monday whispered to Webb.

"Them's the carpenters was buildin' the gallows out back," Webb said. "They was makin' a hell of a racket, an' the judge says, 'Marshal, can't you stop them men from that?' Meek, he says, 'Why, shore, Judge. Put 'em on the jury.' So that's what the nigger done." Webb snorted, and the people near him turned to scowl. He scowled back.

Monday grinned, looking at Meek, who had his legs stretched out in front of him and was idly scraping his fingernails with the point of his butcher knife.

The man who was orating now had reached a high point. ". . . in the honest, if mistaken, belief," he shouted, "that Doctor Whitman was *deliberately poisoning the Cayuse people!* Gentlemen, I put it to you: these unfortunate Indians acted out of simple human concern for the welfare of their . . ."

"He better do better'n that," Webb muttered. "He ain't goin' t' ride no fifty head of horse on a speech like that."

"Fifty head!" Monday said. "That what Tamahas is payin'?"

"Fifty head, the iggerant nigger," Webb said.

Monday let his breath out slowly. "That's a lot o' horse," he said softly. He looked at the five prisoners, huddled together on a bench by themselves, apparently ignoring the trial. Tamahas himself was obviously scornful of the whole proceeding—but then, an implacable scorn was the normal set of his face, so it might be hard to tell, Monday thought.

Webb leaned over to him. "This'n here ain't the best," he said. "They had some military up there a-rantin' and a-ravin', an' he busted two glasses o' water 'fore he wore hisself out."

"Pretty good speech?"

Webb snorted. "Di'n't know any more law'n the Injuns. But he was real excitable."

". . . dying of measles and dysentery, sometimes as many as five a day. Is it any wonder, gentlemen—"

Suddenly from the stairs at the back there came a terrible wail of anguish. On the stairs one of the Indian women had stood and begun to tear her clothing, screaming wildly.

Pratt pounded heavily with his gavel. "Marshal, Marshal, order!"

Meek stood and pushed through the swinging gate of the center aisle, and Monday lost sight of him for a moment. The aisle was jammed with people, and Meek was a short man. Monday soon found he could follow the Marshal's progress by the turmoil as he plowed his way through the crowd.

Several other Indian women on the stairs began to howl a death chant for their people already dead and about to die. The keening wail was uncanny in the crowded room. There was a general shifting and muttering as the wail grated across the ears of the spectators.

"Shut that up!" somebody hollered.

"God damn it, I'm tryin'!" Meek shouted back. Most of the seated spectators had risen to their feet now, shifting and pushing to see, and a babble of talk filled the room under the high wail of the death song.

As Meek reached the end of the aisle, the squaw who had begun the chant saw him coming. She turned and started to run up the stairs, screaming. Meek plunged after her, knocking aside several of the other Indians who had moved in the way. Halfway up the stairs he dived after the woman, catching her by the ankle.

"Hooraw, coon!" Webb shouted across the room. "Go it, hoss, go it!"

The courtroom was in complete turmoil now as people jostled each other in the eagerness to see better, cursing and shouting. Judge Pratt banged steadily with his gavel. Two of the lawyers were arguing loudly in front of the bench. The only still persons in the room were the five prisoners, who watched impassively.

Webb started to pound the butt of his rifle on the floor rhythmically, adding to the gavel-pounding of the judge. He laughed and howled with rage alternately, shouting encouragement to Meek.

The squaw had fallen face forward on the steps when Meek grabbed her ankle, and was clawing wildly at the wood, still screaming. Meek hauled at the leg, dragging the woman down the steps one by one.

Suddenly someone shouted, "Hang the damn squaw too! Hang 'em all!"

Meek stopped suddenly, almost at the base of the stairs. He looked up with shock. It had all been great fun up to that point, but now the tone of the crowd changed.

Webb stopped laughing. With an abrupt gesture he swung his arms to both sides, crashing into the people beside him, who recoiled from the violence, leaving him room. He flicked open the pan of his rifle and knelt quickly, yanking the stopper from his powder horn with his teeth.

Monday had started into the crowd, heading for the first voice of hate that had arisen. He threw himself forward as though breaking his way through heavy brush, but the thickness and immovability of the mass of people made it almost impossible to get through.

He was not halfway there when the enormous roar of the discharging gun filled the courtroom with thunder. There was a sudden gasping silence as the crowd turned in shock. Monday's ears rang loudly with the explosion, but there was no other sound. Almost rigid with the paralysis of fear and startlement, the crowd turned.

Webb stood by the wall in a small clear circle, the muzzle of his rifle still pointed at the ceiling. Above his head the great mushroom of white smoke piled and rolled against the raw boards of the ceiling.

Webb lowered the gun slowly to the floor and leaned on the smoking barrel. He calmly surveyed the hundreds of eyes turned toward him.

Deliberately he leaned forward and spat on the floor. He looked up at them again, closing one eye.

"Y're a damn noisy pack o' niggers. Y'are now," he said contemptuously.

Judge Pratt sat back down, tiny globes of sweat at his hairline. He looked thoughtfully at Webb. Into the utter stillness of the room he said quietly, "Marshal, when you've finished with the woman, eject that man from the courtroom. He will be fined. He ought to know better than to fire a rifle in a court of law."

The crowd began to seat itself again, frightened and silent. Meek looked across their heads at Webb. "Sorry, Judge," he said. "Just a iggerant friend o' mine." He grinned at Webb.

"And of mine," Pratt said absently, looking at the top of his gavel. Then he slammed it down abruptly and said, "Does the defense wish to continue?"

3

Webb was waiting for Monday outside when the trial was over, having permitted himself to be thrown out without objecting. He squatted on his haunches against the wall to the right of the door, watching the people file out. Occasionally one would glance at him quickly, then turn away. There was something about Webb's impassive scrutiny that suggested a man hunting, and it was not a comfortable sensation.

Monday made his way out. "Hooraw, coon," he said, "she's all over." He sat down heavily beside Webb, sighing. "Going to be a bit of a wait for the hangin' though. Account o' havin' them carpenters on the jury, they didn't get the gallows done. An' they won't work tomorrow account it's the Sabbath."

"*Wagh!*" Webb snorted. "Give th' preachers a chancet t' pray f'r them Injuns' black souls. Expect they'll like that."

"Ain't goin' to make no difference at th' end o' the rope."

"Y'iggerant dunghead! Meant the *preachers*. Make 'em feel right godlike. Forgivin' an' all."

"That's fact. Y'know, coon, there's times I ain't real proud to be people."

"How'd the boys take it?"

"Mixed. Tamahas an' old man Kiami took it good. Others looked scared. That Tamahas is one mean son of a bitch, he is now. Meek give'm a glass o' water, an' he knocks it square out o' his hand and busted it on the floor. Looks at Meek an' says, 'What kind of man are you? Give water to me whose hands are still red with the blood of your people.'"

"*Wagh!* Pretty heavy run on water glasses, what with that lawyer an' all besides."

"*Was*, now. Kiami stopped 'em for a minute, though. Judge asks 'em one by one if'n they got anythin' to say, 'n' Kiami gets up and says, 'Kiami has done nothing.' Judge says, 'Then why are you here, Kiami? Why'd you give y'rself up?'

"Kiami says, 'You tell us Christ died to save his people. So we die, to save our people.' Ever'body laughed, naturally, but it made 'em a wee bit nervous."

"*Wagh!*" Webb spat between his feet. "Iggerant dunghead, him. Ain't goin' to do his people no more good'n Christ done his, either."

The last of the spectators were still filing out of the building, murmuring excitedly at the prospect of the hanging. Webb stared at them. "Look at 'em," he said thoughtfully. "Walkin' shitheaps, ever' one of 'em, still warm an' steamy, walkin' around makin' b'lieve they's alive."

Toward the end of the crowd, Meek and Judge Pratt appeared. Meek looked a little worried. The judge, now divested of his robes, walked over to Webb and extended his hand. "Webster, your name is? Allow me to shake your hand, my friend. You wouldn't have twenty dollars about you, I suppose?"

Webb took his hand gingerly. "Hell, no. What would I be doin' with twenty dollars?"

Pratt sighed. "That's what I was afraid of," he said.

Meek stepped forward. "Judge has t' fine y' twenty dollars for shootin' off the gun, hoss."

"Must have discipline in court, Mr. Webster. Even," the judge said unhappily, "if I have to pay it myself."

Meek brightened and smiled broadly. "*Well*, now. *That* bein' the case, here's the marshal right here, Judge, an' he's just the proper collectin' officer. I'll take the twenty dollars now."

Judge Pratt blinked at him. "Meek, if I gave you that twenty dollars the court would never see it. You and your friends would drink it up in an hour."

"Nothin' t' drink in this country, Judge, you know that. 'Gainst the law, 'n' the marshal's closed down all the stills."

Pratt shook his head slowly. Finally he said in a reasonable tone, "Meek, what would I be doing with twenty dollars?" With a last nod to Webb and Monday he strolled off up the street.

Watching him go, Meek said, "Y' know, he ain't the worst nigger ever put on them black robes."

Monday talked Webb into coming with him down to the McLoughlin house to see about the seed wheat he was going to try to borrow. Secretly he felt a little comforted to have the old coon with him, though he knew it wasn't going to make any real difference.

Reluctantly Monday tied up in front of the doctor's house. "Listen, hoss," he said to Webb, "leave y'r rifle here, will y'?"

Webb muttered, but he left the gun sheathed along the horse's shoulder. They walked up the short path to the door, past a neatly painted fence and a well-kept lawn. The house itself was two stories high, white and boxlike, with shutters at the windows.

Monday rapped on the door and stood nervously shifting his feet. In a moment the door was thrown suddenly open and the two men were faced with the great apparition that was John McLoughlin. The man was huge, six feet four and heavy in proportion. His hair was a great mane of white, so light that in his constant movement it seemed almost to float about his head. His eyes were wide with apparent surprise and disturbance, and one hand absently rubbed quick little circles on his stomach.

"Mr. Monday, Mr. Monday," he said excitedly. "Come in, come in. Sir?" He launched his hand at Webb.

"This is—Mr. Webster, Doctor McLoughlin," Monday said nervously. It sounded like a lie, but if you wanted to look at it that way, old Webb *was* Mr. Webster.

"Mr. Webster," McLoughlin said. He pumped Webb's hand quickly and whirled around, his coattails flying. "Come in, come in, gentlemen," his retreating voice said, and they had to scurry to keep up with him. McLoughlin charged up to the second floor, and Monday and Webb had just time to see him disappear into a room at the end of the hall.

"Damn sight too much misterin' goin' on," Webb muttered.

"Now you stop," Monday whispered.

When they entered McLoughlin's study the giant white-haired man was standing behind a great oak desk, frantically shuffling through a stack of papers with one hand while the other continued the habitual rubbing of his stomach. There were several leather-covered chairs before the desk and McLoughlin gestured vaguely at them. Monday and Webb sat down, uncomfortably.

"Mr. Monday, Mr. Monday," McLoughlin said. He sat down suddenly, sweeping one hand across his white mane. "You have no idea. I am so pressed, so pressed."

Monday cleared his throat. "Well, if some other time—"

"No, no no no," McLoughlin said, raising one huge hand. "Quite all right. Webster," he muttered, suddenly pausing for a brief instant to stare at his desk top. "Webster, yes, Webster. You know some of my people, I believe."

"Don't expect I do," Webb said uneasily.

McLoughlin paused, his eyes wide. "No? No? But—were you not with Mr. Gardner's brigade in the spring of 'twenty-five? And with Mr. Smith in 'twenty-eight?"

"Well, yes, I—"

"Good, good," McLoughlin said, relieved. "I was afraid for a moment—you know, the mind, with age—But you've met Peter—Mr. Ogden, and Mr. Ermatinger, and I believe Mr. Panbrun at Walla Walla?" McLoughlin ticked them off on his fingers.

Webb blinked at him, startled. "That was twenty-five years—"

"Yes, yes," McLoughlin said, rubbing his stomach nervously. "*Tempus fugit.* And each new year brings new problems. Mr. Monday, you have no idea. Lawsuits, problems, storage . . ."

"I heard there was some trouble about the land," Monday said, embarrassed. The trouble was simply that the Americans, Thurston most prominently, were methodically stripping McLoughlin of all his holdings in the Oregon Country, their only legal weapon a campaign of hate against the "damned Jesuitical rascal of a Hudson's Bay man."

"Yes, yes, quite. But it has all been turned over to intermediaries for settlement, now, and I am a bit hopeful. I am expecting them momentarily with the papers. But now—" McLoughlin suddenly swept his arms up in a great despairing gesture to heaven. "*Now*, Mr. Monday."

"Sorry to hear about it," Monday mumbled, looking at his hands. He wished he'd picked a less worrisome day to come begging.

"The devil! Mr. Monday, if you'll pardon the expression. The devil!"

"What—ah, what's come up now?"

McLoughlin leaned forward on the desk, his hands lacing and unlacing in front of him. "It is minor, quite minor, I suppose. But just as an example of—in any event. Mr. Monday, I confess to you that I have a terrible fear of rats."

"Rats?" Monday said, beginning to lose his tenuous hold on the conversation. He was not entirely certain whether McLoughlin referred to Thurston or the other kind, and he thought he'd best not ask.

"Rats, Mr. Monday, rats. You perhaps know that in the warehouse at my mill—or, I should say, what used to be my mill—I have a large store of seed wheat. Yes, large stores. Normally it is gone by now, but by hazard I have quite some left. And the rats, Mr. Monday, the *rats* have gotten into it."

"Well, I'm sorry to hear—As a matter of fact—"

"They are attracted to the wheat, and now, Mr. Monday, they threaten *all* my stores. The devil, Mr. Monday, the devil!" McLoughlin rubbed his stomach worriedly and frowned down at his desk. "I am unable to find anyone to take it off my hands, and it is driving me frantic with worry. The *rats*, you have no idea—" Suddenly he stopped, caught by an idea. He leaned forward again intently.

"Mr. Monday, I do not mean to pry, but—have you considered putting your fields in wheat this year?"

"I was figuring to do that," Monday said. "But—"

McLoughlin sat back, disappointed. "But you have your seed already, like everyone else." He raised his hands in a discouraged gesture. "There is *no* one who can take this doubly cursed rat-candy from me. And I am terrified even to set foot in my own warehouse."

"No, I don't have it," Monday said. "But the trouble is, I got no money either."

"Who has money at the *beginning* of a season?" McLoughlin said. "Mr. Monday, are you aware that writing was invented, not to communicate ideas of literary worth, but to keep the accounts of some Phoenician brewers?"

"No," Monday said doubtfully, "can't say I was."

"And that is still its principal use, keeping accounts. If you could consider taking some of this wheat I could make a very attractive price, because of the rats. But it is a matter of urgency; you understand I could not possibly wait until you raised the money."

"If you'd be willin' to carry me another year—" Monday said.

McLoughlin pulled open the drawer of his desk, rummaging around for an account book. "Yes, yes, quite," he muttered nervously. "No question."

When it had all been entered properly, McLoughlin entered the customary "Interest at 8%," which through carelessness he marked as "4%." "Mr. Monday, you have no idea what a relief this is to me. I feel like a free man again." He sat back in his chair, breathing a deep sigh.

"Tell me something, Doctor," Monday said.

"Yes, yes, of course."

"Has Joe Meek been around talking to you?"

"Yes, yes," McLoughlin said hastily. "I see Mr. Joe frequently. Frequently, several times a week. I paid him twenty-five cents yesterday evening, in fact, tax on a cow."

"I thought you'd quit running cattle," Monday said curiously, "Yes, yes, this was for one I loaned some years ago to a gentleman in the valley."

There was a quiet knock on the door of the study and McLoughlin called, "Come in, sir, come in."

A neatly dressed gentleman opened the door and stepped into the room. McLoughlin stood and charged over to him, taking his hand in both his own.

"James, James," he said. "Good to see you. Come in, come in. Monday, you know Mr. Douglas, do you not?" James Douglas was the present factor of the Hudson's Bay Company, having taken over when McLoughlin was forced to resign. There was talk he was due to be knighted, which drove many of the Americans almost mad. Bad enough without a "sir" around.

"Yes," Monday said. "This is Webb—Mr. Webster."

"Nice to see you gentlemen," Douglas said. He gazed speculatively at Webb for a moment, then said, "Webster . . . You were with—"

Webb nodded discouragedly. "Gardner in 'twenty-five, Smith in 'twenty-eight, know a pack o' your boys."

Douglas laughed and turned to McLoughlin. "Well, John, we've settled the mission claim, I think."

"Good, good," McLoughlin said. "These gentlemen were just leaving."

With a great bustle McLoughlin showed them to the door, profuse with thanks and farewells. "And Mr. Webster," he said, shaking his finger at Webb, "I hope no more tricks like that in the spring of 'twenty-six, eh?" He laughed, suddenly frowned and rubbed his stomach rapidly. "Yes, yes, must tend to other affairs."

As the door closed behind them Webb closed his eyes and lifted his face to the ceiling. "Spring o' 'twenty-six," he muttered. "*Wagh!* There's the time I busted a bottle over one of them half-breed Iroquois workin' for Nor'west."

"Hush," Monday said. He was standing near the door, trying to hear the conversation inside. There was a shuffle of papers, and then McLoughlin's voice came strong. It was entirely changed from the frantic anxiety of a moment before, calm and angry.

"James," he said, "this paper obliges me to give Thurston five acres and five hundred dollars, and donate fourteen lots to the Methodist Mission. In addition to which, I must buy back portions of my own land at exorbitant prices. Is that not what it amounts to?"

"Yes, John," came Douglas's quiet voice. "That is substantially correct."

"This is Thurston's doing, at the base."

"No, John," Douglas said. "It is mine."

"You have bound me."

"John, I thought it better to give you one good fever and have done with it," Douglas said quietly. "You are eating yourself to death with worry over these American claims. Let us put an end to it."

After a moment McLoughlin said softly, his voice sounding suddenly tired, "James, the only thing that will put an end to it is my death. But give me my pen."

Monday tiptoed away from the door and down the hall. When they reached the outside, Webb was frowning.

"Y' don't mean t'tell me them niggers know ever' trapper that was ever in the mountains?"

"Damn near," Monday said, depressed.

"*Wagh!* That's *some*, now. Imagine! Rememberin' *me!*" It was an enormously flattering thought for Webb that somebody he'd never seen knew about him. He was obscurely pleased.

"They made it their business t' know what we was all doin'," Monday said. "An' they never forgot nothin', either. If they ain't got it in their heads they got it someplace in their books. HBC allus knew a hell of a lot more about th' American companies than we knew about ourselves."

"Di'n't seem like we never thought much about what *they* was doin'. Less'n we run into 'em in the mountains. Then she was Hannah-Bar-the-Door, for sure!"

Monday loosened the reins from the rail and turned to look at Webb. "Might could be that's why they're still around, an' all the American companies gone under."

"Poor feller," Webb said with unaccustomed sympathy. "Skeered o' rats." But it was a kind of fear he could understand. He'd known a man oncet as was scared t' death o' bumblebees. Good man, too.

"Hya!" Monday grunted, pulling his horse's head around. "There ain't any rats around this country, coon. Not that kind."

"But that nigger said—"

"I *know* what he said, god damn y'r eyes," Monday snapped.

Chapter Nine

That night Monday played an ancient game with the world, and lost again. The great disk of the moon swung up above the river cliffs, threading them with silver, flowing silently across the thickly textured hills of the valley. The river caught the brilliance and carried it in long slow swells toward the sea. At the point of the river's turning there were stately wide whirlpools twisting slowly in the night, carrying the soot-dark shadows of drifting branches and deadfalls.

Monday lay on the bed in the cabin, watching the soft and ghostly light pour in through the little window at the end of the building, making a clean shape of silver blue against the floor's rough planking. With the rapid rising of the moon, the shape shortened and swung across the floor slowly, its angles shifting imperceptibly into new patterns.

He watched the patch of light for a long time before sleep came. He tried to slow down his life, somehow, slow down his eyes, so he could see the actual movement of the light, but he could not do it. Between one second and the next, he could see no change; but in a full minute the sharp edge of light had crept across another crack.

He remembered a watch he had seen once, whose hands, instead of clicking sharply from minute to minute, moved in a smooth slow arc. He had watched that carefully too, and had never caught it moving; the minute hand was suddenly between the lines of the face, and he could not say when it had happened.

He sighed, and shifted his position in the bed uncomfortably. There were so many things a man wanted to see that were just beyond him, a little too fast or slow for the way he lived. He had never been able to see exactly what the fluttering gulls did with their wings, either. And once he had watched a half-drowned wasp walking—for hours, it seemed—trying to figure out the pattern in which its legs moved; what kind of order there was in this complicated thing. But he couldn't keep track of them all at once.

He wondered if it were some defect in his seeing, or if nobody else could see these things either. Perhaps a man was meant to see clearly only those movements that were approximate to the pace of his own life—the moon too slow, the movement of an insect's legs too fast. There were whole worlds he could not understand, because he could not change his own nature to a new rhythm.

People were the same. You were never aware of the changing; but some time later you could look back and say that things had been different before. Webb, Meek, Bill Williams, Trask, himself—all scattered to hell and gone now. A few years ago they had all been sitting around the same fire, lying to one another, cursing, happy. It was almost as though some monstrously slow explosion had burst in the fire itself, blowing them all off so slowly they didn't know what was happening. He tried to picture it all in his mind, where each of them was now, and see if there was some kind of meaning in it, some kind of pattern. But he could not do it. There were too many of the old mountain men, and the space they covered was too large; he could not think like that, could not perceive correctly.

He remembered hanging over the shoulder of that artist fellow that was in the mountains, Miller, his name was, watching him draw, trying to discover the mystery in it. The harder he kept his eyes on the blobs that rolled from the end of the pen, the less he saw; just little black marks distributed at random. He had shaken his head and turned away in puzzlement and then, turning back—there it was: a whole Absaroka encampment, and it took his breath away it was so clear. None of the blots and squiggles meant anything by itself, but when you could see them from a distance, all at once, they made a sort of reality.

It was like that now. He had a terrible conviction that if he could stand back and see everything whole, he would understand it. He would be able to see the picture that was being made of meaningless and isolated events of his life, like strokes of a pen.

Well, there was no time for it now. That was the hell of it, there was never any time. In the mountains if you wanted to take a day and sit around and think about something stupid, that was your business.

Monday grinned drowsily to himself, remembering the time old Trask had sat and watched one of the spoutholes up to Colter's Hell for twenty-four hours running, watch in hand, just to see if it went off regular. It seemed that in the mountains there'd been time for just about anything a man took it in his head to do. Here, it was different. Here, there was always something pressing. Always the sensation of something strong and invisible behind you, never giving you a chance to get things straight before it pushed you relentlessly on again.

The moon had swung until it reached his bed, and the moon-square cocked one corner up. After while it would disappear entirely behind the wall of the house. Monday sighed, discontented, and rolled over, pulling the blanket up around his shoulders in the pleasant coolness of the summer night.

For a moment he was not sure what had wakened him. Then he realized that Webb, who had remained behind in Oregon City in the afternoon, had come in. He was squatted before the fire, his long rifle upright between his knees. Occasionally he poked up the fire, muttering to himself.

"So Markhead says, 'Well boys, we ain't goin' nowhere on foot, an' that's truth.' *Well*, now. Ever'body was real low in the mind . . ."

Monday hoisted himself up on his elbows, blinking with sleepiness.

". . . figurin' as how we'd been come over right smart. Well, up jumps Godin, sayin', 'Hooraw, boys! This child feels like liftin' ha'r . . .' "

Monday swung the blanket back and sat on the edge of the bed, rubbing the back of his neck as Webb continued the recital of a horse raid on the Powder River, that Monday heard a dozen times before.

"What're y' feelin' like, hoss?" Monday said finally.

"*Wagh!* Half froze for meat, this child. Us'ns clean out that deer?"

"Damn near it," Monday said. "We was eatin' all day yesterday."

Webb grunted. "Damn greedy bastards, Meek 'n' that Rainy."

Monday was on his knees at the back, the lid of the cooler raised, poking around inside. "Here's somethin'," he said. "Hell, coon, you wasn't keepin' y'r knife dry neither, I noticed." He unwrapped the chunks of meat and threw them in the pot to boil.

"Man got t' have a little meat," Webb said querulously.

"So," Monday admitted. "Where the hell y' been, hoss?"

"Sneakin' around," Webb said.

Monday stirred the pot with the poker. "What's that mean, 'sneakin' around'?"

"Sneakin' *around*, y'iggerant dunghead! Di'n't I say it? Sneakin' around, politickin', spyin' on people an' such."

The idea of Webb sneakin' around and politickin' struck Monday funny, and he couldn't suppress a laugh. "Damn, Webb. I swear you do get crazy idees."

"*Wagh!* Hell's full o' crazy idees," Webb grumbled. "This child knows all about such, politickin' an' all. He's been politicked by better men than you ever *seen.*"

"Prob'ly," Monday admitted. "But you been in the trade longer'n most, too."

"I been politicked by Ashley, and Billy Sublette, and Fontenelle an' got skun ever' time, too." Webb reminisced. "This child knows all about such. Even saw Pierre Chouteau hisself oncet, in St. Looey. But I turn around and run off slick afore he could smell I had a dollar in my possibles. He'd of got it, sure god. That's politickin'." He nodded sharply to himself with the satisfaction of having fooled even Chouteau, long years ago.

"Well, hoss, y' make any money with y'r politickin'? Y'owe me a dollar, I recollect."

"Hell no!" Webb said disdainfully. "This nigger was just practicin', like."

Monday shrugged. Seemed like a hell of a way to waste a nice evening, but if Webb wanted to practice his politickin' it was his own business.

The old man stared absently into the fire. "Listenin' about what people got to say, 'n' all."

Monday turned to look at him, then back to the pot. "Y' learn anythin' sneakin' around?"

"Not a whole hell of a lot," Webb admitted. "Them city people ain't got one brain between 'em, or just about. Run to a pack, like buffler. Goes against nature."

"Might could be it does," Monday said, waiting.

"Seems like one of 'em gets a idee, they all think like that."

Monday sat back on his haunches, facing the old man. Webb continued to look into the fire. "All right, hoss," Monday said quietly. "Roll it on out."

After a long moment Webb said thoughtfully, "I'm thinkin' it ain't too good a idee for you to go watch that there hangin'."

"So? Account of?"

"Account of y'r woman bein' Shoshone," Webb said.

"They some talk runnin'?"

"Some."

"Brown or white?"

"White."

"Sayin'?"

Webb leaned back against the bench of the table. "Not *say*in' much o' anythin'. More like a smell in the air. *Wagh!* Bad meat, like."

"'Bout me an' Mary," Monday said, poking at the meat with his knife.

"Not exackly," Webb said. "But me, now, if this child was brownskin, he wouldn't get nowheres near them gallows."

"That bad."

"I'm thinkin' it could get that bad," Webb said. "Seems like ever'body's a wee mite nervy."

"Wasn't figurin' to take Mary anyways," Monday said thoughtfully.

"Best like that, t' my thinkin'."

"But I figure t'go myself," Monday said.

Webb shrugged. "Don't see it makes much difference."

"Might could be it does," Monday said. Absently he jabbed a piece of meat with his knife and handed it across to Webb. "This here's about done. No, I helped bring them boys down, and I expect I best see 'er through to the end."

"Stay with the pack all the way." Webb snorted.

"Y'know damn well Tamahas an' them deserve t' swing a bit," Monday said. "This child's all for it. Y'ain't gettin' a rise out o' me like that."

"Ain't trying t' get nothin' out of y'. Y' figure t' prove somethin', go on ahead. It ain't nothing t' me."

"Might could be it's somethin' to me, though. Me an' the territory."

"*Well* now," Webb said, standing up. "We raised sign 'bout a quarter mile from camp, an' sure god it was Absaroka. Good thing, too, it was, else we'd of like t' lost our ha'r besides them horses. . . ."

He turned toward the door and went out. "We trailed after that bunch nigh onto a week. Was Godin as first raised fresh sign, on the Rosebud south o' where she turns . . ."

Monday listened to him mount his bony old horse and ride off into the moonlit night. He rubbed his forehead, staring into the fire. Then he swung the long pothook back away from the flames and went back to bed.

2

Just after dawn on the day of the hanging René Devaux came riding up from Champoeg. The sun had barely cleared the screen of trees to the east of Monday's cabin when Devaux dismounted, throwing the reins over the rail of the porch carelessly.

"Hey, friend of me!" he hollered. "Come out from the cave and look!"

Monday came out, still belting his shirt around him. "What're y' feelin' like, Rainy?"

"Regard! Regard!" Devaux pointed at the rising sun.

The air was supernaturally clear, and the sun rose in an almost tangible aura of power. The light was a physical thing, smashing against the side of the cabin as though to force it into the river. The tops of the trees glowed with sudden incandescence, and seemed to sway away from the relentless pressure of the fight itself. The whole world swelled with a sudden access of energy as the light streamed across it, birthing the new day.

"Mon Dieu, he is very strong today," Devaux said wonderingly.

Monday stretched himself, feeling the sharp heat penetrate his shirt and chest, enjoying the pressure of the light on his face. It was almost like one of the brilliant mountain days, when a man had the sensation he'd never have to eat or sleep again, the conviction that he could steal some of the power of the sun itself and live by that great flood of energy alone.

"By christ!" he said. "Y'know, Rainy, there's some days in this country make you think it's worth the whole winter."

"He going to be ver' hot, this day."

"Be like this forever, f'r all o' me," Monday said contentedly. He looked around at the country, wondering at the terrible distinctness of each leaf, each limb of fir, every furrow of the field. The brilliance of the sun infused every object with a life of its own, an internal glow that illuminated something from the core of creation itself.

"Where he is, that crazy old man?" Devaux asked.

"Got his camp over by them trees," Monday said. "Expect he'll drag ass over directly. C'mon in an' have some coffee."

Devaux hesitated. "No, I stay here. Is not many mornings in the world like this."

"Bastard," Monday muttered. He went back into the cabin, feeling the sudden chill of the shadow, acutely aware of the cutting off of the energy of the great flaming sky. He quickly shoveled a few grounds of coffee and parched barley into the pot, set it to boil and returned to the dooryard.

Devaux was lighting his pipe contentedly, leaning back against the wall.

"By god, Rainy, y're no better'n a lizard lyin' on a rock in the sun."

Devaux gestured absently with his pipe. "Go back in the cave, then, son of a toad. *Crapaud, toi.*"

Monday grinned and stretched his shoulders again, restless with a sudden surplus of energy. At the edge of the field he saw the tiny, infinitely sharp figure of Webb mounting his horse, and the faint tendril of his dying fire. "Here comes the coon now," he said.

"Old Swensen, I saw him," Devaux said. "He is not coming. Says it is a waste of time, to watch Indians hang."

"Even Swensen don't believe in the end o' the world on a morning like this," Monday said.

"You think so?" Rainy said curiously, taking the pipe out of his mouth and looking at Monday. "Strange thing, maybe. Me I wonder who is stronger, Swensen or the sun. I wish I had ask him, now."

"Ask him t'morrow."

"Tomorrow, he will forget what he feel like today." Devaux shrugged, but he was interested to know what Swensen thought on a day like this.

Webb rode up, muttering happily to himself and grinning.

"Some morning, coon," Monday said.

"It is, now," Webb said. "Them Sioux ain't so damn crazy with their Sun Dance. *They* know."

He came to lean against the wall too, chuckling to himself.

"What the hell're you so happy about?" Monday asked.

Webb put his hand level with his heart, sweeping it out to the right, then made the spiral sign for "medicine" from his forehead.

"*Wagh!*" Monday agreed. "*Damn* good medicine, t'my thinkin'."

"Not the sun, y'iggerant nigger," Webb said. "Had me a medicine dream las' night. Woke m'self up laughin'."

"There's some, now," Monday said. "I only woke up laughin' once in my whole life."

"That's cause y're just a boy," Webb said. "Me, I woke up laughin' a dozen times, maybe."

"Sometimes I wake up hollerin'," Monday said. "Hollerin' an' cryin'."

"Hell, that ain't nothin'. It don't take nothin' to wake up hollerin' an' cryin'."

"I'm just sayin', is all," Monday said defensively. "Sometimes I do that."

"Any ol' nigger c'n *scare* hisself 'thout no trouble," Webb said. "But t' wake up laughin', that's somethin' else. T' my thinkin', y' got t' be four different people t' wake y'rself up laughin'."

"Me," Devaux said, "I see only two. One to laugh and one to wake up."

"*Four*, y' dunghead," Webb snapped. "T' make y'rself laugh, y' got t' be surprised, ain't that right? So y' got t' have one different coon t' do the surprisin', an' another t' be surprised."

"Still only two," Monday said, frowning.

"Hold y'r goddam mouth," Webb said. "Then y' got t' have another one t' laugh, an' the last one t' wake up 'cause he hears the laughin'."

"No, friend of me," Devaux said seriously. " The one that laughs is the same one that was surprised, no? And the one that wakes up is the same one who made the surprise."

"Hell, *he* ain't going to wake up," Webb said. "That 'un already *knows* the surprise. Why would he wake up?"

"Because he hear all that laughing going on."

Monday rubbed the back of his neck. "Might could be *three*," he said.

Webb narrowed his eyes viciously. "You got a damn bad habit o' conterdictin' y'r betters, boy. This nigger'll have y'r ass f'r breakfast yet, one o' these times."

"Ain't no reason t' get y'r back up, hoss. But honest t' god, I only see—"

Webb leaned back against the wall. "Don't give a *damn* what y' see. This nigger's figured all that out a long time ago, when I had m' very first laughin'-dream. An' there's four."

Devaux shrugged. "Is very curious, about that."

"Anyways," Webb said contentedly, "this child woke laughin' this morning, an' he ain't goin' t' let any sad-ass niggers like you spoil it f'r him."

"Hell, Webb," Monday said sincerely. "I ain't tryin' t' *spoil* nothin'. I *love* t' wake up laughin', honest."

"Thing about when y' wake up laughin'," Webb said thoughtfully, "y' can't take *nothin'* serious the rest o' the day. It's funny as hell."

"Me, I like to wake up laughing, too," Devaux said, friendly, "but I don't think I ever did."

It was the kind of day everything could happen. The sun, climbing toward noon, remained three times its normal size. The heat, strangely, was not great, but there was a radiance over the land that transformed it, as though a shabby skin had been washed away in the flood of light.

Everything was new, everything was freshened and reborn, as clean
and untouched as had been on the morning of creation.

The body of a man reached out and spread itself on a day like this,
Monday thought. He felt a foot taller, and there was a sensation of
incomparable fullness and tone to all his muscles. The others felt it
too, and they rode in to Oregon City without much talk, simply enjoying
in their bellies the radiance that touched them. Webb did not even
reminisce about the old days; today the present was too real for that.
The old man chuckled occasionally, but Monday knew it was because
of the laughing dream, and not something that had happened a thousand
miles away and a thousand years ago. Even the raw, new gallows behind
the courthouse glistened in the sun. Monday and the others tied their
horses in front and walked around to stare curiously at the
yellowish-white structure; none of them had ever seen a gallows before.

"*Wagh!*" Webb said. "That's *some*, now. Just like one o' y'r goddam
houses, it is."

The carpenters had only finished in the morning, and there was still
the clean odor of freshly cut wood, and tiny piles of sawdust stood like
anthills at several places beneath the platform. On the ground below
one edge there was a long trail of yellowish powder, where the planking
had been trimmed off even.

"Didn't think they looked like *that*," Monday said, walking over to
peer underneath.

The carpenters had built a high, raised platform perhaps fifteen feet
long and eight wide, standing seven feet above the level of the ground.
At the right end a flight of stairs led up to the platform. Two posts, one
at either end, supported the crossbeam, a roughly hewn timber nearly
a foot square.

"I had it in my mind different," Monday said, straightening up. "You
know, just one post, like a upside-down L."

"Hell," Webb snorted. "Y'iggerant dunghead! They got five o' these
niggers t' hang. Take 'em all day, one at a time like that."

"I expect. I ain't criticizing, I'm just sayin' how I had it in my mind,
is all. I never thought much about it."

The center section of the platform was hinged at the back edge.
From under the platform, Monday could see that the front edge was

not supported at all, except by the rope. Tied to a ring at either end of the center trap, the rope passed over the crossbeam and down again at the back of the structure. Passing through two more rings in the frame, it ran low along the back edge. Near the center of the back it passed over a large block of wood.

"Must be five, six dollars worth o' line right there," Monday said. "Not even countin' the nooses."

Devaux shrugged. "Friend of me, is why they want we should pay taxes, to buy rope to hang Indians."

The three had not been the first to arrive. Scattered around were small knots of people chatting, and more were arriving all the time. Most of them glanced only covertly at the gallows. Monday was surprised to see so many women, dressed in bright and festive clothing that shone brilliantly in the sun. The men wore their Sunday clothes, except for a few farmers who had put in the morning in the fields and had come directly to the hanging from work. Monday noticed them glancing apprehensively at the clusters of well-dressed Oregon City people, and realized they were a little ashamed to be here in their work clothes.

"I wonder if I got time t' go see Mary," Monday said.

"Better you wait," Devaux said. "Me, I think they going to start any minute."

"I expect," Monday said. Looking around at the crowd he noticed that there were no Indians at all, not even the tame ones. It appeared that Webb had been right after all, and he was glad he had not figured on bringing Mary; it would have made him tense.

The crowd grew rapidly, and the yard behind the courthouse was soon almost full.

"What the hell's holdin' things up," Webb said, craning his neck toward the building itself. There was a steady low murmur from the assembled people, and it was making him nervous, like the insistent buzzing of a mosquito.

At last there was a flurry of movement in the crowd near the door, and it separated to let a man pass through.

"Here they come," somebody said from the other side of the crowd.

"No, hell, it's just the nooses."

One of the carpenters pushed his way through the crowd. Embarrassed by all the attention, he walked awkwardly up the steps and stood on the platform with the long pieces of rope dangling from under his arm. He peered up at the crossbeam suspiciously.

"Hoist y'rself up with one o' the nooses," someone shouted, and the crowd laughed.

The carpenter turned around and came back down the steps, muttering something to himself. He disappeared into the crowd again, and there was a murmur of disappointment.

The man next to Monday turned and said angrily, "What the hell's the matter with these people? Don't think ahead, don't plan." Frowning, he picked his watch out of his vest and stared at it. "I ain't got all day," he muttered. Monday didn't answer.

After a minute the carpenter came back, still with the nooses under his arm, and a ladder under the other. He climbed the steps again and dropped the heavy Manila line in a pile. He propped the ladder up against the crossbeam and jiggled it into a secure position. He kicked the base to make sure it was solidly seated, then turned to pick up the ropes, and started up.

When he reached the crossbeam he threw the ropes over and straddled the square timber. Somebody started to clap, and there was a little burst of applause. The carpenter looked up and grinned self-consciously, then hastily took one of the nooses and began to fix it to the crossbeam.

"Hey, Bill," someone shouted. "Take a good holt on that rope, 'cause I'm going to borrow the ladder." The crowd laughed obediently, though the man was not on the ladder at all.

The carpenter shinnied along the beam, tying each noose carefully and yanking the dangling ropes to test for security of the knot. The same annoying voice called, "Hey, Bill. You better test 'em better than that. Whyn't y' call for volunteers?"

There was a faint answering laughter, but someone else called out sharply, "Why don't you shut your goddamn mouth?"

"None o' y'r business."

"By god I c'n *make* it my business fast enough." The man started to shove his way through the crowd, but his friends stopped him.

"C'mon, cut it out, you guys."

"We ain't here t' see no rasslin' match."

"Hell," the first voice said, but lower now. "I ain't hurtin' anything."

Monday glanced at Webb, who was staring impassively at the throng of people. "Wee mite nervy," he said. Webb turned and spat on the ground.

Finally the carpenter had finished securing the nooses. He shinnied back along the beam to the ladder and descended. He pulled the ladder away and took it with him down the steps. There was a little more applause, but it was clear that game was over for the time being. A friend slapped the carpenter on the back as he moved through the crowd, and he grinned nervously without turning to see who it was. Most of the people had their attention on the gallows, looking at the asymmetrical hang of the nooses silhouetted against the sky, trying to imagine what they would look like with men suspended from them.

There was another long wait. The novelty of the empty nooses wore off quickly and the crowd began to fidget and shift around. The murmur of conversations began again, and there was much turning of heads toward the courthouse, and much complaining in low voices.

After what seemed an hour, there was another stirring in the crowd by the courthouse door. An Indian woman pushed through silently, paying no attention to the objections, and went to stand directly in front of the platform, staring up at the hanging nooses without expression.

"Tamahas's woman," Monday told Webb, and the old man nodded. Monday watched for the other friends and relatives of the Cayuse chieftains, who had come down with the wagon. None came. Tamahas's woman, dumpy and disheveled, stood alone before the gallows. Gradually the crowd moved a little away from her, until she stood alone in a tiny clear circle.

"What the hell smells so funny?" a voice said, but there was no reaction from the rest.

Suddenly, at the courthouse door, there was a shout. "Here they come!"

This time it was real. The crowd shifted suddenly away, forming an aisle, and the five Cayuse chiefs walked toward the gallows, not looking to either side. Tamahas was first, his face set in contempt, not caring.

He did not glance at his woman as he mounted the steps, his wrists tied behind him with light cord. The man behind Tamahas, unfamiliar to Monday, hesitated at the steps, looking up at the gallows, then at the crowd. He was obviously very frightened, and whimpered. Meek came up from behind and poked him, and slowly the man mounted to the platform. At the top he hesitated again, looking around, and then was pushed by the man behind.

Of the five, Tamahas and old man Kiami were impassive. The other three were in different stages of panic and fear. Meek came behind, herding them silently. The trap swayed and sagged as the five marched across it, bouncing like a plank between ship and shore.

One of the men in the center turned to Meek and began pleading with him. Meek simply shook his head all the way through the argument without saying anything.

"Askin' Meek t' take a knife to 'im instead," Webb said.

"All Indians, they are afraid to hang," Devaux said, his eyes fixed on the figures atop the platform.

"That woman o' Tamahas, she got a lot o' guts," Monday said. "All the rest of 'em scared off."

Meek put his hand on the man's chest and pushed him lightly away. The Indian turned back toward the front and began to cry, whimpering helplessly. Tamahas glanced over at him contemptuously.

Meek began to move behind them down the line, dropping the nooses over their heads and lightly tightening the knots. The blubbering chief in the center could no longer support himself and dropped to his knees. Meek lifted him, with both hands under the Indian's armpits, and hoisted him upright. The trap bounced slowly with the motion, the slack ropes stretching and tightening, stretching and tightening. Meek supported the man with one arm while he dropped the noose over his head. With the feel of the rope around his neck the Indian seemed to be able to stay upright, though he continued to make small noises like a wounded animal and kept his head down, looking at the planks beneath his feet.

Tamahas stared straight out over the crowd and did not flinch when Meek touched him with the rope. Old man Kiami stretched his neck under the noose, like a white man settling his collar more comfortably.

Near the front a man muttered, "Hang the bastards."

Meek stood beside Tamahas with his hands hanging relaxed at his sides. He stared down at the man who had spoken and said quietly, "I'm figurin' to, mister." After he had spoken he continued to stare until the man dropped his gaze to the ground.

Meek started back along the platform. His first steps made the trap sway again, and he stepped off to the solid rear portion. There was no sound from the crowd now, and his boots rang loudly on the raw wood.

He went halfway down the steps and stopped. Taking a piece of paper from his shirt he went back to the platform and cleared his throat.

"This here's the warrant," he said, waving the paper. Then he started to read. "By order of General Joseph Lane, governor of the Territory of Oregon . . ."

The crowd listened to the document in silence. The sun's radiance streamed across the yard, warming and lighting each detail with incredible precision.

". . . five chieftains of the Cayuse tribe of Indians, to wit: Tamahas, known as Little Chief, Kiamisumpkin, Telouikite, Isaiah Chalakis, and Klokamas, having been convicted by a duly constituted jury of their peers . . ."

"What's 'peers' mean?" Webb whispered to Monday.

"Somebody better'n you, I expect," Monday whispered back. "Who else could do it?"

"Them carpenters?" Webb said incredulously.

Monday shrugged, watching.

". . . by the neck until dead. Signed, Joseph Lane, Governor of the Territory of Oregon by appointment of President Polk."

Meek folded up the paper and went down the steps, around to the back of the platform where the rope ran near the edge over the block of wood. Some of the crowd stood on tiptoe to see what he was doing. Meek reached up, but the platform was too high.

Angrily he came back to the steps, drawing his hatchet as he walked. His boots clumped heavily on the steps and he strode across the platform. Without pausing he swung the hatchet as he took the last step, and there was a solid *chunk* as the blade buried itself in the wood. The ends of the rope whipped wildly through the rings as the trap dropped and banged against the supports of the underside and the five Cayuse plummeted.

There was an incredible, inhuman sound as the knots tightened. Three twitched wildly once or twice as their necks broke with the drop. Tamahas and one other began to thrash uncontrollably about, gasping and strangling as the poorly tied knots choked them. Blood poured from Tamahas' nose as he twisted about in great spasms like the convulsions of a dying bird. A rotten smell suddenly filled the air as the sphincter muscles of the three already dead relaxed and allowed their bowels to drain.

His face set, Meek stepped up behind Tamahas, putting both his hands on the Indian's shoulders. He threw all his weight down and there was a tiny dull sound and the neck was broken. Tamahas writhed again in a jerking spasm that sent his legs thrashing briefly.

There was a long, gasping sigh of release from the crowd. Monday looked up at the sky, where the indifferent sun poured joy and energy into the world below.

No, he thought. No, not on a day like this.

He was suddenly aware of an insistent tugging at his side. Unconsciously he jerked his arm away, staring without belief at the brilliant radiance that swept across the yard and the gallows and the crowd and the spasmically jerking bundles that had been men.

The tugging continued persistently and Monday looked down, his eyes unfocused. A small brown girl was pulling on his sleeve, her great dark Indian eyes looking up at him.

"The baby," the girl said. "The baby."

Chapter Ten

It seemed a long time he stood there, staring down at the half-breed Indian girl, trying to puzzle it out. At last he recognized the girl as one of Meek's children. "The baby?" he said.

When he finally realized, something rose in his throat. "Oh god," he said, "Mary."

He wheeled suddenly and began to push through the crowd, frantic with haste. Behind him the little girl came silently, making her way unobtrusively through the unseeing mass of people with their eyes still fixed on the quivering flesh that dangled from the gallows crossbeam.

Monday broke clear of the mass and ran to the front of the courthouse. He cursed his clumsy fingers as he unhitched the animal and swung up, kicking viciously with his heels as he hit the saddle. His horse bolted up into a gallop, almost running down the small dark figure that rounded the corner just as they passed.

The little girl ran a few steps after the galloping horse, then stopped still and watched it go. She looked down at the ground for a moment, and then went to the saddleless horse tied at the raft. She climbed up on the rail and coaxed the horse over, so she could mount. Then she walked him slowly down the center of the deserted street in the gleaming sun.

There was another horse tied in front of Meek's house when Monday reined up brutally, and the animal shied and danced nervously away from his plunging halt. He ran up to the door and rushed into total blindness. After the brilliant clarity of the outside, the dim room was black to him, and he stopped just inside, blinking. "Mary?" he said hesitantly.

"She's in back. Don't worry."

After a second he made out the speaker. It was Dr. Beth, sitting relaxed at the table, with her bag of instruments beside her.

"What's happening? What's happening?" Monday started for the door that separated the back sleeping room from the main room.

"Your wife is having a baby," Dr. Beth said dryly.

The door was locked, and Monday rattled the handle. "Mary? Mary?"

From inside the room Virginia said, "You wait." There was a murmur of low conversation he could not distinguish. Finally Virginia's voice came again. "You wait."

Monday paced back away from the door. "What's wrong? What's happening?"

Beth stood up and went to the cupboard, saying, "There's nothing wrong. Now sit down here and relax your mind." She brought back a tin cup from the cupboard and put it on the table. From her bag she took a quart bottle of watery liquid and poured the cup half full. "Here," she said to Monday. "Relax your nerves."

"I don't need relaxin'," Monday said. He sniffed the cup and it was just whisky after all, so he gulped it down. The burning choked him and made his eyes water, but it felt good in his belly. Beth quietly filled the cup again. "You best sit down," she said. "There's nothin' you can do now."

Monday sat down and ran his hand across the top of his head. From the closed room there was a faint sound that might have been a moan. He started half up again and Beth's strong hand pressed him down.

"It's all *right*," she said. "It's all right. She's in labor."

"Why the hell didn't somebody call me?"

"You're here, aren't you? I sent the little girl soon as I got here."

"Who told *you?*"

"Nobody. I just dropped by to see."

"You mean they were—those two were going to—" Monday stopped. "Oh, god," he muttered. "If anything goes wrong—"

"Nothing's going to go wrong," Beth said. "Here." She pushed the cup over toward him again.

Monday drank, and looked around. The room was more distinct now, as his eyes accustomed themselves to the darkness. He stood up and walked to the front door, then back again. "Why ain't you in there helping?" he demanded.

Beth looked at the table. After a moment she said, "They won't let me in either."

"Why the hell not?" Without waiting for an answer he went to the closed door and put his ear against it. There was only a low rustle of Virginia's voice, and he could not understand what she was saying. He went back to the table. "When did it start?"

"This morning," Beth said.

"Why the hell didn't somebody *call* me?"

"Now sit down. There's nothing you can do except get excited, and that's no help to Mary."

There was the sound of a key in the closed door. Virginia opened it just enough to squeeze through. Blocking it with her body, she turned and locked it again.

"Is she all right? There's nothing wrong?"

"She is fine," Virginia said. "It takes time. Many hours sometimes."

From the closed room there was another moan, louder this time.

"There's something wrong," Monday said. He started for the door, but Virginia stood blocking it.

"No," she said.

"I heard her holler," Monday said. "I want to see Mary."

"She is not hurt," Virginia said. "You understand, she is working. She works very hard now."

"Listen, Virginia, let me see her. Why can't I see her?"

"You give her one more thing to think of," Virginia said. "What she has is enough. She must work now. You understand, when you hunt, you don't want a woman around. This is a woman's work, she does not want a man around."

"God damn it, Virginia! I'm her husband! She *wants* me in there, I know it."

Virginia shook her head. "No. For now, you are just a man. This is between her and the baby now."

Monday stared at her, hurt and not understanding.

Beth stood and took his elbow. "She's right, friend. You're a stranger here. You best sit down and have another drink." She led him back to the table and the cup.

"Listen, that's my baby too," Monday said. He was beginning to feel a little dizzy, and he sat down.

"What you had to do you done nine months ago, and enjoyed it, too. You leave Mary work in peace."

Virginia nodded and turned back to the door, began to unlock it. There was a sudden, surprised grunt of effort from inside, and Monday started up again. Beth pushed the cup toward him and he sat down.

Without turning, Beth said, "It's like I said, isn't it?"

After a moment Virginia said quietly, "Yes." She slipped back into the dark room and locked the door again.

"What's like you said? What'd y' say?" Monday asked.

"Drink up, Monday. There's different ways a baby can come, is all. I said I thought it was coming one particular way."

"How?"

"Head up," Beth said casually.

"What's that mean?"

Beth shrugged. "Means he didn't turn around, is all. Sometimes—" She hesitated. "Sometimes it takes a little longer that way."

Monday reached for the bottle and found to his amazement it was half empty. He decided it must have been partly empty to begin with. "Head up," he muttered. "Don't know what the hell that means, head up."

"It's what we call breech birth." Beth looked down at the table, locking her fingers together tightly and squeezing until she could feel pain, and the knuckles turned white. "Means he'll be a great warrior," she said.

After a while Monday was vaguely surprised to see the stocky figure of Beth silhouetted against the fire, and the light of candles all around. It was a good idea, he thought, the house was so damned dark. The bottle in front of him was still full, and he could not understand having thought it had been half emptied. He reached for it.

The door to the back room opened and Virginia came out again. Her fists were clenched, and her face was wet with perspiration. Her hair, usually pulled tightly back, had fallen down and was hanging disheveled around her shoulders, strands plastered to her cheeks and forehead from the sweat.

She looked silently at Doctor Beth.

"Listen—" Monday started, but his tongue was thick and he couldn't get it all out right away. He had been thinking it out for a long time.

"You come now," Virginia said to Beth.

The stocky white woman stood at the table, resting the palms of her hands flat on the planks. She looked back at Virginia, her face set in an expression of fierce triumph. Finally she nodded.

She turned to the fireplace, where a kettle of hot water still steamed, and began to roll up her sleeves.

"Listen," Monday said again. "I wanna *tell* y' somethin'."

Beth washed her arms and hands carefully, scrubbing with the harsh soap and brush. She held them up in front of her, smiling to herself at how white they were. She turned to look at the Indian woman still standing tensely in the doorway.

"It is good you stayed," Virginia said quietly.

Beth got up and went to Virginia. "Didn't have any notion t' go," she said.

"*Listen!*" Monday said as loud as he could. When both women were watching him he said very carefully, "I ain't no stranger to my wife."

Beth sighed. "No, friend, you're the center of the universe."

She turned toward the bedroom and stopped again, turning back toward Monday. "If you're going to vomit go outside," she said. Then the two women closed the door behind them.

It was a pretty damn stupid thing to say, in Monday's opinion. He snorted. But it was true he could use a little fresh air. The cabin was stuffy, and it made him a little uncomfortable. Carefully he refilled the tin cup, concentrating on it to make himself forget the stuffiness of the cabin.

He hoisted himself up from the table, amazed at what a terrible distance there was to cover before he was standing erect. He leaned on his hands and precisely focused his eyes on the cup. He was quite pleased. He could tell just exactly where it was, by the reflected light from the candles.

Hooraw, he thought. Powerful drunk out, t'night. And such a pretty day, too. He could never remember seeing the sun so big. Experimentally he took one hand off the table, and it upset his balance only a little. He picked up the cup and started for the door. He remembered Mary and began to tiptoe very quietly, so as not to disturb her.

It was not long at all before he had reached the doorframe, and he rested his forehead against it for a minute to think things over. Then he heard the plod of horse's hoofs in the distance. Somebody coming. Good. He'd give them a little drink, if he knew them. If he didn't know them, he wouldn't give them a goddamn drop. That was just how uneasy he was, he wouldn't give them a damn thing.

Carefully he pulled up the door latch. You're a son of a bitch, he thought morosely. Man's got a turrible dry an' you won't even give 'im a little drink.

He walked out the door, and a long shaft of yellow light darted out ahead of him. God damn! he thought. It sure got night quick.

"Hey!" he hollered at the approaching horses. "Who blew out the sun?"

There was no answer, but after a second the horses came into the range of the light from the door.

"*Hooraw*, coons!" Monday hollered. It was Meek and Webb. He grabbed the porch post with one arm and lifted the cup in salute. "*Damn* y'r eyes," he said.

He started off the porch to meet them as they came up, but somehow or other one foot got entangled with the other, and he started to tip forward very, very slowly.

Meek darted forward as Monday pitched headlong off the porch. As the toppling figure lunged toward him Meek grabbed the extended cup with both hands. Monday plowed face down in the dirt, his hand still outstretched. Meek looked into the cup.

"Spill much?" Webb asked.

"'Bout half, I expect," Meek said with disappointment.

"Y're a damn fast nigger anyways," Webb said admiringly. "Give us a drop."

On the ground between them Monday began to vomit, his body undulating limply with the spasms.

"I b'lieve that nigger's sick," Webb said. "Jaybird, you sick?" He nudged Monday with the toe of his moccasin and, getting no response, squatted down beside him. He hollered in his ear, "Jaybird, you sick?" Monday continued to retch violently.

Webb stood up. "I b'lieve he's sick," he said.

"Might could be," Meek said, lowering the cup from his lips.

"Give us a drop of that," Webb said.

"Spilt more'n I thought," Meek said regretfully. "'S all gone."

Webb stared at him, beginning to enrage himself with the thought of it. "Meek—" he started, and automatically his hand went toward the back of his belt.

"Expect there's more where that come from," Meek said placatingly.

They walked up the porch, and as they entered the door there came the wail of a baby in the night.

The two of them stopped, and Webb looked back at the limp body of Monday sprawled helplessly in the rectangle of light from the door.

"*Hell* of a pack o' doin's round here, seems like," Webb said.

The night was clear as thought, and the stars like bright eyes shining.

2

In time the eastern sky turned coppery green and pale, silently diminishing the depth of night. Near the horizon long strings of clouds were outlined in shadow, their edges growing bright with the approaching sun. The predawn silence settled over the Willamette Valley like a mist.

The windows of Meek's house turned light, and sleepers stirred. In the main room three shapeless, blanket-wrapped bundles radiated like spokes from the fireplace, though the fire had long since gone to coals.

Webb lifted his head and looked around. He untangled his arms from the blanket cocoon and straightened his limp hat. He put his head back down on the floor and stared at the ceiling. Next to him Monday's shaggy yellow head shifted, finding an imaginary soft spot on the floor.

The door to the back room opened and Virginia Meek came out, closing the door gently behind her. She went to the fireplace, stepping over the inert form of her husband, and began to poke up the fire. Webb watched her silently as she built a tiny framework of twigs over the red glow in the center. Finally satisfied she was doing it right, he hunched himself up to his elbows, blinking, and extricated himself from the blanket twisted around him. He stretched his shoulders and reached down to get the moccasins he had stacked on the floor as a pillow. He pulled them on and started for the door. As he passed Monday he nudged the back of the blond head with his toe.

Monday jerked, startled, and lifted his head in time to see Webb open the door and step out into the early morning light. He looked around him and said, "Where's Mary?"

"She is still sleeping," Virginia said. "You not wake her up yet."

Monday cleared his throat and struggled up to a sitting position. "That damn Doctor Beth an' her relaxin'," he said, rubbing his forehead.

"You were very relaxed," Virginia said.

"Ain't been so relaxed since I left the mountains," Monday said.

"Sometimes in the mountains," Virginia said, "there were men relaxing as far as the eye could see."

"Wagh! There *were* now."

Meek sat up and blinked. He stared accusingly at Monday. "Who the hell are *you?*" he demanded.

"Damned if I rightly know, coon," Monday admitted.

"Poor doin's when a man has to sleep on the floor in his own house," Meek grumbled. "An' with strangers, t'boot. How's that coffee comin'?"

"It comes as it comes," Virginia said patiently.

"Glad t' hear it," Meek muttered.

There was a rustling of bedclothes from the other room. Monday glanced quickly at the door, then at Virginia, half apprehensively. The Indian woman nodded. He scrambled to his feet and across the room. Behind him Meek grinned widely at his wife.

The back room was somber, shades drawn across the single window. Mary's dark head turned slowly on the pillow as he came in.

He came over to lower himself carefully on the edge of the bed. The baby's tiny head was on the pillow next to Mary, his wrinkled face turned away from her and one small fist clenched tightly by his forehead.

"Well—" Monday said. "Mary?"

The woman brought one hand out from beneath the blanket and Monday took it in his own. For a long time they were still, looking at each other in the half-darkness. Finally Monday shifted his eyes to the baby, the strangely foreign little object that was suddenly a part of his life. It was impossible to understand, somehow. From this day on, his life would be shared by the shriveled, gnomelike little creature so silently sleeping.

"Well, Mary," he said at last. "What—what are you feelin' like?"

"Very tired," Mary said, her voice sounding from far away.

Monday leaned down and kissed her on the forehead.

"He's sort of—funny-lookin', ain't he?" he said, smiling.

"All babies are that way."

"I never, somehow I never thought of him this little, you know. I thought of him around two, three years old or something, I guess."

"Yes," Mary said.

Monday felt a little guilty, because he had no affection for the baby. The only thing he could think of was Mary—just as it had always been. As yet the absurd little face belonged to a stranger, and Monday was very faintly suspicious. He could not picture having someone else around all the time, even a baby, and it made him a little un-comfortable.

"Look how flat," Mary said, nodding her head down at the blanket that covered her.

Monday grinned and bent down to kiss her again. "Just like Sioux country," he said. "Does it—feel funny?"

"Yes." Mary's voice was so low Monday had to lean forward to hear what she said. It disturbed him, and her weakness disturbed him. Her voice was toneless, and there was little life in her eyes.

"Listen, Mary," he said. "This—this is the beginning of something new. Things are goin' to be different from now on."

Mary smiled faintly. "Yes," she said.

"No," Monday said. "It isn't just—just the baby. I mean it *is* the baby, but not—ah, hell."

Mary waited patiently for him to formulate it all in his mind. Monday squeezed her hand and leaned forward. "Mary, it's all goin' to be different. Our life. I been thinkin' about it a lot. Livin' here in the valley, an' all. I never—exactly fit in, just right. You know."

Mary nodded.

"But it's different now. The trouble before was, I didn't have any roots here. I wasn't—*part* of it, somehow."

He straightened up a little and let his eyes go to the baby again. "But now I got roots. My boy's born here. Mary, c'n you see what I mean?"

"Yes, I think," Mary said quietly, listening more to the sound of her man's voice than the words.

"We're part of it now, Mary. We'll fit in, and it's going to be something different. All that other stuff"—he waved his free hand—"it's all gone. We got a baby now, born right here in the colony, an' it gives us—roots, is all I can say. A tie. We belong here now."

He was silent for a long time, looking at the child. "He'll grow with this country, Mary. An' so will we. He'll see it become a state, an' he'll see cities where there's just forest now. Maybe he'll see the twentieth century come, Mary. Wouldn't that be somethin'? T' live in two centuries? The first day of a new century, that's somethin' I'd like t' see. Fifty years ain't old, he'll see it come." He stopped, a little embarrassed. "I'm talkin' too much, I guess."

"No," Mary said. "You talk."

"It's just the beginning, Mary. It's the beginning of a new life for us. This country's going to be rich, and we're here right at the beginning. All it took was the baby to make me feel it, how new it all is. Now we belong, Mary, that's all I can say."

"You want it very much."

Monday looked down at her hand, dark against his own. "Yes. Because—because that's the way it's got to be. And that's the way it will be. Hell, Mary, in a hundred years we'll be—I don't know—ancestors or something. People'll be talkin' about us like we talk about the Revolution. Hell, the Oregon Territory's bigger'n all of England, for all their kings. It's just starting, and we'll help to make it."

"Yes," Mary said softly, and closed her eyes.

"We belong now, is all I want to say really. And everything's going to be different."

The door opened and Virginia came in quietly. "You come now," she said to Monday.

"Just a minute," Monday said, leaning over. "Mary, listen. I'd like to name him, if it's all right with you, I'd like t' name him Webster. Is that all right?"

Mary opened her eyes and looked at him for a long moment. "Webster," she said quietly. "Yes. Yes, is a good name."

"Webster Monday," he said. "Sounds like a governor or something." He laughed self-consciously. "Well, hell. Why not?"

"You come now," Virginia said again. "Let her rest."

Monday kissed his wife again, softly, and stood. She almost seemed to be asleep already. He went quietly to the door, grinning at Virginia as he passed. She went to the bed and straightened the covers, then came out into the main room with the others.

Webb and Meek were sitting out front with their coffee. Monday came up between them and slammed them both on the back. "Hooraw, coons!" he said happily. "Beautiful day!"

Webb choked on his coffee. "Jaybird," he said, turning, "one o' these days—"

"I know, I know. One o' these days y'r going t' have my ass for breakfast. C'mon, cheer up, y' cranky ol' goat. Ain't no good t' be mean on a day like this 'un."

3

The three rode down toward the center of the town and the courthouse, basking in the second supernaturally sunny day in a row. Webb hadn't wanted to come, saying he'd gotten a bellyful of Oregon City at the hanging. "Too bad, coon," Monday said. "I had a surprise for y'."

"What kind o' surprise?" Webb said suspiciously.

Monday shrugged. "If'n y' don't want to know bad enough t' come . . ."

And in the end Webb's insatiable curiosity had gotten the best of him and he had reluctantly agreed to come along, though he wanted it well understood it was just a favor to Monday. Far as the old man was concerned, he didn't give a damn about surprises. Hell was full o' surprises.

The countryside had changed incredibly in Monday's eyes. As they rode, he let his eyes rove over the forests all around, the dirt road, the first frame buildings at the edge of Oregon City. They had all been transformed by a new sense of time, and he could see shadowy shapes all around him. Buildings tall as the firs, stretching up toward the sky. Paved and cobbled streets, with slickly groomed horses pulling buggies. Store fronts of brick and marble instead of raw wood. Transfigured by his new vision of time, the Willamette Valley became the center of civilization, something new on the face of the earth. And something of which Webster Monday was an important part. His son would see it, and his son would be somebody in the scheme of things in thirty years. Growing with civilization, helping to make a society. Hell, there was no end to it.

"Surprises 'r no surprises," Webb muttered. "It's all the same t' me. Y' think *I* give a damn?"

"No, hoss," Monday said cheerfully. "Hell, we might as well just f'get about it."

"Wagh!" Webb grunted discontentedly.

Monday had told Meek about his plan to register the baby as Webster, and he winked at the marshal. He knew it would give the old coon a hell of a kick, to have a baby named after him, and he was looking forward with delight to the filling out of the birth certificate.

They reined up at the courthouse and dismounted. Inside it was amazingly brilliant, the sunlight pouring through the big window on one side of the door and reflecting up from the floor.

"Hooraw!" Meek hollered. "Here's business!"

There was a noise at the top of the stairs and Judge Pratt poked his head out of the door to his chambers. "Marshal, must you shout? There's no one here."

"We got t' register a birth," Monday said.

"So? Whose?"

"Mine," Monday said proudly. "Or anyways, my son's."

"Well, congratulations," Pratt said. "But there's nobody here."

"Ah, Judge," Meek said. "You c'n do it, can't you? We rode all the way in from my place special. Where's y'r clerk anyways?"

"Clearin' stumps," Pratt said. "For a hundred and fifty dollars a year you can't expect him to spend all his time around here. All right," he said discouragedly. "But you should have a doctor, too. Come on up."

The three men tramped up the stairs and into the judge's chambers. There were a couple of chairs and a kitchen table, on which his papers were spread out.

"Doctor McLoughlin's promised to loan me a real desk," Pratt said, "but I haven't gotten around to get it yet. All right, now what do we need?" He started rummaging through a stack of printed forms in the corner of the room, newly run off the press at the *Spectator*.

"We haven't been a territory a year yet, and we already have so much legal paperwork I'm behind schedule," he muttered.

"Well," Monday said in good spirits, "that's because we've got so many laws now."

"My friend," Pratt said without looking up, "there's more truth than humor in what you say. Damn! I can't find any forms that look appropriate. I'll just write it out."

"It'll be legal, though?" Monday said anxiously.

"Oh, certainly. But I can't find—well, never mind."

He took a blank sheet of paper and sat down at the table. He glanced up and saw Webb for the first time. "You don't have—"

"No," Monday said, "he don't have twenty dollars. He's just the guest of honor, so to speak."

"Guest of honor?" Pratt said, puzzled.

"In a kind of way," Monday said slowly. "Y'see, I figured to name the baby—Webster."

He turned, just quickly enough to catch the expression of terrified astonishment on Webb's face. Monday roared, doubling over with laughter.

"There's y'r surprise, coon!"

"*Wagh!*" Webb looked down at the floor, the corners of his mouth twisting. "*Wagh!*"

"Worth comin' for?"

"Well, that's *some*, now." Webb sniffed and scratched his stomach. "Wagh! it is, now."

Judge Pratt, too, was smiling at Webb's discomfiture. He turned back to the paper. "Hell," he said, "I don't know exactly how to go about this. I better just take down the facts and have my clerk fill out a proper form when he comes in. When was the baby born?"

"Last night," Monday said.

"What time?"

Monday turned to Meek. " 'Bout eleven o'clock," Meek said.

"I was sort of asleep," Monday explained to Pratt.

"At a time like that?"

"I had some relaxin' medicine, an' it over-relaxed me."

Pratt suppressed a smile. "How much did the baby weigh?"

"*I* don't know," Monday said. "You need that?"

"Tell you the truth, I don't know *what* I need," Pratt said. "What do you say we call it eight pounds? That's about average."

"Let's call it nine," Monday said. "He's a pretty big boy."

"I imagine he is," Pratt said. "I imagine he is." He wrote down: "9 lbs. 6½ oz." Monday, reading upside down, nodded with approval.

"And your wife is Nez Percé?"

"Shoshone," Monday said. "Virginia's Nez Percé."

"And what's her name?"

"Mary," Monday said. "You know that."

"I meant her last name."

"Monday, naturally."

Pratt hesitated, then looked up. "What was her Shoshone name?" he asked quietly.

"Deer Walking," Monday said, "but listen, Judge—"

Pratt wrote: "Mother: Mary Deer Walking. Shoshone Indian."

"Now wait a minute," Monday said. "Her name's Mary Monday, now."

Pratt carefully wrote: "Father: Johnson Monday. White."

He put the pen down beside the paper and looked up without expression. "Where were you married, Monday?"

"Hell, I haven't got any papers or anythin', if that's what you mean. But she's my *wife*. What the hell difference do papers make?"

Pratt looked down and picked up the pen again. He brushed the feathers across the back of his hand, watching the tips bend back.

"Perhaps none," he said quietly, after a moment. He dipped the pen again, and while Monday watched unbelieving filled in another line.

"Child: Webster, son of Mary Deer Walking. Shoshone Indian. Bastard."

Monday reached across the table and snatched the paper. Crumpling it in his fist he leaned forward and said, "You make that out again, Judge. And you make it out right."

Pratt looked squarely at the hulking mountain man looming over him. Quietly he said, "It was right, Monday. I'm sorry. But it was right."

"Whoa back, Jaybird," Meek said, taking him by the arm and pulling him away from the table.

"He can't do that!" Monday said. "Are your kids bastards? Are they Nez Percé?"

Meek looked at the floor. "Virginia an' me took out papers," he said. "Near seven years ago."

"You can't do this," Monday said, whirling back to the judge. "I'll take out papers, I don't give a damn. Mary's my *wife*, it never even occurred to me."

Pratt looked down at the bare wood top of the old table. "It's too late for that now."

"Listen, Jaybird," Meek said. "Ca'm y'rself down. In the long run it ain't going to make any difference."

"No *difference*—christ, *no difference!*"

Webb moved up on the other side of Monday, saying nothing.

Monday tore his arm loose from Meek and lunged across the table, grabbing the front of Judge Pratt's coat, pulling him half out of the chair. "You put it down," he said viciously. "Webster Monday. You put it down like that. Webster *Monday!*"

Pratt said nothing, and did not raise his hand to free himself. He looked up at Monday without expression, waiting.

Meek slammed his fist on Monday's wrist, breaking his grip. Monday straightened up, looking from one of the men to the other. Pratt straightened his lapels calmly. "I could do that, Monday," he said quietly, looking at his hands folded on the table. "But it would just be changed. Legally speaking the child is son of Mary Deer Walking. I'm sorry."

"You're sorry? You think you're sorry?"

"C'mon Jaybird," Meek said. "We best go now. We c'n come back after while."

Monday closed his eyes, his fists clenched at his sides. Finally he opened them and looked at Pratt.

"Come back? Why come back?" His voice was cold and even now. "Fill it out."

"Monday," Pratt said, "if I had the power to change—"

"Fill it out," Monday said. "You ain't got any power. You nor any o' the rest of us. There's nothin' human got any power, just the law."

"The law is made by men, Monday. And in the long run—"

Monday snorted. "In the long run, in the long run. Son of Mary Deer Walking. That's a death certificate an' you know it. But what the hell. It don't matter who you kill as long as this shitheap of Oregon City got law. All right. Fill it out."

"Please try to understand—"

"FILL IT OUT!" Monday shouted. His body shuddered once and he shook off the hands of the men on either side angrily. The three of them stood and waited while Judge Pratt took up the pen again and began to fill it out.

Chapter Eleven

He stopped at the top of the cliff across from his field and looked long. In the evening glow the river was coppery and molten, like a flow of liquid fire. The sun was almost behind the little cabin that crouched like a tiny, frightened animal in the midst of the cleared fields. Below him, in the eddy of the river's turning, driftwood swung in long circles, sometimes brushing against the bank with a crisp, crackling sound. The sandy beach of the point, where he had given Webb his swimming lesson, was in shadow now, deserted and peaceful.

He had cleared it all, perhaps fifty acres. He had seen it happen, bit by bit, first in his mind, then in reality. With the aching muscles of his back and arms, he had known what it was to fall the trees, to change the face of the land. The great piles of slash burning like beacons in the night, lighting the whole field, the ashes scattered in the fall wind, and soaked into the earth by the rains of winter.

Seven years.

Seven springs, bursting up out of the ground with the incredible beauty that astonished him as a miracle each time it happened. Seven summers of sweetness, lush with green, and the forests lying still under pale skies.

And seven winters; winters of misery and depression, the sky a leaden plate that weighed on his shoulders and mind for long months while the land outside the tiny cabin soaked up the moisture of the air, absorbed the endless drizzle of the dark Oregon sky. And then spring again, and the new miracle.

The rain, he thought. It's the rain that kills me. While the land took nourishment a man died, for half the year or more. The land profited and was indifferent to the parasites that clung to its broad back. And in the end, there was no way he could touch it, not in any sense that mattered. If the fields were left for a year they would sprout of themselves, and the forest would creep in from the edges. In ten years— wilderness again, as though he had never lived and passed this way, never poured his anguish into that dark earth. He was transitory, he and all his kind. The land would remain, and the cleared spaces were no more than momentary irritations of the skin, insignificant, temporary, ephemeral. The land did not care.

Seven years, and what have I got?

A horse, a cabin, and a vague sensation that time had passed. In the mountains he'd had three horses and he bitterly recognized that his dismal plank cabin was a poor substitute for the cheer and light of a skin lodge. The mountain years had been full and rich. Each year had its share of wildness and excitement, and was crowded with events and memories; it was a life. Here, the murky and indistinct recollections of a long winter one year, a year there was no snow at all, the year the chimney burned.

The year the chimney burned, he thought bitterly. An hour and a half of the year that had been worthy of note.

In '44 the Provisional Government had passed a law prohibiting Negroes in the country. It had seemed like a good idea at the time; the Oregon country would be free. But they had forgotten to pass a law prohibiting the slavery of whites. And as he thought back, that was the thread that ran through the last seven years for him. Slavery to the land, to the society, living with a constant sensation of being trapped in a small dark room. He wondered if the mountain life had been as free as he remembered it, or if his mind was tricking him. And, in the end, was freedom important? No one here thought of it, talked about it. How long had it been since he'd even heard the word, except in a political speech? It was not something to be proud of. Here they were contemptuous and embarrassed; freedom was a child's game, something for infants and Indians. Here a man had more important things to think about than freedom.

"Hya!" Monday said softly, nudging his horse into motion again. He passed behind the screen of trees and began to descend along the trail toward Swensen's place.

And now there was the boy, little Webb. No one's fault but his own. It would have been so simple, any time, to have a regular marriage with papers and all. But it had never seemed important, he had never thought.

It was typical. He had never really been willing to accept this new world he was living in. He had never committed himself fully, and now he had to pay for it. Or the child had to pay for it. You couldn't have it both ways; in the end it was all or nothing. To live, you had to play the game according to the rules, whether you liked it or not. And his trouble was that he had never been willing to do it that way; he'd thought he could drift along without taking a stand either way. But it was impossible.

"Well," he said aloud, "I expect ever'body's got to grow up sometime."

His horse flicked his ears at the sound of Monday's voice, then let them drop again, and moved slowly along the trail in the thickening dusk.

Doctor Beth's animal was tied at the front of Monday's cabin when he reached it, and there was light from inside.

"Sorry to just barge in," the woman said as he entered.

"Don't matter," Monday said.

"You don't look too chipper for a brand-new father," Beth said.

Monday shrugged. Automatically he went to the fire and began to poke around for a live coal, but he had been gone too long and would have to rekindle it entirely.

"I wanted to have a word with you," Beth said, watching him.

"Tell you the truth, I'd—Could it wait? I'm feeling a little low in the mind." He took a piece of kindling and began to shave a fuzz-stick with his knife, watching the thin pieces curl back from the blade.

"Won't take long," Beth said. "And it's—more or less important."

Monday shrugged again. The knife slipped, severing one of the shavings completely, and it annoyed him. "Roll it out, then," he said.

Beth leaned back against the table, watching the flickering flame of the candle that stood on the mantel. "You know," she started, "the baby came like I said it would, head up."

"So."

"That kind of birthing is hard on a woman."

"I expect all birthing is," Monday said. He put the fuzz-stick upright in the ashes and began to build a tiny structure of kindling around it.

"That kind is worse," Beth said flatly. "Now it's over and done with, I may as well tell you there's one hell of a lot of women don't live through it."

Monday looked up, startled. "You—"

"That's why I stayed," Beth went on, without waiting. "I figured Mary was going to need more help to get through it than just Virginia."

"Oh, my god," Monday whispered. "I didn't know—"

"Now listen, Monday," Beth said. "It's over now, and it's all right. There's no call to start getting scared this late in the game. It's over, we were lucky, and that's that."

"There's nothing wrong, I mean, Mary's not—"

"Mary's torn up pretty severe," Beth said. "She had a damned hard time, and it's going to be a while before she gets over it. That's what I wanted to talk to you about."

"I'll be good to her," Monday said. "I'm not going to—"

"The thing I want to say is, with a birth like this, all the damage isn't to her body."

"What do y' mean? Somethin' wrong—"

"Just let me finish, Monday, just let me finish, all right?"

Monday nodded, watching the woman's eyes.

"I seen a lot of breech births, and they do something strange to a woman," Beth went on. "I tell you frankly I don't know why. I just don't know. But sometimes, for a long time afterward they—think different. Sometimes for six months, sometimes even a year. They're depressed. They're scared, as near as I can tell. When you go through something like that, it scares you bad. In other words, there's likely going to be times that Mary's worried and upset, and you won't know just why. But there's a reason. There's a reason for everything."

Monday rubbed his forehead, trying to understand. He stood at the fireplace and took a locofoco from the little box on the mantel. After striking it, he applied the bright flame to the fuzz-stick. Suddenly there was a little column of flame in the center of the kindling.

"I'm just saying, be a little careful," Beth said. "She's going to be taking things very serious. She's going to get low in the mind and want to hide in a corner. She's going to feel like nothing's worth doing, you understand? And you have to remember that she's not thinking the same as you're used to. You want to be careful, and not upset her too much."

After a moment the kindling had caught, and Monday began to pile larger wood around. "You know," he said, "the baby's a bastard. A half-breed Shoshone bastard."

"Babies are babies," Beth said indifferently.

"Might could be," Monday said bitterly. "The law don't think so."

"Listen, Monday," Beth said. "Don't blame the law for somethin' you should have thought of nine months ago."

"Sure. It's my fault. I know it. I'm just sayin'."

"Just feelin' sorry for yourself is what you're doin'."

"Might could be," Monday said. "Don't matter what you name it."

"Listen, my friend," Beth said. "You best forget about your own disappointments for a while. Seems to me you best concentrate on making life a little bit pleasant for y'r woman. You ever ask her what kind of life she wants?"

"She's my wife," Monday said. "She wants what I want."

"You ever ask her?"

Monday stood. "Thanks for comin' by, Beth."

"All right," she said, standing at the table. "I'm pokin' my nose where it don't belong. But one thing is my business, Monday. I'm just telling you that Mary is going to be—scared and miserable for a while. You're going to have to remember."

"I'll remember."

"All right. That's all I ask. Be good to her. Don't let her get too upset." She walked to the door and opened it. She stopped in the doorframe and turned back. "And for christ's sake," she said with exasperation, "quit feelin' like the guilt of the world's on your back.

You're just a man, Monday, you're not Jesus Christ. Everybody makes mistakes."

She went out, closing the door softly behind her. Monday methodically fed the fire a little, and swung the coffee pot in on its long hook.

2

He brought Mary and Little Webb home a few days later, borrowing Swensen's wagon for the trip. It was something new when they came into the cabin, as though it had never happened before. In a way, Monday felt that he would think of his life in the valley as beginning this day.

Mary stood in the doorway, holding the tiny figure of the child. Silently she looked all around the room: the fireplace, the bed, the cupboard at the back and the little window beside it. She seemed to Monday more like a bride than a mother, silently considering the house to which her man had led her, where she would live her life from now on.

There was a clumsily arranged spray of flowers on the bed, gathered hastily just before Monday had left for Oregon City. Mary saw them, and smiled gently. She went over to the bed and carefully put the tiny, bundled baby down. Picking up the flowers, she turned to Monday.

"Well," he said, embarrassed. "You're home again, Mary."

"Yes," she said.

Monday took her shoulders gently in his hands and leaned forward to kiss her on the forehead. "You best sit down," he said. "Don't get too tired."

She sat at the edge of the bed, and the movement partially wakened Little Webb. He squalled, and Mary picked him up, holding him against her breast and rocking gently. Over the child's head her eyes continued to rove about the room, taking in each detail, as though she had not lived with them all for seven years. She said nothing, and Monday could not tell what was passing through her mind.

Suddenly, for no apparent reason, he saw her eyes fill with tears, and she bent her head, resting her cheek on Little Webb's downy head.

"Mary," he said softly. "Mary, what's the matter?"

"Is nothing," she said. "Just—just happy to be—home again." She gestured to the room.

Monday sat down beside her and put his arm around her shoulder. It was strange, he thought, how a woman would cry when she was happy.

"Mary," he said, "this is the beginning for us. Right now."

Mary rocked back and forth with tiny, slow movements, soothing the child.

"Do you remember what I said, Mary? About having roots now?"

"Yes," she said. She was humming to the child, a song without melody, like the flight of a bee.

"I've thought a lot about it," he said. "I've thought about the last years, and all the trouble we've had getting—I don't know, getting settled. Being a part of all this. And I know what's wrong, I know what's been wrong."

Mary lifted her head, her eyes seeming almost luminous in the dusky interior. She waited calmly for her husband to continue, but Monday saw the hope that flickered behind her silent gaze. Her tear-filled regard disconcerted him, and he looked down at the tiny round head of Little Webb, now silent again. Absently he reached out with his free hand to touch the fuzzy skull of the baby gently with his fingertips.

"It's been—me, I guess, all the time. I never really put my back into it. I never really tried hard enough."

She looked at him for a moment in silence. Then the tears welled up again, and she looked back down at the child in her arms. "You work very hard," she said softly.

"It ain't that so much, it's—I don't know, I just wasn't willing to do a lot of things you got to do to get along. I figured to just work my land, an' let it go at that. But you can't do it that way. A settlement ain't just land, there's people, too. And I guess I never really got it straight that I had to work at getting along with the people, too. I never really tried.

"But—from now on, Mary, I'm really going to try. From now on we're going to be part of this country, Mary. Not just squatting here on the river, but really part of it. Do you—can you see what it'll mean?"

"Yes," Mary said. "Yes, I can see."

"We'll see more people, get out more. I know it's been awful lonely for you here, without anybody to talk to or anything. But we'll change all that. We can do it, Mary. We've just got to try."

Monday got up and paced over to the bed, becoming excited with his vision of the future. It was going to be all right, he thought. The business at the courthouse, all the rest of it—it was all part of a pattern, and he was only now coming to see it. It had been his own reluctance to make the changes the new life required that had been at the root of his troubles all the time.

"I'm going to give Little Webb something to be proud of," he said. "From now on, we're going to be part of this territory. An' if it means doin' a few things I don't feel like—well, that's too damn bad. I'm going to get along here. Mary, do you see what I mean?"

"Yes," Mary said. "Yes, I see. It will be better for you that way." A tear dropped from her cheek and glistened on the child's head. Tenderly Monday touched it.

"Better for all of us, Mary," he said gently. "It's going to be all right, from now on." But he couldn't tell if she'd heard him or not.

In the next weeks he settled into it, working with a sense of purpose he'd never known before. Enlisting the help of Devaux and Peter Swensen, he got the wheat in in five days, working from first light until it was too dark to see. The two men were, he thought, indifferent workers, but it went all right. Peter had a tendency to drift over to Rainy and engage him in a discussion about the end of the world, but Monday finally put them on opposite sides of the field, and it went faster after that.

Only Webb would have no part of it, and Monday was obscurely disappointed. The old man had simply snorted contemptuously at the idea of "helpin' some poor bastard dirt-clod," and wandered off into the hills to see how things were there.

Monday knew where he was going now, and it was a good sensation; it was what had been missing in his life before. He finished each day aching in every muscle, tired with a different fatigue from what he had known, a strained tightness from the constant repetition of the same movements hour after hour. It was not something he liked, but he figured he could get used to it. He could get used to anything, now; he knew where he was going, he knew what he was working toward.

Mary slept a great deal during these days, almost as much as the baby. Monday had many hours alone, sitting before the fire in the evening, thinking things out. In his mind he noted different jobs to be done, new approaches, plotting out his plan of attack as carefully as though it had been a horse-raid in the mountains.

He put aside his own feelings bit by bit. What was pleasant, what was enjoyable, ceased to be a matter of importance. He began to test his endurance against the work, against the compromises that had to be made, as he had tested his strength against the purely physical problems of the mountains. Deliberately, he forced himself to go to the Oregon City mill and make arrangements for the grinding of the wheat in the fall. He was polite, refused to take offense at the unfunny comments about mountain men farming. After the percentage had been established he stayed at the mill, leaning back against a rail and talking with the other farmers; weather, the prospect for the crop, the hundred small variations of the same comment.

At first he was self-conscious about it, feeling as though he were pretending to speak some foreign language and making a fool of himself with his exaggerated casualness. But he found the other farmers took it all for granted, thought nothing of it. It was the way life was. At first they had regarded him with the suspicion he had grown so used to in seven years, but after the first encounters this too diminished. He found if he shook his head and said, "Looks like a bad year," half a dozen times or so, it was considered conversation.

In a fashion it was absurd, and he knew it. But he told himself it was part of the big game—one of the rules, and he would learn it as he would learn all the rest of them. He had set himself to play the game, and he would play it to the bottom.

He made several trips into Oregon City that could have been avoided, simply to talk, to make himself part of the community that centered in the town by the falls. And the strange thing was that he found the game was not as complicated as he had expected. As long as he didn't say what he thought, but contented himself with the ritual repetitions, he got along very well. There was not, after all, much to talk about in this new world he was entering. Weather and crops. That, and trouble. He quickly learned that you didn't talk about what you enjoyed, but only about things that gave you trouble. It was a funny contrast, he thought, with Webb. The old man was constantly telling himself stories about the times he'd had fun, the times he'd loved. Here it was not like that. The well was dry, you thought the lettuce was going to rust (though it hadn't rained now for nearly six weeks), that bastard Brown hadn't returned the hoe he borrowed a year and a half ago. It was serious. It was all serious, and as long as you didn't forget that, you got along fine. Life was one long series of problems to be solved, and that was what was important. It was grim. But that was how it was, life.

He was a little surprised by the ease of it, for he had expected something that ran much deeper. But all you had to do was float along with the surface, say the expected things, and there was no trouble. You could remain your own man inside. As long as you made a gesture for the sake of appearances, they left you alone.

So he talked the meaningless talk, and listened to the sarcastic gibes at neighbors and friends, and occasionally essayed one or two himself. It didn't matter what they were, as long as they were critical. To himself he shrugged. Another unwritten rule, and as easy to follow as any other. In a sense, all you had to do was detach your mind from reality, and follow the lead of the others.

Mary continued listless and depressed. Monday was glad now that Dr. Beth had warned him what to expect, or he would have been seriously worried. She was very silent, and very weak. She moved about the house as slowly as when she had been big with child. She spent as much of her waking time as possible outside the cabin. Whenever it could be done, she took her work out to the porch. She often stared out at the hills with her work forgotten in her lap, and at those times she seemed very far away. She seldom smiled these days, and he sometimes caught the glint of tears in her eyes as she looked out over the ridges and hills of the valley.

Watching her, he was more than ever certain he had made the right decision in trying to make himself a part of the valley community. He could realize how terrible her life must have been before, married to a man that was always somehow apart from the others, always an outcast.

The thing that was difficult was that it was so hard to talk to her. She lacked interest in everything.

"You know," he'd start, "it's a damn shame Peter doesn't work that mountain o' his. Damn good land up there."

"Yes."

"It's a waste, t' my thinkin'. If he ain't going to work it, he'd ought to give it up t' somebody that would. It ain't right just to leave it sit there, lyin' idle."

"Yes."

"Peter's a hell of a nice ol' hoss, but you know, he's bone-lazy and there's an end to it."

Mary just looked at him.

It was either that or the inevitable uninterested "Yes." Sometimes he thought if she said "Yes" just once more he'd go out of his mind. And then he'd have to remind himself that, in a sense, it wasn't Mary at all, but her—strange condition, and he would have to try to ignore it.

The biggest problem in the future, he knew, would be to work Mary into this new world, too. In small ways he was beginning, trying to interest her in the little things that went on. When he'd been to Oregon City he'd repeat the conversations for her when he got home, telling her the gossip, what people were doing, what they were saying. Her silence made it difficult, and it infuriated him when her gaze absently wandered off over the hills. But he doggedly continued, with the same grim determination he was learning to show in everything.

Sitting before the fire in the evening, he'd plan the next few steps ahead; perhaps, before too long, they'd get somebody to stay with Little Webb and go into town Saturday night for the dances. Once in a while there was a sort of theater performance got up by the local people, and it wouldn't hurt any to be seen at one of those.

That was the main thing; to let it be seen, let it be known that they were taking part, both of them, in the life of the valley. He was no longer running wild and alone, separated from the rest of them by some mysterious and unbridgeable chasm. That he was, finally, one of them, and ready to do what was necessary.

In the last weeks of June he saw it happen, saw that he was in fact beginning to be wholly accepted. When he entered a store in Oregon City, the conversation no longer stopped; he joined in easily and naturally, and thought it was going to be a bad year for wheat and hoped they didn't have another winter like the last. It worked. It was purely mechanical, but it worked, and he had a growing sense of triumph. When he had finally set his mind to it, he had been able to do it. The wasted seven years were behind him now, and how stupid it had all been. All they wanted was for him to play the game, and he could have done it any time, had he understood, had he been willing to commit himself to it. But now he was doing it, and steadily the life he was building began to take shape.

3

Beneath his grim satisfaction with the progress he was making, there ran one strong and bitter current of torment. Hovering always at the back of his mind was Mary, and the most basic lack of all, the problem that showed no sign of improving: the physical distance that continued to exist between them. He thought he could understand it; but it was not a thing he could live with, understanding or not. Through the last months of pregnancy he had not made love to her at all, out of fear for the child. And after Little Webb's birth, Doctor Beth's cautioning had made him hesitant.

But his simple physical longing was becoming intolerable. To feel their bodies twined together again, to feel the sudden soft release when they merged into one, to hear the tiny animal call of pleasure in Mary's throat as he thrust into the warmth of her body, plunging deep and long. The movement of their hips together, the softness of her breasts beneath his hands, the feel of her thighs gripping him, tightening and releasing in the rhythm of joy . . .

Waiting he could understand; but there was an end to it, there had to be an end to it. It had been weeks now since the birth of Little Webb, and still she did not turn to him in the night, caressing his belly softly until he awoke aroused and moved to feel the hardness of his own flesh in her. He had waited for her to make the first sign that she was ready to receive him again, and perhaps that was the mistake. It was not changing as time went on; she remained distant, unresponsive to his touch.

Well, hell, he thought. Nothin' changes less'n you make it change. It was not simply his own desire in question, but in some way the whole problem of Mary's detachment from the world around her, the world in which she would have to take a part, sooner or later.

He was working to build a place for them here, but he knew that before Mary could take her place in this world she would have to take her place again as his woman. It would have to begin there. He would have to bridge the distance that existed between them, before all else.

The more he thought of it, the more he was convinced that if they could share the joy of their bodies again it would bring her back from that strange land she lived in now, just out of sight. Back to him, and back to the real world. She had no contact now, she was not moved. But in the joy of physical love, in the sweeping tide that carried them both, she would find herself again. The barrier would be broken, one time for all.

In the end he saw that the choice could not be hers; she was waiting too, without volition. Waiting for him. Her indifference would have to be broken, for both of them. Now she was only a half-wife, sharing his house, but not his body. It was not right for her, and it could not go on. And what she was incapable of doing for herself, he would have to do. He knew that after the physical act of love, she could not remain indifferent, could not remain—apart. They would be together again, and it would be the beginning.

He was elated when he had worked it out in his mind and seen clearly what was involved. His "kindness" had been an absurdity. No woman wanted to remain without the fullness of her man within her; it was insane, un-normal. What contact could be expected when there was not even the most basic contact of all, the meeting of flesh with flesh? None. It was no wonder her lethargy continued, no wonder the wall remained between them. And if she was at first reluctant—it was the strangeness. And she was, after all, his wife. In the end he knew she would realize the importance.

He watched her as she bent over Little Webb's cradle, crooning softly to the baby, settling the light blanket around his tiny body. The simple curve of her back was a delight to his eyes, and he realized with a sense of anguish how much he had missed the touch of her body.

She finally stood straight, silent again, looking down at the cradle. She came back to the table where Monday sat, and as she turned he took his eyes away from her, strangely embarrassed, and looked at the fire.

"You need nothing?" she said softly.

"No," Monday said, shaking his head slowly. "Nothing."

"I am very tired," Mary said. "I go to bed."

Monday nodded.

He listened to the rustle of calico as she took off her clothes, the slow, measured whispering of the fabric against her skin. Watching the fire he could see it clearly in his mind, and had no need to turn. The slim triangle of her back, the full breasts and softly curving belly, the gentle swell of her thighs . . . He suddenly realized his fist was clenched tightly on the table in front of him, and deliberately relaxed. He was obscurely annoyed with himself for being so tense; there was nothing so damn strange about a man wanting to make love to his wife.

Deliberately he calmed himself and waited a few minutes after he heard the slight creak of the bed and the soft sounds of the covers moving. The fire was dying, and normally he would have let it go, but tonight he wanted light, he wanted to be able to see his woman. He went to the woodbox and got other small log, putting it carefully in the center of the coals that still glowed bright orange and red. He watched until the tongues of yellow flame began to lick up the sides of the wood, then turned and went to the bed.

Mary was lying on her side, her face toward the wall, as she had slept since the birth of little Webb. As Monday took off his shirt he let his eyes caress the gentle curve of her hip beneath the blanket, a soft hill raised from the plain. Always now, she slept with her face turned from him; it was part of it. Before the baby she had always been turned toward him, watching him undress, lifting the covers to welcome him to the sight and comfort of her body. He had missed the welcome, but tonight he was almost grateful that she did not watch him.

His throat was tight with anticipation, but he consciously kept himself in control. As he sat on the edge of the bed to remove the heavy boots, he felt her stir slightly, still awake. He lifted the covers and slid under, moving far over so the length of his side rested gently against her back.

He lay still for a long moment, letting the peace of sensation seep into him, savoring the light, tantalizing touch of her skin. He must not hurry. He must be gentle, as gentle as though he had never known this woman before.

The wood had fully caught now, and long shadows danced against the walls and ceiling. Watching the shadows, he let his hand rest on her full thigh, almost absently.

After a moment he turned to her, dropping his arm over her naked body. He felt the softness of her flesh stiffen as he moved, and then relax again. He waited.

His hand rested just below her breasts, and slowly he began to caress the taut muscles of her stomach, soothing her gently, letting her feel the love in his fingers. He pressed harder against her, feeling the urgency of his own rigid organ pressing between her thighs. He kissed the back of her neck softly, and stroked the length of her body from the full rich breasts to the crisp triangle of hair between her thighs that seemed electric to his touch.

She moved slightly, and he stopped again, waiting for her to turn to him. But she remained facing the wall, and her tension did not ease. He ran the tips of his fingers along the inside of her thigh, gently, questingly, feeling the softness of flesh warmed against flesh, the tiny mound that lay beneath the masking mystery of the dark matted hair that curled against his palm.

He probed gently, hoping to feel the warm curving thighs open to welcome him, to feel the pressure as she thrust against his palm with desire. After a moment he took his hand away and gently clasped her shoulder.

"Mary," he breathed in her ear, gently pressing her shoulder toward him. She did not answer.

He closed his eyes for a moment, then tightened his grip firmly on her shoulder and pulled her toward him. Unresisting, she turned on her back, but her eyes remained closed.

With a sudden motion he swept off the blanket and threw it to the floor. He raised himself on one elbow and leaned forward to kiss the deep warm valley between her breasts. He stroked the inside of her thighs gently, and at last felt the release of her tension, and her legs parted slightly as she relaxed.

He slid one leg over her body; deliberately he let his weight swing over to rest between her thighs, moving gently. He searched with stiff anxiety in the tangled hair, and suddenly felt the moist warmth of her opening to receive him. He penetrated her body slowly, letting himself enter gently, long, until at last the flesh of their groins touched, and he leaned forward to rest the weight of his chest on her soft breasts.

"Mary," he whispered.

He began to move his hips slowly, rhythmically, and with a sense of terrible relief heard her gasp, with the old and loved sound of wakened passion.

He raised his head, wanting to see again the love in her eyes. The flames were high, and the firelight cascaded across her cheek. His own breath caught sharply in his throat.

Her face was twisted and disfigured in a mask of loathing and revulsion that struck him like a physical blow. He recoiled suddenly, his eyes wide with shock, and in the suddenness of the motion twisted back to the side of the bed.

Instantly Mary turned back to the wall. Monday lay still for a moment, staring terrified at the ceiling, where the same shadows spun and danced.

He felt the sudden shaking at his side as Mary's body began to jerk in the rhythm of silent sobbing.

He turned to her again, instinctively putting his hand on her shoulder. As he touched her she stiffened again, and he jerked his hand away as from a fire.

"Mary," he said desperately, "Mary, I didn't know—"

When she could control herself enough to speak, he could barely make out the words. "Don't hate me," she said, her voice strangled with anguish. "Don't hate me."

"Mary, my god—" He closed his eyes. What have I done? he thought desperately. What have I done?

"Mary," he said aloud. "It's all right, Mary. It's all right."

But he knew it was not all right, and even as he tried to think of some way to soothe her, even as he murmured things that had no meaning, he sensed the black shapes of guilt dancing along the wall, and the fire twisted his shadow into something he could not recognize.

Chapter Twelve

Nothing was ever said about it. Monday could not find words to ask the questions that were in his mind, and Mary could offer nothing. Their daily life went on as though it had never happened; the incident existed in a vacuum, with no relation to what had come before, and no effect on what came after.

Monday did not know why it had happened, and could not ask; the shock and pain of that remembered mask of loathing were too much for him to bear. He did not know who was at fault, if there was a fault, and could not ask. In the end, he supposed, it was his own stupidity—and yet, the only thing Mary had said was, "Don't hate me." And what did that mean? That she took the responsibility, that the failure was hers? He didn't know, because there was no way to ask.

Finally, the only thing he could see to do was to ignore it. As far as possible, pretend it had never happened. There was no use hashing it over and over in his mind; torment with no end, anguish without result. Deliberately, in the days that followed, he put it away from his mind and turned to things more tangible, things he was capable of dealing with.

If this—distance that existed between them was not to be bridged so easily as he thought, there remained the other problem, of bringing Mary into the world he was making for them. There at least, there was something he could do. There, he was not helpless and confused.

As he thought about it, it became more and more clear that the first steps would have to be made inconspicuously. The first breach in the great wall would have to be made without drawing too much attention, without causing a lot of talk and raised eyebrows. Something perfectly natural.

And a few days later it occurred to him; it was obvious. There was one occasion everybody would be out for, and Mary's presence would not be at all remarkable; it would even be expected. The one truly exceptional day of the year, Independence Day, the Glorious Fourth.

The morning of the Fourth dawned brilliant and clear, and Monday was at once nervous and excited. He paced restlessly on the porch, waiting for Mary and Little Webb. For the third time he stuck his head in the door and said, "Mary, you just about ready?"

"Almost," she said. "You wait."

"I been waiting an hour," Monday complained.

"Not ten minutes," Mary said.

Restlessly Monday went out to the borrowed wagon and ran his hand along the top of the wheel. The already harnessed horse looked at him curiously, and Monday patted him absently on the muzzle.

The sun was just over the horizon. The service in Oregon City wasn't scheduled to start until ten o'clock, but Monday was already afraid of being late. He wanted today to go just right, and it would be a bad sign to be late right at the beginning.

Finally Mary came out, carrying Little Webb. She was dressed in her best calico, red and white. Monday had seen it a dozen times before, but somehow he stood speechless when she came out of the cabin into the sun, and was standing on the porch.

"My god!" he said, staring at her.

"There is something wrong?" Mary asked hesitantly.

"Wrong! No, my god, you're beautiful! It's perfect."

She had carefully brushed her long black hair until it shone in the sun with the gleam of charred wood. The smooth, tan skin of her face was like satin, and Monday thought he had never seen a woman so beautiful before.

"It is all right?" she said anxiously.

The old longing leaped up in him again. He swallowed heavily and went over to touch her on the shoulder. "It's—fine," he said softly. "It's wonderful."

From her arms the baby looked up at him silently, great dark eyes without expression. Monday gave him a finger, and Little Webb grasped it tightly.

"Come on, Webb," Monday said, smiling. "Your first Independence Day. Few more years you'll realize what it means, Independence Day. Somethin' pretty important for the Big People."

He helped Mary up on the high wagon step and went around to the other side. He climbed up, shook the reins and the horse started off. The wagon was an extravagance, and he knew it. It was going to cost him a dollar extra at the Oregon City ferry, but what the hell. He'd had to borrow the money from Swensen anyway, so it didn't make much difference if it was two dollars or four. And today he wanted to be respectable. He had a feeling it was going to go well. He wanted it to be perfect.

The sun already warm. They lost it when they passed beyond the cleared space of his field and into the fir-canopied trail that led north over Peter's Mountain, and the early-morning air was cool. Mary shivered a little and hugged Little Webb closer to her breast.

"Mary," Monday said quietly, "you scared?"

She shook her head, looking down at the floorboards.

"No reason to be," Monday said. "It's going to be all right. On the Fourth nobody's going to be—I mean, all the little things don't matter. The Fourth's too big for people to be mean."

"Yes, I hope."

Monday grinned. "By god, I'll bet you don't even know what Independence Day is for, do you?"

Mary shook her head, still looking down. "In the mountains, it was for liquor, mostly."

The big man laughed. "Wagh! It was now! We always did 'er up brown, an' that's truth. But what it means is, it's a celebration of when the United States got her freedom from England. It was about seventy-five years ago. They had a war. When I was just a boy there used to be some Revolutionary soldiers around, an' then there was really doin's. It ain't so patriotic as it used t' be, with all the parades and speech-makin' and what all."

They reached the turning point where the trail down to Monday's point joined the main road, and swung off to the right. Absently, Monday talked on about the Revolution and why it was important, trying to cheer Mary a little, trying to interest her in the celebration as something more than an ordeal. Much of it, he knew, was meaningless to her. She had heard the names, Washington, Jefferson, Adams, but she didn't connect them with anything. And he was completely beyond his own depth when he tried to explain why the colonies had been established in the first place.

"The point is," he finished helplessly, "it's sort of a celebration of freedom. The big day for the United States. That's why there's always big doin's. You understand?"

Mary nodded silently. After a moment she said, "History—it is very long here. Much longer than in the mountains."

Monday laughed. "Longer than either of us got any idea. And listen, Mary, this afternoon we'll go aboard a real ship, would you like that? The government sent a ship, just in honor of the Oregon Territory. It ain't much, just a sloop-of-war, the Portsmouth, I think. But she's lyin' in the river, an' there'll be a reception this afternoon, prob'ly. Would you like that?"

Mary stroked Little Webb's head, and the baby wriggled restlessly in her arms.

"Anyway," Monday said, "there's a surprise for you."

Two surprises, in fact, in order that she would not feel so much alone. Monday waved as they neared the little frame church, and Joe Meek waved back. With him was Virginia, and the three children stood silently to one side. As Monday helped Mary down, they all came forward solemnly to shake hands and peer curiously at the baby she held. Mary crouched down and pulled the blanket away from the tiny face for the wide-eyed appreciation of the Meek children.

"How y' feelin', hoss?" Monday said.

"Right lively," Meek admitted.

Monday drew him off a little to the side. "Say, Meek, listen. Did y' get ahold o' Webb?"

"Wagh! I did. He's comin'."

"Good," Monday said with satisfaction. "More familiar faces around, better it'll be."

"The coon says he ain't missed a Fourth o' July in sixty years or better, an' he ain't fixin' t'start now."

Monday laughed. "He's goin' to find 'er a bit dry after the mountains."

"Well, now, far as that goes," Meek said, "after the hollerin's done here, I figured I might go about a bit o' marshalin'."

"Hell, Meek, on the Fourth?"

"Happens there's a still over to Linn that the marshal must've overlooked. Can't have them kind o' doin's."

"Wagh! Might could be you'd need a bit o' help t' break 'er up?"

"Just might could be," Meek admitted. "Y'know, them shine merchants get a bit riled when the marshal shows up with his ax."

Monday clapped him on the shoulder. "Well, Marshal, I see my duty plain enough. I'll just give you a hand."

Mary and Virginia had been talking, their voices low and inaudible. When the men came back, they fell silent and looked up.

"Soon's Webb gets here we'll go on in," Monday said.

Other settlers were arriving all the time, some of them men Monday had talked to in the mill or in the Oregon City stores. He waved as they pulled up, stopping the wagons around the perimeter of the little square in front of the church. They waved back, cheerfully enough, and it gave Monday a good feeling.

"The old man," Mary said. "He is coming too?"

"He's comin'."

She looked up into his face, and after a moment said quietly, "Thank you for my surprise."

Monday grinned at her.

Webb came in about ten minutes later, slouching in the saddle and peering around suspiciously. Beside him, to Monday's surprise, rode René Devaux, looking chipper and happy.

"Hey, Rainy, what the hell're you doin' here? You ain't even American."

"Is true," Devaux admitted. "But me, I am a great celebrator anyway."

Webb looked down at Little Webb and wrinkled his forehead. Very carefully he said, "What're y' feelin' like, hoss?" Little Webb didn't answer, and Webb straightened up. "Ain't very bright, is he?"

"Let's go on in," Monday said.

The little group moved over to the church and began filing up the steps. Thurston stood just at the door, shaking hands with everybody who passed.

"Well, Monday," he said. "Seems to me this is the first time we've had the honor of your presence here."

Monday extended his hand. "Well, you know, I'm not too much on church-goin'."

"In time, in time," Thurston said. "Marshal, how are you?"

"Rollin' along," Meek said.

Thurston pointedly ignored all the others, the women, Webb and Devaux.

Inside, the church was dark. After the brilliance of the summer-morning sun, it seemed cavern-like. Webb sidled over to Monday and said, "What's that nigger doin' shakin' hands out there? He ain't the preacher, is he?"

Monday frowned. "No, but—hell, I don't know, coon. That 'un shakes hands ever' chance he gets."

Meek said, "I hear tell when Thurston left Iowa he swore he'd either be in hell or Congress in two years."

"That's four years ago," Monday said. "Don't look like he's going to make 'er."

"No, but he's still got his eyes on Congress."

"Hell's closer," Webb muttered.

"Let's move up an' sit down," Monday said. People were coming in the door, and the little group of ex-mountain men was forming a bottleneck.

"This child's goin' t' stay back here," Webb said. "These here places make me nervous."

"Don't you go duckin' out, now," Monday said.

The two families moved down the aisle and took a pew about halfway toward the pulpit on the right side of the aisle. The seven of them, not counting little Webb, took up nearly the whole thing. Mary went in first with the baby, followed by Monday and the Meek children and Virginia. Joe sat on the outside, stretching his legs comfortably in the aisle. There was a steady drone of conversation and laughter, and Monday wondered if it was this way for regular religious services.

Finally Thurston closed the door at the rear, cutting off even the little light that came in. Now the two windows behind the pulpit were the only source, and dust-defined sunbeams poured through, unfathomably bright against the comparative obscurity of the rest of the room.

The pulpit itself was on a low platform that ran all the way across the end of the church. Behind it was arranged a row of chairs, the places of honor. The little building was used for all public meetings, and it was arranged now for its non-religious functions, except for the pulpit itself.

Thurston and a few others came along the side aisle from the back, mounted the low step to the platform and took the chairs. They were all members of the Mission Party, Monday noticed. He wondered what kind of politicking had insured that none of the more liberal American Party got places on the platform. He shrugged to himself. If there was one thing that didn't interest him it was the political quarrel that split the Oregon Territory in two.

Somebody started to applaud as Thurston reached the platform, but he frowned, and the applauder stopped suddenly. There was a nervous scraping of the chairs as the dignitaries took their seats. Then silence. They were all dressed in black, very dignified. They sat with their hands folded in their laps with an attempt at calm and succeeded only in looking very ill at ease.

There was a long wait. Thurston peered off to the right frowning very slightly. Someone in the audience cleared his throat noisily.

Meek tried to engage one of the Methodist preachers from down in the valley in a staring contest, but the other looked down, embarrassed, at his folded hands.

At last the Reverend Andrews entered from the side and walked across the platform, his face set, looking neither at the seated dignitaries nor at the crowd in the tiny church. He strode to the pulpit with a few sheets of paper in his hand. His long, dour face showed no expression. He was clean-shaven, and the heavy bones of his face were like planes hacked out of a stone.

Meek leaned over to Monday and whispered, "Wagh! Bringin' up the heavy artillery."

Monday nodded. Andrews was a hard man, one of Thurston's, more political than religious. Though with the mission settlement it was often difficult to tell where one left off and the other began. Monday had a moment of uneasiness. Andrews, with his rigid Scot Puritanism, was one of the American Party's most implacable enemies, and the dedicated adversary of anything that smacked of frivolity.

Andrews leaned forward, bracing both hands against the edge of the pulpit, his head lowered, looking at his notes. Gradually the murmur of conversation quieted, until there was only a low buzz.

Suddenly his head came up, and his savage black eyes scanned the room. Instantly the last remaining sound was arrested. He held the crowd immobile for a long moment, as if debating whether to speak to them or not. Then he relaxed, pushing himself away from the pulpit, and began to speak in a slow, strong voice.

2

"Friends," he said quietly. "Fellow Oregonians." He paused, and there was no sound. Satisfied with his control, he continued, beginning in an almost conversational tone.

"Seventy-four years ago today, and three thousand miles from this place, the Continental Congress created a sovereign nation under God, The United States of America."

He paused, looking down at the floor. When he looked up again there was a trace of a smile at the corners of his mouth.

"That sounds simple enough, does it not? In less than five seconds I have said it: 'created a sovereign nation under God.' Is that what we are gathered to celebrate this Independence Day?"

He paused for a moment. "No," he went on. "It is not. The celebration of the Fourth of July is a symbol, as the Cross of His Crucifixion is the symbol of Our Lord Jesus Christ. The Declaration of Independence itself is merely a scrap of paper, gentlemen, a scrap of paper. And further, I spoke in irony when I said the Continental Congress created this nation. They did not. This nation—this continental nation—is built, not on a scrap of paper, but on a foundation of blood and agony. The Founding Fathers, to whom we pay our respects, signed a brave document, yes. But it remained for the common man to give flesh and life to that document; to make a living reality of what that declaration described.

"It was our fathers and our grandfathers who wrenched this continent from the tyrannical grasp of King George, and they did so, many of them, at the highest price of all. Let us, indeed, give credit to the men of vision and genius who conceived this free nation. But let us not ignore those men of strength—ordinary men like yourselves—who fought the war that made it real! The soldiers of the Revolution!"

There was applause, as was inevitable at the mention of the Revolution. When it had subsided Andrews leaned forward on the pulpit and stared out across the rows of pews.

"Yes, applaud," he said. "Our ancestors suffered and died that you might be here to applaud. Here, in the Territory of Oregon, by the great Pacific Ocean. The men of Bunker Hill and Lexington and Concord had never heard the word Oregon, and yet they fought for it and died for it. Many of them did not understand why they had to die in the cold and mud of Valley Forge; but they fought and died because they had faith in the vision of their leaders.

"Is it their sacrifice that we celebrate today? Their faith in the continental destiny of that borning nation seventy-four years ago? Or is there yet more, on this day of days?"

Monday glanced at Meek, and the marshal shrugged. He couldn't see what Andrews was getting at either.

"We would like to believe that the soldiers of the Revolution were all men of high ideals, fighting for the principles of the Declaration of Independence. But we know it was not so. Vision—true vision—is given to some few men by the grace of God. And to the rest is given—faith.

Faith to follow the vision of their leaders, and, if necessary, to die for that vision. And this, gentlemen, is the true greatness of the Revolution.

"Again and again the Book refers to Our Lord in the image of the Shepherd; He who guides, He who keeps his flock safe from harm, and sees to their well-being. 'The Lord is my shepherd, I shall not want.' And the Lord has led us to the green pastures of Oregon, and He has led this nation to grow and fulfill its destiny from ocean to ocean.

"I pose a question, and it is not merely rhetorical. Through following the shepherd, the flock remains safe. And what happens—I ask you to contemplate seriously—what happens if, in their confidence, the flock ceases to hear the shepherd's call? Begins to wander over the green pastures, without leadership? They are decimated by the ravaging hordes of wolves that skulk just over each ridge.

"For make no mistake—the wolves are there. At this moment even they are licking their chops, wanting no more than the opportunity to descend in ravenous hunger and devour us! At this moment even there are agents of foreign tyrannies living amongst us, biding their time until they can strike the death blow to this colony!

"And worse, gentlemen! Claiming rights to this land. Land that was bought by the blood and sacrifice of our ancestors. Our forefathers died that we might possess this continent and make it fruitful. And I say continent because it is not simply a matter of one more nation in the world, but a continent-nation, the greatest single achievement of mankind, the greatest nation that has ever been seen on the face of the earth!"

There was a great wave of applause, and some shouting. Meek leaned over again to Monday. "McLoughlin just lost another five acres," he whispered. Monday grimaced.

"Very well," Andrews continued, when the uproar had quieted. "But, when it comes to translating your noble sentiments into action—that is perhaps a different question. For I will tell you plainly, you have ceased to hear the voices of your shepherds. You tolerate what is intolerable, you clasp the viper to your bosom. And you gather here today to celebrate a historical occasion. But hear me! I tell you that Independence Day is not a commemoration—it is a reminder! For the

battle is not yet won, the Revolution is not yet over. The sacred trust
our ancestors bequeathed to us has not been kept.

"We are all soldiers in this great Revolutionary Army, and our task
will not be completed while there remains one single Jesuitical king's
man in the whole of the Oregon Territory!"

"Run the bastards out!" someone shouted, and there was a roar of
agreement. Monday glanced toward the back, where Webb and Devaux
stood near the door. Catching his eye, Devaux shrugged and pursed
his lips. He brought his right hand casually up to his mouth and made
the mountain sign for "talking at great length."

Andrews paused, leaning forward on the pulpit again when the
cheering and acclamation subsided.

"This danger, then, is clear. But there are others. Dangers surround
the flock, and because they have ceased to hear the voices of the
shepherds, they risk destruction. This colony exists as an island of
Good, surrounded by a turbulent ocean of Evil and Decay. The savages
of the hills threaten us with their primitive brutality, yes. But there is
more. The moral decay of these barbaric children of Satan threatens
us even more than their bloody tomahawks.

"It was President Madison himself who pointed out the evil tendency
for a tiller of the soil to revert to herdsman, for herdsman to revert to
hunter. The downward chute to Hell is easy, there is no question of
that. Mankind, unclean at birth, must struggle perpetually against the
forces of Evil that would drag him back to the primitive, to a life of
irresponsibility, wandering over the face of the earth, godless and
soulless.

"This is why the grinning wolves of the mountains must be rooted
out and destroyed. They are the living representatives of Satan, with
their nomadic existence, their worship of Satanic gods. It is not the
physical harm they do, but the terrifying moral danger they represent.

"It has been said the eternal vigilance is the price of liberty. And so
it is—but, do you conceive, can you understand what eternal vigilance
means? It does not mean posting guards on a fortification. Eternal
vigilance means not merely physical protection, but watchfulness,
watchfulness. The shepherd must ruthlessly eliminate the dangers to
his flock, and so must the shepherds of civilization. Eternal watchfulness

for sin, for weakness, for those elements of decay and disintegration that threaten the very security of the civilization for which our forefathers died.

"Let me tell you exactly how the necessary eternal vigilance operates; I need go back no farther than six years, to the year eighteen forty-four, here in the Oregon Country. In that year, you will remember, the Provisional Government passed resolutions interdicting both liquor and Negroes from the country.

"The interdiction of liquor is, of course, obvious. The terrible degradation wreaked by spiritous liquors is, unhappily, well known. But observe for a moment the second interdiction, against men of color. In keeping with the spirit of the colony, this law was passed to prevent the insidious entry of that devil's institution, slavery. But, did the lawgivers content themselves with prohibiting slavery? No! They struck far deeper, at the very core of the problem, making it a criminal offense for any man of color, free or slave, to be found in Oregon! One so discovered was to be sold to the lowest bidder and conveyed back to the slave states, after the price of passage had been repaid by work here.

"I cannot communicate my admiration for the men who drafted this resolution, for they were men of foresight. Rather than attacking a mere symptom—slavery—they clear-sightedly struck at the very foundation of the disease, and that foundation is the simple existence of the black man.

"Where the black exists, the possibility of slavery exists, and even that possibility was avoided by those men, devoted to making this land free.

"It is not, in short, the Negro himself, but the way of life he represents, that is a threat. Equally, it is not the savage with his tomahawk that jeopardizes the well-being of this civilization—but the way of life he represents.

"Thus, we can see that the danger is not always apparent, except to those who see clearly; that is to say, the shepherds. And for the shepherds of this colony to succeed in what may justly be described as a God-given task, they must have the obedience and the cooperation of the flock. As those brave men of the Revolution had faith in their leaders, so must the people of this territory have faith in theirs, endless faith, faith to do what must be done, faith to sustain them through the years of eternal vigilance that are our lot.

"But this community has not, I am sorry to observe, always manifested that singleness of purpose that has characterized the growth of this nation. Their vigilance has been halfhearted, ineffective.

"I speak now of a taint, a stain, a corrosion that rots from within, which has been permitted to exist. I speak of the fabled wolves in sheep's clothing, the elements and agents of Satan, slinking silently amongst the flock. The elements of savagery, skulking unperceived in our midst, which pose as great a threat to the security of the community as the more obvious deviltry of the Jesuits.

"In short, I speak of certain individuals of this community whose actions more closely resemble those of the savage than those of civilized men. Conscienceless individuals, men without moral strength, unwilling to listen to the voice of the shepherd.

"Men whose manner of dress, manner of speech, manner of thought, reflect not the millennia of civilization since Our Lord Jesus Christ, but the primitive savagery of Satan's children.

"The blood shed on the battlefields of freedom, Bunker Hill, Concord and Lexington, has been hallowed by history. And yet these men dare—dare, I say—to mingle this sacred blood with the taint of savagery! To satisfy their unnatural lusts they stop at nothing, sending forth upon this green land of Oregon the unclean spawn of animal couplings, neither red nor white, the taint and decay and ineradicable blot of mixed-blood children, fouling the—"

Meek was standing at the aisle. Calmly, and without a word, he walked up to the pulpit, where Andrews watched him come in astonishment. The minister's face had suddenly turned from the twisted caricature of anger and hatred to surprise. He raised his hands in front of him in a faint gesture.

Meek grabbed one shoulder and half-twisted him around. Gripping him by the seat of the pants and the collar, he dragged the long dark figure down from the platform and up the aisle, still silent, his face expressionless. At the back, René Devaux quickly reached out and opened the door. As Meek went through, the little Frenchman held the door for him, bowing deeply from the waist. Outside, Meek heaved with all his strength, sending the long figure of Andrews tumbling in the dust of the little square.

Meek stood on the step with his fists on his hips, watching. Andrews raised himself to his knees, but went no farther. Meek spat in the dust, then wheeled and went back into the church. About half the assembly was standing, staring unbelievingly toward the door, and all the other faces were turned toward him.

"All right," Meek said. "Show's over. Get the hell out of here."

On the platform Thurston sat unmoved, watching it all carefully, while on either side of him the other dignitaries were agitated, showing shock and consternation. Monday watched Thurston's face, fascinated by its immobility and calm. Thurston caught his glance, met it casually, then turned away, dismissing him.

Monday turned to Mary, but she seemed almost not to have heard or seen any of it. She was looking down at Little Webb, stroking his still fuzzy head lightly, with love.

Chapter Thirteen

It was past noon when they reached the cabin again. Mary strangely, seemed wholly unmoved by Andrews' vicious denunciation. For the first time Monday was almost grateful for her strange state of lethargy and inertia. Nothing could touch her deeply, hurt her deeply. She was too involved with subtle interior currents to be affected by the outside world. There were times, he thought, when it could be a considerable advantage.

His own strongest feeling was regret that he had not been the one to throw Andrews out of the church. At first he had told himself it was because he was so far from the aisle—there was nothing he could have done. But, in fact, he had not been moved to do anything. He realized miserably that he would probably have sat through whatever was to come, head hanging lower and lower, accepting whatever vileness Andrews chose to dispense without protesting; allowing himself to be shamed.

The comparative darkness of the cabin was like a refuge. Mary crossed the dim room and put Little Webb gently on the bed. The baby had fallen asleep again for the greater part of the trip, but now he woke and began to squall. It was very rare for him; Monday thought he was probably the most silent child ever born. Sometimes he was disconcerted by the baby's quiet regard, so distant and uncomprehending.

Mary crooned to the child, tucking the blanket carefully around him. The wailing continued, and at last she picked him up from the bed, opened her dress and gave him the breast. He settled down quickly, closing his eyes.

"He was hungry," Mary said, smiling at the little face.

"Mary—don't feel bad. You know, about what Andrews said. It's just one man." But in his mind he saw the heads turn to stare at their pew, faces full of hostility.

"No," Mary said quietly. "It is not important, that." She shrugged gently, jogging the child's head. Little Webb opened his eyes briefly, reprimanding, then quietly clutched the breast again.

"I'm sorry it turned out that way," Monday muttered, almost to himself. "I hoped—I don't know, I hoped things would be sort of new starting today."

"It is nothing," Mary said. After a moment she repeated absently, "Nothing. It is just the same."

"Mary, there's one more thing."

"Yes."

"I have to go back."

"Go back?" she said softly.

"If I don't go back—I mean, if I let the bastards drive me now, there's no end to it. Can you see that?"

She nodded slowly.

"If I let 'em run me out like this they'll figure I'm ashamed or something. Hell, I don't know. But I got to face 'em down."

Little Webb had fallen asleep again. Gently she disengaged him from the breast and tucked him back under the blanket. With her fingertips she lightly caressed the still wrinkled forehead, and the child did not stir. She stood from the bed and turned to Monday.

"Yes," she said, "it will be all right."

He kissed her lifted forehead. "Thanks, Mary. We've got to fight this thing through. You understand that."

"Yes. I understand now, better than before. You must do what you have to do."

He went outside and unhitched his horse from the borrowed wagon. Hurriedly he saddled and mounted. Mary had come to the door and watched silently.

"I'll be back early," he promised.

He sat for a long moment, looking at her framed in the doorway. Her eyes were glistening, and he was afraid she was going to cry again, and he couldn't stand to see it. He pulled the reins suddenly and wheeled the animal off to the trail.

Mary watched until he was out of sight and the dust had settled back to earth and there was no sign left of his going but his absence.

She leaned back against the doorframe and let her eyes rove over the distant ridges lying open and clean under the summer sky. The timbered hills of the horizon were endlessly far, wavering in the heat like the images of dreams dissolving.

She went back into the cabin, closing the door behind her. In the dimness, cut off from the light of the sun, she went to the bed and sat looking down at the sleeping figure of the child, her hands folded quietly in her lap. For a long time she remained. Then she stood, shaking her head as though to clear her mind, and went back to the cupboard.

◦═⧓═◦

"Hell," Meek said, rubbing the back of his neck. "That mouse-holler preacher don't amount to a damn."

"How'd Virginia take it?" Monday asked him.

Meek shrugged. "Y'know, Virginia, she's pretty hard about things like that. She's seen 'em come an' go. Long as she's got the house an' kids an' me, she don't much give a damn."

Monday shook his head.

"Anyways," Meek said, "I got half a notion Thurston put that stuff in that speech his own self. You seen him up there, ca'm as ca'm. *He* wa'n't surprised none. Me, I think he was just throwin' a rock in the pool t'see what jumped."

"Well, he knows now, sure god."

"Mary's all right, I expect?"

"She's all right. She's—hell, I don't know, seems like she's so moody lately I can't tell *what* she's thinkin'."

"It'll pass," Meek said. "That's the one thing we're allus sure of, coon. It'll pass. What d'y' say we go down to that there boat, cheer y' up a bit?"

"Tell y' the truth, I ain't much got the heart for it," Monday said.

"Nothin' t' give a man heart like a leetle sip o' rum," Meek said. He stood up and looked down at Monday, still leaning back against the porch post. "C'mon, hoss, do y' good. Rainy an' Webb's already gone down."

"All right," Monday said, standing. "How come you didn't go down with 'em?"

Meek grinned at him and flipped the reins of his horse off the rail. "Oh, I figured as how you might be comin' back."

Monday looked at him, surprised. *"Wagh!* You ought t' go on the stage like one o' them mind-readers."

"Hell, you ain't the hardest man in the world t' figger out," Meek said. "Littler the mind, easier it is t' read. C'mon."

"By god, I believe I'd like a little bit o' rum. Relax me some."

"None o' that damn relaxin'," Meek said. "Last time you got relaxed the front yard smelled bad f'r a week."

"That was different," Monday said defensively.

2

They reached the riverbank about a hundred and fifty yards from the beginning of the wagon road that led down to the ferry.

The sloop-of-war *Portsmouth* lay at anchor in the middle of the Willamette, her graceful bowsprit pointing upstream. The mid-afternoon sun was brilliant, picking out the ripples of the river in sharp flashes of silver, glinting from the polished fittings of the ship. The sails were neatly furled on the yards, and there was a strong feeling of peace about the long, slim shape of the vessel.

As they watched, there was a flash of white from the hills across the river, and seconds later the boom of a cannon explosion, echoing across the placid Willamette surface.

"Where the hell'd they get that?" Monday said.

"That there's the twelve-pounder McLoughlin brought over from Vancouver," Meek said. "They been shootin' her off ever' now and then all day."

"Hell of a waste o' powder," Monday said glumly.

"What's Independence Day 'thout a cannon or two?" Meek demanded. "Anyways, it don't take near as much powder just t' make a noise as it does t' fire ball."

"She's mighty pretty sittin' out there," Monday said, looking back at the *Portsmouth* and the stars and stripes that streamed from the flagstaff at the stern.

"She is, now. Just like a picture or somethin'." Meek started his horse off toward the wagon road and Monday followed. They left their animals near the top of the bank and started down the road to the landing on foot. Halfway down they rounded the corner and met Devaux and Webb coming back up.

"Hooraw, coons, where's y'r stick floatin'?" Meek said, puzzled.

Webb squinted at him, wrinkling his nose as though by way of answer. He lifted his hands, fists clenched, in a gesture of helplessness.

"*Enfant de garce!*" Devaux exploded. "You know what he says, the animal! You *know?*"

"Whoa back there, Rainy," Monday said. "Who you talkin' about?"

"That dunghead down t' the boats," Webb muttered.

"He say *two dollars*, the animal! Two dollars to rent a little boat to go out there."

Monday lifted his eyebrows in surprise. "Jesus god! Meek, ain't that against the law or somethin'?"

Meek shook his head sadly. "No sir. This here's a free country, man's got a right to make his livin' how he sees fit. Me, I never interfere with a man's profit. It ain't moral." He dug into his pocket and brought out his marshal's badge. As he pinned it on, his chin tucked down to see, he said, "On t'other hand, I never let a man's profit interfere with me. Who's down there?"

"Heap o' shit with teeth," Webb offered.

"Me, I don't know the name. The animal, the *bête!* Is half bald, him, with little spectacles." Devaux made circles with his thumbs and forefingers, holding them up to his eyes to demonstrate.

"Little Billy Macon," Meek said, grinning. "Come on, deputies."

Devaux shook his head. "You try that deputy thing once before. Me, I have to swim the river, just for the honor."

"There ain't going to be no trouble this time," Meek said. "Little Billy got hisself a order o' copper tubing up from San Francisco 'bout a month ago. Ain't but one thing a man'd want copper tubing for, an' that's a still. But you don't say nothin', all right?"

Monday shrugged. "Hell, I suppose it's worth a try."

They rounded the last corner before the landing in a group, Meek marching slightly ahead. At the edge of the raw plank dock there were half a dozen tiny skiffs tied up. The short, stocky man heard them coming and turned around. Seeing Devaux and Webb he set his jaw defiantly and folded his arms decisively across his chest. "No pay, no boat," he said. "That's all. I tol' you oncet, you men. Now get out of here."

About fifty yards out from the dock was one of Little Billy's skiffs, laboriously being rowed by two of the Indians from the Methodist Mission down-valley. It was obviously the first time they'd ever tried to row, and the little boat zigzagged erratically, the only determinable direction being gently downstream. As passengers the skiff held Thurston and four others, all Methodist Mission dignitaries. From time to time the annoyed, sharp voice of Thurston came over the water as he tried to discipline the Indians into doing something they were incapable of doing.

Meek smiled warmly. "How's business, Billy?" he said conversationally.

"*Some* of it ain't bad," Billy said pointedly, staring at Webb.

Webb leaned on his rifle and stared back indifferently.

"Glad to hear it, Billy," Meek said. "Wisht I c'd say the same." He shook his head sadly. "Ain't allus pleasant, bein' marshal."

"Ain't allus pleasant bein' a ferry hand, neither," Billy said defensively.

"I expect there ain't no way to make a livin' altogether pleasant," Meek said absently. "On t'other hand, bein' a ferry hand, y' don't have to bring down a lot o' trouble on y'r friends."

Suspiciously Billy shifted his eyes from Webb, and glanced at Meek. "What's that mean?" he asked.

"Hell, I ain't one t' bore y' with *my* troubles," Meek said. "But, just f'r example, y'take moonshinin', now."

Little Billy unfolded his arms and cleared his throat.

"Sometimes I find out a real good friend o' mine's been makin' shine, y' know," Meek told him confidentially. "Then I got t'crack down on him just like if he was a stranger."

"Ah—is that a fact?" Billy said.

"Yup, fact. Five hundred dollars and ninety days," he said slowly. "Lot o' money, five hundred dollars. Lot o' time, ninety days. When y' think about it." He grinned at Billy.

The ferry hand cleared his throat again and blinked, trying to smile back at Meek. "You, ah, you have any—trouble? Lately, like?"

"Matter o' fact . . ." Meek said discouragedly.

With an emotion something like awe, Monday thought he saw Little Billy's eyes fill with tears. The stocky man blinked again, all his concentration fixed on Meek's next words.

"Matter o' fact," the marshal repeated, "I've heard one or two things that make me feel real bad, Billy. *Real* bad."

"Whatever y' heard it ain't—Listen, Meek, I got a wife and kids," Billy blurted. "We been good friends f'r a long time, ain't we? I allus been a good citizen here, ain't I?" He held his hands out toward Meek.

"Hell, yes, Billy. Why y' think I'm here? I got t' check on what I heard."

"Listen, Meek. Marshal. It ain't true. Hell, maybe a little wine—"

"You're right charitable, Billy, but I'm afraid I just got t' go out t' that sloop an' see for m'self. Me an' m' deputies, here."

"Sloop?" Little Billy said. "Sloop?"

"Hell yes," Meek said with a puzzled air. "I heard there was liquor aboard her, an' I got t' check her out. What'd y' think I was talkin' about?"

Little Billy wheeled around suddenly and stooped down, beginning to unwind the lashing of a little green and white skiff with a crudely painted "6" on the bow.

"*Well*," he said, with nervous cheerfulness. "You wa'n't plannin' to *swim*, was you?" He laughed a little, and with a spasmic gesture handed the rope to Meek.

"Shouldn't that go in the skiff?" Meek said. "I don't know nothin' about it, but it sort o' seems like foolishness t' stand here holdin' a rope in m' hand."

"Oh, hell yes," Billy said. "Don't know what I'm thinkin' about." He threw the free end of the line into the skiff. "Ain't m'self today, Joe. All the people comin' an' goin'. You know." He clapped Meek on the shoulder.

"Climb in, deputies," Meek said.

With straight faces the three mountain men stepped down into the skiff warily and settled themselves. Webb got in last, stepping too far to one side, and the little boat rocked wildly.

"This here nutshell ain't seaworthy," he complained. "Ain't you got somethin' that'll holt still a little?"

"Sit down, coon," Monday said. "You're rockin' the boat."

"Boat's rockin' me, y'iggerant dunghead! That's what I'm *sayin'*."

"Now cut out all that there arguin'," Meek said firmly. "We got t' put our hands on them lawbreakers. Right, Billy?"

"Right, right," Billy said. "Go get 'em, Joe. I holt her while you get in."

Meek got in the skiff with great dignity. For a moment they all sat there looking at one another. "Well, for christ's sake grab an oar," Meek said impatiently.

"There's two of 'em," Monday observed.

"Me, I got t' save my strength," Meek said, leaning back contentedly in the stern. "Never c'n tell when a shine-merchant'll get violent. Can y', Billy?"

The ferry hand had grabbed a boathook and was pushing them anxiously away from the dock. "*No* sir!" he said. "Can't be too careful with lawbreakers."

With a discouraged shrug Devaux picked up the other oar and clumsily inserted the pin in the oar lock.

"Don't lose them oars," Billy called over the widening distance.

"What is wrong with you, Bony One?" Devaux asked Webb. "You don't take an oar."

"Hell, son," Webb said complacently. "This nigger's *way* too old for them kind o' doin's. You pull smart on that, hear?" He began to fumble in his shirt for his pipe and tobacco. Contentedly he assembled stem and bowl and began to take pinches of stringy tobacco out of the pouch.

After a couple of false starts which set the boat rocking crazily, Devaux and Monday got their rhythms together and began to pull steadily, moving the little skiff out toward the anchored sloop.

"Some doin's," Monday muttered. "One too old an' the other too weak."

Meek winked at Webb. "Both too smart, that's the ticket."

Webb leaned back against the side, giving the skiff a permanent heavy list to starboard. "Right pretty day, f'r the kind o' day it is."

Meek leaned his head back on the stern, in the pillow of his clasped fingers. "It *is*, now," he said. "Just the day f'r a little boat ride."

3

There was an oddly insect-like air about the little skiffs approaching the still sloop; like so many stiff-legged beetles scurrying around the corpse of a dead mouse.

A boat from the sloop itself, manned by sailors, was heading toward the Linn settlement, on the other side of the river. Meek watched it with interest; the smooth, straight progress, the tiny wake it left behind. The skiffs approaching the sloop were, for the most part, in various degrees of uncontrol, oars manned by hands more accustomed to reins and plows.

"By god," he said to Monday and Devaux, "strikes me you boys got one hell of a lot t' learn about seafarin'."

"There's a oar available—any time you want—to teach us," Monday said, grunting. He was on the low side of the skiff—Webb had refused to settle in the middle—and his oar dug deep with each stroke, pulling the boat around to port.

"Listen, friend of me," Devaux said. "Don't do it so hard, and we go much better."

"I got to *pull*, don't I?" Monday complained. "You ain't doin' it hard *enough*, that's what our trouble is."

"Now boys," Meek said tolerantly. "Don't argue. Just pull."

"You bastards—got to—row back," Monday said.

All in all though, they weren't doing much worse than the other visitors. The "official" boat, containing Thurston and the other well-dressed gentlemen, had drifted downstream steadily under the inept handling of the tame Indians. It was making up the distance now, approaching the *Portsmouth* from astern. Glancing up between strokes, Monday noticed with amusement that two of the dark-suited white men were now at the oars, and the Indians sat hulking in the bow. He would have been willing to stake all he owned that Thurston was not one of the rowers. He could imagine the hard-faced little man boiling inside and dreaming of what he would do to the incompetent Indians.

"Hooraw, boys," Meek said encouragingly. "Now we're runnin'. I should o' been a sea captain. I got a natural talent for it. Hey, matey?" He nudged Webb with the toe of his boot. The old man opened one eye and examined the admiral carefully. *"Wagh!"* He snorted. He turned his head sharply and spat over the side to show his opinion of the career Meek was mapping out for himself. The boat tipped suddenly with the motion and Monday's oar plunged deep below the surface.

"Cut *out* that goddamn stuff," he said. "I almost lost the oar."

Webb turned back and shrugged indifferently, settling himself comfortably against the thwart. It made no difference to him. He'd swim if he had to.

They were near enough to the sloop now that they could hear the voices of the crew and guests. There were not too many people aboard, but the light flashes of high laughter and the flickering of brightly colored dresses gave a very cheerful atmosphere. As they approached, Monday determinedly tried to pull in rhythm, so they wouldn't careen around so much.

There was an opening in the ship's rail, from which depended a rope ladder. On deck stood a tall, thin man Monday judged to be the captain. The boat of Thurston and the missionary party pulled up to the ladder about twenty yards in advance of their own. A rope was thrown to a waiting sailor on the *Portsmouth*'s deck, and the dignitaries climbed up the ladder. The captain bowed courteously and shook hands, gesturing at the length of his ship and smiling broadly to make them welcome. A smiling, handshaking knot of men formed at the top of the ladder as the rest of the guests mounted.

The captain saw the boat of the mountain men approaching and shouted down to the Indians in the missionary boat, "Cast off there, cast off." The rope was thrown down and the skiff drifted back along the hull of the *Portsmouth*, bumping once in a while as the Indians ineffectually tried to shove themselves away. Finally it cleared the stern, and the Indians took up their oars discouragedly and plunged them in the water, drifting off with no clear idea of where they were supposed to go or how to get there.

Meek waved and shouted, "Ahoy the *Portsmouth!*" in his best admiralty fashion.

The captain grinned and waved back. Thurston came up to his shoulder, and the captain leaned over to hear what the small man was saying. Slowly the smile faded and his face hardened as he watched the skiff approach.

The little boat bumped heavily against the hull of the sloop. "Sorry, gentlemen," the captain called down. "All full up for the moment. Come back later." He turned back to Thurston. "Let me show you—"

"Hey, Captain," Meek said, smiling.

The uniformed man turned. "I said come back later. Put ashore."

Meek stood in the stern, starting to protest again. The captain leaned forward on the rail, his face angry.

"Put ashore, I say! Put ashore! There's no room for your kind on this vessel!" He wheeled and called, "Mr. Cole, Mr. Cole!" Another uniform came running up. The captain looked down at the mountain men and said, "Mr. Cole, see that these men go ashore. Under no circumstances permit them aboard. They're troublemakers." He turned back to Thurston and the others, now smiling again. "Come along," he said. "I think you'll be interested . . ."

Without a glance back the missionary group moved away from the rail and out of sight. At the top of the rope ladder the mate stood blocking the opening, his legs spread and his face hard. "Shove off, you," he said viciously.

Meek was still standing, looking up at the mate. He licked his lips, thinking, and then suddenly sat down again, rocking the skiff.

Devaux finally shrugged, put his oar against the hull of the sloop and shoved away. When they were a few yards out, Webb said, "Well, admiral?"

"That son of a bitch," Monday growled. He shoved his oar into the water and let it dangle there.

After a moment Meek said, "Y'know what I'm going t'do?"

"No," Devaux said, without interest.

"I'm going to get me a black suit one o' these days," Meek said. "Wagh! I am, now." Suddenly he grinned. "But f'r right now, I got a turrible dry."

"Th'ow y'in the water," Webb said absently. He had been little moved by the goings on, simply watching it all from beneath the floppy brim of his hat.

"Head over t' the west bank," Meek said.

"What the hell's that goin' to do?" Monday said.

"This nigger's goin' to have a drink f'r the Fourth, government or no government," Meek said. "C'mon, deputies. Pull."

"Just a goddamn minute," Monday said. "*You* was supposed t' row back."

"We ain't goin' back," Meek explained. "We're still goin' across. Ain't we?"

"Well, yes, but—"

"So," Meek said decisively. "Haul away, boys. We're bound for Australia."

"All I say is, I hope there's a drink in Australia," Monday said gloomily.

"There is boys, there is," Meek said contentedly. "Pull, now."

4

Just north of Peter's Mountain the Twality River emptied into the Willamette, coming from the west. It went by various names—Twality, Quality, Tualatin—and at this time of year was so shallow it scarcely merited one. As it neared the Willamette it coursed over a rock-strewn bottom, not more than a few yards wide. In winter it was a dirty brown flood, but by the middle of summer the water was clear and fresh.

It was a walk of perhaps two miles or more from the point they had left the skiff, just below the Oregon City falls. There was a well-defined foot-trail along the bank for the better part of the way, and the going was fast. When the four men turned in at the Twality, they were abruptly slowed by the thick brush and soon abandoned the bank entirely, to wade up the middle of the stream.

"Goddamn it, Meek," Monday said. "You sure you know where you're goin'?"

"Hell yes, I know," Meek said impatiently. "I been savin' it. Don't y' trust me?"

"*Wagh!*" Webb snorted. "I recollect one time I follered you up t' the Snake—"

"That was different. We was lost, then."

"We sure as hell was, an' you didn't help none, neither. 'Foller me,' y' said, real cheerful. 'I know a shortcut,' y' said. Took us four and a half days t' get a half-mile from where we was."

Meek shrugged. "Ain't nobody perfect. All I got t' say, you niggers sure don't want a drink very bad."

"Drinking I am for," Devaux said. "All this walking I am against."

"Well, she's just a couple hundred yards now," Meek said. "You want to go or not?"

"Lead on, Marshal," Monday said grimly.

"An' if'n it ain't there," Webb said calmly, "y' best take a good holt on y'r topknot, boy."

Monday stopped suddenly, the water swirling around his calves. "Listen," he said. "We oughtn't t' make so much noise, we're like t' get shot."

"Naw," Meek said. "Nigger as runs it, he's in town. I looked."

"*Politickin*', by god!" Webb said admiringly.

"Oh, I got a hair o' the black bear to me, if it comes t' that," Meek said modestly.

"Me," Devaux said, "I esteem you both. Can we go now?"

When they broached the little clearing a few minutes later they were suddenly assailed by the odor of sour mash. The clearing was tiny, not more than fifteen or twenty feet in diameter, and in the center stood the distilling apparatus, the big vat raised above the fire site, the brightly glinting worm of copper tubing.

"Right pretty," Webb said admiringly. "*Right* pretty." He began to prowl around the edge of the clearing, poking into the brush with the butt of his rifle, looking for the stored whisky.

There was a loud, dull clang as he connected with a huge camp kettle, but to everybody's disappointment it was empty. Monday finally found the whisky itself, cached in a burned-out stump on the side opposite the river. "Hooraw, coons!" he said happily, hoisting a bottle. "We're in business."

Monday clamped his teeth down on the protruding cork and tugged it loose. He took a swallow of the water-clear liquid and gasped. "Whoo!"

When the bottle had gone around the circle once it was half emptied. The pressure of haste gone now, the four men squatted on the ground and contemplated the label-less container.

"Is not whisky, that," Devaux said. "Is merely alcohol."

"Well, hell," Monday said contentedly. "We c'n make whisky out of 'er if it comes t' that."

"Waste o' time an' tobacco," Webb grumbled. "Gimme that there bottle if'n y're so damn particular. Alcohol's good enough f'r this nigger."

"No, Rainy's right," Meek said. "It ain't fittin' to be drinkin' plain alcohol on Independence Day. We ought t' have honest-t'-christ whisky."

"This nigger's against the whole thing," Webb said menacingly.

"Well," Monday said reasonably, "this here's a democracy, ain't it? An' the Fourth o' July t' boot? Let's vote on 'er."

Webb stood up defiantly. "I ain't votin' on nothin', y'dungheads. One nigger with brains is more like t' be right than three without. Y're just gangin' up on me is all."

"That's what democracy *means*," Monday said. He glanced over at Meek, and the marshal gently put the bottle down on the ground.

"I vote f'r whisky," Meek said, keeping his eyes on Webb.

"Me too," Monday said.

Devaux had sneaked the bottle when Meek put it down and said nothing for a moment. When he found his voice he said, *"Et moi."* He blinked unhappily.

"Whisky it is," Meek said, and launched himself from his squatting position in a long dive that caught Webb just as he was standing, throwing the old man to the ground. Monday was right after him, grabbing Webb's knife hand and slamming it on the ground. He threw all his two hundred pounds against Webb's shoulder, pinning it to the dirt while Meek struggled with the other.

Webb's legs flailed frantically in the air as he struggled, but the weight of the other two held his shoulders pinned tightly. Devaux watched interestedly, then drained the last of the bottle and stood up. "Is terrible drinking, that. You will thank us in a minute."

"Get the hell out o' here," Webb snarled, "I'll kick y'r balls off."

"Me, I have no envy to be kicked like that. I come around to the other end." Reaching carefully over Webb's immobile shoulders, he probed in the old man's shirt and pulled out his tobacco pouch. "*Le voilà,*" he said.

Turning quickly he dragged the big kettle out of the brush and emptied the tobacco into it. He got another bottle from the burned-out stump, yanked the cork, and poured the contents ceremonially into the kettle, on the tobacco.

The act having been accomplished, Webb seemed to lose his energy. "You *bastards,*" he said miserably. "You lousy, dunghead, tobacco-stealin' bastards!"

Meek let go Webb's shoulder and jumped back, but the old man did nothing. He sat up, cursing, but made no motion to attack.

"What d'y'know," Meek said, marveling. "We busted his little spirit."

"This nigger'll bust y'r little ass one o' these days," Webb muttered, rubbing his shoulder.

Devaux was methodically opening all the bottles stored in the tree trunk and emptying them into the kettle. Gradually the clear liquid took on a brownish stain from the tobacco.

Monday came over and looked into the kettle. "Stir it up a little bit," he said.

"Friend of me," Devaux said patiently, "then the tobacco goes all over."

Monday shrugged. "Anyways, I think y'ought t' stir it. It ain't darkening up very fast."

"There is not much tobacco," Devaux said.

Webb hoisted himself to his feet. "Y'mean you dungheads ain't going t'put nothin' in? Y'call that *fair?*"

"Who said anythin' about fair?" Meek asked curiously. "That's just the way it works. It's a free country," he added mysteriously.

"Free, hell!" Webb spat. "You dungheads stole my tobacco, *that* ain't free."

"Free f'r them in the majority." Monday shrugged. "C'mon, Rainy, hurry up. How's it comin'?"

"Is a mistake to rush a thing like this," Devaux said reprovingly. "Is ver' delicate, whisky-making." He bent down into the kettle and dipped his tongue in the swirling liquor. "What we need," he said, frowning, "we need a little molasses. Or maybe pepper."

"Well, we ain't got any. This'll do," Monday said impatiently.

"If you are in such a hurry, you should have voted against the whisky," Devaux said. "Now it has to age."

"Well, hell," Monday explained, "I didn't think it was going t' *take* so damn long. How'd I know you was going t' get so fancy?"

Devaux shrugged. "Is all equal to me. You want to drink before is made up proper—is your business."

"Good." Monday grabbed one of the empty bottles and lowered it into the kettle. He brought it out half full, with the suggestion of an amber tint. There were flakes of tobacco floating in it, and if he looked closely he could see the oily little brown streams diffusing into the whisky.

"You see?" Devaux said. "Now you swished up the tobacco."

"How's she go, hoss?" Meek said, watching Monday's tentative sip.

Monday grimaced, picked something off the tip of his tongue. "Ain't too bad, if'n you avoid the pieces."

"Wagh!" Webb snorted with satisfaction and picked up a bottle.

"You see, I was right," Devaux said. "You should not have swished up the tobacco."

"Still better'n what Billy Sublette used t' sell," Monday said complacently.

"He used t' cut 'er with water, is why," Meek said. "Three t' one for a starter an' more later, when nobody could see too good."

"How the hell d'you know?" Webb demanded. "You was allus the first nigger on the ground, come Rendezvous."

"People used t' tell me later what happened," Meek explained.

By this time they had all settled down with their respective bottles in a tight circle around the kettle.

"Was all different in Hudson's Bay," Devaux said. "You know, that Ogden, he never allowed any liquor in camp. Never. He was hard, that one."

"*Was* he, now!" Monday said. "*Never?*"

"Never," Devaux said. "No cards, either."

"Hell, I seen cards a many a time in Nor'west camps," Webb said. "An' liquor too."

"Yes," Devaux admitted. "But he did not *allow* them, is what I am saying."

Meek got up and went to the still, looking it over carefully. "Real nice job, that," he said absently. He kicked at the vat once, but nothing in particular happened. Finally he reached up and wrenched the coil of copper tubing loose.

"You boys want t' hear this here worm sing?" he asked.

While the others looked on interestedly Meek rummaged in his pocket, holding the worm down to drain the fluid from it.

"God damn," Monday said morosely. "That's a hell of a waste, what you're doin' there."

From his pocket Meek brought up a shiny bugle mouthpiece.

"This here's sort of a loan from the US government," he said. He pounded the mouthpiece into the opening of the copper tubing and raised the improvised bugle to his lips. He blew a long, resonant blast and looked down with a pleased expression.

"Wagh!" Webb said admiringly. "C'n you play a tune, I mean, c'n y' change 'er any?"

"No, I don't know how," Meek admitted. "I used t' do this without any mouthpiece, but sometimes I'd cut my lip up on the worm, like that." He blew the horn again. "So I sort o' borrowed this here mouthpiece from a bugle that was lyin' around." He blew another long blast.

"Me," said Devaux, "I like violins. Me, I am amorous of violins." He blinked, getting sad as he thought about violins.

"I ain't really amorous o' nothin' but women," Monday said. "An' only one o' them." He leaned back on his elbows and closed his eyes. "Whoo."

"Y'know," Meek said, "I hear there's two kinds o' alcohol. If'n y' get holt o' the wrong kind, y' go blind or die or somethin'."

"Y'iggerant dunghead!" Webb snorted. "Y' *believe* that?"

"That's just what I heard is all I'm sayin'."

"*There's* a pack o' lies," Webb said. "Them preachers in*vent* that kind of idee, just t' scare y', is all."

"Might could be," Meek said. "Never scared me too much, though."

"That's cause y're too dumb. Y're supposed t' be worryin' all the time did y' get the right *kind* o' alcohol, an' eventually y' quit drinkin' altogether cause o' bein' scared to get the wrong kind. That's why they make up that kind o' stuff, them."

"Always somebody tryin' t' scare a man," Monday said. "Always somebody that don't *allow* somethin', like cards or somethin', or try to scare y'."

"Here," Meek said, grabbing Monday's bottle. "You best fill up again. You're gettin' glum."

"No, I ain't gettin' glum. But I get tired o' people all the time not *allow*in' stuff, an' tryin' t' scare a man."

"Don't pay no *mind* t' that kind o' stuff," Webb said. "That's all."

"Sometimes y' *got* to," Monday said. "They's always somebody on y'r back."

"Not mine," Webb said complacently.

"That's 'cause y're alone," Monday said. "It ain't so easy f'r the rest of us." He spat a fleck of tobacco from the tip of his tongue.

"Don't spit it out," Webb encouraged him. "Chew it. Anyways, *ever'body's* alone, whether he likes it 'r not. Don't y' even know that? Me, I like it."

"That's all right," Monday said. "That's all right for you t' say."

"I ain't just *say*in'. That's the way it *is*. Y' got your choice, y' run alone like a man, or y' run with them sheep." He made a vague gesture in the direction of Oregon City. "Ain't I right? Meek, ain't I right?"

Meek looked down at the ground. "I don' know," he said.

"When y' get to the bottom of it, ever' man jack's alone in this world. Y' come in alone, an' you'll go out alone. An' in between times you're alone."

"What you don't see, hoss," Monday said. "There's times a man got to run with the sheep or go under."

"I ain't sayin' nothin' about that. I'm just sayin' it's one or the other."

"Friends of me," Devaux said slowly. "Me, I think you are both wrong."

"Rainy," Webb said, "if'n there's anythin' that riles me, it's a drunk that contradicts his betters."

"I excuse myself," Devaux said politely. "But you are both wrong. Me, I am not alone, and moreover I do not run with the pack. For me, there is the Conspiration."

"Conspiration?" Webb said suspiciously. "I don't b'lieve that's a real word."

"*Mais si*, is a real word, conspiration," Devaux said.

"That's like when y' get together t' plot somethin', " Meek said.

"Is like a secret society, but the Conspiration is not secret. Anybody can see it. Me, I go anywhere, an' there are others like me."

"Where the hell you get a idee like that?" Webb demanded.

"My *père*, he tell me before I leave Montreal, he say, 'René, never forget you are part of a great conspiration. No matter what happen, there are other members of the Conspiration, and you will know them.' An' he was right moreover, him."

"How d' y' join this here Conspiration?" Meek asked.

"You do not join it," Devaux said. "It exists. You are part of it or not. There is no joining."

"So what d' y' *do?*" Webb said. "Y' plot things, like Meek said?"

Devaux shrugged. "Do? You do nothing. Maybe help each other once in a while. Mostly nothing."

"Ain't a hell of a lot o' point to 'er, then," Meek said.

"Ah!" Devaux said. "But friend of me, when you see the Conspiration, you *know*. It is that somewhere in the world—everywhere—there are others like you. And after that, you are never alone. There is always the Conspiration."

"No!" Webb snapped, suddenly angry. "A man's dead alone, an' the sooner he realizes it the better off he is."

"Whoa back, boys," Meek said. "Ain't no use arguin' while there's still serious drinkin' to do."

"No arguing," Devaux said. "Me, I have no envy to argue."

"Drink up, drink up!" Meek said, swishing his bottle around in the kettle. "Why the hell's ever'body so serious all of a sudden? Rainy, I think what happened is your 'pair' or whatever y' call 'im dropped y' on y'r head afore y' left Montreal."

"That," Devaux said, "is very probable. But it does not change the facts." He shrugged. "The Conspiration, it exists."

Meek looked at the little Frenchman, who was completely serious. "Rainy," he said, "y're either a lunatic or y' got the answer t' one hell of a lot o' problems with that there Conspiration."

"Me, I am a lunatic," Devaux admitted cheerfully. "An' moreover, I have no problems, me." He dipped his bottle in the kettle and pulled it out. "Now I wish we have not put the tobacco in," he said morosely. "And I wish we had some violins. Me, I am amorous of the violin."

Chapter Fourteen

I

Is 'at dunghead goin' t' *sleep?*" Webb demanded after a while. Meek leaned over and nudged Monday. "Jaybird, you goin' t' sleep? Webb wants t' know."

Monday opened his eyes and raised his head off the ground. "No, I ain't goin' t' sleep. I'm just restin' my eyes." He put his head back down.

"You know," Devaux said, "he don't tolerate whisky, that one."

"This nigger don't tolerate it neither," Webb muttered. "He plain *likes* it."

"Well, you got t' remember," Meek said. "This here is two, three times stronger'n what we got in the mountains. Mebbe four. I don't know. How the hell should *I* know? Y' shouldn't of *ast* me!"

"*Wagh!*" Webb tipped his bottle up for a long time. When he brought it down he said, "Y'know what I say? I say this is one hell of a Independence Day. I ain't shot off my gun even *oncet.* Just sittin' here gettin' stupid drunk with a bunch o' sad-ass dungheads."

"Is not as lively as some," Devaux admitted, looking at the mouth of his bottle.

"What I mean is, I ain't had any *fun,*" Webb complained. "That's what makes me mad, I ain't had any *fun.*"

"Me too," Monday muttered, dragging himself up to a sitting position. "Me, I vote it's a hell of a Independence Day."

"I ain't votin' on nothin'," Webb said. "I'm just sayin'. You niggers is all *crazy* with y'r votin'. I ain't *votin'* it's a hell of a Independence Day, I'm just *sayin'.*"

"All right," Monday said. "I'm just sayin' too, then. The bastards won't let y' have any fun. Makin' speeches t' come over you, won't let y' on their damn little ship."

"Hey, regard," Devaux said. "You woke up."

"I was just restin' my eyes," Monday explained.

"That was a bad thing, that captain and all," Devaux said musingly.

"An' what's more," Monday said, "*I* don't b'lieve they got any *right* t' keep us off'n that ship. We're citizens, ain't we? An' that's a government ship, ain't it? It *belongs* t' us, sort of. They can't keep us off'n it."

"Not me," Devaux said. "Me, I am not a citizen."

"Meek," Monday said. "You know all about law an' things. They got any right t' do that just because we ain't dressed right?"

"They done it, didn't they?" Meek said.

"Me, I'd just as soon not be in the United States if that's the way it's goin' t' be," Monday muttered.

"I'll tell y' what let's do," Meek said. "Let's sink 'er."

"Sink who?" Webb said.

"That ship. The *Portsmouth*," Meek said. "Let's sink 'er."

"Wagh!" Monday said softly, thinking about it.

"Right t' the bottom o' the river," Meek said gleefully.

"Never done nothin' like that," Webb admitted. "By god, that sounds like a hell of a good idee, Meek. Let's do 'er!"

"Me, I don't think I can," Devaux said glumly.

"Why not?"

"Me, I am not a citizen."

"Y're a deputy, ain't you? That's practically the same thing," Meek said.

Monday frowned slightly. "Y'know, I think you got this deputy thing wrong, Meek. I think it must be more complicated than that."

"Mebbe so could be," Meek said cheerfully. "Ain't nobody objected so far, though. Listen, what d' y' say?"

"Hell, I say fine, but *I* don't know how to sink a ship."

"They got McLoughlin's cannon up on the hill, ain't they?" Meek said. "It's perfect, y' couldn't ask for anythin' better. We'll just put 'er under slick with that cannon."

"By god, she's worth a try," Monday said, scrambling to his feet. He wavered a little and put his hand on his forehead. "Whoo! Di'n't know it *got* so drunk out this time o' year. Hooraw, coons, let's go."

"Hold up, there," Webb said, and the other three turned to look at him.

"Now don't you go gettin' cranky, hoss," Monday said. "Else we'll vote on y'again."

Webb's face was set in a contemptuous grimace. "You so damn hell-fired eager. Ain't y' forgettin' something?" He gestured to the whisky kettle.

"*Wagh!*" Monday said. "Damn near did at that. Best bring 'er along."

"Me," Devaux said, "I just take a little bottle. I had enough, almost."

"It ain't f'r *us*, altogether," Monday said reprimandingly.

"Hell it ain't," Webb snapped. "Who's it *for* if it ain't f'r us?"

"F'r them poor survivors," Monday said. "That's how it is when there's a tragedy at sea. Y'give the survivors a drink. It's sort of traditional."

"I s'pose that may be right, though I don't much give a damn myself about survivors," Webb said dubiously.

"Y'know," Monday said, "if'n we have t' vote again, y' may not live through it this time. It's risky stuff when y'ain't in the majority."

"Moreover," Devaux said, "is you and Meek got to carry it, because we rowed."

After a little arguing for the sake of appearances Webb gave in and agreed to carry the kettle at least halfway. But he insisted that the question be reopened at the halfway point. When this was agreed, Webb squatted down in front of the kettle and put his arms around it. His hands did not come together on the opposite side. With an enormous tug he got it off the ground and stood wavering for a moment, just his face showing above the rim. His eyes had a wild glare as he stared at the others from behind his load. Monday turned away so as not to laugh and make him mad.

"It's too damn heavy," Webb said angrily. Slowly he stooped back down, gently resting the kettle on the ground again. "No man living or dead that could carry that thing."

"So much the better," Monday said. "That means we got plenty of drinkin' to do."

"That damn kettle's solid cast iron, y'iggerant dunghead. *That's* what's heavy."

"Listen," said Meek. "One of us take each side an' it'll go fine, all right?" He lifted up the bail and gestured for Webb to take the other side.

"See? That does 'er slick. We're off!"

They made their way through the brush at the edge of the clearing and started down the bank, Devaux and Monday holding bushes aside for the kettle-bearers. When they reached the very edge of the stream, the kettle was gently lowered by all four.

"You're doin' fine," Monday encouraged, "you're doin' real good."

Webb scowled at him, but took the kettle bail again. With Monday and Devaux cheerfully leading the way they waded downstream. Behind came Meek and Webb, their free arms outstretched for balance, the kettle swinging precariously between them and occasionally banging against their legs.

"God damn it, Meek!" Webb complained. "You're doin' that a-purpose. Holt *on* t' that thing."

"Here's a slippery rock," Monday said. "Watch the moss, now."

"Watch y'r own damn moss," Meek said. "*You* want t' carry this thing?"

Monday shrugged. "Just lookin' out f'r y', coon. 'Cause, if anythin' happens t' that whisky we'll have t' kill y'."

With the overbalancing weight of the kettle and the slipperiness of the bottom, the going was uncertain and tended to be spasmodic. But in reasonably short time they had reached the mouth of the Twality, where it emptied into the broad flood of the Willamette.

"This is halfway," Webb said firmly. He sat down on the bank and took off his moccasins, pouring the water out of them.

"No, it ain't *nearly* halfway," Monday said.

"I ain't carryin' this damn thing a step farther than halfway," Webb said.

"Listen," Meek said in an injured tone, "*I'm* doin' half the work." "*Wagh!*"

"Now don't worry, hoss, we'll let y' know. Y' ready t' go again?" Monday considerately helped Webb up, but the old man brusquely shook him off.

They started downriver toward the falls, keeping to the flat edge of the water where they could, occasionally detouring up the bank a little when there was no path at all. Webb was unrelentingly suspicious of Monday's estimate of distance, and insisted every thirty or forty yards that they'd passed the halfway point.

"Now, listen, hoss. It just *seems* like that because it's farther goin' back than it was comin'."

"Farther! Just exactly the same, y'dunghead. How c'n it be farther?"

"F'r one thing account of y'r judgment's got a bit cloudy," Monday explained. "Anyways, it ain't very far from Christmas t' New Year's, but she's one hell of a stretch from New Year's t' Christmas. Now ain't that right?"

Webb closed one eye and peered at him, his teeth clenched. But Meek interrupted just as the old man was about to speak, saying, "C'mon, boys. We'll never get there if we stop an' argue ever' ten feet."

"Oh, we got lots o' light, yet," Monday said, feeling cheerful.

2

Still, the sun was behind the hill when they reached the cannon emplacement. There was a road of sorts high on the hill above the river, and the cannon was about twenty yards below that level, perched on the edge of a narrow rock outcropping that dropped fifty feet into the river.

They put the kettle down at the roadside, and Monday wiped his forehead. He had held out as long as he could, but Webb had finally sat himself down beside the trail obstinately. He refused to say a single word, and Monday, realizing the end had come, took over with Devaux. He was secretly satisfied that he had managed to get Webb to carry it well over halfway.

Meek dug in his pocket and got his marshal's badge, and pinned it carefully dead-center on his belly.

"Wagh!" Monday said. "That's a hell of a walk, comin' back. I tol' y' it was farther."

"Me, I'm glad we brought the whisky," Devaux said. "If we had some violins it would be perfect."

"Hell, I'd be sober by now if'n we'd of left it," Meek said. "Now shut y'r traps an' follow me." He started down the path toward the rock outcropping. Devaux and Monday followed with the kettle, Webb behind. From the trail they could hear the sound of voices and laughing.

There were only three men left at the cannon, and empty powder sacks were scattered around the rock. "All right, boys," Meek said loudly. "Clear out, now."

The three farmers looked around, startled. "What's the trouble, Meek? We ain't doin' no harm." One of them glanced behind the marshal to the three who had followed him down the path. He saw the kettle and looked puzzled. "What the hell's that?" he said.

Meek looked around. "That there's cleanin' fluid," he said. "You boys been shootin' this here gun off all day, now we got t' clean it."

"*Cleanin'* fluid? Cleanin' fluid for a cannon? Meek, I never heard—"

"Now look here, friend. We ain't come t' discuss y'r ignorance. Now you just clear out an' let us get t' work."

Reluctantly the farmers looked at one another, then back at Meek and the others. Finally one of them shrugged. He stuck the smoking punk upright in the ground beside the cannon. "All right, but listen. We promised t' get this here cannon back t' McLoughlin two hours ago."

"Don't you worry about that. I seen him just ten minutes ago an' he says, 'Let the boys have their fun. But you get that gun cleaned up.'"

Scowling, the three men began to trudge past. One of them sniffed as he passed the marshal. "You been inter that cleanin' fluid y'r own self, Meek," he said enviously.

Meek winked at him. "Might could be I have. I expect there's enough left f'r the cannon an' you boys too. Jaybird," he said, turning, "let these here boys have a bit o' that cleanin' fluid f'r their rifles."

They did, and Devaux let them have the bottle he'd brought along to carry it in. The three farmers finally wound off up the path in better humor.

"*Wagh!*" Meek said gleefully. "Let's put 'er under, boys."

The *Portsmouth*, now in shade, lay peacefully at anchor just a little downstream from their cliff. Meek kicked the one remaining powder sack with his toe, and looked out across the river at the sloop.

"That's a hell of a long shoot," Monday said dubiously. "Y'think we c'n reach 'er from here?"

"Hell, yes," Webb said. "This nigger knows all about such. She's just like any other rifle. More powder y'put to 'er the farther she goes."

"Well, we best load 'er up good, then," Meek said.

"Friend of me," Devaux said dubiously. "What we going to use for ball?"

"Rocks, I expect," Meek said, rubbing the back of his neck. "That's all we got, ain't it?"

"Listen," Monday objected. "You ain't going to sink a sloop-of-war with *rocks.*"

"Why not? Put enough powder behind 'em, y' c'd prob'ly sink 'er with straws."

"Me, I think we must have a trial shot. For range."

Meek looked doubtfully at the powder sack. "I ain't sure we got enough powder for but one shot," he said.

"Hell, you put all that powder in there it'll fill up the whole damn barrel," Monday said.

"Well, that's about what she's goin' t' *need,*" Meek said. He pointed out to the sloop. "Look at that, that's one hell of a long shoot, y'know."

"That cannon's goin' t' blow up, sure as hell," Monday said.

Meek shrugged. "Well, I already owe McLoughlin so much I expect the price of a cannon ain't goin' t' make much difference. You boys start gettin' rocks, an' I'll put the charge to 'er."

"How you going to aim, you don't make a ranging shot?"

"Just like a rifle," Webb said. "Listen, this nigger knows all about such. Whyn't you back off an' lemme fire 'er?"

"No," Meek said firmly. "This here was my idee an' I get t' shoot 'er off."

Monday dropped some rocks beside the muzzle of the cannon Suddenly he squatted on his heels and looked seriously up at Meek. "I don't think you know what y're doin'," he said.

"What *I* wish," Meek said, "I wisht I c'd get in a little bit o' practicin'. It ain't ever' day a man gets t' sink a warship. I'd like t' do 'er just right."

"I know what you mean," Devaux said. "Me, I find the attitude admirable."

"Well, I expect we'll just have t' trust t' luck," Monday said.

There was a creaking of wagon wheels on the road above, and the snuffling of a horse. The noise ceased and Webb jumped up excitedly. "Load 'er up, load 'er up! Somebody's comin'!"

"Dépêche-toi!" Devaux said, running up to grab the ram. Meek began to shovel powder frantically while Monday stood by with the rocks.

"Is enough, is enough!" Devaux said. Almost pushing Meek out of the way he began to ram down the loose powder. Meek ran over to the smoldering punk the others had left upright in the ground and began to blow it into glowing red.

He ran back and poised the punk over the cannon's touch-hole.

"Wait a minute, dammit," Monday shouted. "Lemme get the *rocks* in!"

Webb started to laugh and kick the whisky kettle, making a loud bell-like tolling.

"Get out o' the way, get out o' the way!" Meek said. "Here she goes!"

Monday jumped back away from the muzzle, laughing. "Run f'r y'r lives!" he hollered.

He and Devaux scurried back toward the path. Holding his free hand over his ear and squinting down at the touch-hole Meek lowered the punk. For what seemed a long time nothing happened.

Then, suddenly, there was a brief flash of smoke at the punk, and the cannon bellowed, spitting a huge gout of puffy white smoke twenty feet out over the edge of the cliff. The little machine leaped wildly in the air and jumped back three feet or more, falling over on its side with rolls of smoke still piling out of the barrel.

Meek looked down at it wide-eyed, astonished at the violence.

"Did we get 'er?" Webb demanded. He ran out to the edge of the cliff again and peered at the *Portsmouth*. The sloop floated placidly on the dusk-dark surface of the river, undisturbed.

"We didn't get 'er," Webb said, turning accusingly toward Meek.

Monday and Devaux came out to look. "I don't even see any splashes," Monday said disappointedly.

"I forgot to aim," Meek said, lifting his hands and letting them drop again.

"But the rocks," Devaux said, puzzled. "Where did the rocks go?"

"Well, we done somethin' wrong, that's all there is to it," Meek said firmly. "That's what happens when you get in too much of a hurry."

"But the rocks," Devaux said again, disturbed. "Where did the rocks *go?* Did you put them in?"

"I didn't get 'em *all* in," Monday said. "Hell, with that dunghead standin' there ready t' touch 'er off, I didn't figure t' hang around—"

"Y' had too damn much powder in there, Meek," Webb said. He was crouched down looking at the cannon. It lay helplessly on its side, trails of blue smoke still streaming out of the muzzle and rising straight into the still air of afternoon. "It ain't supposed t' fall over like that."

"Mr. Joe, Mr. Joe," came a voice behind them. John McLoughlin stood at the trail, his eyes wide and the great mane of white hair seeming to float around his head like a low cloud. With one hand he rubbed his stomach rapidly.

"Mr. Joe, what—what are you about here?" McLoughlin asked excitedly. "This will never do, Mr. Joe, never do!"

"Well, we—we was just celebrating a little, Doctor," said Meek in a friendly way.

McLoughlin bent over and sniffed at the kettle. "Yes, yes," he said abstractedly. "But Mr. Joe, this will never do. You had some sort of projectile there. Dangerous, Mr. Joe, terribly dangerous."

"Wagh!" Webb said happily. "That there's the idee. We figured t' sink that there little boat slick."

McLoughlin raised his eyes. "My cannon," he said to heaven. "My cannon." At last he looked back down at the men, glanced at the cannon, started to say something, and stopped. He shook his head helplessly, setting the loose hair into motion again.

"We'll clean 'er up good as new, Doctor," Meek assured him. "We even brought the cleanin' fluid."

"Yes, yes, Mr. Joe," McLoughlin said. "I see that. Mr. Joe, can you imagine the situation if you had succeeded in sinking that vessel? With *my* cannon?"

"Well, hell," Meek said hesitantly. "I didn't exactly think about—the thing is, Doctor, a man's got his dignity."

McLoughlin shook his head again. "Gentlemen, I must ask you not to avenge your dignity with *my* equipment. An American warship! *My* cannon! Mr. *Joe!*"

"Well, anyways," Webb muttered cheerfully. "We got a good bang out of 'er."

"Me," Devaux said, "I had a great envy to see it sink, that boat."

3

It had been a pretty good Independence Day after all. The grand attempt had cheered them all considerably even though, strictly speaking, it had not accomplished its purpose. Meek was genuinely chagrined when he thought of the possible consequences of sinking an official representative of the United States Government with McLoughlin's cannon, and he set himself to humility and cooperation, dragging the little machine up the trail and helping load it into McLoughlin's waiting wagon.

"By God, though," he told McLoughlin, "if'n you hadn't of rushed me, we'd of got 'er sure."

"Mr. Joe," McLoughlin said resignedly, "my life consists of arriving somewhere five minutes before utter disaster."

At the end of the day everything seemed to get very complicated. If Monday had had his way, he would have curled up on the spot and gone to sleep. But the wagon had to be taken across to Oregon City on the ferry, explanations had to be made to Little Billy, who seemed unable to understand exactly *why* his skiff had been left on the wrong side of the river. After a careful consideration of the condition of the mountain men, he finally realized he was much more likely to get it back by towing it across himself. It would have been difficult to predict the final destination if any of the four had undertaken to row it back. The question was finally settled by McLoughlin, and a five-dollar bill changed hands in the deepening darkness.

When the cannon had been established back in McLoughlin's yard, Meek regretfully rode on off toward his house at the other end of town. Monday, Webb and Devaux began the long ride down the valley.

"Listen," Devaux said suddenly, just as they reached the edge of Oregon City. "We forgot the whisky again."

"Wagh! We *did* now!" Webb snorted. "Damn! I b'lieve you boys is drunk, do a thing like that."

Monday shrugged, unable to worry about it seriously. "Me, I don't care. That's a hell of a jaunt back, now."

"Is right, that," René said, after a moment.

"Me, I vote t' go back an' get 'er," Webb said.

"I ain't votin'," Monday said. "I'm just goin' home."

"How the hell *come!*" Webb said plaintively. "Ever' time you bastards want t' get y'r own way you vote on it. How come it don't work for *me?*"

"Friend of me," Devaux said, "you do not understand the essential. Before one votes, he makes certain he is the majority, or it does not march properly."

"Your trouble, coon," Monday said, "is you been a minority all y'r life."

"Ain't goin' to be no different, neither," Webb muttered. "You bastards think you change the way things *is*, just by votin' 'em to be different."

The night was fine and pure as they rode along the east bank. There was a sharpness and clarity to the stars that Monday had seldom seen. They hardly seemed to sparkle at all, points of brilliance in the fathomless sky. The moon was not risen, and the depth of blackness was almost supernatural. They could see none of the trail, but let the horses find their way.

"Why the hell is summer so much better than winter?" Monday said absently.

"Is a question of light," Devaux said. "Here there is no light, eight months a man lives with no light, and the wet and the cold."

Monday shook his head. "Y'know, every winter I think I can't stand it any more, I figure I got to leave. But I'm too damn low t' do it in the winter, an' when spring comes, it's so good I forget all about it."

"Is crazy, that," Devaux said. "Me, I quit thinking in October, then it does not derange me, the winter."

"When d' y' start again?" Webb asked.

"May. Good years, maybe the middle of April."

"What if y' f'rget to turn y'rself on again?" Monday asked him.

Devaux shrugged. "Makes no difference," he said. "I forgot one year, and nobody noticed."

Monday laughed and stretched himself up in the saddle. The unpleasant cloudiness of the whisky was leaving him, but the sensation of well-being and peace remained. After the discouragements and rebuffs of the first part of the day, it had been good to have a little fun, without worrying about it. The cannon's explosion had wiped out the bad taste in his mouth from the sermon of Andrews and the *Portsmouth*.

"This must be the best summer there ever was in Oregon," he said. "I'll bet the summer of 'fifty goes down in history as the best summer there ever was."

"Y'iggerant dunghead, *that* ain't the kind o' thing they write history about. Ain't nobody cares what the weather's like."

"Look at Valley Forge," Monday said. "Ever'body knows that was a real bad winter, what with all them Revolutionary sojers freezin' their feet off and all that kind of stuff."

"That's different," Webb said. "That's when a man's miserable, sometimes they pay attention to that. But they ain't nobody gives a damn when a man feels *good*. I read one hell of a heap o' history, an' I tell you plain, it ain't about when a man feels good."

"Seems like it ought to be, though," Monday says. "Seems like the times a man feels good are important, too."

"What ought t' be ain't what is," Webb said. "Ain't nobody cares."

Monday looked up and watched the bright star-points jog the rhythm of his horse. "They's sure a vast lot of 'em, ain't there? One of these days I'm goin' where I c'n see what the stars look like in the winter, too."

"Is just the same, I think," Devaux said.

"No they ain't," Webb said decisively. "They's in different places."

"How can that be?" Devaux said. "The sky is the sky."

"Hell, I don't know *how*," Webb said. "But they are. I seen 'em many a time in the mountains. You c'n see 'em good there."

"I never noticed when I was in the mountains," Monday said. "I guess I was never interested."

"That's 'cause you was too young," Webb said. "Man got to get a little sense before he gets interested in lookin' at the stars."

"Me, I don't see how they can be different," Devaux said. "I am also commencing to have bad in the head."

"Whyn't you put up at my place, if'n y're gettin' a headache?" Monday said.

"Maybe I do that, me."

"Look," Webb insisted. "Days is shorter in the winter, ain't they? That proves things c'n change."

"That's just because of the rain an' clouds all the time," Monday said. "You just can't see the sun is all."

"God *damn*, y're a arguin' son of a bitch," Webb said.

It was well past midnight when the three were finally on the trail that led down to Monday's cabin. There was no light, and Monday figured the candle Mary usually kept had burned down. He was, he realized, a lot later than he had figured, having promised to be back early.

They tied their horses outside and Monday went up on the porch. When he opened the door he was assailed by a rotten odor.

"Jesus Christ," he said. "What's that smell?"

He started across the room toward the mantel and stumbled on a chair. "Damn it! Just a minute, I'll get some light."

He fumbled on the mantel for the little box of locofoco matches and the candle. In the blackness the match flared, blinding him with its sudden brightness.

"Mary!" he called. "Wake up, we got company."

He touched the wick and the yellow flame streamed up, dark shadows leaping out toward the wall. He started to turn, catching an unfamiliar shape out of the corner of his eye, but he was too late. In a fraction of a second he saw Webb's hurtling shape, and then the old man's rifle butt plunged into the pit of his stomach, doubling him over. Webb lifted his knee, crashing viciously into Monday's face and throwing him backward from the fireplace to sprawl unconscious against the wall.

Webb looked at him for a moment, then turned back to look up at the gently swinging form of the woman suspended from the beam.

"That is no answer," Devaux said, his eyes fixed on the contorted face that witnessed death by strangulation. "He will wake up some time."

"Couldn't think o' nothin' else," Webb muttered. After moment he went over to the bed, lifted the heavy pillow from the swaddled bundle there. He looked down at the blackened and twisted tiny face and clenched fists for a moment, then gently put the pillow back.

He turned back to the center of the room.

"Me," Devaux said, "I thought all Indians afraid to hang."

"This don't prove no different," Webb said. After a moment he blinked and said, "We best cut 'er down."

He picked up the overturned chair and reached for his knife. Against the wall three heavy shadows danced to the soundless music of the candle's flame.

Chapter Fifteen

They buried her toward the river, next to a clump of blackberry where she had gone every day, in season, to pick the full sweet berries. The late-afternoon sun slanted flat along the river, golden red, making flame bursts of the trees on the other bank.

Monday tamped down the tiny mound with the flat of his shovel. He squatted, resting his forehead against the handle, looking at the ground between his feet. He was numb, wholly numb. After the initial grief of waking he had sunk into suspension, doing what had to be done without thinking about it, moving slowly, unconscious of the passing of time.

Webb leaned on his own shovel and watched the back of Monday's head.

"Y' figger t' mark it any way?" he said. "Cross or somethin', maybe."

Monday looked up. He passed his hand across his forehead. "Mark it?" he said. He frowned and after a moment repeated, "Mark it. No. I know—I know where she is." He looked at the pile of fresh-turned earth, the color of a newly plowed field. "She's right—here," he said. He turned away, his eyes closed.

They walked slowly up the slight rise to the cabin. At the porch Monday absently knocked the dirt from his shovel blade, as though he were returning from any other day's digging. There was a sharp flash of anguish as he lit the candle inside, a clear, stopped vision of turning to catch sight of the dangling, shapeless form in the center of the room. For a long time, every time he lit a candle it would be there, just at the edge of his sight. He would always be just on the verge of turning, catching a glimpse . . .

He shook his head and blew out the candle. The house was already cool, though the sun was not yet down. And it was empty. He went back out on the porch and sat with his back against the wall, watching the thunderous silent reds and purples of the dying day.

"What d'you want, hoss?" Webb asked him.

"Go away," Monday said. "Leave me alone."

Silently the two men saddled their horses again and mounted. Webb sat slumped in the saddle for a moment, frowning down at the neck of his animal. He guided the horse a few steps until he was just opposite Monday.

"Listen, coon," he said.

Monday looked away from the sunset and turned to the old man, his face blank.

"Y'know down t' the coast, there's a two-hump mountain. Round fifteen miles this side o' Solomon Smith's I hear."

Monday nodded absently. "Saddle Mountain they call it. Ain't much of a mountain."

"Reckon t' take a look at 'er anyways," Webb said.

Monday nodded again.

"Y'understand?" Webb demanded. "This nigger's headin' down there."

"All right," Monday said indifferently.

The old man sat quietly for a moment, looking at Monday. Then he clucked to his horse and turned off on the trail, Devaux riding silently beside him.

Monday turned his attention back to the setting of the sun, watching the shifting colors and the changing shapes of clouds without interest. When the colors had faded and there remained no more than a thin, copper-green stain in the western sky, he got up slowly and went back into the cabin. Mechanically he kindled a fire in the fireplace and watched the yellow flames begin to work at the wood.

He went to the cooler below the floor in the rear and fumbled around among the paper-wrapped packages until his fingers touched the cold smooth surface of the bottle. He brought it back to the table and sat down. For a minute he stared at the growing fire, motionless. Then with a sudden gesture he yanked the cork out of the bottle and tilted it up, letting the raw fire burn his throat and savoring the pain of it. He put the bottle back down, blinking to clear his eyes.

"That's all," he said to the fire. "There's nothin' more to take away.

The fire flared and he watched it uninterestedly. After a while he put his head down on his arms and began to weep.

It seemed not grief so much as utter emptiness. A great vacuum had been made in the world, and the world did not acknowledge its existence. Night came and the stars came out, and somewhere in the sky the moon was riding, tonight a pale sliver slipping through the blackness. "Fingernail moon," she called it. Was that Shoshone? Or had she made it up? Now he would never know. There were many things he would never know now, all the answers to the questions he had not thought to ask. There was always time tomorrow for the forgotten questions of today. Until time ceased suddenly, and it was too late to ask.

In the tiny lagoon by the river, a frog lay half beneath the water, great bulbous eyes peering about at the world, a thick voice croaking in the night. A doe drank placidly at the beach, her forelegs in the water. She shook the droplets from her muzzle, sparkling in the moon, looked around her, and bent to drink again. Small animals rustled in the brush.

Too late for questions now, and in any event there were few enough answers. The ultimate answer was always the same; absence. Nothingness. Emptiness. There was now no reason to do anything. To light the fire was futile; it burned the wood and was gone. A man ate and his body used the food and it too was gone, having served no purpose but to keep him alive enough hours to find more food. An endless cycle of inutility, without reason, cause, or outcome.

A raccoon hunched silent by the river, puzzling at the bright and tantalizing image of the moon that wavered before it, infinitely attracting, infinitely mysterious in its shining. The raccoon looked around, black eyes bright and searching.

It was all over now. Hollowness, the ringing emptiness and gray cycle of day on day, planting, harvesting so you may survive the winter to plant and harvest again, under the cold indifferent sky.

By the lagoon a snake waited patiently, moving silently from time to time toward the frog's hoarse croaking. The raccoon tentatively reached out one fine and agile paw to touch the surface of the flickering moon. Shrews darted from their tree-root nests and foraged in the night with the terrible voracity of hunger. Owls flew.

2

Night emptied itself into the ocean. The eastern sky stretched thin and pale across the endless forest, and in time was visited by a hollow sun that climbed the day in a furious masquerade of life. Night passed; day came. The animals of darkness sought shelter in the dawn silence, and the animals of light blinked at the world.

Monday woke, remembering, and stood suddenly at the table. The fire was out. He sat back down again, resting his head on his arms, as he had slept. After a while he rose and went outside, not noticing the light except as absence of a darkness that had existed before. He walked down the slope toward the river and the blackberry patch. There was no one there. The little pile of dirt rested inert in the dawn, dark from the moistness of the night. During the day it would dry again, becoming light gray, and then the night wetness would come again, making it dark.

Summer would end in a flurry of rain that wet it down, and the leaden sky of winter would press it, flatten it, and when the spring came again grasses would begin to grow. Another summer, another fall—perhaps there would be clear, bright days in fall—and another winter . . .

He turned and went back into the cabin. The day stretched out vacantly before him and he did not know how he was to fill it. He made a small fire because it seemed appropriate, and there was nothing else to do. He stared at it, thinking about fires and cooking, his mind drifting aimlessly. He stood up again suddenly and looked around the cabin, but nothing had happened there. He absently swung the coffee pot in over the tiny pyramid of flame. After a moment he went outside and sat on the porch, but there was nothing to see. When he came back in, there was an acrid smell in the cabin, and he realized he had forgotten to put water in the pot. He swung it out away from the fire, watching the thin tendrils of oily blue smoke that drifted from the spout. Then he sat down again, his elbows propped on the table and his head supported by his hands, trying to remember if there was anything to do. There was nothing.

The day went in tiny spurts of consciousness, spaced by long intervals of unawareness. He discovered himself standing on the riverbank, watching the current, but could not remember coming down. He became aware that he was sitting again, staring at the fire, but the last he remembered clearly he had been standing. Somewhere.

The trails his mind followed into the future had all been blocked, save one. And that had begun to spiral in upon itself, twisting and writhing like a gut-shot coyote, without purpose or direction. The current of time had become unchanneled, losing self in an endless futile whirlpool that swirled around him, leaving the center still and empty, with only the vague awareness of motion at the perimeter.

The sun swung up and passed the center of the sky, and the level of the water-clear whisky in the bottle dropped slowly. He discovered as the morning passed that by spacing swallows he could maintain a blurred sensation of unreality, without emptying the bottle too quickly. In a circle around him as wide as his arms could reach, everything was unreal. Beyond that, perhaps there was solidity and actuality; but beyond the radius of his arms, nothing was important. It was a state that suited him, and what little concentration he could gather up he devoted to maintaining a veil between himself and the world around him. The numbness did not in any way remove pain, or longing; but it blunted the sharp edge of importance and made it more difficult for the lance of sudden anguish to dart unexpectedly into his mind.

The drifting bubble of futility remained whole until mid-afternoon. He had lost the conception of time, since there was nothing to mark one hour off from the next. It was all one, what existed and was no more, and what would be. The isolation of the cabin at the end of the trail was a help, for there was no distraction other than the silent progress of the sun. When he could hold his mind to it better, he thought he could maintain the silence and the lack of motion forever.

When he heard the soft plodding of a horse approaching he did not look up from the table.

When the door opened he was momentarily blinded by the brilliance of the afternoon sun that came flooding into the obscure dimness of the room. He looked over without interest and saw the thick figure of Meek silhouetted briefly against the cascading brightness of the doorframe. Then the marshal closed the door behind him and came to sit on the other side of the table from Monday, his face seeming somehow loose, without tone.

"You look like hell," Meek said after a moment.

Monday raised his shoulders in a light shrug. He lifted the bottle and rubbed his cheek with the smooth, cool, surface, looking over Meek's shoulder.

"Feelin' sorry for y'rself ain't goin' t'help nothin'," Meek said.

Monday said nothing. Meek put the flat of his hands on the table and looked around.

"Webb here?" he said.

Monday shook his head. "No."

"Where's he at?" Meek said.

"Down t' the coast," Monday said absently. He tilted the bottle up and took a long swallow.

"Where at down t' the coast?"

"Saddle Mountain, maybe."

Meek looked down at the table and swept a crumb off with the flat of his hand. "He tell y' that?"

Monday nodded.

Meek was silent again for a moment. Finally he pushed himself up and stood looking down at Monday. "You best come in t' town," he said.

"Don't feel like comin' in t' town."

"You best come in anyways. There's trouble."

Monday half laughed, turning the bottle in his hands, but the sound was faint. "I got troubles enough here," he said absently.

"Troubles past is past," Meek said without sympathy.

Monday inclined his head indifferently.

Deliberately Meek leaned over the table and slapped him with the back of his hand, his face set. "Straighten up, Jaybird," he said coldly.

Monday recoiled, his cheek stinging, anger beginning.

Meek braced himself against the table edge and said, "Get y'r gear an' come in t' town with me, hear?"

"No call t' do that, Meek," Monday said quietly.

"Call enough. There's trouble an' we're both in it up t' the ass. Preacher Andrews is dead. Webb kilt 'im last night."

Monday looked up, finally reached. He returned to the world with a sense of loss, his eyes cleared and he saw Meek's drawn face for the first time. He stood up unsteadily and looked down at the table planks, trying to sort it all out in his mind. "What happened?" he said finally.

Meek shrugged. "Put a hole in his gut the size of a punkin' an' took off."

Meek turned and started toward the door.

"Wait a minute," Monday said. "How come you're so damn sure it was Webb? There's other people hated that bastard."

Meek turned at the doorway and looked silently at Monday for a moment. "You find me another man in a thousand miles o' here that'd take the scalp."

Monday looked down at the table again.

"Get y'r gear an' come on."

3

Thurston was waiting for them in the dusk when the two horses pulled up before Meek's house. The small man's smooth face was hard and expressionless as he watched Meek and Monday dismount.

He stared coldly at Monday as he approached. Without taking his eyes away from the big man, Thurston said to Meek, "Why isn't this man handcuffed?"

"Handcuffed?" Monday said, looking up. "What the hell for?"

"Forgot t' tell y', Jaybird," Meek said disgustedly. "Y're under arrest. Court issued a warrant for y' this morning." He pushed past Thurston without looking at him and went in the house.

Monday heard Virginia's quiet voice say, "I did not let him in." He could not make out Meek's answer. Thurston stared at him for another long moment before he spoke.

"You had better come inside, Monday." He turned abruptly and followed Meek into the house.

Monday stood dazedly for a moment. He glanced at his horse, decided against it, and slowly followed the other two men. Inside, Virginia was just closing the door to the back room. A sudden image flashed across his mind at the sight of the door; a dark head almost lost in the whiteness of the sheets, the distant lassitude in her eyes, the softness of her hand on the blanket. . . . He closed his eyes for a moment, shocked physically by the suddenness of memory and pain. His fist clenched spasmodically.

When he opened his eyes Meek was coming back from the cupboard with a bottle and two tin cups. He clanked the cups down on the table and poured them half full, pushing one toward Monday.

Meek sat down heavily on the bench. He sighed once and lifted the cup, making no motion toward Thurston and saying nothing.

"And now illegal liquor," Thurston said contemptuously.

"Looks that way," Meek acknowledged dryly.

"Really, Marshal—" Thurston began.

"This is my house," Meek said flatly.

"What the hell am I under arrest for?" Monday said finally.

"That should be obvious," Thurston said. "As an accessory to the murder of the Reverend Andrews."

"Can they do that?" Monday said to Meek.

"Done it," Meek said.

"The arrangements for the interment have been made," Thurston said.

"Glad t' hear it."

"And the posse has been organized. The men will gather here at six o'clock tomorrow morning. You will swear them in, Meek."

For the first time Meek looked up at Thurston. With his eyes fixed on him, Meek took another deliberate sip from the cup. He smacked his lips and Thurston turned away with an expression of faint revulsion. Meek looked back at the fire.

"You're quite the organizer," he said.

"Someone has to do it," Thurston said sharply.

"Seems like posse-organizin' is the marshal's job," Meek said.

The room was cold and barren with hostility. Thurston finally snorted.

"You take too much on yourself, Governor," Meek said.

"Don't call me Governor," Thurston snapped.

"Slip o' the tongue," Meek said. "I forgot you ain't made it yet."

Thurston leaned forward, one hand braced against the table. "Meek, I'm not here to trade insults."

Monday finally looked up from the cup into which he had been staring during the exchange between the other two men. "Just what the hell *are* you here for?" he said quietly.

"To find out once and for all where you two stand."

Meek laughed shortly.

"Amuse yourself," Thurston said. "The posse will be here in the morning."

"Never needed a posse in my life," Meek said. "If I go after Webb I c'n do it alone."

Thurston laughed and took his hand away from the table. "Meek, you are utterly mad, do you understand that? Do you think you could be permitted to go after that killer alone? A personal friend?"

Meek reached back and got the bottle again, refilled his cup. "Meek's got friends," he said, watching the stream of liquid. "Marshal's got no friends."

Thurston shrugged. "A pretty theory."

"Thurston," Meek said slowly, "I hate your guts."

Thurston pursed his lips. "Pity," he said. He finally turned to Monday. "And you, my friend, are going with the posse."

Monday looked up at him incredulously. "Oh, no," he said. "I'm under arrest, remember?"

Thurston was silent for a moment. Then he said quietly, "Within ten days someone is going to hang for this murder. I don't care who it is. Do you understand me? This is your last chance in Oregon, Monday. And yours, Meek," he added. "That posse will set off in the morning and the two of you will be with it. It takes a beast to track a beast."

He turned suddenly from the table and walked out.

After the door had slammed behind him, neither of the others said anything for a long while. Finally Meek let his breath out explosively and slammed his cup down on the table. "Well," he said, "at least all the cards're face up now."

"Wagh! they are. Like the old woman said t' the cow with one foot in the milk pail, 'Get in 'r get out.' "

"Y'know what my problem is, Jaybird? I'm a honest man."

"Last chance in Oregon," Monday murmured contemptuously.

"Oh, I expect if it come t' that he c'd run us out slick enough. Run me out, anyways, an' hang you."

"Hell, he can't hang me. Not for somethin' Webb done."

Meek shook his head. "Jaybird, far's he's concerned we're all of us just as guilty as the old coon. An' this town is just about hot enough he could arrange it."

Monday looked down at his cup again.

"Well, I don't expect the hoss'll get caught less'n he wants to," Meek said.

Monday looked up suddenly. "Maybe he wants it," he said slowly.

Meek shrugged. "That's his own doin's, then."

"I don't know what t' do," Monday said helplessly. His shoulders ached and his head had begun to blur again from the liquor.

"If'n I was you," Meek said, "I b'lieve I'd take out when the marshal went t' sleep."

"Hard on the marshal."

Meek jerked his head impatiently. "That'n I c'n get by. Me, I'd head f'r the hills, like Rainy."

"He lit out?"

"He knew about it, I expect. Said he thought he'd wander off an' see his Conspiration a while."

Monday rested his forehead on his hand. "Well, that's just it, Meek. That's just exactly it. Rainy's got his Conspiration. Me, I got nothin'."

"Best think on it anyways."

"I thought about it. I thought about takin' out. But I got no place t' go." He looked up again helplessly, spreading his hands. "I just got no damn place in the world t' go."

He sat up late and, as the whisky ran out, began to sober. He lost the sense of confusion that had blanketed him, and his mind seemed to whet itself on the rough stone of fatigue and purgation. He felt empty still, but his mind cleared, and out of exhaustion he began to see things clearly, as they were, without the masking aureole of emotion.

More than the murder was involved, more than Webb, more than some abstract principle that might be called either justice or vengeance. Justice, he thought, was not in the game, or someone would have to pay for the death of Mary. The only question was—who? Andrews had paid for it, in equal coin, but it was a gesture of vengeance that had not touched the guilty. Thurston? Oregon City? Or himself. A way of life; could you convict a way of life for murder? Perhaps that, eventually, was the question that lay silently at the root.

He also became convinced that Meek was wrong. Thurston could not arrange the hanging of a man who had done nothing. Law was still administered by men like Judge Pratt, and the temper of the people would not move that one. But it was also clear that the murder had been a windfall for Thurston, giving him a tangible focus for the hatred, a lever to work against the indolence of the sheep.

One thing was strange; in thinking of Thurston he was never able to isolate the image of the dapper, hard little man. In Monday's mind there was always a shadowy crowd behind him, a constant faint murmur of assent.

In the lassitude of his drained emotions, Monday did not hate Thurston. He could never remember hating anyone, it was a feeling that seemed to be beyond his range. Thurston acted out of pressure, the pressure of the eternal shadowy crowd behind him. Like a rock dislodged by an avalanche he was, at root, incapable of controlling his own direction. Perhaps the rock, too, had illusions of leading the thunderous slide, but in the end all power came from the mass behind, and in time that mass would overtake and swallow the insignificant individual, and another take his place. In the end there were not leaders and followers, but only the relentless and inevitable rush of the mass, carrying everything before it.

He half laughed at his own image in the darkness of the cabin. It was just as well not to be in the way. But what did you do when you looked up and found you *were* in the way? Saw the wave of stone descending.

While Thurston could not hang him, there was no question that, with the power of the avalanche behind him, the little man could run Monday out of the Oregon Country. Could run them all, and the more he thought of that the more he thought it was what Thurston had in mind. With the murder of Andrews as his lever, Thurston could make life in the settlement intolerable for all the mountain men. All the *ex*-mountain men, Monday thought. We're nothin' now, neither one thing nor the other.

And in the end he came back to the same realization; there was no place to go. They were the pariahs, the ones that didn't fit. They smelled of wolf, and in any settlement it would be the same. Suspicion, hatred, sidelong glances in the streets. Like the Indians. Andrews had said it, something like. It wasn't the Indian's hatchet that was dangerous, but the simple fact that he existed.

Monday sighed, feeling the ache in his shoulders and the small of his back intensely. He got up from the table and grabbed the blanket Meek had left out for him. He took off his moccasins and stacked them for a pillow. Lifting his legs stiffly, he tucked the edges of the blanket under, one after the other, and let his head rest on the soft leather, looking up at the ceiling. He felt numb and without will.

He closed his eyes and played an old game with himself. He imagined that his feet faced the other direction and the fire was to his right, instead of the left. He tried to sense the presence of the table on the *left* side, he visualized the door as being at his head. After a moment he felt it that way, and opened his eyes suddenly. There was a shock, as the physical reality abruptly contradicted the image he had firmly in his mind.

There was an odd contrast between Thurston's usual cajoling reasonableness and the blunt hostility of the evening. And Monday wondered if it might not have been deliberate, an attempt to make them angry. If he and Meek did refuse the hunt for Webb, so much the better for Thurston. It would show the shadowy crowd they approved of murder, and were thus guilty themselves. And that would be the end. Another year for them, perhaps, but finally the rolling avalanche would swallow them up, as in time it would swallow Thurston himself, crushing them all beneath the mindless, thundering weight.

He rolled to one shoulder, moving his legs to untwist the blanket. He watched the dying fire for a while, then closed his eyes again and shifted his head into the hollow of the moccasin pillow.

A man was nothing but crazy to run uphill against a rock slide. But there was a chance to survive if he went along with it. The only chance he had. Go along or go under.

Chapter Sixteen

The old man rode steadily through the night, twisting up through the hills that ranged along the west bank of the Willamette. As the sky behind him lightened with the coming dawn he was emerging on the broad flat called Twality Plains. It would be nearly a full day's ride across, and he was tired. At dawn he stopped for a few minutes to stretch himself and sit with his back against a tree while the horse grazed. They had a long way go.

"Wagh!" he muttered. "This nigger's gettin' too old f'r this kind o' doin's."

There had been a time, and it did not seem long ago, when forced marches through the night were nothing to him. A bad cast of the dice and he might sit the saddle for forty-eight hours or more, running from the Bloods, chasing the Crows. It didn't matter in the long run, a few hours' sleep after, and he was fit again. It was all different now, but he had not really learned to pace himself. He still demanded as much as ever of the bony old cadaver in which he lived, and was always surprised when it gave signs of objecting.

"Hya!" he called. Obediently the horse came over and waited while the old man mounted. "Move," he said, nudging with his heels.

The sun was warm on his back as the morning grew, and he let it soak into him gratefully. The horse plodded steadily along and the old man half drowsed in the saddle. From under the brim of the loose felt hat he watched the country go by, green-black of the ever-present firs, the greenish gold of ripening wheat in the fields he passed. There was a lot of settling on these plains, he thought.

Several times he passed within shouting distance of cabins, but he did not stop. Ahead of him there was only an endless gentle rolling of the land, soft hills all crested with a fur of evergreens. The silence was good. The sun warmed him and warmed the land, a golden flood that rolled gently with the hills, filling the earth and sky with light.

"Pretty country, right enough," he said admiringly, looking around. A little soft, a little bit too rich, but pretty for all of that. No country for him, but he could see how a man might learn to love it.

Toward midday he stopped again. He gently guided his animal into a clump of fir, far enough in that he could not be seen from the trail. He did not expect anyone, but the middle of the day made him a little nervous. He figured he would have a good twenty-four hours before they took after him in earnest. He picketed the horse and stretched himself beneath the heavy web of branches to sleep for an hour or so.

Above him there was a light breeze, threading softly through the limbs, disturbing them just enough to make a steady rustling that was strangely comforting. The sun came through in tiny spots, but the canopy of fir was too dense to let much in. He slept in the shelter of a green grotto, with the ground beneath him soft from the packed and matted needles.

He wakened quickly when it was time. He looked around him at the mass of brush, and he might have been anywhere. The world ended in undergrowth a few feet from where he lay. He sat up, blinking. He was still tired, but the nap would carry him through to the end of the day all right. He intended to have a full night's sleep tonight, and tomorrow morning it would all be new.

He leaned back against the tree under which he had slept, wriggling, scratching his back comfortably, grateful for the simple physical sensation. He sighed and sat still for a moment, his bony wrists hanging over his knees, his head bent, letting himself wake up fully.

He untied the fresh scalp that hung from his belt and put it beside him on the ground. He pressed and smoothed it with his hands, trying to flatten it out, but it had begun to stiffen as it dried, and remained half folded. He looked down at it, the dark brown hair that seemed both unnaturally short and the wrong color. It wasn't like a scalp a man might be proud of, he thought. The long, sleek black hair, the hair of a fighting man who kept it long just to challenge you to take it. It wasn't really a scalp at all, just the hair of a dunghead white man. It didn't mean anything; wasn't worth a dance. And in any event, there was nobody left to dance for his victory.

"Wagh!"

Absently he fingered the two long locks that hung beneath his hat, braiding one of them and shaking it out.

Twenty-four hours, maybe more. They wouldn't find the body until morning. And then they'd do a vast lot of running around before they finally buckled down to do anything about it. He chuckled a little, thinking of the confusion. When *he* wanted to go, he got up and went. Didn't have to tell nobody, make a pack of damn fool arrangements. Just go, when he got it into his head to go. That was the way he liked it. He mounted again and started off.

He left the scalp of Andrews lying on the ground to rot as the year turned round. It had disappointed him, and he didn't have to do with things that disappointed him.

The sun was ahead of him now, as he rode into the afternoon. The brilliance and heat made the earth itself seem luminous and, despite the shade of his hat, he had to squint to see. Light rose up from the ground in waves that shifted before him, distorting the solid reality of the hills and forests into shivering planes of distance.

By the middle of the afternoon he was within sight of the first peaks of the Coast Range rising abruptly from the gently rolling country of the plains. In the waves of heat that stood between him and the mountains was an impression of flowing water, as though he looked at the distant peaks through some soft and golden sea.

In his mind he checked off another point with the sensation of satisfaction. Now he had seen it, the Coast Range. As he had seen the Bighorns and the Medicine Bow and the Wind Rivers and the Tetons and the Blues and the Cascades. As he had seen a hundred ranges that had no name, but were clear and sharp in his mind.

As mountains went, the peaks of the Coast Range did not amount to much. Not really mountains at all, just bigger hills, he thought. Still, he had set his mind to see them, and he had seen them. Sometimes at night, just before he went to sleep, he liked to go over in his mind the mountains he had seen, numbering them off, bringing them again before his eyes with the perfect accuracy of his imagination, caressing the granite cliffs that dropped a thousand feet, glissading over the long basalt slopes, counting the folded layers of red and gold and a thousand colors without name as he had seen in the canyon of the Green River. He counted his mountain ranges as a miser counts his money, each piece carefully examined and dropped into the box of memory.

He sat for a moment, guarding the first sight he had of this new range, storing it away carefully with the others. Then he nudged the horse into motion again and moved off slowly toward the peaks that swam in the heat of the afternoon.

2

Monday was wakened by the sound of voices outside the cabin. He sat up, blinking the sleep from his eyes, and kicked the twisted blanket away from his legs. From the closed door that led to Meek's bedroom he heard a lower murmur. Meek opened the door and leaned out.

"Made y'r mind up, hoss?" he said.

Monday nodded. "Ain't much choosin' t' do, when y' get right down to 'er."

Meek looked at him for a moment. "All right," he said finally. "Go on out an' make the boys t' home." He came into the main room and lifted his rifle down from the pegs over the fireplace. "I got t' check this here gun," he said. In a louder voice he called, "Virginia! You 'bout ready?"

Virginia's gentle voice from the bedroom said, "A minute, Joe."

"Virginia's takin' the kids over t' Doc Newell's."

Monday nodded. He stood up and went to the door, opened it in the bright morning sun. There were fifteen or so men clustered outside talking, and he could see another half-dozen coming, among them Thurston.

The conversation stopped when he came out on the porch, and several of the men looked at him curiously. For a moment they were silent. Then one of them, with whom he'd talked often at the mill, said in a jocular tone, "What the hell are you doin' loose, Monday? I heard they was a warrant out f'r you."

Monday rubbed the back of his neck ruefully. "That's fact," he admitted. Thurston and the other five men had drawn near now, and Monday added in a voice loud enough for them to hear, "Except it must o' been some kind o' mistake, though. Y'know, there's *some* around here gets awful excited when things ain't organized just right."

There was some laughter, and the men near the porch turned to grin at Thurston. "*That's* sure god truth," somebody said, snickering.

Still mounted, Thurston rode up to the porch and looked coldly at Monday, who leaned casually against a post.

"Well, Monday?" he said, unsmiling.

"Well, Thurston," Monday said affably.

There was a moment of awkward silence, and one of the farmers turned away, stifling a laugh. Thurston glanced angrily at him, then turned back to Monday.

"Are you decided?"

Monday looked up in surprise. "Why, surely," he said. "Are you?"

"What does that mean?" Thurston snapped.

"No harm intended," Monday said. "Just didn't seem reasonable a man'd set himself for a few days' hard ridin' dressed like that."

Thurston was neat in his dark coat and vest, as usual, and made an odd contrast with the other members of the posse, farmers dressed in their worn denims and heavy, dust-gray shoes.

"I thought maybe there was a church service or somethin'," Monday said. "Say, any o' you fellows got a little tobacco?" The man who had spoken to Monday first grinned and stretched out his tobacco pouch. The rest of them were watching Thurston with unconcealed amusement. Monday slowly unfolded the pouch and got out his pipe. He let himself slide down the post until he was sitting on the porch.

"The way I dress is certainly no concern of yours, Monday," Thurston said sharply.

"No sir," Monday said, a little humble. "Just seems like it sort of—spoils the organization, like."

"What kind of game are you—" Thurston broke off as Virginia came out of the cabin, followed by the three half-breed children. They walked quickly off the porch past Monday, not looking at anyone.

"Where's Meek?" Thurston demanded as the woman passed. Virginia did not answer, but moved through the crowd with her children, not even turning to acknowledge that she had heard.

"Try pretty please," Monday said absently. He tamped the tobacco down in the pipe bowl and handed the pouch back. He looked calmly up at Thurston. "Do we get t' wear them little blue hats again?" he said.

This time the laughter was general, and the farmers made no attempt to suppress it. It was obvious they were thoroughly enjoying Thurston's discomfiture. The amusement stopped suddenly, cut off by the echoing roar of a discharging gun inside the house.

For a moment the crowd stood frozen with shock. Then Monday leaped up and slammed through the door, just in time to see the bedroom door open and Meek appear, supporting himself with both hands, his face white and twisted with pain.

"Meek! What hap—"

"She went off." Meek grunted.

Monday grabbed him under the arms and supported him. The right leg of Meek's denim trousers was blackened and there was a dark, wet stain spreading through the lower part. Monday helped him back into the bedroom and put him on the bed. The long rifle was lying on the floor, the barrel still smoking, and the room was full of blue smoke and the acrid smell of burned powder.

A dozen men had piled into the house after Monday and clustered around the bed. Monday snatched out his knife and ripped the trouser leg down from the knee.

"Checkin' the flint," Meek said, with effort. "She—went off." The bedclothes were absorbing a spreading brown stain. The hole was clean, through the fleshy part of the calf, and the blood that drained from it was very dark.

"Somebody go for Doctor Beth," Monday snapped. There was the sound of running feet across the main room, and in a second the loud "Hya!" as the man mounted and set off at a full gallop.

"It ain't bad," Monday said, sponging away the blood with the corner of a muslin sheet. "Didn't get the bone. Y're damn lucky, Meek."

Meek grunted.

"Any dunghead that'd check his flint with a full charge in—" Monday broke off suddenly and glanced up at the set face of Meek. The wounded man opened his eyes slightly and met Monday's regard steadily.

Thurston had shouldered his way through the crowd and was standing at Meek's head. "Meek," he said evenly. "You did this deliberately."

There was a vaguely discontented murmur from the crowd behind Thurston, and Monday straightened up to stare at the smaller man.

"Thurston," he said, "you go too far."

"By *god*, you do," one of the farmers said angrily. "I know you set your cap against these boys, but you got no call t' say somethin' like that!"

Thurston whirled to look at the speaker, but the other did not turn away. The balance had suddenly shifted. Meek was too well liked. Another farmer pushed forward and said, "No man goin' t' shoot hisself just t'spite you, Thurston. Now you leave off, hear?"

There was a general mutter of agreement.

Monday bent back down to Meek. "How y' feelin', hoss?"

Meek clenched his teeth and moved his leg slightly. The brownish stain was now nearly eight inches across on the bedclothes, but the heavy flow of blood seemed to have lessened. Meek looked up and tried to grin. "Smarts some," he said.

"Take it easy, Joe," somebody said sympathetically.

"Ain't got much choice," Meek said.

Thurston wheeled and left the room, passing through the crowd of men who stared at him without expression.

A few minutes later Dr. Beth came striding up the porch with her instrument case, panting a little from the hard ride. She plowed into the crowd without a word and leaned over the bed, examining the wound.

After a moment she straightened up. "Get out of here, you men," she said. "Get, now!"

Slowly the group filed back out into the main room, muttering in an undertone.

"You get out, too," Beth said to Monday. She wiped away the new blood from around the wound. "This is nothing," she said finally. "Just a flesh wound. You're a lucky man, Joe, if she don't infect."

Monday looked down at Meek, whose face was not now so distorted with pain.

"Well, Marshal," he said.

"Just Meek," said the other. "Man can't do much marshalin' with a hole in his leg."

"Kind o' the hard way, ain't it?"

"Ever' man's got t' find his own way," Meek said. "In this hooraw she's devil take the hindmost."

"Monday, I asked you to get out of here," Beth said.

Monday looked at Meek for another moment. He went to the door, stopped and looked back.

"Take care o' y'rself," he said.

Meek gestured casually. "I'm out of it," he said.

Monday shook his head and went out into the main room.

"Good luck, Jaybird," Meek called after him.

Monday heard Beth say, "You're damned happy for a shot man." He could not hear Meek's answer. He closed the front door of the cabin behind him and walked out on the porch. The heads of the talking men all turned toward him. Thurston stood apart, alone.

"Well?" Thurston said.

Monday looked at him, then let his eyes shift over the crowd of men waiting expectantly. He stepped down off the porch.

"He's got better'n a full day's start on us," Monday said. "An' he's travelin' alone. But we c'n make it up."

"We don't even know what direction he headed," one of the men objected.

"Maybe Monday knows more than we," Thurston said.

"Maybe I do," Monday said evenly. "He's headed down t' the coast, Saddle Mountain."

"How do you know that?"

"It don't matter how I know," Monday said. "If we take a boat downriver to Skipanon landing we c'n make up the start he's got on us."

Thurston came over to him. "Monday, if you're leading us astray to give him time—that's a hundred-mile trip . . ."

Monday shrugged. "Frankly, I don't give a damn. You got any better ideas?"

Thurston was silent, then turned away. The carpenter named Bill said, "Look's like we got t' take Monday's word or forget it. It's a big country."

"Yeah, but what *I* want t' know is, who's t' pay passage on the boat," one of the others said.

Monday spread his hands. "This here's more or less official, ain't it? T' keep law and order in the territory? I expect the territorial government'll pay."

"That'll take months, the way them boys work."

Monday looked at Thurston. "Well, them as has money might pay now, an' the territorial government'll pay 'em back when they get around to it."

"Hell, I got no money," somebody muttered. "I didn't figure it was going t' cost a man any *money* t' be on this here posse."

"Lessn y' lost y'r taste for huntin'," Monday said to Thurston.

"All right," Thurston said finally. "It can be arranged. But I'm warning you, Monday, if this is a ruse of some sort, you will regret it."

"Maybe we best settle that out right now," Monday said, rubbing his neck. "Seems t' me you ain't so eager t' get Webb as you appeared yesterday. You want him or not?"

"I'll have him," Thurston said. "A vicious murder like this can't be overlooked, Monday, even if one of your friends committed it."

"Well, now," Monday said. "You're making a big thing out o' that. But it ain't me draggin' my feet an' makin' speeches. I'm ready t' go."

"If you two are going t' stand around making faces at each other we ain't none of us going any place," somebody muttered.

"Take y'r choice, Thurston," Monday said. "I'm trying t' get along. If you don't want me on this hunt, you just say so in front of ever'body an' we'll know where we stand."

Thurston looked at Monday, then at the twenty or so men who stood waiting, their faces impatient. He turned and walked back to the sleek bay mare and mounted. "Come along, then," he said. He turned the horse and started off toward the center of town and the boat landings at the edge of the river. Monday watched him go silently. Gradually the others mounted and set off behind the small man.

It was surprising, Monday thought. But not really, in the end. He watched the train of horses form behind Thurston. They followed whoever moved first or talked loudest. It was just damn near that simple.

He shook his head in wonder and mounted. They ought to make Young's Bay at the mouth of the Columbia by nightfall, with luck. Then, in the morning, it would start.

3

The sun was already beginning to lower steadily when the old man reached the steep hills that were the first ramparts of the Coast Range. They began abruptly, sweeping up from the plain without transition, and he was pleased. It was clear and distinct; here the plain ends, here the mountain begins. There was a cleanness that satisfied something in him.

A stream ran along the foot, and the old man briefly considered making camp there, then decided against it. He was certain he had a good twenty-four hours, but if somebody should come up behind, it was too exposed.

He dismounted and walked down to the edge of the stream, knelt beside it to drink. He had only a few hours of daylight left, a few miles into the hills, and the chances were he'd have to make dry camp. Beside him his horse dipped into the water, the reins dragging beneath the hoofs. The old man straightened up and looked around him, stretching his neck and letting the water settle. Then he bent down again, wanting to fill his belly. There was nothing so treacherous on the trail as the sudden appearance of thirst, which took a man's mind off everything else and made him careless. He didn't want that to happen.

After a few minutes he mounted again and started up the trail that wound across the range. He rode slowly into the sun, not hurrying, letting the animal find the pace that suited her. His first day or two in mountains he did not know was always a great pleasure for him. He liked to go without haste, letting the structure and appearance of the land soak into his bones, looking everywhere, listening, watching, feeling.

It was a constant miracle, and he had never lost his sensation of wonder at the variety of the world. Everything different, everything unique, each stone and tree and blade of grass different from every other. Behind each apparent likeness there was a thin, bright core of difference, and in the end, no two things were really like. It was a thing he had always loved to feel, the basic solitude of each thing that existed in the world. Without possible number, and his brain whirled when he tried to think how *many* things there might be, if you could count them.

The sun disappeared behind the hills ahead just after he crossed the first ridge. He rode a little farther on, just to understand the feeling of dusk in these hills.

Finally he moved off the trail a few yards into the brush and made camp. It was perfectly arbitrary; he would sleep where the night had caught him, and he knew he would not remember the camp. He liked to have at least an hour to look around and pick a campsite, so he would remember it, be able to bring it back to his mind at some other time. But he did not feel he had the time, and that hour was better used this day in going farther on. Tomorrow might be different.

He picketed the horse and settled down, permitting himself to realize for the first time just how tired he was. There was a tension across the back of his shoulders and his neck was stiff. The muscles in his forehead were strained from squinting ahead into the sun all afternoon, and he rubbed the back of his hand across them, trying to work out some of the strain.

Finally he sighed and went over to the saddlebags. He had filched some jerky from Monday's larder, and he took out a handful of the leathery black strips and went back to sit under a fir, resting his back against the rough bark. Absently he chewed on the strips, staring unseeing at the brush ahead of him. The jerky had been overdried and was brittle. He decided tomorrow night he would have to have a camp with water so as to soften it up a bit.

The pearl gray of the sky, dimly glimpsed through the mat of limbs above him, was darkening rapidly when he finished. In the deep forest of Oregon night came too quickly, and the old man was jealous of

light. He got out his blanket and rolled himself up, fidgeting around
to locate a position where the stones and fallen sticks on the ground
did not dig into his old frame too deeply.

He let his mind wander, enjoying the unnamable period that was
neither waking nor sleeping. Before he had left the mountains, the real
mountains, he had made himself out a sort of list. It was in the way of
a promissory note to himself, things he granted himself for the pleasure
of it. Sitting around his lodge fire at night, he had carefully constructed
in his mind the shape of events that might occur, and had chosen
between them.

He was nearly at the end of his promises now, having seen the sun
rise and set on the Columbia River, having ridden through the
Wallowas, having observed the habits of the high plateau people he
had passed in the east, having seen his first tame Indians.

There were three things left, and as he drowsed he regretfully
realized that he would not be able to do them all; there was not time
enough left. He wanted to see the ocean, he wanted to climb to the top
of Saddle Mountain, which he had been told was the highest peak of
this range, and he wanted to see some of the men he had known, who
were now settled down on the coast: Ebberts and Trask and Solomon
Smith, all of them on the strip south of the Columbia they called Clatsop
Plains.

He would not have time for all that now. One of his promises to
himself would have to be broken, and it made him uncomfortable.
When he settled his mind to do something, it ate at him if he could
not do it. But he would have to give up the idea of seeing the men. The
land was more important, in the end.

He was beginning to feel the pressure of time. Twenty-four hours
was not really much, when you thought about it. When you had to
pick your spot, and make whatever preparations the site seemed to
require.

Though he remembered how much the Gros Ventres had been able
to do in Pierre's Hole, in just one night. After Godin shot the headman
they'd holed up in a cottonwood grove, the whole damned village.

He chuckled a little to himself, thinking about it. *Some,* now, he
thought sleepily. They must have worked like beavers all night, because

by the next morning they'd made a regular little fort inside that cottonwood grove. And *wa'n't* Billy Sublette surprised when he sneaked in there to look!

"Him an' Sinclair an' that crazy Boston nigger a-crawlin' on their bellies. Billy parts some bushes an' *wagh!* Ball catches ol' Sinclair right atween his eyes an' Billy hisself takes one in the leg. *Well,* they come a-slidin' back with big eyes. Nobody never did figure out how them niggers got such a fort built up in one night."

Of course, there had been a whole village of Gros Ventres to work that night in Pierre's Hole, eighteen years ago. And he was alone. That made the whole difference right there; he was alone.

He woke with the false dawn and was on the trail again fifteen minutes later. By the time the first direct rays of the rising sun touched him he was several miles from where he had slept.

He was now coming into country that suited him better. With the ending of the flat land the ugly traces of man ended. Here there were no scars on the face of the land where man had cut and burned and ripped the earth with his filthy metal plows. It was something he could not understand, this mindless violation of what existed and was good; the insensate drive to make the world conform to man's size and comprehension, the violent rape of the earth by which he spread his ugly and diseased seed. It was a futile thing, a witless viciousness, and there were times when the thought of it made the old man sick. He did not understand any of it, and yet he had seen that, for some, there was a meaning and importance that escaped him, and that was frightening. They gained something from all this ugliness and destruction, something he did not know. They broke their lives against the stones of the earth, and killed joy and freedom with their grimness, and seemed to think their lives were good in proportion as they suffered in destroying what was natural.

He shook his head, and the long black locks swung beneath his hat. "Pack o' dunghead bastards, ever' one of 'em." It made no sense, and it infuriated him that the insistent plague of humankind should spread so quickly through this senseless massacre of the earth.

But here there was only the trail to mark man's passing, a fragile thread that twisted through the hills that had existed since the world began. They were all around him now, the timeless hills, matted thick and black with forest, ahead, behind, on all sides. They stretched away in endless marching ranks, and in the vastness of the hills the trail was no more than the silken thread of a fallen spider web. It served, briefly, and would be gone again with the new morning; gone in the lifetime of a man. There would be other trails to other destinations, as the whimsy of the spreading disease determined. And they too would disappear, swallowed in the brush that swelled in one season to fill up the scratches man had made. They would all be gone. And man would be gone. And the hills would remain.

It was just after the middle of the day when he began to think he had crossed the crest. It was a difficult thing to tell. Hills towered ahead and behind, cutting off his view, but he thought the trail was going down more often than up, now. It was a strange thing, this mountain he was searching for, strange that the highest peak should be so far from the spine of the range itself. He shrugged, indifferently. Each range was unique, and this one no less than the others he had known.

He came out on a clear slope, inexplicably free of heavy timber, solid-packed with brush chest high. He looked across the little valley at the hills on the opposite side. While the sides of the ravine were steep, there was something soft about the peaks. They were rounded and somehow gentle. Like the flesh of the earth, as the mountains of his home were like the bones themselves.

Squaw tits, he thought absently, looking at the rounded hills across the valley. *Les Tétons*, old Pierre would've called 'em. But old Pierre called everything *tétons* that had any faint likeness to a woman's breasts. And since all mountains are somewhat like, Pierre was a happy man; the world was full of *tétons* for his appreciation.

The thought made the old man obscurely unhappy, reminding him of the only *tétons* he gave a damn for, the range between Pierre's Hole and Jackson's Hole; standing tall and awesome. He had tried to climb the tallest of them, too, to stand on top and look around; but he could not do it. He had tried three times and had never found the right way to do it. It was one of the great defeats of his life, and he had never forgotten it. But he was secretly a little proud of the mountain for having resisted him.

"Wagh! That's a *mountain*, now," he said to the horse.

He glared across at the wooded slope of the opposite hill defiantly, suddenly ashamed of the softness of its contours, the gentleness of the peak.

"Squaw mountains." He leaned over to the side and spat deliberately on the trail. Roughly he jerked the reins and started off again. As he passed beneath the trees, his vision of the other hill was cut off.

"Goddamn bad country to go under in," he muttered. "Soft, *wagh!* Men soft, mountain soft." In some strange way he was humiliated for the softness of the land, as though it were himself.

Old Pierre was dead now, damn his eyes. Never could trust a Iroquois, anyway.

"*All* gone under now," he said, chuckling to himself. "Ever'one o' the dungheads." Damn good riddance. He suddenly reined up, the abruptness of the gesture making the scalp locks swing across his chest.

"Hya!" He wheeled the bony horse around and drummed his heels into its ribs viciously, startling it into a gallop. Reaching the open spot on the trail again, he reined back and slid off the saddle while the mouth-sore animal was still rearing.

"Damn soft squaw mountains," he muttered, throwing the reins on the ground. He walked to the very edge of the trail and stood facing the hills with his hands on his hips.

"TEVANITAGON!" he shouted across. He waited for a moment, but only the faintest of echoes came rippling back, "Tevanitagon . . ."

"KAYENQUARETCHA!"

It was unsatisfactory; the echo was so small he could hardly hear the names. He wanted the mountain to shout back at him, but it was too soft.

"MIAQUIN!

"KARAHOUTON!

"SAWENREGO!"

One by one he screamed the names of every Iroquois trapper he could remember. When he had finished, he stood silent for a moment, watching the waves of light roll over the peaks, molding them in shadow and sun. All around him was a smothering silence, all other living creatures frightened by his rasping, harsh voice.

"They was *men*, by God," he said softly.

His horse had stood quietly through the whole of it, accustomed through the long years to the inexplicable insanities of the man. He picked up the reins and mounted again.

"We best move on right smart," he told the horse. He wanted to have time to look for a decent campsite tonight; he had not liked the blank anonymity of last night's camp. It gave nothing to remember.

It was good to hear their names again, though, he thought. He was glad he'd done it. Maybe he'd give this squaw country somethin' to think on, hear the names of men like that. Damn their dirty brownskin souls.

"All gone under now," he said to himself.

Worthless dungheads all, but he missed them. And there'd be nobody to shout his name for him, nobody left at all.

He threw back his head and screamed into the sun.

"WEBB! ME, WEBB!"

Then he let his head drop forward in silence. He rode on, hunched over the saddle horn, letting the horse go on its own toward the mountain where he would make his stand. He didn't care about it any more, one way or the other.

I

The breakers rumbled in Monday's ear, and he thought he could feel the vibration of them through the sand of the beach itself. He shifted his position in the blanket cocoon, digging a little hole for his hip in the sand. He glanced at the watch fire, with its two lonely guards, and snorted. Right in the middle of Clatsop Plains and they mount a guard, he thought. When daylight came they'd be able to see two, three cabins around the little bay; and in any case the Clatsops hadn't made any trouble for anybody for twenty years or better, and then not much. They were good and tame.

He shrugged to himself and shifted again. He couldn't seem to get comfortable, couldn't get to sleep. Around the fire, dimly lit by the flames, were the blanket rolls of the other members of the posse. They looked like the droppings of some monstrous dog that had come out of the sea to foul the land.

God damn, he thought, that's somethin' Webb'd say. He was even beginning to think like the old coon.

They were scared, all of them. Always scared. They huddled around the fire, staying close together for comfort and security, sleeping peacefully under the eye of the guards. He wondered vaguely what the hell they'd do if something actually happened. He was obscurely tempted to give a wild whoop or fire off his gun or something, just to watch 'em run. Scared of the dark, scared of the mystery in it.

And the trip down on the steamboat had been a farce, more like a children's picnic outing to the beach than anything else; a children's game he soon grew bored with watching. They weren't really interested in chasing down Webb. For many of them he supposed it was just a sort of holiday. Somebody told them they had to do it, so they did it. But they didn't care about Webb, they weren't interested. They weren't interested in anything except standing around the mill and predicting doom and disaster for the coming year.

It had been so easy to take the lead away from Thurston in the morning. As long as you were one jump ahead, the crowd was with you; always on the side of the man who could humiliate somebody else. It was the one skill truly worthy of admiration, because it was the one they all envied.

But there was no permanence to any of it, no real malice. They shifted back and forth like seaweed swinging in the tide, they drifted with the prevailing wind, soft, pliable. Because, at root, they did not care. They simply needed somebody to follow, like any other herd. As long as they did not have to be responsible for their own actions they were content.

All that he could understand. What he did not really understand was how there could be strength. How combining ten soft men could make something hard. And yet he knew it was true. At some point the herd, only contemptible, became the avalanche, which was irresistible in its power. It was this transformation he could not comprehend, could not visualize. The power of combination that made it possible for the avalanche to swallow up a man like Webb, worth a dozen of them.

And if it had been easy for him to take the lead from Thurston, it was no less easy for Thurston to take it back, on the way down. It was he who had given the long river passage its air of holiday, digging up whisky some place, passing it around to the eagerly outstretched cups, smiling, winking, conspiratorial. Monday wondered vaguely how it came about in Thurston's mind that whisky ceased to be Sinful when it became Useful.

He had watched with disgust, depressed and unwilling to make the effort to do anything. He wasn't interested in a battle of authority with Thurston, and in the end it was probably his own indifference that would settle it. He had even taken his own pitiful dollop of whisky, thanking the little man automatically, cursing himself when he saw the faint grin of triumph on Thurston's face. In the long run it didn't matter. He had stopped Thurston from rolling over him in the morning, and that was all he wanted. He was here. There could be no backhanded rumors about the murderousness of mountain men. He was here, playing the citizen, and the fact was enough.

The rollers swept across the face of the ocean, driven by the power of a thousand rollers that followed. They touched bottom near the coast, reared up and arched, fell smashing against the sand with the rumble of distant thunder. Foam and spray scattered in the night winds like a thousand filmy spider webs wrenched loose from the deep green mass. One after another they followed, endlessly the same, and the bursts of thunder were lost in one another, tangled and muted and transformed into the steady rumble that shook the sand.

He was here, and that was enough. He was not guilty.

The sky was light long before the sun appeared. Blocked off by the humped peaks of the Coast Range, the sun never came to the coast itself until an hour or more past real dawn.

The assorted farmers stirred around the fire with first light, blinked and sat up, wondering why they were here. Some of them had never seen the ocean, and it was a bewildering sort of thing, a thousand flat miles and nothing in sight, like the plains of the Midwest they had crossed to reach the promised land of Oregon.

"What the hell do y' suppose is on the other side?" one of them said.

"Japan, they say."

"Must be one hell of a long way," said the first man, staring fascinated at the endless expanse of nothingness.

" 'Bout as far as the moon, I expect."

"Hell, it's farther than *that*. I c'n *see* the moon."

Monday saddled his horse and rode over to where Thurston was giving orders about the preparation of the morning meal.

"I'm goin' t' ride over t' Solomon Smith's," Monday said. "Get a idee from him about the lay o' the land."

Thurston looked up at him suspiciously. "Thought you'd been down here before."

"I have," Monday said.

"All right," Thurston said after a moment.

Monday turned his horse away and started walking him down the beach. He had gone only a few yards when he heard Thurston's voice behind him call, "Monday!"

He reined up and turned in the saddle to look back.

"I expect you'll be coming back?" Thurston said.

"I'll be back."

The men gathered around the fire were all looking at him, and Monday realized Thurston was starting his day's campaign early. It was just a gibe, something to put a little doubt in the minds of the men who overheard. He started off again, shaking his head.

Monday cut across the long sand spit to the half-moon bay that was the outlet of some river or other. The tide was in, and the bay a shining circle of water, perhaps a quarter of a mile across, the surface lightly rippled in the breeze that came gently off the sea. He skirted the edge, a row of low sand bluffs at his left, and in half an hour was within sight of Solomon Smith's cabin.

There were three Indian women sitting against the wall of the cabin, sunning themselves as they worked at some task Monday could not see. As he approached one of them got up and scuttled inside the cabin. The other two moved away.

Solomon appeared at the door, his long figure seeming to stoop as he came out, the ever-present pipe clenched in his teeth. Monday rode up, greeting him, and dismounted.

"What're y' feelin' like, Solomon?" he said, extending his hand.

"Pretty fair, Jaybird. How's y'rself?"

"Good enough."

"Have a pipe?" Solomon said. He handed over his tobacco pouch and Monday lowered himself against the wall in the sun.

"What the hell's goin' on, Jaybird?" Smith said curiously. "What's all the hooraw about?"

Monday looked up, a little surprised. "How'd you know there was a hooraw at all?"

Smith laughed, taking the pipe out of his mouth. "Hell, y' can't unload twenty armed men an' a barge full o' animals without somebody gettin' a bit curious about it. Where'd y' sleep?"

"Up the beach a little ways. It was nearin' dark when we got to the landing, so we just come down a bit an' settled in."

"Looks like a war," Smith observed.

"Approximately," Monday said. "Posse. Y' remember old Webb?"

Smith nodded. "Been up t' the valley for a month or so, him."

"He killed a man couple o' nights ago."

Solomon looked down at the ground. "Allus was sort o' wild, Webb." After a moment he added, "What makes y' think he's comin' down here?"

"Told me so," Monday said.

Smith looked at him in surprise, but said nothing. Monday asked him about trails in to Saddle Mountain.

"No problem," Smith said. He picked up a stick and began to draw in the dirt. "There's the big trail that goes across the mountains into the valley," he said. "Running east and west. 'Bout ten miles inland it gets cut by a north-south trail. South branch runs all the way down to Killamook country. North winds around a bit and ends up at Saddle Mountain, more or less. Clatsops used to think it was a sacred mountain, had ceremonies o' one kind and another. Highest peak around."

"No more."

"No more," Smith said. "Not for years. Y' can't miss the branch. There's a big cairn o' rocks where the Killamooks leave trading stuff sometimes."

"Thought this was all Clatsop country around here."

"It is. Sort of unofficial agreement. Long as the Killamooks stay to the trail, nobody'll bother 'em up to the crossroads. Sometimes when they get bored they bring a batch of junk up and leave it at the cairn. Clatsops go take what they c'n use, leave junk o' their own."

"Don't seem reasonable."

Smith shrugged. "Both of 'em convinced they get the best of the bargain. It's just a way of passin' the time anyway. If you turn off north at the cairn you'll get there sooner or later."

Monday stood. "All right, Solomon. I thank y'."

"Any time. Wish y' could stay for a bite t' eat," Solomon said.

"Maybe I'll stop by when all this is over," Monday said. "I been meanin' to get down an' see you an' Trask an' whatnot, but I never get around to it. How's things goin'?"

"Good and bad. The gold strike in California left me without any men up here, but they're driftin' back, poorer than when they left."

"Same in the valley, pretty much. How's Trask?"

"He's figurin' to leave, settle down in Killamook country."

"Thought he was satisfied here," Monday said.

"Bridge is never satisfied," Smith said. "But he got swamped by the gold strike, too. Can't do much with a depopulated country."

" 'Spect not," Monday said. "Well, too bad t' lose a good man up here."

Smith nodded. "Though in a way," he said, "it's prob'ly better this way. Bridge is kind of hard t' live with. He's pretty independent."

Monday looked at the other man curiously. "You too?" he said after a moment.

"Me too, what?" Smith said, puzzled.

"Nothing," Monday said. "It ain't important. I best get back."

He mounted again and leaned down from the saddle to shake hands with Smith.

"Say, Jaybird," Solomon said. "What'd Webb kill that man for?"

Monday heard himself answer automatically, as though it were someone else speaking. "For me." It was not what he had intended to say.

2

The second night out the old man was lucky. Just about the time he began thinking of a campsite, the trail crossed a small river. It was the only stream of considerable size he had passed since he left the flat country, and he was grateful for it.

There was a wide meadow on the other side, rich with ferns and grass, held between the arms of the river's curve. At the very edge of the water was a running border of cottonwoods.

The stream ran swift and shallow, boiling white water over the rocky bottom, churning the air-clear water into milky froth that swirled away down the current. At its deepest the stream did not reach his horse's belly. They forded easily, and the horse scrabbled up the tiny bank on the other side, into the cottonwood thicket. The old man dismounted and worked through the narrow barrier to the clear meadow, three or four hundred yards across at its widest point. He left the shelter of the trees and stood looking around him.

The sun was below the hills to the west now, and the sky was turning bright with the glow of the reddening dusk. There was a quietness settling on the land, and he stood motionless for a long time, savoring the sensation of change that came each day. The day creatures were searching their homes, going into silence; the night-runners had not yet come into voice.

He breathed deeply, listening. At last he returned to the grove and brought out the animal that waited patiently for him. It was probably not too smart, but he wanted to sleep in the clear. He didn't like the brush of this country, the matted wall that hindered and hobbled you and forced you to follow trails where someone else had passed. He wanted space and light around him, it was how he felt free.

He let the horse wander over the meadow, searching out that perfect mouthful of grass that was always promised, and always a few steps farther on. He spent a few minutes gathering branches for his fire, then settled himself down a few yards from the thicket, lying on his side with his head supported on one hand, just looking.

The silence grew deeper with the dusk, and he followed it with his mind, trying to guess the exact center point between the night and the day, the precise moment when the day sounds were completely gone. Like a stone thrown in the air; there had to be a moment of perfect rest before it began to come down. He was convinced that between the night and the day there must be an instant of perfect rest, when all life ceased. A hundred times he had tried to discover it in the dusk, and always failed.

By the river bank a frog croaked, and the old man grimaced. The night sounds had begun. He had missed it again. But he thought he had come closer this night than ever before; it was a half-victory.

In a few minutes the dark was full of sound and life around him. They were coming out quickly now, as though the frog had been a guard to announce the freedom of the night. As he went back to the little stack of wood he had gathered he heard the rustling of small scurryings and movings in the cottonwoods. A light breeze had come up, and the grasses of the meadow swung gently back and forth in ranks.

Good moon, too, he thought. Lopsided and red, almost full, hanging swollen just over the eastern peaks. Five minutes and it would be small and pale, riding fast to the top of the sky. For some reason his favorite moon had always been the lopsided one. There was an absurdity about it that pleased him—a little off-balance, looking as though it were about to tip over.

As he watched, he saw a thing he loved; the silent, ghostly swoop of an owl across the smoky red face of the moon. It was the silence of it that made him wonder. Strong wings beating, that should have made a thundering in the night. But there was nothing. All other birds were coarse and unlovely with their flappings and clumsiness. Some of them could glide with a certain grace; but none flew like the owl, in silent dignity and solitude.

Gradually the moon lost its fire and turned cold and silver. The light of it streamed across the surface of the swift-running stream, broken and shattered and carried away by the infinity of currents and countercurrents that roiled the surface. The brilliance darted and flickered along the ripples faster than his eye could follow. When he had stared at it long, his eyes went out of focus, and there was nothing but the swirling, mingling patches of brightness. Haloed brilliance independent of moon and water; light alone, existing and dancing in the deep blackness of the night, dancing to its own unheard music.

At last he sighed and shook his head. "Wagh! Moon-doggin' again." But he was beginning to feel better, just the same. Silliness, nothing had changed in the world around him, but he was beginning to feel calm.

" 'Nother couple days I ought t' be feelin' right peart," he said aloud. It was good to be back again. And with the best of omens, too, the flight of the owl, the good moon. Everything was going to be clean and pretty. It was going to work out all right.

The predawn light was a brilliant overcast. The meadow and its bordering trees glowed with a light of their own. The sky itself was softly luminous, shading evenly and gently from east to west. The cool, diffuse light was wholly neutral. Objects were not seen by light and shadow, as in full sun, but simply by their form, illuminated softly from all directions at once.

He woke more quickly this morning, and was satisfied to observe it. He was coming back to life again, once away from the numbing and dulling influence of man and his doings.

Part of it was that, after two days and nights, he was beginning to get the feel of this range, beginning to become a part of it. From his leaving himself open and wholly receptive, the shape and form of the land seeped into him, changing some inner balance to correspond. It led, as always, to a feeling of growing contentment, a feeling of being part of the world again. When in the society of men he had a sense of terrible isolation from the real world, because he had no time to listen, and to see. There was always the suspicion, rapidly becoming conviction, that something was happening. Sometimes he had to run out someplace to sit quiet and see what the world was doing; to be still and listen to the roots talking. The veil of emotion and noise and shallowness that was always associated with the presence of human beings hid the world from him and made him tense.

Now it was easing, and as he rode in the morning he was relaxed, throwing himself open to the shape of the hills and the texture of the trees he passed.

It was a land that lived by water, drawing its life from the earth soaked by nine months of rain. The thick and irritating growth of brush that forced him to follow a traveled trail was part of it; all the growth seeped up out of the ground. In the east, even in the range of mountains on the other side of the Willamette Valley, it was not like that. There the heavy growth was high up, as though it grew from the power of the sun, leaving the surface of the earth itself more clear, more spacious. Here, as he let himself feel the character of the land, there was a sense

of closed corridors, of thickness, of darkness in the forest itself. It was
water country. In the sun forests there was a sense of distance and space
he needed. Room to move about, room to breathe, freedom to cut his
own trail in any direction that suited him.

That was the big trouble here, he thought, with all the firs and spruce
and trees of gloom. It was a country that lived by wetness, and he was
a sun man, himself. He shrugged. It was something new to learn, and
he had always been very curious about the way it went between a man
and the world.

Thick as hair on the back of a dog, he thought. And him a flea
wandering around. Naturally, a flea was better off; a flea could run
along the top if he had to. Suddenly the old man had a wonderfully
clear picture of himself scampering along the tops of the forest with
ease, running along the matted surface under the open sky. He laughed
aloud, and the horse pricked up its ears.

"Wagh! That's *some*, now. Wish't I c'd do 'er!"

It was an image of such brilliant vividness that it pleased him
unreasonably every time he thought about it, for the rest of the day.

Just after noon the trail began to show signs of heavier use, and the
old man knew he was coming into the sphere of the coastal settlements.
He was sure of his mountain by this time, but the trail seemed to be
skirting several miles to the south of it. He stopped the horse and looked
around, frowning. He did not relish the idea of cutting straight across,
not with the massed brush that seemed to grow thicker as he approached
the coast.

He eased the horse into motion again. He had some hours of light
yet, and would follow the trail until he was certain he had no choice.
He was more watchful now, approaching civilization, but in a certain
way less receptive. He scanned the brush and forest on either side, for
signs of man's passing, and lost some of his satisfaction in simple
perception. It was like the difference between looking at a piece of meat
with great joy, because you were hungry, and examining it carefully
because you thought there were maggots in it.

By the middle of the afternoon he was very jittery, and it was with
a double sense of relief and apprehension that he came to the crossroads,
where a six-foot-high cairn of rocks stood sentinel. The continuation

of the trail he was on, heading toward the ocean, abruptly grew to the proportion of a road. The trail coming in from the left was also heavily traveled. To his right, heading north toward the mountain, there was much less sign of use.

He nodded to himself with satisfaction and quickly turned off on the north-winding path. In a few minutes he was out of sight of the stone cairn and the meeting of the trails.

He stepped up the pace a little, wanting to put some distance between himself and the frequented place. After an hour he eased off, losing the uneasy sensation that there was somebody behind him. Twenty-four hours. They would be in the mountains by now, probably somewhere just before his last campsite, or if they had been pushing, they might even have reached it by now. He would have all day tomorrow to pick his spot on the mountain and get ready.

He had been on the mountain path for nearly two hours, and it had become obvious that it was very seldom used. It had narrowed considerably, so that his thighs were often scraped by the brush on either side. There were a number of deadfalls across the way, and for each he had to dismount, lead the horse over, or find a way around. The horse was becoming a handicap.

In the heat of the afternoon he was sweating heavily and the increasing effort was tiring the animal more rapidly. When the trail crossed a tiny creekbed he decided to stop for a few minutes.

The stream was almost dry this late in the summer, having been nothing much to begin with. The white, rocky bottom wound through the woods, bright in the light of the sky like bones drying, with only a faint trickle of water in the center. The old man dismounted and squatted by the dry bed, looking at it, not thinking of anything in particular. After a bit he roused himself and unstrapped the saddlebag to get his tin cup. He took it into the middle of the creekbed and dipped up half a cupful.

He waited a few moments until the mud settled in a fine sediment, then drank, sipping the fresh coolness slowly. At the moment he felt that a cup of clear water was perhaps the finest single experience in the world, and he didn't want to waste any of it. He knew he would feel the same about eating when he made camp, and sleeping when it was time to sleep, but that didn't matter. For the time, his cup of water was sufficient.

He shook out the cup, stuffed it back in the little saddlebag. It took so little to make a man really happy. He sat for a moment beside the creek, thinking. Then he unsaddled the horse and stripped the bags off. He took the long rifle out of its leather pocket and cradled it across his knees.

The animal grazed slowly along the edge of the dead stream, and the old man watched her for a while. They had gone a long way together, the two of them, shared a lot of mountains between them, a lot of cold rivers.

"Wagh!" The old man grunted. "Y're a terrible ugly critter, though. Y'are now."

The horse was too bony, the points of her bones seemed about to poke through the skin, and her ribs were always faintly visible. She was getting old now, the bony old skeleton. She'd seen better days, they'd both seen better days. The old man wondered vaguely if the horse missed the traveling brigades, missed being picketed at night with twenty other animals like her, browsing companionably in the darkness of the night.

The animal nosed aside the ferns and grabbed a mouthful of grass. Chewing contentedly she looked over at the old man, then back down to the grass. The old man thought about the winter times, the starvin' times, when he'd spent more hours of the day stripping cottonwood bark for the goddamn animal than he spent getting food for himself. A waste of time, but the animal was life itself. A man without a horse was a dead man, a nothing.

Funny thing was, no matter how much she had to eat, the old rack of bones never put on any flesh. He supposed there was some just plain *built* bony, him and the useless old skeleton that browsed contentedly under the ferns.

He picked up the rifle and went over to the animal, rubbed her neck and pulled on the mane. The horse looked up, tried to nibble one of the long black scalp locks that dangled on the old man's chest, then turned back to the hope of nourishment that never seemed to do any permanent good.

Coolly and without emotion the old man raised the rifle and placed the muzzle behind the animal's ear and pulled the trigger.

The hammer fell with a loud clack and the flint sparked. The old man looked unbelieving down at the open, unprimed pan. He blinked, clearing his vision, and tightened the grip of his fist around the rifle. He wheeled suddenly away from the animal and walked off a few steps, yanking the plug from his powder horn with his teeth.

He began to curse softly as he poured the powder, because his hand was shaking. It was a thing he could not stand, wasting powder. There was no reason for it.

Chapter Eighteen

I

The sun was well above the hills when the long, ungainly column of horsemen wound around the little bay. As they passed the Clatsop village built at the mouth of the river they became less a posse than a parade. The inhabitants of the village all came out of their lodges and lined the trail, watching them pass, curious, saying nothing. The village dogs barked constantly with a high, annoying yap-yap that got on Monday's nerves. He was glad when they were past, headed out along the trail the Indians called the Big Road.

The land was partially cleared around them, and the Big Road was well traveled. Going was easy, and they made good time. For the first few miles the Big Road ran next to the river, nearly due south, paralleling the beach and less than half a mile inland. Then the coastline bulged out with a great hump of the headland Neahseu'su, and the river skirted around the inland side. Before long the column had trended away from the sea, and the steady rolling sound of the surf disappeared behind the bulk of the head. The land around them was still flat; but now the foothills of the head rose abruptly a half-mile to the right, and to the left were the first risings of the Coast Range. From both sides small creeks began to empty into the river.

It was going to be one hell of a hot day. There was an oppressive thickness to the air this close to the ocean, like a feather comforter made invisible. It was very still. The horse's hoofs raised tiny puffs of dust that did not dissipate until shattered by the passage of the next horse. Toward the end of the line the dust was unpleasant and made it difficult to breathe.

The men had lost the shrill gaiety that characterized the boat trip down. It wasn't so much like a holiday now. They rode with their eyes narrowed against the brilliance of the morning sun and the cloud of dust that enveloped the column. There was little talking between them, and what little there was consisted of sullen complaints.

It would be better, Monday thought, when they reached the timber again, and shade. There would not be the dryness of the dust, and the heat would not be so intense. He had become increasingly depressed as the morning wore on; and uncertain. But there was no way to change it now.

Again he had the powerless sensation of running before the avalanche. There was nothing he could do, no way to stop the landslide once it had begun. All he could do was keep running or be swept under. It had gone too far to stop.

Where did it begin to be inevitable? Webb had asked him in so many words to come back to the mountains; that he might not die. And yet, was that a choice, a real choice? There was nothing in the mountains any more. A drifting, aimless life, living each day for its own sake. Nothing. But in refusing, perhaps he had dropped the last stone that started the fall. After that, the end was certain, and he supposed everything that had happened could have been guessed at. If you could see, if only you could see clearly. That each blot of ink, meaningless, in the end made a picture. But you could never see in time, it was one of the rules of the game. A man could never know what slight movement of his hand was important until it was too late to change. And then there was nothing to be done. You went along. In the end there were no real decisions to make, it was all inevitable, you did what you had to do. Thurston did, Webb did, he did. All of them pushed by something beyond their comprehension, beyond their control. All of them, knowing or not, pushed by the following avalanche. He could not be responsible for it, he could not be guilty of it.

By noon they were filing beneath the webbed roof of limbs again. Gray with dust, the column was a ghostly snake threading through the deep green-black of the forest. Monday rode silently in the middle of the line, his horse as gray as the others. They were all indistinguishable, one from the other.

Bill the carpenter pulled up alongside Monday's mount. "Hell of a day," he said.

Monday nodded. His shirt was plastered to his back with sweat, and rivulets washed away the dust in tiny streams down his face.

"Y' think we'll catch him?" Bill asked.

"We'll catch him," Monday said.

Bill shook his head dubiously. "Awful damn big country t' go a-chasin' one man in."

"Different if he's waitin' for you," Monday said.

"Think he's waitin'?"

Monday nodded.

Bill thought about it, frowning. "Me, I don't like that much," he said.

Monday shrugged. "Just the way it is."

They rode in silence for a few moments before Bill said, looking around him, "You know this here Saddle Mountain?"

"I been around it once," Monday said.

"Hard going? Me, I don't like climbin' mountains and things like that."

"Not much to it," Monday said. "Just a nice walk uphill."

"That's good."

"Pretty easy place to set a mousetrap, though," Monday said.

"How so?" The other man frowned, and Monday was faintly pleased.

"The two peaks ain't but about a quarter-mile apart. Little razorback ridge in between 'em. A man tryin' t' cross that ridge, he's about two hundred feet below the peaks. Pretty easy target from either side."

"Well," Bill said hesitantly, "maybe we'll catch up to him afore he gets up there."

"Ain't likely," Monday said. "He'll be headin' for high ground fast as he can. I expect he'll just get up there an' try to pick us off one at a time."

"Well," Bill muttered, "I just hope nobody gets hurt, is all."

"Jesus *christ*, man!" Monday said, finally at the end of his patience. "What the hell you think we're *here* for?"

Startled by Monday's vehemence, Bill looked up at him, and Monday was disgusted by the fear so evident in the other man's loose face.

"Hell, y' don't have t' get *mad* about it," the carpenter said. "I ain't got nothin' t' do with this anyway."

"You're here."

"So are you, far as that goes," Bill said defiantly.

"Sure. We're all here," Monday said morosely.

The other man reined back his horse and drifted down the line.

They were all here, Monday thought. It was a kind of puppet show. Would they have any notion if they saw the old man over the sights of their rifles that they were looking at a man of flesh, like their own? He doubted it. Everything outside their own skin was part of the puppet show. Like the malicious gossip at the mill, there was no sense of real persons, of real harm. It was just a way of passing the time. The only man for whom it was real was the old man who waited for them, because death is real.

"Damn their eyes," he whispered. "God *damn* their eyes." His throat felt tight, as though he wanted to holler, but he did not. He rode along with the column and behind him the carpenter assuaged his hurt feelings by cursing Monday and all like him.

By mid-afternoon Monday was tense. At every bend in the trail he expected to see the crossroads, and it did not appear. They would have made up the start Webb had, perhaps even gained more than that. The endless jogging of the horse became a steady irritation. On either side the trees passed without end, a continuous wall of foliage that was exactly the same. Nothing changed, and they might as well have been riding in a circle for all the sense of progress.

He had the crazy notion that they were going to meet Webb coming the other way. They would round a bend and there he would be, slumped indifferently in the saddle, coming toward them. *Then* there'd be hell to pay.

And what if they were ahead of him? What if they got up to the mountain and found Webb behind them? Who was hunting, and who being hunted? Maybe in the end that was the real question: who was the hunted? Gradually he eased up toward the head of the column, out of the insane conviction that if they did meet Webb coming the other way he wanted to be the first to see him.

When they did reach the crossing point of the trails, Monday had an instant of terrible shock, seeing Webb standing impassively waiting for them. But even as his heart jumped, he realized it was not a man, but the cairn of rocks that marked the informal trading site between the Killamooks and the Clatsops.

He swallowed heavily, looking at the cairn. Thurston's beautiful bay pulled up beside him and they rode the last few yards to the cairn side by side.

"Well, Monday," Thurston said.

Monday looked at the trail that led off to their left, toward the mountain. "I think we best leave the horses here," Monday said.

"Give your friend more time?" Thurston said.

"You may as well quit," Monday said evenly.

Thurston shrugged indifferently. Monday turned to the others, who were pulling up around them.

"This trail ain't used much," he said. "We'll make better time on foot." He dismounted and began to take what gear he needed out of the saddlebags.

The others sat their animals, waiting. Finally Thurston shrugged and swung gracefully out of the saddle. The rest then began to dismount, and Monday knew without caring one way or the other that if he had taken the lead yesterday morning, it was all over now. There was no question of who was running the show. It didn't matter.

When they swung off on the trail Thurston said, "Monday, since you've been down here, why don't you come up front here?"

"So you can keep an eye on me?"

"So you can show us the way," Thurston said, smiling amiably.

An hour on the new trail, and Monday was a little surprised by the pace Thurston was setting. The little man, whatever else he might be, was not soft. He could march with the rest of them, and better than most of the farmers. Monday figured he was politicking again, proving something. He was never done with proving something.

The stillness of the afternoon heat was broken by the sudden ringing echo of a gunshot ahead.

Monday stopped abruptly in the trail. Thurston looked at him, then back at the trail ahead.

"There he is," Monday said.

"Yes," Thurston said thoughtfully. "There he is."

Now the question was answered. There was no doubt who was the hunted.

2

Shortly after he left the creekbed, the trail began to trend east, gradually rising along the flank of a ridge. In a short time the lowering afternoon sun was almost behind the old man. Now only one valley separated him from the double-peaked mountain, and he figured there would be a live stream at the base.

He looked down slope at the almost impenetrable wall of foliage. Absently he played with the end of one of the scalp locks, wondering if he had missed a trail that would have taken him in the right direction. The one he followed was definitely heading east, and up. He decided to give it another half-hour, then cut straight across.

There was no question of finding a man-trail now; he was too far in. As he walked he scanned the brush on either side of him, evaluating the slight breaks that might represent an animal track down toward the river. He passed several in the next half-hour, small, old, not recently used. When he reached one that appeared a little more fresh he turned off without hesitation, forcing down off the slope toward the valley bottom. The brush closed in around him, plucking at his shoulders and legs.

The soil was both rocky and dusty under his feet, and in a short time the blanket-bottoms of his trousers were covered with reddish-gray dust and his moccasins merged indistinguishably with the trail beneath them. The loose rocks rolled and jabbed and pounded his feet through the thin leather. It was his last pair, and a hole had already started in one sole.

All in all, groping through the brush was not as bad as he had anticipated. The trail he followed was not completely overgrown yet, and he figured it had probably been used in the spring as a main track

down to the river. Then the deer would have changed, for reasons of
their own, and one day the trail would be completely deserted and left
to go back into brush. It was a sense deer had that men lacked: to use
it for a while, then give it back to the world, freely.

Thinking of the brush, he had overprepared himself for the
unpleasantness, and the reality was satisfactory by comparison. He
reached the river a little more than an hour later and began looking
for a camp.

It was a fair little stream, even this late in the season, and he supposed
it probably had a name. Fifteen or twenty feet wide, flowing through
the corridor of timber at the valley bottom with the endless shifting
grace of light and water that never tired. Flowing down from a
mountainside, winding through the forest in light and darkness, passing
ten thousand ferns that nodded and dipped, ten thousand firs that stood
by its banks. Without fatigue or hunger or the aching the old man felt.
It was getting so he was tired by the end of a day, and grateful for the
chance to rest a bit and think over what he had seen in passing. Once
it had not been that way; he had pushed on into the dusk and been off
again before dawn. There was so much to see ahead, so much to do.

The point where the deer trail met the little river was disappointing.
There was a small, relatively calm pool, but otherwise it was no different
from any other point on the bank. It was a good little river, he thought,
too good to waste on a camp he would not remember. He started
downstream.

The cold water felt good to his feet, but the river bottom was even
rockier than the slope he had just come down, and he had to walk
carefully. Here in the bottom of the valley itself he was shielded from
both the warmth of the setting sun and its light. It was dark and cool,
with spatterings of brightness catching the ripples and glinting off to
trees at the side, speckling them with shifting spots of silver.

In a quarter of an hour he had found a landmark that satisfied him,
a huge boulder on the north bank. It was perhaps twenty feet high, soft
with moss and ferns, ponderously leaning out over the flowing water.
Opposite the boulder was a flat space in the shape of a tiny triangle,
with one side facing the river and another facing a small inlet, not much
more than ten feet long.

He climbed out on the flat space, which he was already thinking of as "camp," and sat down, looking across the stream at his boulder. The camp space was rocky and small, but it would be all right; it was the boulder that counted, something pleasant to see and think of. He watched for a little, while the sun-blots crept and shifted over the green furry surface, fading and brightening in an unpredictable pattern as the trees moved gently and the sun lowered behind them.

Finally he nodded with inner satisfaction. It was all right, he felt comfortable. It would be a good place to spend the night.

3

The stillness of dusk; a time almost perfectly neutral, a suspension, filled with the promise of depth and solitude in the night to come.

The old man gathered wood, enjoying the changing shapes of his camp in the changing light, seeing how one tree began to recede into shadow and another, by contrast, move forward for his attention. He moved quietly in the warm grayness, picking up a stick here, a larger slab there, and carrying them two or three at a time back to his rocky little point. It was an inefficient way to get wood together, but he didn't mind. He liked to spend the calm expanse of dusk in a calm manner; it was insanity to do anything else.

He did not need much wood, and there was not only the question of the fire, but a question of timing. He thought he was going to like this little camp very much, and he wanted things to go properly. It was most satisfying for him to finish laying the fire and have it ready to light at the precise moment in the growing darkness when it seemed to him that he needed a little more light. It was, in the end, perfectly unimportant. But there was a certain contentment for a man in feeling that he has well suited his actions to the changes of the world around him.

It was a kind of contentment the old man had not felt for a while now, ever since he got mixed up with the man-ugliness of the settlement. There it always seemed that he was running counter to something, always conscious of conflict, of tension. He couldn't let the world take him along, because of the noise and stink of the man-world. He shrugged as he kindled the fire, and put the thought away from him. It was over, now. This was not the place to be worrying about it. He filled his little cup half full of water, dropped in a couple of tiny pieces of flaky white suet from the pack. He put the cup by the fire where it would boil quickly and got a handful of the jerked deer. The jerky was in flat sticks like hardened leather, eight or ten inches long. He broke a few of them in half and stood them on end in the cup. They were still too long, and stood up out of the cup like a fistful of bark. When the water neared the boiling stage, he turned the strips end for end, to let the other half soften a little.

When he was finished it was a little softer. Not much, but enough to make a difference—and he had a cup of weak broth to drink. It was not like fresh meat, but it was better than no meat at all. He chewed on the rubbery strips and watched the orange and gold reflections of his fire ripple in the water, almost as though a tiny sun were burning just beneath the surface.

Slowly the balance of light changed. The western sky grew dark, and in the east was the pale glow of the rising moon, not yet visible above the trees. The old man put one last stick on the fire to last until he was asleep. He made a halfhearted attempt to clear away some of the larger rocks before he rolled up in his blanket, but he knew it wouldn't make much difference. If you got rid of the rocks you had the holes they left. It was better to try to fit yourself around the worst spots.

With the setting of the sun the night had become pleasantly cool. He took off his moccasins, which were still wet from the wading. The dust he had collected on the slope had formed a fine, silty layer of mud inside. He rinsed them out carefully, scrubbing away the soapy-feeling layer. Ruefully he noted that the hole in the right sole had grown considerably from the rough pounding down the rocky slope. He stuck his little finger through the hole experimentally, then shrugged. He washed his feet and put the moccasins back on to prevent them from shrinking up so badly in the night they could not be worn tomorrow.

He pulled the blanket over him, tucked the edges under and rolled over to his side. He could see both the fire and the reflection of it in the tiny inlet beside him. He glanced up at the light and eerie glow that preceded the appearance of the moon, and realized there would be a time in the night when the great disk would be overhead in the space between the trees, directly over the river. Then he would be able to see both the moon and its reflection in the still inlet. It would be pleasant, but would not happen for a couple of hours. He thought he would like to wake up for it, to see two moons at the same time.

A fly or something buzzed near his ear, and he sleepily swatted at it, hoping it was not a mosquito. Mosquitoes were a damned nuisance. They said the ones that buzzed weren't the ones that bit you, but the buzzing ones were the ones you swatted. It didn't seem fair, but he supposed it was probably true. There was nothing to guarantee that things would be fair. He wondered vaguely if a mosquito could see the end of its own nose.

He wakened without being startled, and at first could not understand why. Then he realized he had promised himself a look at the overhead moon, and it was the sudden increase of light that had brought him out of sleep. It was almost directly above, framed between the wall of trees that edged the river. The night was very clear, and the markings on the face of the brilliant disk were sharp and distinct. For the thousandth time the old man tried to make some sense of them, tried to make them fit into a comprehensible pattern, tried to see the man in the moon. He never could. Everybody else saw the man in the moon, and a dozen times people had tried to explain to him, but he never could see it. To him there were gray patches, and he was perfectly familiar with their shape; but he could not make pictures out of them. It was the moon, with its uniqueness, and resembled nothing but itself. It was sufficient.

He glanced over at the reflection in the inlet, where the moon's twin wavered luminously in the darkness. The inlet was not as calm as it had appeared. The reflection lengthened and shortened and occasionally broke, distorting the perfect symmetry of the brilliance that hung overhead. He wondered if it would be possible to make it hold completely still, and be the perfect, flawless duplicate he had seen in his mind when he had thought about it before. In an odd way it seemed possible to him that in the reflection he might be able to see the pictures, even though he could not see them in the moon itself.

The more he thought about it, the more it seemed to be a good idea. He had always wanted to see the man in the moon. He unwrapped himself from the blanket. His fire was still glowing faintly, and he threw on one of the pieces of wood he'd been saving for morning. As it flamed up and lit a small circle he surveyed the problem.

The mouth of the inlet was only about eight feet wide, and there was already a fallen log damming part of it. One end of the log rested up on his bank, and he thought if he could get that end into the water across the mouth it might do the job. It was too heavy to lift, but he thought he could pry it off with a lever of some kind. He looked around the edges of the fire circle until he found a windfall about six inches through at the base.

He dragged it back to the fire and hacked off a few of the more troublesome branches. With the lever he waded to the river side of the log and thrust the thick end beneath, wedging it in the stones of the bottom. He heaved up, but the end of the lever slipped and the log dropped back to the bank. He took a more secure purchase and tried again, and this time it worked perfectly. The end of the log rose from the bank and slid down the lever with a great splash to lie directly across the mouth of the inlet.

The splash completely destroyed the moon's image, scattering it in wild ripples and flecks of brightness that darted on the surface. He climbed back up on the bank and squatted on his heels to wait for the disturbance to die down and the whole image to return. When the ripples had settled, he found the reflection still wavered and moved. There was undoubtedly a current coming in from somewhere, probably around the end of the log, where it did not fit perfectly against the bank.

He sighed, and gathered up some stones and twigs to dam the gap. He had to go back into the water to do it, and his legs were getting cold. He packed the sticks and rocks into the open space, sealing them in with mud. It would wash away, but it might last long enough to get the moon still for just a moment. There was not much to packing the end, but when he had finished the improvised dam he had to wait again for the ripples to subside so he could see if it had worked.

It had not been enough. The reflection still wavered and distorted itself. The current must be coming in under the log itself. It was more complicated than he had expected, building a trap for the moon.

He went back into the water again. Patiently he began to wedge stones at the bottom of the log, filling spaces between large ones with smaller ones, and scraping up gravel from the bottom to dam whatever holes he had left. He worked as quickly as he could, but plugging most of the eight-foot length still took him almost twenty minutes.

When he got back to the bank and looked in the water there was no image at all. The moon had passed over the clear space above and was behind the trees again on its slow and certain journey to the other side of the world.

Chapter Nineteen

The morning light was thin and cold. The sky was clear, and the old man knew it would be hot. But the thickly grown river valley was like an undersea canyon, and he was submerged beneath fathoms of green that filtered out warmth from the light that reached him, seeping through the leafy roof like a winter rain.

It was all right. When he opened his eyes and looked around him, he knew he had sloughed off the last of the protective skin, the horny coating of blindness and insensitivity he had grown to protect himself from the rawness of others' emotions, from the ugliness of their doings. This morning the world was new again, as it should be every morning. Washed clean by the night of all its tensions and confusions, pure and virgin under the sky. A new day, full of surprises and new things to see and new wonderings and maybe even an answer or two. A new day, free and limitless, to be lived for its own sake.

There was still little warmth in the air when he had finished eating. He would have to get moving to get the dampness out of him. He gathered up his little gear and stuffed it in the pack. As he stood taking one last look around the campsite for forgotten articles, his glance flickered over the little inlet, with its absurdly ineffectual dam. He grimaced, and a sudden thought occurred to him.

He shrugged out of the pack and knelt at the end of the pool away from the river. Slowly dipping his arm in, he tried to see if he could feel motion at that end of the inlet. It had just passed his mind that it might be an outlet for a spring, rather than an inlet of the river.

But he could feel nothing. He stood again, wiping his hand absently on his trouser leg and staring down at the pool. Well, he would never know, now. He had tried to make a trap for the moon and failed, and he would never know exactly why.

He wriggled his arms through the pack straps again, and waded into the river, walking carefully on the rocky, slippery bottom. At the other side he glanced back at his dam, the mud and sticks now nearly washed away, leaving things as they had been before he came.

He turned and started up the brushy slope. Beside him the great boulder, thick with cascading ferns and moss, was a silent, massive sanctuary for small creatures that live in eternal dampness.

Today he was alive again, and he was glad to be himself once more, without the callous layer that came from rubbing too much against human beings. As he moved upward toward the mountain's foot the damp-stiffness worked out of his muscles quickly. The brilliant newness of the day was strong in his belly. He was raw and open again, letting the world come into him and taking pleasure in the deep invasion. His eyes saw more, his ears heard more, his mind collected and arranged and patterned the information his senses brought him precisely, sharply. Details of almost invisible fineness engraved themselves on his mind without effort; the myriad infinity of textures and shapes and sounds that were the forest. The saw-toothed edge of a sunlit leaf against a shadow-somber fern, the crook of a branch at his elbow, the hushed breath of a fir limb sweeping the air, gently. And with the increased sensitivity there came the eerie, almost forgotten sense of lightness, as though he had thrown down a fifty-pound pack. It always happened when he was fully himself. It was how he liked to live, sharply, and how he liked to see, clearly.

He was climbing steadily now, though the ground was not yet rising steeply. Occasionally, through breaks in the screen of trees ahead, he could see the outlines of Saddle Mountain's double hump. He was approaching from the southwest, and part of his view of the mountain itself was obscured by a minor peak. The little peak rose perhaps a hundred and fifty feet above the surrounding ground. It reached well above the level of the trees, standing absurdly naked and compact like a dungheap in short grass. From the top he thought he would be able to get a fair look at the countryside, and the mountain itself, less than half a mile from the flat-topped little pinnacle.

The animal trails thinned out, disappeared, started again. The brush was heavy on the uphill slope, and going was slower than he had hoped. When he finally reached the top of the little promontory the day was far along, near noon. The sun was full on the face of the mountain now, picking out the folds and crevices of the peaks sharply.

He put his pack and gun on the ground and sat down to empty his moccasins of the rocks and gravel they had accumulated on the walk up from the river valley. He poured out two miniature waterfalls and banged the soles together to dislodge the last fragments.

He was well above the tree level here, but looking to his left he was unable to see the ocean, fifteen miles away, and it disappointed him. The western horizon was blurred and indistinct in the gray-blue sea mist. In fact, he was not certain he could have seen the sea itself, even granting the day were clear enough. He looked up toward the mountain face that rose abruptly a half-mile distant from him. If he could see it at all, it would be from up there.

Absently he tamped his pipe full while letting his eyes rove over the slope leading to the minor peak, looking for trails. From here the brush looked almost like a tufted meadow, but there was not a sign of a trail anywhere, and he knew the undergrowth was probably over head height.

He finished stuffing his pipe and lit up. He sat then for nearly half an hour, still as a rock, with his hands clasped in front of his knees, studying the configuration of the mountain.

Finally he knocked out his pipe and stuck it in the broad flap of his hunting shirt, where it rested hot against his ribs. He stood up and stretched, spreading his arms wide against the sky. He picked up his gun and began to climb down from the small peak, swinging around the base and starting up the first gentle slope of the mountain itself.

After an hour and a half the terrain grew more and more rocky, a litter of stones, gravel and reddish-brown dust. The trees began to thin noticeably, leaving occasional tiny meadows.

When at last he reached the edge of the timber the trail he was following was running almost horizontal along the mountain flank, heading west. Just beyond the trees was the widest meadow he had yet seen, slanting down the mountainside to his left. Outcroppings of rock studded the slope, and on the other side was a long, straight rib of rock extending downslope. Above and to the right the small peak rose, rocky and bare of trees.

He squatted at the edge of the meadow and considered the long rock wall, absently plaiting one of the long black braids that hung beneath his hat.

He picked up a stone and tossed it from hand to hand for a moment, while he studied the meadow and the wall and the peak above. Finally he shrugged and stood up. He heaved the rock out toward the wall. It fell far short, clanked against another stone in the meadow, and everything was silent again.

It was worth keeping in mind, if he didn't find anything better. The wall would make a nice little fort, but he wanted to get higher. He moved out around the edge of the trees and started up the small peak.

Beyond the trees the terrain was a tumbled mass of rocky debris; loose gravel, occasional large boulders. The loose rock slid out from under his feet and scattered down the slope, the stones bruised his feet through the thin leather of the moccasins.

He had to rest once before he reached the top. He squatted, his bony wrists dangling over his knees, facing downslope. The sun was dropping more quickly now, and taking on a reddish tinge. This side was nearly all in shadow now, but farther off to the east the sun still caught the tops of other ridges, picking out the peaks like tiny match flames in the shade.

Finally he started up again, and shortly afterward reached the big boulder that seemed to be the peak. He looked around, checking the ground from the point of view of cover. The little peak sloped down to the razorback ridge, tumbled rock again. The opposite peak, a quarter of a mile away, was somewhat higher, and more flat-topped. He thought it would probably be a better place to make his stand. Satisfied, he sat down with his back against the boulder to look around for the pleasure of it, and watch the day die.

He had almost forgotten how sweet it was to be on a mountain, isolated and above the land. Below him and on all sides the thick, matted forests stretched away along slowly undulating ridges. A few miles south of him was the sudden sharp hump of the ridge he had been on the evening before. It was the only real break in the land worth noticing. All the other ridges, harsh and tiring in reality, were flattened by distance and his height, seeming inconsequential.

It was an odd thing, and one that always delighted him, the way the land flattened out when you saw it from a mountain peak. On the trail the next ridge always seemed to tower over you, hovering like the breaking crest of a wave, an ordeal, a challenge. But from here it was obvious that these little ripples couldn't bother anybody; they made the difficulties of the trail seem minor. It was just a different way of seeing.

His one real disappointment was that there was only a blurred transition from sea to sky, off to the west. He couldn't really be certain of the horizon; it was not the sharp, clean dividing line he had pictured in his mind. Maybe it would be clearer in the morning.

He thought he heard the faint sound of falling rock on the other side, the side he had come up. A deer, browsing high the lateness of the afternoon, searching out the last of the sun. If he could get some fresh meat the day would be just about perfect.

He stood up and walked around the side of the boulder to look.

2

An hour and a half after they had heard the shot, the column came to the point where the trail crossed the dry creekbed, and found the old horse. The animal lay with its legs pointed stiffly out to the side, and flies were buzzing around the pool of blood that collected below its head.

"Kilt his horse, by god!" one of them said wonderingly.

"Wonderful," Monday said. "You're a real genius, now."

"Don't get smart, Monday," Thurston said.

One of the farmers was kneeling beside the animal in fascination. Finally he stood up again, unconsciously wiping his hand across his trouser leg. "Don't seem t' be hurt or nothin'," he said. "What do you suppose he done that for?"

"Same reason we left ours at the crossroads," Monday said. "He's got t' be movin' faster."

"Well, hell, he di'n't have to shoot 'im."

Monday said nothing aloud. Ain't figurin' t' leave no way out, he thought miserably. There would be no loose ends of Webb's life hanging around. Bit by bit everything the old man had was being left behind.

Thurston was looking apprehensively at the trail where it continued into the heavy forest, disappearing in a few yards. "It wouldn't be difficult to ambush the party in there," he said thoughtfully.

Monday snorted. "What's wrong with right here?" he said.

The men looked around them. Except for the creekbed, the forest was dense and impenetrable all around them. There was any amount of cover available, just for the taking. They looked at one another, grouped in a tight bunch around the animal, guns unloaded.

Thurston turned angrily to Monday. "Why did you let us make targets of ourselves? Are you leading us into some kind of trap?"

"You're alive, ain't you?" Monday said. "I figure he's headin' for the mountain, an' he won't make a stand before he gets there."

"Why? How can you be sure?"

"I can't," Monday said. "That's what I figure. That's the way he is."

"Damned little to go on," Thurston said.

"Huntin' men ain't a sure trade," Monday said. "My opinion's all you got. Take it or leave it."

In the end Thurston turned away. Monday looked at the western sky. "He's still got better'n an hour on us," he said. "We best push on till dark, make camp, and get an early start in the morning. If you approve, of course," he added to Thurston.

Thurston shrugged, his insouciance returning. "Whatever you say, my friend. I get the impression we're more or less in your hands. "

Monday looked down at the blackening wound in the horse's head. "That's funny," he said absently. "I get the same impression." He looked up at the mountain peaks, barely visible above the screen of trees. The others followed his glance, from the dead horse to the heights. There was a low conversation between four or five of the men standing around the horse.

Finally one of them laughed nervously. He shrugged his pack into a more comfortable position and walked hesitantly over to Monday and Thurston.

"Mr. Thurston—" he started politely.

"What is it?"

"Ah—there's a couple of us—well, we decided to go home."

"Go home!"

Monday grinned a little and looked down at the ground.

"Yeah," the man said hesitantly. "Me, I mean I didn't want to come along here anyhow, you know?"

"Don't be ridiculous," Thurston snapped. "You can't just go home. That kind of talk does nothing but make trouble. You men are on a posse, not a picnic outing."

"Well, that's what we thought we'd do, though," the other said. The four other men came up to stand sullenly behind their spokesman, looking neither at Monday nor at Thurston.

"Look, Mr. Thurston," the first man said reasonably. "Me, I got a wife and kids, you know? I got to think about them. And I got wheat to get in."

"The last resort of cowards," Thurston said contemptuously, "Wife and children. Do you think your wife and children are safe while that maniac is loose?"

"Mr. Thurston," the other said doggedly, "I ain't fixin' to argue with you. I know you c'n come over me slick." He glanced down at the dead horse. "I don't care whether you call it coward or whatever. But I figure to go home." The little group behind him muttered a sort of wordless agreement. The first man was standing his ground, embarrassed but adamant.

"Let me tell you something, my friend," Thurston said. "If you back out now, you will regret it the rest of your life."

"Yeah," said somebody in the crowd. "But it's like t' be a longer life."

There was a little laughter, and Thurston wheeled to survey the main group angrily. "All right," he said finally. "How many other cowards are there here? If you leave this posse, you'd better start packing when you reach home."

Slowly they began to divide, a few more coming to stand with the original deserters, looking embarrassedly at the ground.

"Just let me look at your faces," Thurston said coldly. "I want to remember you."

"Me, I was figurin' to go take a look at that California gold anyways," somebody said, but it had gone too far now. There was no answering laughter.

Through the exchange Monday had said nothing. He looked at the ten men who had decided to stay, and figured it was a question of fear either way. Some were more scared of Thurston than of Webb, that was all. He shrugged.

"I say let 'em go," he said finally. "This here army's a sight too big for comfort anyways."

"No one asked your opinion," Thurston said.

Monday grinned at the ground and rubbed the back of his neck. There was nothing Thurston could do about it. He was losing half his men, and that was that.

After having stared at the deserters, Thurston suddenly turned and picked up the pack he had put on the ground. Without a word he started down the trail again.

Slowly, and with relief, the group of deserters turned back the other way. A few of the remaining members looked enviously after them.

"Now's the time, boys," Monday said, watching them.

"Well, hell—" One of them shrugged, looked at the ground for a moment. "I s'pose we might as well see 'er through," he said. He picked up his pack and started after Thurston. One by one the others reluctantly followed.

Monday came at the end of the line, shaking his head in wonder at the ways of men.

It seemed almost lonesome in the morning, with only a dozen men; and silent ones, for the most part. On a few faces there was obvious regret that they had not gone off with the others; but it was too late now. Thurston had improved the evening by delivering, in a companionable way, his opinions of the deserters and his predictions for their future. By the time he had finished, the talons were well dug in, and Monday thought there would be no more to take the back trail.

The longer he ran with this bunch the more baffled he became, watching them sway back and forth before the wind, watching Thurston politick them unceasingly. The establishment of his authority was as natural as breathing for the small man; he did it automatically, without thinking about it. And always a chance comment dropped here, an observation there, to fertilize the suspicion of the others for Monday.

Thinking back on it, Monday thought he had probably made a mistake on the first morning. Thurston saw him as a threat now. And slice by slice he was cutting him back to size. A mistake—but what the hell else could Monday have done? Let himself be cut out without fighting? In the end it didn't matter. No matter what he did, it was wrong.

Bill the carpenter had been one who stayed. In the early light he came over and sat down beside Monday, rolling a cigarette casually. "Nice morning," he said, looking up at the sky.

"So," Monday said.

After a moment, Bill said, "Say, that old man, now."

"What about him?"

The cigarette paper tore across, and the carpenter cursed it. Holding the ruined cigarette carefully so as not to spill the tobacco, he reached in the pocket of his denim jacket for the book of papers.

"I expect he's a pretty good shot," Bill said. Others of the group had begun to drift over to listen.

"Expect he is," Monday said. "Thing is, he won't get a shot at all until we're out o' the timber. Chances are we can make it up t' the rock without him knowing. *If* you walk soft."

"Y'really think so?"

"Listen," Monday said, gesturing to the wood around them. It was full of sounds, rustlings of animals, scraping of limbs, a steady murmur of life and movement.

"If we got a trail it shouldn't be too hard," Monday said.

"After we get out into the open, that's a different story. He's got his eyes, then."

"All right, you men," Thurston said. "Pack up and let's get moving."

The men started to drift off to their bedrolls.

"Think you'd best charge y'r guns this morning," Monday said quietly. He pulled the plug from his powder horn and poured. "From here on in all bets are off."

The others looked at one another, then silently went to get their gear together and load their rifles.

They wound down into the little river valley silently. Monday was amused at how quiet a dozen men could be if they got scared enough. The morning wore on, the sun rose above the trees, and the heat increased.

Just after noon they were filing along the flank of a tiny ravine and could see the mountains plainly. Monday was leading, with Thurston just behind. He was setting a good pace, hoping to make up a little more time, and the others followed silently, without complaint.

Suddenly Monday stopped, looking over toward the rising ground. He gestured with his hand and squatted on his heels. Thurston sat down beside him, pulling a handkerchief from his vest pocket to wipe his forehead. Monday peered out at the little promontory, and finally pointed.

"See that little butte?" he said quietly to Thurston.

"Yes, what about it?"

"Y'see them three big rocks up there? One by the edge, the other two close together in the middle?"

"Yes, yes," Thurston said impatiently.

Monday brought his finger down and rested his wrists on his knees. "One of 'em ain't a rock," he said.

Even as they watched a tiny figure stood up beside a boulder and stretched his arms wide. It was like watching a theater show from a great distance. The figure disappeared for a moment behind the rock, then reappeared, starting to descend from the little humped peak. Almost immediately they lost sight of him, as he merged with the rock face in the distance.

Monday turned to Thurston, his face without expression. Thurston met his glance for a moment.

"Well, let's go," Monday said. "We picked up another half-hour."

Old coon's getting careless, he thought. Then he remembered that Webb would be figuring on having a good start over them. He would not have been able to guess they could make up so much time by taking a steamboat downriver. He didn't know the country, and it was costing him dear. Monday shook his head. They would catch him now, before he had any time to fort up.

"Let's go," he said again, sharply, irritated. "You comin' or not?"

As the column filed past the clear space, each of them glanced at the promontory, where just a moment ago their quarry had stood.

The silent hot sun swung over the top of the sky. Silently they followed the rocky, dusty trail that zigzagged up the face of the smaller of the two peaks. In a couple of hours the top of the small promontory was below them and when they came to clear points they could see that the land around was beginning to flatten out now. They were above the terrain, and as their steps lengthened into yards and the hot hours of afternoon passed, the horizon drew farther and farther away, until at last they could see the Cascade peaks, tiny on the horizon, still white-capped with snow. Hood, Rainier, Adams. Tiny cones, almost indistinguishable, like bleached anthills across a wide plain.

The going was steeper here, and they did not make as good time. Most of them were not used to climbing, and once or twice they had to stop for a few minutes. The sun swung down, and as they neared the edge of the timber the western sky took on a reddish tinge.

The trail came to a long meadow that stretched down to the left, barricaded on the opposite side by a straight wall of rock, looking almost man-made in its regularity. Monday stopped again.

The trail itself swung out around the trees, heading up into the open rubble of rock. Leaving the shelter of the trees, a man would be perfectly exposed to the natural fortress of the rock wall.

The more he looked at it the less he liked it. No, he decided finally. That don't shine. There was a limit to the extent he could trust his notion that Webb would be at the top; and he had reached the limit. He backtracked, moving back into the secure anonymity of the thick forest.

"What's the matter?" Thurston said.

"Could be a mousetrap," Monday said. "There's a perfect set-up over there. We best take another way."

He went back along the trail two hundred yards or so. There was still forest above, and he wanted to stay with the cover as long as he could. He started straight up the side of the hill, hoping to gain a few hundred more feet of height before he had to go into the clear. The others followed reluctantly. After fifteen minutes he saw the clear light of the sky through the trunks of the trees, and knew he had gone about as far with forest cover as was possible. He stopped and waited for the others to come up with him.

"Spread out a little," he said quietly, "and take it easy, for christ's sake."

The others ranged themselves to either side. This high there was not too much brush, and the relative clear gave them a chance to move. When they were set in a long line across the face of the hill, Monday moved forward.

They reached the edge of the woods, where there was a sharp dividing line between the cluttered rocky slope and the trees. A hundred yards above them was the crest of the smaller peak, silhouetted now against the redness of the setting sun. Monday studied the slope, looking for some kind of cover for a dozen men.

Suddenly, at his left, one of the men darted out into the open, slip-running across the slope to the shelter of a boulder. Behind him a little stream of rocks slid down.

Goddamn idiot, Monday thought. Wants to skirmish a little. Another silhouette appeared at the top of the peak, coming around the boulder. For what seemed an eternity it stood still.

"*Get back!*" Monday shouted. On either side of him there was the crashing thunder of exploding powder.

Chapter Twenty

Half blinded from staring into the setting sun, the old man saw nothing of the shaded slope for a moment, except the mass of darkness that was the edge of timber, a few hundred feet down. Then, astonishingly, a sudden line of white flowers seemed to bloom at the forest's edge; the shock, the final echoing roar of the guns that rolled off the mountain slope and seemed to hang in the air.

An invisible hammer smashed into his side, jerking him around and back, off balance. His foot slipped into a tiny crevice in the stones, and he fell to his side with the sound of the blast still in his ears.

The side of his body was lost in a fog of numbness, and he could feel only an enormous pressure like a great, inexorable ram pounding against his side. As he fell, with his foot wedged in the crack, he felt a dull, sudden sensation in his leg that was not like pain, but like the grating of two stones together somewhere deep inside.

He was still for a moment, his right cheek rammed into the gravel as he fell. He blinked once, staring at the stones that rested just before his eyes. In his mind was the sharp vision of the white blossoms of smoke erupting suddenly from the dark bank of trees like a row of miraculous flowers. Slowly, he began to feel the sharp points of gravel digging into the side of his face.

Then it came; then the pain came.

His leg suddenly exploded into brittle shards that speared up through his groin. He lost his breath and gasped sharply, clenching his eyes shut without volition. He heard the thin, animal bark of pain, and knew it was himself. He tried to raise himself on his arms, but his arms did not move. He was heavy, a great stone seemed to have fallen on the side of his chest with blind and massive force, shoving him into the ground, deeper and deeper. His chest began to throb against the crushing weight, and a steady pulsating roar of blood sounded in his ears.

The first wave passed, and for a second he could breathe again. He opened his eyes and found he was staring into the blood-colored western sky. Then the pain shattered his leg again, and the red sun swooped suddenly down to fill his field of vision with the smoky, hot color of blood and wash away all other sight. The descending ocean of red poured over him and he let himself go, to pass into the profound depths where sound and sight were drowned in the softly throbbing waves of redness.

He did not know how long he floated there, drifting deep within a pulsating cavern of redness; drowned in the measureless, throbbing heart of some great beast that might have been the world. He twisted and revolved slowly, moved by heaving tides he could not comprehend, conscious only of the relentless contraction and release of the monster heart, pulsing slowly, thick waves of pressure beating against his mind, the thunderous roar that echoed down the wide caverns into a blackness that hovered just beyond.

Gradually he became aware of a dizzy feeling of rising, and the gravel that pressed at the flesh of his cheek pushed him harshly up through the murky redness. He moved toward a thin veil that was the surface, and passed it with the sensation of puncturing a membrane that separated two worlds. The edges of the wound drew away from him and he emerged into consciousness.

He discovered himself lying on his right side, head downward on the slope. The edge of the sun was still just visible, so he could not have been unconscious long, a minute, perhaps two. He lifted his face from the ground, and heard the tiny, faint rattle as pieces of gravel dropped away from his cheek. Others he could still feel embedded in the flesh. The enormous pressure remained on his left side, and he knew he would have to relieve that before he could move. Slowly he turned his head to look, blinking.

He was vaguely surprised to find that nothing rested on top of him after all. Still the sensation of throbbing weight persisted. The side of his hunting shirt was torn at the left, and a wet black stain spread around the edges of the rip. He could feel a thin, oily flood moving down across his belly, a sensation vaguely like insects crawling. From the loose hem of the shirt lying on the ground a little rivulet of blood appeared, moving in a sluggish stream to the edge of the leather and pouring itself into the absorbent ground.

He put his head back on the ground for a moment. He drew his right arm back and tried to push himself up. The effort made a dull explosion in his side and he gasped again. Slowly he raised his upper body, trying not to jar the explosion into existence. He had lost the power to make his muscles act unconsciously. He had to concentrate on each motion individually. The elbow braced, the shoulder and back set, then tense, then moving. He thought carefully of each step.

He came up resting on his forearm on the third try. He looked back at his side again, puzzled, unable to believe the weight he felt so clearly did not exist. But there was nothing except the ragged rip in the leather and the spreading stain. He deliberately and slowly moved his left arm, closing his eyes tightly as the sensation of weight turned slowly to a flood of dull pain.

But there was no choice. He had to get up, no matter what it cost. They would be coming for him. He set his teeth together, and his lips drew back in a silent grimace. He breathed deeply twice, and felt a new, sharper agony somewhere inside him. He rested his left forearm on the ground and slowly let his body turn so that he was belly down, supported on his forearms, his head hanging low. The flood of pain from his side swept up, subsided. He tried to inch his left leg forward, but it did not respond. Regretfully he let the weight of his body settle on his left arm, and moved the right leg. The motion tensed the muscles of his left side, and the dull, throbbing explosion rumbled again. He ignored it, his eyes clenched tightly shut, and brought his right knee up.

He found no way to avoid producing the pain again, and with this realization it was a little easier. He would just have to live with it. Methodically he hauled himself up until he was sitting on his right hip, his body braced against the stiff right arm.

He looked down at his left leg to see if he could determine why it did not respond. The lower part was wrong. His foot lay limply on the ground, though his knee was turned upward.

It was a weirdly disturbing sight, the angles were all wrong, the lower part seemed have lost its relation to the upper.

He reached down with his fingertips, touching the leather, moving slowly down the length of the leg. He found something more solid than flesh, like a rock beneath the leather. Puzzled, he pushed it a little harder; suddenly threw his head back as the bright flash of pain exploded, blinding him momentarily.

When the first brilliance of agony had passed, he reached behind his belt for the butcher knife. He inserted the point up near the knee of his trousers and ripped down the length. He slowed the movement of the knife as he reached the hard point, and worked carefully to the side. The leather fell away on either side, revealing a jagged shard of bone that protruded from his calf near the front.

He looked down at it for a moment, then turned his eyes to his side again. The ball had plowed into the rib cage, but well to the side. Tenderly touching it, he could not tell how many ribs it had smashed in passing. Every time he moved a thin, screaming pain echoed somewhere deep inside. He could not tell exactly where it was, and that seemed strange. It felt as though the whole side of his chest was full of glassy splinters, and he thought it was probably true. The heavy, half-inch lead ball erupted when it hit something hard, and smashed bone like a hammer. Some inner part of him was pierced by the shards of bone each time he moved, but he could not locate the pain accurately enough to know what part.

He looked up and saw that he was only a few feet from the boulder against which he had rested to watch the sunset. His rifle still stood upright, resting on the butt. It seemed uncanny that it should not have moved, that it could have remained quietly standing while the whole world exploded and erupted.

He dragged himself over to it. Slowly he eased himself around so he was sitting with his back against the stone again, his useless left leg stretched out ahead. He pulled the rifle down to his lap, laying it across his knees. It was hard to breathe, the effort of moving cost too much in pain, and he could not get enough air. He hung his head for a moment, concentrating only on the breathing, until he felt he had regained enough to go ahead. At the edges of his vision were the vestiges of the red ocean, and each time he moved, they closed in slightly, and he had to wait. When he could no longer see the stains of red at the edges of his eyes, he lifted his head again and reached for his powder horn.

It was difficult to charge the gun with the barrel horizontal across his lap, but he could not stand up. He poured a little powder in, then stood the rifle on its butt beside him and tamped it lightly on the ground to settle the load. He repeated this three times, until he thought it was about right. Normally he loaded without even thinking, but when the charge was divided into three it was more difficult to tell. He pushed the butt away from him, holding the barrel, and drew out the long ram. He forced the patch and ball down securely, replaced the ram in its socket beneath the barrel, and drew the butt back into his lap.

When at last he had primed the pan, turned the flint to a new edge, and hauled the heavy hammer back, he felt better. There was nothing he could do about his leg, or his side. But the others came now, there was something he could do. He was not helpless, the old man. He was ready for them now.

The dangerous thing was that his senses had come untracked. He could not tell where the pain was that was inside him, he could not sense his body accurately. He could not tell how much time passed, except by judging from the darkness. His inner sense of time had gone, and it might be seconds or hours. He simply could not tell. He did not know how long he waited for the others to come, only that they did not come, and the sky went dark in the west.

The moon rose behind his boulder, invisible to him. He sat silent and waiting in the sooty shadow, while on either side the rocks began to glow with a ghostly luminescence. He listened as carefully as he was able, but his own mind was full of sounds, and he could not always distinguish the sounds of the night from the sounds his own mind made.

With the coolness of the night a breeze had begun to sweep up from the valley, rustling the trees below, fitfully shaking the scrubby brush of the rock slope. The sussuration of the wind was twined and tangled in his perception with the sound of his own blood rushing strong and hissing in his ears.

The shadow in which he hid grew short with the rising of the moon. Still the others did not come, and at last he knew he was forced to make a decision. He could remain, or he could try to go.

He looked down at the razorback ridge that connected his small peak with the larger one, less than a quarter of a mile away. On either side of the ridge the ground dropped sharply away, the flanks specked with brightness of light rocks in the moonlight. The ridge itself twisted like a bright snake, dropping down from where he sat several hundred feet, then rising again to disappear into the heavy body of the other peak. The massive face of the peak itself was silvery and distinct in the moonlight. The old man could not tell if the moon was supernaturally bright, or if the impression was simply part of the derangement of his senses. He could make out detail on the opposite face that he thought would be impossible in normal moonlight. If the detail was real, the moon was awesomely bright this night. He twisted his head to the side, trying to look up, but the moon was still beyond his vision.

There was something at the back of his mind about the moon, something it seemed important to remember. He tried to think about it, but was not able to keep his mind in one place. It drifted, floating on the substanceless light like a swirl of smoke gently moving in a shaft of the brilliant moonlight. His vision kept coming back to the image of the line of white flowers appearing suddenly at the darkness of the forest's edge, all spread in a line. It was an astonishing sight, it was perhaps the most amazing thing he had ever seen.

It was the moontrap, he thought, that was what he should remember. But remembering, he could not understand what it meant. He had tried to build a moontrap, but it had not been right. It was very simple, and there was no importance in remembering it.

The shadow drew in slowly until it reached the lifeless foot that hung uncertainly at the end of his left leg. Half the moccasin was in light, and as he watched the white glow spread like a bloodstain down to the ankle and began to ascend the calf.

He was suddenly frightened. He did not want to see that brilliance reach the splintered bone that stuck out beyond his ripped trouser leg. He was convinced that when the ghostly light reached that shard of bone something terrifying would happen. He did not know what, but the conviction was strong in his belly. All around him the stones seemed to glow from within, burning coldly with an unearthly flame of their own. If that happened to the bone that protruded from his leg, he thought the pain would be unbearable. He would have to protect himself. He would have to go. He looked down at his leg again and the moonlight had crept up a little higher. He did not have much time.

Deliberately he let himself tip over to his right side, resting on his elbow. He inched around until be was pointed down toward the ridge. He lowered the hammer of the rifle to half-cock. Grasping the muzzle with his left hand he began to squirm down toward the ridge, dragging the gun loosely behind him as the left leg dragged.

He tried to keep the tension out of the muscles of his left side, but he could not do it altogether. He drew himself up over his right forearm. Bracing there, he dragged the right leg up under him. Then the forearm forward again, draw the body up to it, pause, then the right leg.

Each time he drew himself up he had to tighten the muscles of his belly, and there was the dull thump of pain in his side. There were two distinct pains; first the dullness as the muscles contracted, then the sharp, fiery splinter as something happened inside, as a bone shard darted deep in some part of him that should not be touched.

The dead weight of his body rested on his right hip each time he dragged it forward. The rocks scraped mercilessly at the leather, and when it had been gouged away began to work at the flesh beneath it.

After the first effort, something had given way in his side with a soft sensation. Shortly he began to feel the tickling-insect sensation of flowing blood down his belly again, but there was nothing he could do about it. It became one of many sensations that confused him at first. The wild mélange of pain from the leg, and from the side, the new sensation of tearing in the flesh of his right hip as he dragged himself slowly over the brutal rocks, the scraping of his side and elbows and the flowing of blood across his belly.

There were too many feelings. He could not keep track of them all. The muscles of his back occasionally twitched, and there would be momentary burning irritations like the sting of a nettle. They were not real. He did not know where they came from, except that he could no longer perceive his body accurately, and it was signaling things that did not exist.

He had to forget about the feelings, it was all he could do. Some of them existed, some of them did not exist, but all were equally real. All he could do was forget them, because he could not distinguish and there was not sufficient room in his mind to hold them all. He forced himself to think only of the one thing that was important, to move. Elbow forward, drag. Leg up. Elbow forward, drag . . .

He was astonished as his glance caught the boulder he had left. He thought he had been crawling for several hours, but the rock, now outlined with the silver fire of the moon, was only a few yards away. He looked down at the ridge and could not see that he had gained at all. He would have to use something much closer for a reference point, or he would never be able to discern any progress.

He chose a flat slab of rock that leaned against another, about fifteen feet away. As surely as he had turned his mind from the pain, he turned it away from the ridge and the peak at the other side. There was only the leaning slab. That was his goal. The rest did not exist. He reached his elbow forward again.

He tried closing his eyes for a few movements, to see if he could surprise himself with the progress he had made. It did not work well. He tended to lose his balance with his eyes closed. And when he lost his balance it required a tensing of muscles to keep him upright, and then there was the quick succession of dull pain, sharp pain, and the knowledge that the puncturing sliver of bone had penetrated deeper into his life.

Even that was not so bad as the terrifying sense of someone watching him when he closed his eyes. He looked around, but there was only the bright, indifferent eye of the moon, staring down from a vastness of sky that was deeper and higher than he could ever remember.

He stopped often to rest, when the always threatening veil of redness crept in at the edges of his sight. It was hard to rest, he hated it. He wanted to move, he wanted to go on. The only thing that was real was the dragging of his useless corpse over broken ground, the land tearing at his flesh. He wanted to do that. He wanted to move and the anger and hatred welled up in him when he had to stop to rest.

He set himself to it viciously, finding a fierce joy in doing it. The moon stared down, and watched him.

"I'm goin'," he muttered. The moon did not believe he could do it. The moon thought he was a helpless old man, all alone and almost dead and unable to do what he had to do.

"I'm goin'. Wagh!"

The leaning slab of rock was passed. He did not remember passing it, and looked back over the long bright barrel of the rifle to see that the rock was fifteen feet or more behind him. He clenched his teeth in satisfaction. He was doing it.

He looked forward again, and pretended that the ridge seemed a little closer. As he had lost the ability to distinguish between the world outside and his own mind, it was not exactly pretending. If it seemed closer in his mind, it was closer. It was simple. The rock over which he dragged the beaten body was a product of his mind. He had created it and the moon to watch. It was his joy to do this. It was his life.

He stretched his arm forward again, and it passed from the light into the sudden blackness of a moon-shadow. He saw it disappear, and drew it back again, badly frightened. He looked at it, back in the light again. It had not been cut. It had seemed to him it had been cut off, thrust into the nothingness of space, ceasing to exist along the sharp line of shadow. It was another trick of the moon.

He looked up. It rode very high, and tiny. It seemed incredible it should be so tiny and yet give so much light. But the sky was so large, it deepened above him to infinity, and just beyond the last reaches of depth hung the moon, watching.

He grinned. The moon was testing him, to prove his worth. The great white eye of the world was watching impassively to see if he could do it. The moon did not care, one way or the other, but it was interested in watching him.

He put his arm forward into the shadow again, tapping with his fingers to be certain the ground was there. Reassured, he dragged himself up, and his head passed into the nothingness. He looked back. His legs were still in the light, cut off by the shadow-knife just below the hips. He almost wished he could leave them there. They were doing little good. He could not even remember if his right leg was still working or not.

He went on. The moon crested above him and began to swing down toward the sea. In time it was no longer above, but ahead of him, and then he understood it better. The moon could not wait. She was watching him, the great white eye, but she would not wait for him. He would have to keep up.

It helped. In time it became clear to him that the world had ceased to exist in the shadows. There was only emptiness, an emptiness created by the moon. Where there were no rocks to tear at him, he could move more easily. The luminous lovely moon was dissolving the earth around him.

He went a little more easily then, moving westward in the track of the moon. Time and pain were lost and drowned in the sweet curve of moving light that drew him on.

Only once was there trouble after that, and then he fell over a low step along the ridge. It was not more than three feet, but he lay crumpled at the base for a long time, the redness that was the enemy of the moon having overcome his sight. The silver light revived him in time, and he began again. He closed his mind off to all sensation but that of moving. It was so complete that he thought he had let go of the rifle, and had to look back to see if it and the useless leg still dragged along.

He did not remember crossing the base of the ridge and beginning to ascend the other side. He remembered only the brilliant light he followed, a light that filled him completely and left no room for pain or thought.

But the moon in time touched the crest of the peak above him and gently, softly, began to slide down out of his sight. It was time, he thought. This was where he was supposed to be. He faithfully dragged himself as long as the faintest sliver remained above the hill, but when it had gone, he stopped.

He was finished with his journey now. He was alone again. He looked around him. The opposite slope, the peak from which he had come, was now in the silvery light. He was tired and he would rest here.

He was almost surprised to find how high he had come, following the moon. Now only one thing remained for him to do. Just a few feet uphill, he saw a rubble heap of rock. That was it.

He dragged himself behind the heap, and at last put his head on the ground. The rocks dug into his forehead comfortingly. After a moment he lifted his head again. He would make a fort. Somewhere in the back of his mind he thought he had twenty-four hours to make a fort in. He didn't know where the idea had come from. Things had happened so confusingly, ever since the blooming of the miraculous smoke-flowers. But time had become meaningless and it didn't matter if there were twenty-four hours or twenty-four years. There was no time, only movement, and all movement followed in the moon's track. He was bitterly ashamed of himself. Dragging himself like a gut-shot animal while the moon glided with her white perfection so easily and smoothly across the sky. But there was nothing to do about it. It was just the way things were. The moon was perfect, but he was only a man; the way the world was.

He began to try to arrange the rubble into a sort of wall that he could lie behind. He would have to lie on his right side, though by now he could no longer distinguish one side from the other with precision. The right one was pretty badly torn up too, he thought, from all the dragging. He hoped it would be all right.

He did not seem to make too much progress with the wall. The stones would slip from his hands, and sometimes he would forget what he was doing, and find himself sitting numbly staring at the rock he held. Then he would place it carefully with the rest, and reach out to find another with his fingers. The moon having left him, he did not see very well.

He put his head down and thought perhaps be would rest a little before he did anything else. He couldn't remember ever having been quite so tired. He was sorry the moon had left him, but he realized it could not wait. It made him a little lonely.

He opened his eyes again. Suddenly he smiled, blinking. The eastern sky, just above the horizon was faintly light. He felt a joy that was stronger than the pain surge inside him. The sun was coming. And smoothly as the moon in its perfection it would glide upward in the sky. It was perfect, and there were suddenly tears in his eyes. He had never in all his years thought of anything so beautiful as the slow and perfect course of sun and moon swinging through the depth of sky, balancing each other, lighting the day and night. It was a miracle.

He put his head down, no longer feeling lonely, knowing the sun was coming. He loved the moon, but he loved the sun more. He looked once more at the lightening patch of the horizon and closed his eyes.

He loved it all.

Chapter Twenty-one

After the blast there was enormous agitation up and down the line as men scampered back into the full shelter of the trees to reload.

"We got him!" somebody called excitedly. "We got him, honest to god!"

"He just ducked behind that rock, you damn idiot!" a voice answered.

Monday stood looking at the spot of sky next to the rock where the silhouette of Webb had appeared. The sudden apparition, a moment of utter stillness, and then it was gone again. It was too sudden, like some sort of miracle.

"I'm dead *sure* I hit him!"

"I got eyes too. He jumped back just before we shot."

"He ain't fired back, has he? Has he? That means we got 'im."

"Hell, he's just sittin' there waitin' for somebody t' show," the skeptic answered.

"Monday!" the first man called. "What d'you think? Did we hit him or not?"

Monday did not answer for a moment, the after-image of the dark form strong somewhere inside his eyes. Finally he looked down at his own rifle and gently lowered the hammer.

"Well," he said at last, "there's one sure way t' find out. Go up an' look."

Someone laughed, a strained tight sound in the reddish dusk. "Not me, friend."

Behind the trees Thurston came scrambling through the brush to Monday's side. "Well?" he said.

Monday turned to look at him. "Well, what?"

"What do we do now, mountain man?"

"It's gettin' dark," Monday said absently.

"I can see that, thank you," Thurston said. "What do we do now?"

Monday shrugged, looking down at the ground. He frowned. "Take him now or wait for morning," he said. He shook his head confusedly, his mind not on his words. When he looked back up at Thurston his eyes were full of puzzlement, as though he had expected to see someone else.

"What's wrong with you, Monday?"

"Nothin'," Monday said slowly. "Nothin's wrong with me."

"Your gun hasn't been fired," Thurston said.

Monday looked distractedly down at the rifle. "Misfire, I suppose."

"You sup*pose!*"

Monday shrugged.

"Monday, pay attention, will you? Should we follow up now, or wait until morning?"

Finally Monday brought his attention back, and his eyes lost the glazed indifference that veiled them. He looked around, at the rocky slope above, at the dim shapes of the men he could see through the trees, finally faced Thurston.

"We best wait till morning," he said. "Ten more minutes an' we'll be shootin' each other."

Thurston watched him carefully for a moment in total silence. The debate was still going on along the line as to whether or not the old man had been hit, but even those who were convinced of it had no enthusiasm for going to check.

"All right," Thurston said finally. "Bill!" he called. "Come over here a minute, will you?"

The carpenter came slowly through the brush, picking his way methodically around the clumps.

"We'll camp for the night and take him in the morning," Thurston said.

Bill shrugged. He looked at the ground for a moment, then glanced up at Monday. "That what you say too?"

Monday nodded. "No fire," he said. "An' you best scatter your bedrolls around in the brush. No use makin' it too easy if he decides to do a little night-runnin'."

"You think that's a possibility?" Thurston said.

"Possibility of anythin'," Monday said. "I'm just sayin', is all."

"We'll set a few men to watch," Thurston said.

"All right," Monday said. "I'll take a watch."

Thurston looked at him. "No," he said. "No, that won't be necessary. You'll need all your energy tomorrow."

After a moment Monday snorted. "You just won't get off my back a minute, will you?"

"Why, Monday. I'm trying to look after your condition. We're depending on you." Thurston smiled humorlessly in the growing dark.

"You're sure damn worried about my condition," Monday said.

"Yes, my friend," Thurston said quietly. "I am."

Four men were picked to make up the first watch, and their alternates chosen at the same time. The night would be very short with the summer full on them, and their altitude. By four o'clock there would be enough light to begin. Grumbling, the men began to distribute their bedrolls, and by the time they had finished it was full dark.

"Where's your roll, Monday?" Thurston asked him.

"Over here," Monday said, pointing to the small fir with his pack and gun resting against the tree. "Why?"

Thurston shrugged negligently. "Just curious."

Monday tilted his head, but there didn't seem to be anything to say. He got out his blanket and began to settle down. Just as he had his legs raised stiffly to tuck the edges of the blanket under, he saw Thurston's shadowy form bend over by the guard post nearest Monday. He was there for only a moment, then moved past Monday's bedroll toward his own.

"Sleep well," he said as he passed.

Monday rolled over on his side. "Y're a trusting bastard," he said quietly. "Y'are now."

From where he stretched, wrapped tightly in the cocoon of wool, Monday could just see between the tree trunks a tiny patch of the rocky slope leading up to the little peak. The gigantic full moon had hung on the eastern horizon just before the sun went down, and rose into the darkening sky rapidly. It was as brilliant a moon as he had ever seen, and he watched the bluish light flood over the rubble and debris of the slope, casting sharply defined shadows.

He watched the shadows shift, picking a reference point where a shadow just touched a stone. It had soon changed, pulling gradually away from the stone with the pace that was always just too slow to see.

He counted the illuminated stones that he could see in his rigidly blocked field of vision. A few minutes later he counted again. It was always around the same number, as nearly as he could tell. While some disappeared into shadow others slowly emerged. It was just the way it was, without pattern. Some vanished into the black nothingness of shadow and others came up to replace them in the light. It was all measured in a slow rhythm of the world he could not understand or hear.

He sighed and rolled over to his back. Through the mat of branches above, the patches of sky he could see seemed very light, and only a few of the brightest stars were visible. There was too much moon, and it fit the whole sky, as well as the land below.

He watched the shapes of the dark limbs above occasionally moving gently in the night breeze that seemed to flow up the slope from the valley below. He started to count, and stopped himself, disgusted. It was pointless, and it made him obscurely angry that he should be forever counting tiny objects in small patches. The trees that blocked his view of the slope were a frustration, and the limbs that cut the night sky into a thousand bits and sections were a frustration. He could not see, and he felt closed in, muffled.

Out in the clear it would be different. Up on the peaks, looking down with the sky stretching out. He would have a different view from up there. Webb would be having a different view now.

Then the image he had so carefully avoided flooded sharply before his eyes. The moment of stillness, the figure beside the rock, seeming no more real than a cut-out paper man pasted against the red sky. The roar of the rifles in his ears and the gouts of white smoke that leaped out toward the sharp man-shadow.

He wondered how badly Webb had been hit. There had been no mistaking the spasmodic jerk of the body before it disappeared behind the rock. He had been hit, there was no question of it in Monday's mind. The only question was how badly. The heavy impact of a ball could spin a man around just by grazing him. It was hard to tell, it was impossible to imagine.

He tried to think how it might be for Webb now, where he was, what he was thinking. On the other peak there was a chimney of sorts in the rock, out of sight of this peak. Monday had seen it before, but it was no use. A man going up the chimney, back braced against one side and feet on the other, was just a mark. But—in the night . . . Webb could make it down in the night. While the posse was rummaging around on their bellies in the morning he could be moving silently through the woods toward the horses. Then up to Astoria, maybe. From there a ship, down to San Francisco, or up the Columbia. That would be it, upriver. Past the Willamette, up to the narrow straits and the beginning of desert country. The high plateau and the long dry days, and the final glorious relief of the Blue Mountains. Across to the Snake, and Pierre's Hole, where the Tetons reared up against the morning sky like the ramparts of Paradise, and Jackson's Hole on the other side, and the Wind River beyond . . .

Monday looked up at the segmented, blocked sky above him. After a long moment he sat up, untwisting the blanket from around his legs. He fumbled in his pack for his powder horn and the little leather possible sack. In the almost-blackness of the deep woods he put the blanket silently aside, picked up his rifle and started toward the perimeter of the guard circle.

"Who's that?" The man's voice was shaky, and it was impossible to distinguish fear from anger in the tone.

"It's just me," Monday said quietly

"Jesus, you scared me. You shouldn't do something like that."

"Sorry," Monday said.

"What the hell are you doin' up anyways?"

"I'm goin' t' take a piss, if it ain't against the rules."

The guard laughed. "Well, I don't know," he said.

Monday laughed with him and moved into the brush on the other side. He started down the slope, heading for the trail that led to the open meadow he had avoided so carefully.

Behind him the guard carefully estimated ten minutes. Then he sighed and stood up. He made his way hesitantly over to the blanket roll that was Thurston's. He squatted beside it and shook the small man's shoulder.

"Mr. Thurston," he said. "Mr. Thurston, wake up."

Thurston's head came up quickly, and he whirled to face the other man.

"What is it?"

"You were right, Mr. Thurston. He's gone."

Thurston was silent briefly. "So now there are two wolves on the mountain," he said finally, almost to himself.

"What'd you say, Mr. Thurston?"

Thurston sighed. "All right," he said more loudly. "Wake up the others."

When he was out of sight of the guard post Monday began to move more quickly downhill, sliding sometimes, almost falling as the rocky litter of the slope slid out from beneath his feet.

He reached the trail a few hundred yards below in short time. The moonlight was incredibly bright, and he moved fast toward the open meadow lying ghostly and silent in the pale glow. The rock wall that stretched along the opposite side was silver and black. He trotted across the meadow and scaled the wall. He was still out of sight of the main peak, but only because of the slow curve of the hill. He would skirt the side of the razorback ridge if he could, staying off the crest itself in case one of the posse should chance going to the top of the small peak. He was beginning to feel a panic urgency and stepped up his pace, skirting around the bulge of the mountain.

They could make it down the rock chimney in a couple of hours, the two of them, and be gone before Thurston and his pack even woke to begin the hunt again. If they pushed, Monday was sure they could get several hours' head start. If Webb was not hit too badly. But that was something he could not consider now; he would deal with it when it came.

The horses were picketed down by the cairn. They could make it while Thurston and the gang were still looking for them on the mountain, with a little luck. Monday grinned to himself. Somebody in the posse was going to have to ride double going back. Since Thurston's beautiful bay was the handsomest animal of the lot, that's the one they would take. Too bad, my suspicious friend, Monday thought. Won't there be a hooraw then!

There was a grove of firs standing downslope from the ridge itself, starting just below the crest. Monday rounded the last hump and stood looking up at it black and somber in the bright moon, the deep foliage sucking in the light, like an emptiness. After a moment he started up toward it.

And then? After?

After—they could choose their trail as they liked. Down coast maybe, down into Killamook country, or even farther. Or upriver and back to the mountains. Hell, it didn't matter, it would all work out in time. It would take care of itself. But right now they had to get out of here as best they could.

Under cover of the fir grove the light of the moon was sharply diminished, and he had to slow a little. The thicket was much more brushy than the open rock slopes he had been traversing, and he cursed his own clumsiness as he stumbled through.

A little downslope from him in the brush, a doe wakened, startled, and spread her nostrils in the cool night air. She froze, head up and silent, listening to the passage of the great animal only a few yards from her. Her great dark eyes caught the moonlight like pools of deep water. When the crashing had diminished, she dropped her head to nuzzle the softly spotted fawn that slept beside her undisturbed. She licked at its ears, and it rustled up into wakefulness and looked around. Softly she pressed it with her muzzle, nudging it gently to its feet. She began to move through the brush silently, away from the crashing sounds that had wakened her, away from the unknown menace of the great night-running creature. The fawn followed, still blinking with sleep, and they sought shelter in the lower part of the thicket.

When Monday emerged at the edge of the grove, the moon was far over in the west, and dropping fast. The eastern sky was already lightening, though it would be more than an hour before true dawn. He had almost forgotten how early the light came this high on a mountain. With the growing brightness they would not have much time. The main thing was to get to the rock chimney without being seen. Not knowing exactly where they were, the posse would be hesitant about traversing the ridge, and that would give them a little advantage. Once down the chimney, they had won; the whole posse would have to go all the way back down the other peak, as they had come up, and it would take hours longer.

He scanned the opposite slope carefully for several minutes, trying to guess where the old man might have gone to ground. The slope was littered with boulders and rocky rubble, and he might have holed up anywhere; it was impossible to tell. He spotted a pile that looked as though it had been stacked deliberately, and thought for a moment that was it. But then he saw that there were others, and there was no way to tell if one of them was any different from the others.

He left the edge of the grove and started down into the depression of the saddle, staying a little down from the crest. It was all rocky again, out in the clear, and boulders studded this slope too. Shortly he reached the lowest point, about thirty yards below the middle of the razorback itself. He stopped again to look, but even in the increasing light of predawn, he saw no more than he had seen before.

"Damn," he breathed.

Well, it didn't matter. He would find him all right, one way or the other. And then it would be all over, the whole seven-year nightmare. Back to the mountains, free, as if it had never happened. In a year it would all be wiped out of his mind, Oregon City, the things he had done, the indecision, the compromises. One year would do it; he could change it all. One year of watching the sun rise out of Sioux country and pass midday with the Absaroka, and afternoon with the Nez Percé, and end the day sinking into the sea while the coast people watched, Clatsops and Killamooks.

And Oregon City would be just a distant name, out of a long past dream that was slightly unreal now. One year. It would be easy to change things, if he could just get away. He could cut it off clean, everything he had done in the past seven years, cut it off sharply and start a new life. The old one would not cast its shadow into the future, he was sure of it. A clean break.

The thought of being free of it all excited him and added pressure to the sense of urgency. "Well, we got to get out of here first," he said.

He started up the slope, almost running now. The whole eastern sky was a pale and coppery green. The sun was coming fast. He gave up all attempt to move inconspicuously, and the tiny cascades of rock rolled down from his feet as he scrambled across the slope, heading for the top. They could not possibly hear him at this distance, anyway.

The first shot exploded in the ground next to his feet, scattering rock fragments. Instinctively he dived headlong into the shelter of a boulder, hunching himself behind. He was panting hard, half from the effort of scrabbling up the slope, half from the frightening suddenness of the shot.

He grinned to himself. "Crazy ol' coon," he said. Shoot at anything that moves. It hadn't occurred to him that Webb might mistake him in the dim light for one of the posse. He was sorely tempted *not* to call out, just for a little while, and let the old man think the others were after him. Serve him right, give him a little scare. But the thundering echo of the shot was too much in the silence of the coming dawn, and they'd be coming. There wasn't enough time for jokes, and the inevitably growing light in the east was cutting their chances every second.

"*Hooraw, Webb!*" he hollered. "*It's me, Jaybird! I'm comin' up!*"

He stood up and started around the boulder. The second shot crashed into the top of the rock next to him and whined off over the slope. Monday stood paralyzed and still for a moment, looking at the puff of smoke that rose into the still air from the pile of rocks fifty yards uphill. He saw the barrel of the rifle tilt in the air and disappear behind the little wall, to be reloaded.

"WEBB! IT'S ME!" he screamed again.

The gun barrel appeared again and lowered to the rock wall. This time Monday saw the top of the old man's limp hat, and knew there was no mistake. He could see. He darted behind the boulder again, just as the third shot roared in the morning stillness and slivers of rock sprayed into the air where he had been standing.

2

She's too late for that, Jaybird, the old man thought sadly. She's just too goddamn late.

The heavy recoil of the gun was more terrible than he had expected. As it slammed back in his shoulder, he had felt the soft, breaking sensation in his side again, and the tickling of the blood flowing down his belly. Now he rested the barrel of the rifle on the top of the wall and put his forehead on the stock for a moment. He looked along the barrel, but the boulder was lying still and silent.

Three's all y'get, he thought. He couldn't give him any more than that. Not when each shot tore him up worse inside. After firing the first time he knew that it was different from ever before. Every time he fired the big old gun, it killed him a little. There were only so many shots left; he had enough powder, but he was short of life. He couldn't afford to waste any more.

He leaned back against the ground and pulled the gun into his lap. He worked slowly and evenly to reload. He placed the patch over the muzzle and pushed the ball slightly down to seat it in the barrel. He shoved it down with the ram and tapped lightly, without strength.

He was sorry about the way it was, he was sorry about the Jaybird. But there was nothing he could do about it.

I'm comin' up, he thought. Just like that. It's me, I'm comin' up.

He peered over the top of his little wall, but Monday had not appeared again.

He caught a brief motion in the sky out of the corner of his eye, and looked up. A hawk, aroused by the sudden blasts of thunder in the dawn, wheeled smoothly around the opposite peak in a wide circle, gliding easily over the razorback ridge, its head lowered and swinging slowly from side to side, watching.

The old man blinked. He watched the gentle glide, watched as the sleek bird swept past just above his own level, out over the ridge.

"Hello, bird," he said.

He started to cough, spattering blood on the stock of the rifle and his hands. He turned his head away and waited until the spasm had passed. Then he spat on the ground, trying to clear his throat of the blood that seemed to be choking him.

There were tears in his eyes when he raised his head again, and he blinked to clear his vision. He looked around the sky but he could not see the hawk, and he could not turn to see behind him.

He heard a noise on the slope and looked down just in time to see Monday dart behind another boulder, farther down than the one he had left.

You best go back t' y'r boys, Webb thought. He didn't understand, Jaybird, he'd never understood how it was.

I'm comin' up. It made the old man angry to think about it. Some one o' these days he'd have to understand that there comes a point when you can't just say "I'm comin' up" any more. A point when you've made up your mind, whether you know it or not.

The hawk had swept in a wide circle behind the old man, and now it came into sight again to his right, sweeping silently out of the sky to course above the barren peaks that were its hunting ground, and see what strangeness there was there.

It passed almost directly over the boulder behind which Monday now hid, and the old man chuckled. The action brought more blood into his throat, and he spat it out. But he couldn't stop the chuckle. He knew what he'd do if *he* were the hawk.

The hawk swung up over the ridge, paralleling the lay of the land. It dipped one wing slowly and came around in a great circle to pass over the crest of the razorback again.

"Shit on 'im, bird," Webb whispered softly.

He wanted it with all the strength that was left in his torn body. But the hawk swung across the ridge to the other side of the mountain and out of sight again.

Monday made another dash down the slope. In his terrible haste he slipped and fell, just short of shelter. The old man looked at him down the barrel, then lifted his head again.

Get up, y'iggerant bastard, he thought. I could've had y' slick.

It was better to let him go, the old man thought. He'd known a lot of cowards in his time, and they were always better alive. It hurt more, it went on and on that way, and never ended. And all of 'em the same. Look different on top, but all of 'em the same. Never willin' to go all the way. Take a branch trail because it looks a little easier, always figuring you can come back if it ain't right. Then another, and another. But it didn't take many of them before you couldn't go back any more. The choice was made, whether you were willing or not.

I'm comin' up.

No. No, it's too late for that. It ain't that simple, I'm comin' up. It's too late to run any more.

Monday was now down into the lowest depression of the saddle, a couple of hundred yards below the small grove of trees, He left the shelter of the last boulder and started up the opposite slope to the security of the fir thicket.

The old man watched him climb contemptuously, a tiny figure scrabbling up the rocky slope. Still, he was sorry it had to be this way. They'd run together, he liked the Jaybird when it came to that. But there were times when a man had to choose who was going to be with him. And this was one of the times. He didn't want the Jaybird with him now.

Sorry, hoss, he thought.

He was surprised to find tears in his eyes. He blinked and shook his head angrily. It don't matter a damn to me, he thought.

The hawk swirled back, coming this time from the left, a dark, swift arrow in the sky. The old man watched it pass again. He lifted his rifle a little, by way of salute.

Monday had stopped in the middle of the opposite slope and was looking uphill at the fir grove. The old man followed his glance and saw another figure appear at the edge of the woods. Even at this distance, when the men were tiny, he recognized the small dark-suited man. He had a name, but the old man couldn't remember it. The faint sound of voices came to him, but he could not make out the words.

"Listen to'm," he muttered. "They're talkin' to each other." He coughed blood again, and this time could not shift his head to the side. It trickled from his mouth after the coughing was finished, and stained the front of the leather shirt, mingling with the blood of animals long since dead. Weakly he pushed the scalp locks over his shoulders, so they wouldn't be spoiled. He wished the hawk would come back. If the hawk came back, he would talk to it.

Monday half turned on the slope, pointing down toward the base of the ridge, still talking, explaining something. The small dark figure at the edge of the grove slowly raised the rifle, and the old man saw the tongue of white smoke leap out down the slope. The crash echoed between the peaks just after, roaring in his ears. Monday doubled over suddenly and kicked backward, knocked off his feet. He tumbled a few yards down the slope, dislodging a tiny avalanche of rocks beneath him. He rolled up against a small boulder and stopped.

C'mon, get up, the old man thought. That ain't no way t' die. But the crumpled form did not move any more.

The old man blinked again.

The tiny figure at the woods lowered the gun and rested the butt on the ground, looking down at the boulder. After a moment he walk-slid down the slope and bent over the crumpled form. At the edge of the trees the old man saw other figures moving. The man stood up, still looking down at Monday. Then he turned and called something up to the others.

A whole line of men came out of the dark obscurity of the fir grove and made their way downslope. They collected in a tight circle around the boulder, looking down at the dead man. The old man heard the tiny chatter of their voices, like distant birds. He wished he were sure of his load, he wished he could see more clearly. But with every second the number of shots he had grew less. He would have to be sure.

A wave of redness swept in at the corners of his vision, and he rested his forehead on the rifle butt again. Loosely he spat out the blood that was collected in his throat. His breath was coming raspingly now, he could hardly make his chest work, and a froth of blood formed at his mouth.

Suddenly he felt warmth on his face, and opened his eyes. The first red crescent of sun had appeared above the horizon. He looked at the flaming brightness, but he could not get his eyes open all the way. He wanted to take it all in his eyes, he wanted to be blinded by the radiance and brilliance of the great flaming disk.

He looked down the slope again, and the circle of men around the corpse had disappeared. His vision was coming and going in waves of blurriness now, but he could make out the motion. He saw them spread across the slope in a line, seeking out the protection of boulders, frightened, cautious, careful.

Come on, he thought.

He blinked again, but he could not clear away the liquid, shifting haze. His head wavered as he watched, and he knew he could not wait. He had not time to wait for cowards. He had never had time for that.

He put his head down again, trying to gather up the strength that was in him. He would charge them. If they wouldn't come, he would charge them. The way it used to be. With the shrill defiant shriek keening strongly across the peaks. He would do it, just one last time. To show them what a man was.

He lifted his left hand to support it against the wall and was surprised to find there was no pain at all from his side. Staggering, he pulled himself up until his chest was resting on the wall. His mouth hung open and loose. With one last brutal thrust, he raised himself erect above the waist-high pile of rocks.

He opened his eyes. From his left there came the swift shadow that was the hawk, swinging past him and swooping up into the space above the ridge. The terrible cry of hate died in his throat, and he watched the pitiless grace of the great bird of prey as it rolled easily on one wing.

Below him on the slope, a thunder roared, and the great white smoke-flowers bloomed mysteriously in the dawning sun.

The old man raised his rifle high.

"Hello, bird," he said.

The wall in front of him exploded into shards and dust, and the massive hammer smashed his frail body and broke the bones of his chest.

Startled by the thunder, the dark and silent hawk slid down the sky and over emptiness again. An updraft rustled softly in the feathers of its breast, and it gave its body freely to the unseen currents of the world.

There was time. It would all pass. The mountain would remain when the gross and roaring animals had gone, and in a later time small creatures would be lying on the sun-warmed rocks. Then the solitary dwellers in the wind would come to rake the sky with their sharp wings, for this was their way and the way of the world. It had been so since hawks first hungered in the sky. It had always been so.

The draft lifted it in a sweeping spiral that rose slowly into the vast silence of the new day.